A Woman's Fortune

Josephine Cox was born in Blackburn, one of ten children. At the age of sixteen, Josephine met and married her husband Ken, and had two sons. When the boys started school, she decided to go to college and eventually gained a place at Cambridge University. She was unable to take this up as it would have meant living away from home, but she went into teaching – and started to write her first full-length novel. She won the 'Superwoman of Great Britain' Award, for which her family had secretly entered her, at the same time as her novel was accepted for publication. Her strong, gritty stories are taken from the tapestry of life.

Josephine says, 'I could never imagine a single day without writing. It's been that way since as far back as I can remember.'

Also by Josephine Cox

JOSEPHINE
COX

A Woman's Fortune

HarperCollins*Publishers*

HarperCollins*Publishers* Ltd.
1 London Bridge Street,
London SE1 9GF

www.harpercollins.co.uk

Published by HarperCollins*Publishers* 2018
1

A catalogue record for this book
is available from the British Library

ISBN: 9780008128234 (HB)
ISBN: 9780008128579 (TPB)

Set in ITC New Baskerville Std 13/17pt
by Palimpsest Book Production Limited, Falkirk, Stirlingshire

Printed and bound by CPI Group (UK) Ltd, Croydon CR0 4YY

MIX
Paper from
responsible sources
FSC® C007454

For my Ken – as always

A special message from Jo

A little note to my readers to say sorry for the length
of time you've been waiting for this book — but here
it is. I've not been able to write these past months,
but I'm better now thank goodness. So thank you
for your patience, which is much appreciated.
I went through a trying time health wise,
and needed a bit of time to recover. But I'm
back on track.

Thank you for the extra help given by my long-
standing copyeditor Yvonne, and to my editor Kim
— thank you very much, you're a good friend.

Many apologies and thank you for your loyalty,
which I'm so grateful for.

Jo x

PART ONE

The Leaving
July 1954

CHAPTER ONE

Shenty Street, Bolton, Lancashire

SHE'D SEEN HIM around here only a couple of times before, a scruffy-looking man with his cap pulled low and his collar raised high. He had a furtive air, not looking directly at anyone in the street and skulking in the shadows instead of greeting folk with a cheery 'All right?' in the usual way. Round here, everyone knew everyone else – and their business – so Evie was certain this man was a stranger. And, from his manner, he was up to no good.

The question was, what did he want with her dad?

She'd now come into the kitchen to make sure her brothers, Peter and Robert, were getting on with their homework, leaving her mum and Grandma Sue folding the dried clothes ready to be ironed. Now, standing just inside, the back door partly closed to conceal her, Evie watched her father and the stranger. The two men faced each other in the shadowy alleyway between the Carters' house and the next row of terraces. Evie could plainly see both men in profile, her father taller, younger and more handsome than the weaselly-looking fella. The stranger was saying something in a voice too low for her to hear and then Dad, who had been smiling, no doubt laying on the charm, muttered something in return and began to look less happy. The next moment the man, his expression aggressive, was wagging a finger in Dad's face. Evie was surprised to see her father's shoulders slump and he no longer met the other man's eye. She was half ashamed to be snooping and half afraid that here was bad news on the way and she ought to see if she could do something about it before her mum heard. This wouldn't be the first time Dad had got in a bit of a tight corner, and Mum had lost a bit of her sparkle of late.

Since Evie had left school to help her mother and Grandmother Sue with the washing business she was more aware of what everyone in the family was up to. It wasn't always bad news with Dad, but there had been some weeks when money was especially tight after he'd had a long evening at the pub, celebrating or commiserating some event with 'the lads', especially if the bookie's runner had been there collecting the stake on some nag that Dad had been told was 'a certainty' to win and make his fortune, and which had eventually cantered in well down the field.

Michael Carter was never down for long and, with his irrepressible high spirits, would shrug off his setbacks and carry on regardless, sweeping aside any difficulties as if they weren't happening. But Mum was sometimes impatient with him these days, and the older she got the more Evie could see Mum's point of view. Somehow Dad's jokes weren't as funny as they used to be, and Evie understood why her mother was beginning to look worn down and her smile had grown, like herself, thin. You couldn't live on laughs, after all.

What was that word Mary had used when Evie had once confided how annoying Dad's charm could be when you recognised how he worked it on you? *Exasperating.* Mary Sullivan, Evie's best friend, was clever. She always had her head in a book and knew a whole dictionary of good words. She even *had* a dictionary, so Evie reckoned 'exasperating' was probably exactly the right word for her father.

Evie glanced to where her brothers were labouring over their schoolwork at the kitchen table. Their heads were down in concentration so she risked opening the door a fraction wider and craned her neck through the gap. The two men were talking intently but their voices remained low. Then the stranger, with another jab of his pointed finger, turned and disappeared from view. Evie waited a minute, then made a show of opening the back door wide and treading heavily up the alleyway to greet her father where he had moved to stand in the open in front of the house. The summer's evening sun was low between the rows of back-to-back houses and for a moment a golden beam shone through the sooty air directly onto his face, showing his furrowed brow and his tired eyes with a fine trace of lines she had never noticed before. He was standing with his hands in his pockets, facing into the sun with his eyes closed, almost as if he were praying. Suddenly Evie saw that her handsome dad looked older than his years.

Michael Carter looked up at his daughter's approach and turned to her, his smile instantly back in place.

'You all right, Evie?'

'Just taking a rest before I tackle a pile of ironing. Grandma's got a bit of mending to do so I said I'd iron. She's really feeling the heat today.'

'Well, your gran's got her own insulation,' he said, winking. 'It's certainly hot work for a July evening.'

'It is that. But Gran will be taking the good stuff back early tomorrow, so we need to get on.'

'Oh, leave it, lass. Don't be beating yourself up. It'll wait for you.'

'That's what I'm afraid of, Dad. There'll be more tomorrow and I'll not have Mum or Gran doing my share. Gran's complaining about her feet, and I don't blame her. She's been on them since seven this morning.'

'She's a tough old bird, and a good 'un. Don't tell her I said so, mind.'

Evie and her father exchanged smiles.

Michael called across to Marie Sullivan, who lived in the house opposite and was sweeping dust off her doorstep. 'All right, Marie? Tell Brendan I'll see him for a drink later.'

'I'll tell him.'

He waved to old Mrs Marsh, who lived next door to the Sullivans, and who was out rubbing Brasso onto her doorknocker. Mrs Marsh was known to be house-proud. 'Evening, Dora. That's looking good. I'll find you a job at ours, if you like.'

'Give over with your cheek, Michael Carter,' she grinned.

Evie laughed along with her father. This street was home. She knew no other, and nor did she want to. But the question remained, who was that man with the creeping manner who had caused her father's smile to slip? She took a breath and decided to plunge in.

'Dad . . . who was that man?'

'What man?'

'Here, a few minutes ago. In the ginnel.'

'Here, you say?'

'Ah, come on, Dad. Talking to you. Just now.'

'Oh, *that* man . . . '

'Yes, *that* man. I don't think he lives round here. Is he a friend of yours?'

'Well, I wouldn't exactly call him a friend, love . . . '

'What then?'

'What?'

'Oh, for goodness' sake, Dad, do you have to be so *exasperating*? Who is he and what does he want, lurking round here? Is everything all right? Only you didn't look too pleased and it set me wondering.'

Michael turned the full beam of his smile on Evie, but she noticed that it didn't quite reach his eyes. 'It's a bit of business, that's all, love. Nothing for you to worry about.'

Evie fixed him with a hard stare. 'If you're sure, Dad,' she said doubtfully.

'As I say, sweetheart, nothing to bother yourself over. Or your mum.' He looked at her meaningfully until she nodded. 'Now why don't you go and look in the pantry where I think you'll mebbe find a bottle or two of cold tea cooling in a bucket on the slab. That'll help that ironing along, d'you reckon?'

Evie knew there was no point pursuing the matter of the stranger so she shrugged off her anxiety as Michael took her arm with exaggerated gallantry.

'C'mon, let's see if the boys have abandoned their homework yet. Your cold tea and ironing await, your ladyship,' he grinned.

'Too kind, your lordship,' Evie beamed, and, their noses in the air in a pantomime of the gentry, they spurned the alleyway and the back door, and let themselves in through the front, laughing.

~

'I don't know what you two have got to be so cheerful about,' Grandma Sue said, easing a swollen foot out of a worn and misshapen slipper. 'My ankles are plumped up like cushions in this weather. It's that airless I can hardly catch my breath.' She slumped down on one of the spindle-back kitchen chairs and began to massage her foot.

'Here you are, Gran, a cup of cold tea,' said Evie, emerging from the pantry and putting Gran's precious bone-china cup and saucer down on the kitchen table beside her. Sue had been given the china as a present when she left her job as a lady's maid to get married. No one else in the family would even think of borrowing it, knowing that the crockery was doubly precious to Sue because it had not only survived the war, it had outlasted Granddad Albert, too.

'Here you are, Mum . . . boys.' Evie placed mugs of the tea, which was no longer particularly cold, in front of her mother, Jeanie, and her younger brothers. Peter and Robert were frowning over their school homework, applying themselves to it with much effort and ill grace.

'Thanks, Sis,' Peter smiled on her. 'I'll just get this down me and then I'm off out to play football with Paddy.'

'Football, in this heat?' Sue shook her head and smiled. 'You're a tough one, an' no mistake.'

'Lazy one, more like,' said Jeanie, taking off her pinny. 'What have I said about not going out to play until you've done your homework?' She sat easing her back, then removed the turban she wore when she was working to try to prevent the steam from the copper frizzing her hair. As her mother raised her arms and pushed up her flattened curls, Evie noticed how sore her hands were. Mum liked to look nice but it was difficult in this heat, with all the steam and hard work. In winter it was even worse, though.

'It's too hot to do schoolwork. It's the play next week and no one's bothered about doing sums when there's the play to rehearse.'

'But you're not even in the play, are you, Pete? Isn't it just the little 'uns that are doing the acting?'

'I'm in the choir *and* I'm playing the whistle,' said Peter. 'You can't have a play without music.'

'That's right,' Robert had his say as always. 'Pete's got a solo.'

'Two solos,' Peter corrected. 'Anyway, it's only one more year before I'm fourteen and then I can leave school. I can read and write already – what more do I need when I'm going to be a musician?'

'A musician, is it now?' smiled Sue. 'I don't know where you get such fancy ideas.'

'Fifteen,' Michael corrected, coming out of the pantry with a second bottle of cold tea. 'You can't leave until you're fifteen.'

'But that's not fair. Evie left at fourteen. Why can't I?'

'Evie left to help Mum and Grandma Sue with the washing,' Michael reminded his elder son, not for the first time. 'The authorities turn a blind eye if you've got a family business to go into, especially when it's the best in Bolton.' He beamed at Jeanie and she rolled her eyes at his nonsense.

'And if I don't get on with that last pile of ironing I might as well have stayed at school,' Evie said, getting up and moving to the ironing board, beside which was a pile of pretty but rather worn blouses.

'I could always go and help you at the brewery until the music takes off, Dad,' Peter went on, adding innocently, 'I'm sure we need the money.'

'And you wouldn't be spending it in the pub like Dad does either,' Robert said, unwisely. 'Or betting on horses.'

Typical, thought Evie, in the brief silence that followed. When would Robert ever learn to keep quiet?

Jeanie, Sue and Michael all spoke at once.

'Shut up, Bob, and get on with your homework. I won't have you cheeking your father,' said Jeanie.

11

'I think you're asking for a clip round the ear, my lad,' said Sue.

'Ah, come on, son. A man's got a right to have some fun,' said Michael.

Robert lowered his head and began snivelling over his exercise book while Peter got up very quietly, collected his books into a neat pile and sidled over to the door.

'I'll see you later,' he muttered and left, taking his mug of tea with him.

Sue eased herself off the chair and made for the living room, where the light was better and where she kept her workbasket. 'I'll just finish that cuff on Mrs Russell's blouse and you can add it to the pile. I'm that grateful for your help this evening.'

'Oh, and I've found one with a missing button. Do you have a match for this?' Evie followed her grandmother through with a spotlessly white cotton blouse and showed her where the repair was needed.

Sue turned to her button box and Evie went back to the ironing, mussing up Robert's fair hair supportively as she passed. Robert was still sniffing over his schoolbooks, writing slowly with a blunt pencil. The distant sound of Peter's voice drifted up the alleyway from the street, Paddy Sullivan answering, and then the dull thud of a football bouncing.

'Right,' said Michael, 'I'll be off out. See you later, love.' He planted a kiss on the top of Jeanie's head and was gone. Jeanie didn't need any explanation.

She got up and took her tea into the living room to sit with her mother.

'Let's hope he comes back sober,' Sue muttered under her breath.

'He's usually better on a weekday,' Jeanie said loyally, 'and it's Thursday as well, so I reckon there isn't much left to spend anyway.'

They each lapsed into silence with a sigh.

~

Evie shared the attic bedroom with her grandma. It was hot as hell that night, as if all the heat from the street and the scullery and the kitchen had wafted up into the room and lingered there still. It was dark outside, although the moon was bright in the clear sky. Sue was lying on her back on top of her bed, her head propped up high on a pillow and with the bedclothes folded neatly on the floor at its foot. She was snoring loudly. Evie thought she looked like an island – like a vast landmass such as she'd seen in the school atlas – and Sue's swollen feet, which Evie could just see in the dark, looked enormous, being both long and very wide. Poor Gran, thought Evie, it must be a trial carrying all that weight on your bones in this weather.

It was Sue's snoring that had woken Evie and now she was wide awake and too hot to get back to sleep. The bed seemed to be gaining heat as she lay there and the rucked-up sheet was creased and scratchy. Lying awake and uncomfortable, Evie thought of the weaselly stranger she had seen earlier, how Dad had swerved her questions and obviously didn't want her to know anything about the man. He'd more or less admitted it was a secret from Mum, too, and therefore from Grandma.

I bet it's about money, Evie thought.

Her dad had a job at the brewery loading drays and doing general maintenance. She had long ago realised that it wasn't very well paid. Despite Jeanie's scrimping and all the doing without, though, Dad didn't seem to care. He just carried on going for a drink or three, and enjoying what he called 'a little flutter' on the dogs or the horses. 'You have to place the bet to have the dream of winning,' he had explained to Evie. 'A few pounds is the price of the dream.' Sometimes he did win. Mostly he didn't.

The laundry helped to support them. For someone so old – she was sixty-three and didn't care who knew it – Grandma Sue was full of go, always trying to think of ways to improve the little business. She offered mending and alterations, and had found new customers away from the immediate neighbour-hood – people with a bit more to spend on the extra service.

Enterprise, Mary Sullivan had called it. 'Everyone admires your gran,' Mary had said. 'She doesn't sit around being old, she gets on with it.' Evie had to agree that Grandma Sue was amazing.

Evie looked at her now, lying on her back, snoring like billy-o, and grinned.

Getting up silently, Evie went to stand in front of the open sash window, desperate for a breath of cool fresh air. The rooftops of the houses opposite were visible but, from where she stood, there was no one in sight in the street. She lingered, breathing deeply of the hot, sooty air, leaning out and turning her head to try to catch any breeze.

Then she heard the echoing sound of approaching uneven footsteps and recognised her father coming down the street, weaving slightly, not hurrying at all, although it must be very late as he was the only person in sight. But – no, there was another man. Evie hadn't heard him, but suddenly the man was right there, outside the house. She leaned out further to see who had waylaid her father; it was the man she'd seen earlier. In the quiet of the night their voices drifted up to her, and her heart sank. Something was not right.

'I told Mr Hopkins what you said and he isn't prepared to wait that long,' growled the stranger. 'He wants his money now.'

'And I told you I don't have it,' Michael said. 'I'll pay him what I owe, I promise, but I need more time.'

'Mr Hopkins says you've had long enough. He'll be charging the usual rates from now.'

'Please, I can get it all by next month. I just need a bit longer to get sorted, that's all.'

'I'll be sorting you out if Mr Hopkins doesn't see his money soon,' snarled the man, leaning in close. Evie felt hot all over, the beginnings of panic flipping her stomach.

'Next week, then,' she heard her father pleading. 'I'll get it by the end of next week. C'mon now, I can't say fairer than that.' He tried for a friendly tone, a man-to-man kind of banter, but Mr Hopkins' man was not to be charmed from his purpose.

'Next week it is, then,' he said, 'but there'll be interest, too, don't forget. You should have paid up straight away, Carter. It's going to cost you more now. I'll be back to collect what you owe. All of it, *and* the interest. And if you don't pay – and I mean every pound of the debt – I wouldn't want to be in your shoes. You won't be able to talk your way out of it with Mr Hopkins. Let this be fair warning to you.' It was a dark warning.

The stranger seemed to melt away in the darkness, and Evie slowly sank down to the floor beside the window. She had a sense of trouble. Oh dear God, *every pound*. Dad owed Mr Hopkins pounds! And he had only until the end of next week to pay. And tomorrow was Friday already. How on earth had Dad got himself into that kind of mess? It couldn't be a bad bet on the horses. That might have wiped out his wages but wouldn't have led to such a debt, surely. Maybe this Mr Hopkins was a moneylender. Oh good grief, this was serious . . .

She sat numbly thinking about pounds of debt for a while, then got up stiffly and crept back to bed. Sue's snoring had subsided, thank heaven, and she was blissfully asleep. Evie lay down and tried to work through the situation in her head. Who else knew? No one, she guessed.

Evie wished that she didn't know, and her father's secret was so terrible that she couldn't unburden herself by sharing it with anyone, especially when her mum and grandma were so tired after working all hours doing laundry. She didn't want to worry them until she knew what was going on and how bad things were. First she'd have to confront Dad and see what he had to say, though she didn't hold out much hope of getting a straight answer. She'd already tried asking about the stranger and he'd pretended there wasn't anything wrong. No doubt he'd try to fob her off with some tale when she questioned him about what she'd overheard . . .

It didn't occur to her to leave the matter to her father to deal with alone. Now the truth was out she couldn't sweep it under the rug and forget what she knew. That was the kind of thing he did, and look where it had got him. He needed to face facts and do something about the trouble he was in. That awful man had sounded dangerous.

She tried to think of people who might be able

to help. The Sullivans were good friends. Perhaps she should go to Mary and Geraldine's father, Brendan. Dad might listen to Brendan. But it wasn't the Sullivans' problem and it would be unfair to burden them. Besides, money was probably tight there, too, as there were so many of them.

What about Billy? He was such a good man, so reliable, and she knew he'd do anything for her. But he hadn't got any money, she was sure. He was a postman but he hadn't been all that long in the job. He'd got his mother to support, too, as his dad had been killed in the war. And anyway, why should Billy give over whatever savings he might have to help her dad? But he was so wise, maybe he'd know of a way out of this mess . . .

Who did she know who could lend Dad the money he owed to this Mr Hopkins? Evie racked her brains but could think of no one. The most well-to-do person she knew was Mrs Russell, whose blouses she had been ironing that evening. But then she remembered the mended cuff Gran had worked on, the missing button and how worn the once-fine fabric now was with repeated washing. Mrs Russell was a step up from Shenty Street, but she was widowed and lived on what she had, which was not much. And anyway, Grandma would die of shame if the Carters took their problems to Mrs Russell. So would Evie herself, for that matter.

The burden of her secret and the anger she felt towards her father kept Evie awake until the early hours, when she eventually fell into a restless sleep. It was with heavy eyes and a heavier heart that she faced the next morning.

~

'You're looking peaky, love,' Jeanie remarked to Evie as they finished their breakfast of bread and scrape. 'I've got the copper heating and if you help me fill the dolly tub first, you can go with your gran to Mrs Russell's, if you like? Your dad's already gone and Pete can see to Bob so there'll be no one under my feet.'

Evie filled the dolly tub with hot water, then put in some washing soda, followed by some small items from the latest bundle. Then the sheets went in the copper with more washing soda and Evie pushed them underwater with some long wooden tongs.

'Help me load up, then.' Michael had made the trolley for them out of some orange boxes set on a frame with two axles, some pram wheels and a steering column handle. The box part was lined with an offcut of old sheeting to prevent splinters snagging the clothes. Evie laid the ironed and neatly folded bed linen inside, then placed the blouses carefully on top and covered them with a piece of fabric to keep off the dust. This had been Sue's idea, to keep the clothes clean and dry, and she'd fashioned the mac to fit snugly over the boxes like a pram cover.

19

Evie nearly blurted out her worries about her dad to Sue before they were two streets from home, but then she remembered her resolve of the previous night: not to say anything until she simply had to. There might yet be a way to deal with the mess Dad was in without spreading the worry around.

Mrs Russell lived not far from Queen's Park, and Sue and Evie cut through the back alleys, chatting about their washing schedule. But it didn't stop Evie worrying that the end of next week was the deadline for her father to pay back Mr Hopkins. She fell silent while Sue chatted on, unaware of her grand-daughter's preoccupation.

'. . . We'll go to the boys' play, I reckon,' Sue was saying. 'I think we need to get tickets. I hope there's no charge for them. I'll ask Peter. It's no use asking Bob, bless him.'

Before long, they arrived at Mrs Russell's, a tall old-fashioned red-brick house that had been divided into two. Sue opened the gate and Evie wheeled the pram up along the tiled path, then round to the back door. A rose bush was in full bloom in the small front garden and she noticed its delicate scent was like the perfume Mrs Russell wore.

Mrs Russell's 'girl', Annie, opened the door, beaming at Sue and Evie.

'Come in and I'll go and tell the missus that you're here.'

Sue and Evie unloaded the trolley, passing the

items between them to lie neatly on a chair in Mrs Russell's large kitchen.

Annie showed them to the sitting room, then went to make a pot of tea. Mrs Russell's sitting room was like the lady herself, all pink and white and pretty.

'Good morning, Mrs Goodwin. And, Evie, my dear, how lovely to see you. Please, sit down. Annie will bring us some tea,' Mrs Russell greeted them.

Evie liked Mrs Russell, who was always friendly and fair and didn't treat Grandma Sue as if she wasn't fit to set foot in her house, as a couple of the women who sent them their washing did.

'How did you get on with that cuff that needed your expert attention?' asked Mrs Russell.

'I'll show you. Evie, love, will you fetch that blouse so Mrs Russell can see?'

Evie did as she was asked, admiring the soft colours of the wallpaper, so different to their home on Shenty Street with its constant smell of washing soda and damp sheets draped over the maidens. How quiet this house was, too. Kind of restful . . . Evie glanced into another room opening off the corridor before she reached the kitchen. There was a large comfy-looking sofa, and a small pile of books that looked as if they'd been read a lot. A piano, far bigger than the one at the school, stood at the window end.

Mum would love to sit there and sing a few songs around that piano, Evie thought. So would I . . .

She knocked on the kitchen door and retrieved

the blouse, then Annie followed her back with a tray of tea and some plain biscuits.

Mrs Russell admired the mend, which pleased Sue, although Evie knew that it had been an easy job for her, and then the two women drank their tea and chatted while Evie sipped hers and gazed round the room, daydreaming about living in such a house. On a side table in a smart frame there was a photograph of a man in air force uniform. Evie guessed it was Mr Russell.

'Well, must be getting on,' said Sue as soon as she'd finished her tea.

Mrs Russell counted the payment for the washing into her hands and Sue put the coins in her jacket pocket and thanked her for the tea.

'Annie will bring round the next wash on Wednesday morning as usual, Mrs Goodwin,' Mrs Russell assured her.

'Thank you, Mrs Russell. I'll see you next week,' answered Sue with a smile.

Then Annie showed Sue and Evie to the back door where they'd left the trolley.

'She's so nice,' said Evie as she wheeled the empty trolley back along the footpath.

'And a good woman. Doesn't think that just 'cos she's seen a bit of money she's any better than the rest of us. But poor woman lost her husband in the war, like Granddad Albert. She's got no children either and I think she might be a bit lonely. It's family that's important, not how smart your house is. Always remember that.'

'Yes, Gran,' said Evie, though she thought it would be nice to have some pretty things at home as well as her family.

The thought of family started her worrying about Michael and Mr Hopkins' man again. The coins Mrs Russell had paid Sue for the washing and mending would go nowhere towards a debt of *pounds*.

~

By the time Evie and Sue had wheeled the trolley as far as the top end of Shenty Street, they were both hot and tired.

'Look, there's Billy,' said Sue, seeing the postman pushing some mail through the last letterbox in the road.

'Hello, Mrs Goodwin. Hello, Evie. That's lucky, seeing you now. I've just finished my round for the day. Been up since cockcrow.'

'So have we,' Evie smiled. 'Best bit of the day, first thing.'

'I'll take the trolley home and you can join us in a minute, Evie,' suggested Sue, fully aware that her granddaughter and Billy had a special fondness for each other.

Evie had never been so glad to have a few moments alone with Billy. All the way home the worry about her father's debt had festered and she couldn't keep it to herself any longer. Billy was so wise and, not being family, he might be able to see straight what needed to be done.

Evie perched on the low wall at the side of the end house and Billy sat next to her, putting his empty bag down at his feet.

'What's up, Evie? You look like something's fretting you.'

'Oh, Billy,' her brown eyes filled with tears, 'it's a family thing really but I don't want to worry Mum and Grandma unless I have to. Trouble is, it's too big. I don't think I can deal with it on my own.'

'Is it your dad?' Billy knew Michael Carter had a reputation for being feckless but then a lot of men round here put their beer and their bets before their families. 'What's he done that's so bad you can't even tell your mum and grandma?' He'd heard Michael had been placing some heavier bets lately, more than just the odd shilling. He hoped it hadn't got out of hand.

Evie told Billy about the creepy man sent by Mr Hopkins and what she'd heard in the night.

'Oh, Evie, Hopkins is bad news,' said Billy, lowering his voice. 'He runs a card game. I've heard all sorts about it: that it's held upstairs at the King's Head. It sounds as if your dad's been playing cards there and has run up this debt.'

'Cards? Are you sure? Not horses or dogs? What do you think's going to happen, Billy?'

Billy thought better of telling Evie everything he'd heard about Mr Hopkins. 'Let me think . . . Hopkins will want to get the money off your dad if he can. Maybe your dad can agree to pay it back a bit at a time.'

'But it's pounds already. That might mean it's never paid off!' Evie was indignant.

'I don't see that he's any choice if he can't pay it all. He has to take responsibility, love.'

'But I'm afraid if I tell Dad all this he'll take no notice of me. He never likes to face up to problems and I'm sure he'd rather carry on as usual at the pub and betting on the races than pay what he owes Mr Hopkins. And I don't want Mum and Grandma to be scrimping and doing without because of what Dad owes, Billy. They've been working so hard and Mum's getting all worn out, and Grandma's feet are so swollen in the heat and she's bone-tired. She should be sitting down in a comfy chair and drinking tea like that nice Mrs Russell, not working to keep Dad in beer and card games.' Evie felt hot, angry tears springing to her eyes.

Billy put his arm around her shoulders and drew her to him, wrapping her in his comforting embrace.

'Do you want me to talk to your dad?' he asked after a minute in which Evie's tears subsided as he hugged her against his jacket.

Dad might take some notice of Billy, who was

older than she, and a man, of course, but she felt the responsibility for her family should be hers.

'Shall we both talk to him?' she suggested. 'I think he'll listen to you but it was me that found all this out, and he *is* my dad, after all.'

Billy stood up and took her hand. 'I'll come round this evening after he's had his tea and we'll say our piece then, all right?'

'Thank you,' said Evie, giving Billy a hug. 'I'll see you later.'

Billy kissed the top of her head, then let her go. As he took up his bag to go back to the depot, he watched Evie walking back to her house halfway along Shenty Street. Before she disappeared down the passage she turned to wave with a little smile and Billy felt his heart lift.

He retrieved his bicycle from where he'd chained it to a lamp post, worried about Evie's future.

Mr Hopkins had a reputation as a bully and there were some nasty stories about him. Billy didn't want anything violent to happen to Michael Carter. He was Evie's dad, and Evie's happiness was very close to Billy's heart. She was a hard worker and everything she did was to help her family, even giving up school, for all she loved it, to help her grandmother with the washing business.

As he cycled back to the mail depot, Billy resolved to help Evie in whatever way he could. She was an angel and he would never let her down.

CHAPTER TWO

Evie met Harold Pyke from down the road at the back of her house as he was leaving.

'What did Mr Pyke want?' she said, going into the scullery.

'He brought us some peas from his allotment. Says they're the first of the season,' Jeanie said.

Sue was wringing out some garments from the dolly tub and putting them in a large bucket, her hands red-raw from the morning's work. She winked at Evie and looked sideways at Jeanie, who was poking stray curls back under her turban with a damp hand.

'Just an excuse to come round and admire you in your pinny, if you ask me,' laughed Sue.

'Go on with you. He was only being kind,' said Jeanie, though she looked pleased.

'It wouldn't be the first time Harold Pyke's come round offering veg,' said Sue. 'You want to be careful, our Jeanie. He'll be asking for something in return before long.'

'Well, what a thing to say!'

'Don't encourage him, then, lass.'

'I can't help it if the fella's taken a shine to me,' Jeanie gave a comical but telling little grin.

'Not just that fella, either,' said Sue. 'I'm not surprised he's bringing round peas, the way you've been tossing your hair around. It's nice to have the peas and that, but be careful not to fascinate him with your smiles and tossing your curls around.'

'How can I toss my hair when I'm wearing a scarf?'

'It's what you were doing, turban or no turban. And, as I say, there are others, too. That Derek Knowles, for instance. And Patrick Finlay from round the corner. We're not doing their washing for nowt but a cabbage and a bit of flirting.'

'I'm a happily married woman and I'm certainly not labouring over a hot copper for a cabbage or a bag of peas, so don't you worry.'

'So long as you've got that straight,' said Sue. 'Now, our Evie, what's Billy's news?'

'He's coming round later, after tea.'

'He's always welcome. He knows that,' said Jeanie.

Evie wished the business of her father's debt wasn't the reason for Billy's visit, but maybe with his help it could all be resolved without upsetting Mum and Grandma. Evie was feeling better now she'd spoken to Billy.

As she carried the bucket of clean wet clothes to the mangle in the outhouse, she decided not to worry any more about her dad until she had to. There was work to be done, and plenty of it.

~

It was mid-afternoon when the boys erupted into the house. Jeanie made them each a jam sandwich – thick bread, thin jam – and they went off noisily to play in the street with Paddy and Niall Sullivan, passing the Sullivan boys' sister Mary on their way out.

'Hello, Mrs Carter,' said Mary from the back door.

'Come in, lass,' Jeanie called out. 'That frock's come up smart, hasn't it?' she added to Mary. The school summer dress was second-hand, and Sue had altered it to fit Mary a treat. School uniform was expensive and Mary didn't mind that hers wasn't new. She was well aware how fortunate she was to be allowed to continue at school and study, the only one of the seven Sullivan siblings to do so.

'Mrs Goodwin's done a stupendous job with it,' said Mary.

Stupendous – whatever next? thought Jeanie.

'Is it all right if Evie and I go for a stroll up to the park? I won't be keeping her from her work, will I?'

'I've just finished,' announced Evie, beaming at

her best friend. 'Gran says she's got mending to do and I'll help Mum with the tea, so we won't have to be long.'

Mary looked to Jeanie for confirmation.

'Best get going, then,' Jeanie smiled.

Mary produced a paper bag of bull's-eyes from her pocket as the girls went outside and Jeanie could hear them giggling as they skipped down Shenty Street as though they didn't have a care in the world.

She smoothed down her pinny and put the kettle to boil, pleased to hear Evie's laughter. Her daughter had been oddly preoccupied today. Evie worked hard, and Jeanie worried that she sometimes forgot Evie was only sixteen, barely a woman yet.

Sue and Jeanie were enjoying a few minutes' sit-down with a well-deserved cup of tea when they recognised Michael's heavy footsteps approaching.

'Got the sack, didn't I?' Michael told them, untying his work boots before hurling them through the open back door in a show of temper. 'There was a mix-up about the maintenance of some pipes and there was a bad leak this afternoon and a lot of beer was lost. Mr Denby called me in. It was like he'd made a note of every single thing I've ever missed. I reckon he's had it in for me for a long while.'

'Oh, Michael!' Jeanie's face was completely white. Deep down she knew her husband was a slacker. He sometimes went into work the worse for wear from the night before, but he was popular at the brewery with his mates and it hadn't occurred to her that he might be less popular with his boss.

Sue kept quiet but her expression was grim.

'Couldn't you go and ask him for another chance?' Jeanie suggested quietly.

Michael gave a hollow laugh. 'No hope of that. I told him he could stuff his job and I was well out of it. He never remembers when I've done summat properly, only when he wants to pick holes. I told him that straight. I've had it with smarming round Denby, at his beck and call all day.'

'But he's the *boss*, Michael.'

'Aye, well, not any longer,' muttered Michael. 'I'll be my own boss from now on. I'll answer to no one. If you women can do it then so can I. I can tout my skills around, earn some money from my own gumption.' He gave a brief smile. 'Give folk a bit of the old charm, butter 'em up, like, I'll soon have plenty of satisfied customers.'

'Like you did Mr Denby, you mean?' muttered Jeanie.

Sue passed Michael a strong cup of tea with sugar in it. 'I think Jeanie means you'll need to find paid work straight away,' she said diplomatically, trying to keep the peace. 'It can take a while to build up customers when there's only you to do it.' She was fond of her son-in-law but she thought he lived too much by his belief in his luck, and not enough by hard graft.

'Look, I'm sorry, love. It's not your fault,' he went on, taking Jeanie's hand. He lifted it to his lips and planted a kiss on her rough skin. 'Mebbe I do need to find work with someone else. I'll have a look around and see what's going. There's proper house-building now – I'm sure I'll be able for summat. I'm going to have to be,' he added quietly, sounding unusually forlorn.

Jeanie got up and hugged him to her. 'Don't worry, you'll find a new job,' she said. 'In the mean-time the washing's going well and we can take in some more for a week or two, just to tide us over.'

'I'll ask around at church,' said Sue, though they were already working to capacity. 'That's where I heard about Mrs Russell, after all.'

As the two women rallied their own spirits and tried to pull him up with them Michael felt even worse. He wondered when would be the best time to break the news of his debt from the card game, realising even as he considered it that there would never be a good time. Maybe if he held his peace something would turn up . . .

'Dad, you're home early,' said Evie, appearing with the boys at the back door. 'Here, have one of these sweets – they were giving them away at the shop 'cos the box got wet or something. Anyway, they're all right.' She passed round the sweets and then looked properly at her parents.

'What? You two are a bit gloomy. You haven't had

bad news, have you?' she asked, wondering whether her father had told her mother about the debt to Mr Hopkins. Then again, it might be something quite different that was making them look so down; perhaps they'd heard someone was ill or even dead.

'Evie, would you go and collect Bob, please – you've probably seen him playing in the street – and Peter, too?'

'Yes, Mum.'

Evie's stomach was churning by the time she'd rounded up her brothers and they all trooped into the kitchen where their parents and Grandma Sue were now sitting round the table. Whatever it was, it was very serious.

'Mum, Dad, tell us. What's happened?' asked Evie.

'I'm out of work, lass,' said Michael solemnly.

'Oh, Dad . . . ' Peter said. 'But you'll find another job.' He sounded confident.

'Of course, Pete. I shall have to.'

'Will we starve?' asked Robert, looking anxious. 'Will we have to go and live in the woods, and eat berries and boiled nettles?'

'Give over your nonsense,' said Jeanie. 'I don't know where you get such daft ideas. We've got the washing, and your dad's going to find another job, so in a week or two it'll all be back to normal.' She ruffled Bob's hair and gave him a reassuring smile.

'But it won't be,' Evie blurted out. It was as if her mouth suddenly had a mind of its own.

They all turned to look at her and in that moment her suspicions were confirmed: Dad hadn't told Mum and Grandma Sue a word about the debt. It was time to face up to the truth. She couldn't keep quiet a second longer, as if she didn't know, while Mum and Grandma Sue tried to make the best of things and Dad sat there taking them in, pretending it was all going to be all right.

'What do you mean, love?' asked Sue. 'There's no need to get upset. We'll manage somehow.'

'I mean, what about Mr Hopkins? How on earth are we going to pay what you owe him, just from the washing, Dad?'

Michael sat open-mouthed and there was total silence. It was broken by Sue, who sprang to her feet with surprising speed, looming over Michael, her face a picture of fury.

'And who the hell is Mr Hopkins?' she roared.

~

'Right, Mum, I'm off to see Evie,' said Billy, putting a cup of tea down beside his mother's armchair. 'Have you got everything you need? I won't be late.'

'You're a good lad, Billy. I'm right as rain, don't you fret.'

Billy wasn't looking forward to helping Michael Carter sort out his problems repaying Mr Hopkins. Being a postman, Billy tended to know more than most what happened in several neighbourhoods, though he wasn't a gossip. He'd heard of at least two men who had been beaten up when they couldn't pay Hopkins, and some who had had their possessions taken by Hopkins' men in payment of their debts. Billy had thought before now that, what with Michael's drinking and his betting, if it hadn't been for the laundry the family would probably have gone under.

Billy got as far as the corner shop on Lever Lane, at the junction with Shenty Street, when Geraldine Sullivan emerged, rummaging in her handbag and bringing out a packet of Craven 'A' cigarettes.

'Hello, Gerry. Just finishing work, are you?'

'Yes, it's been a long day. Mr Amsell does the evening papers but it's my job to sweep up and tidy the storeroom. I'll be glad to get home and take these shoes off – and these stockings. It's that hot in the shop.' She fanned herself prettily and Billy tried not to think about her taking off her stockings.

Geraldine Sullivan was a real looker, with her glossy dark hair and her big blue eyes. If Mary had more than her fair share of brains, there was no doubt that her elder sister had got the beauty. Geraldine had worked at the corner shop ever since she'd left school. Billy thought she was seventeen or eighteen now but it was hard to tell, what with her red lipstick and her hair always nicely done. She had an easy way with the customers and Billy thought Mr Amsell had realised her beauty was an asset behind the counter as well as her manner, because he knew of several men, old and young, who would choose to go to Amsell's shop just to be sold a paper by Geraldine Sullivan.

'It's the way her hand brushes mine when she counts out the change,' Patrick Finlay had joked. 'Gives a man hope.' Patrick Finlay was sixty if he was a day, and was sweet on half the women in the neighbourhood, including Evie's mum.

'I hope Ma's got something nice saved for my tea,' Geraldine was saying. She laughed and added, 'That's if Da, Stephen, Jamie, Paddy, Niall and especially Cormac haven't scoffed it all.' Cormac was her youngest brother, aged five, who of all her siblings resembled her most. Plump and cute, he looked like a dark-haired cherub.

Billy joined in her laughter. 'Aye, you want to watch out for the little 'un. I reckon he's got the appetite of a brickie.'

Geraldine offered the open packet of cigarettes but Billy shook his head.

'No, thanks. That's one vice I haven't taken up,' he smiled.

Geraldine lit her cigarette, tipped her head back with a flick of her hair and blew a plume of smoke into the air. 'Why, Billy, what vices have you taken up, then?' She looked him directly in the eye. 'Do tell. I'm interested.'

'Ah, man of mystery, me,' Billy replied.

'I like a mystery,' Geraldine said. 'That's what we need round here, a bit more excitement, don't you agree?'

'Mmm . . . ' Billy nodded, unsure quite what he was agreeing with. Still, it was pleasant strolling down to Evie's in easy and attractive company, and fortunately, before Geraldine's flirting got too much for him, they reached her house.

'Thanks for walking me home, Billy. Always nice to see you.' She gave the merest wink, produced her key from her bag and opened the front door. 'See you soon,' she promised with a glamorous red smile over her shoulder, and closed the door behind her.

Phew, that Geraldine is getting to be quite a girl, Billy reflected. Not many round here had her style. She reminded him of Elizabeth Taylor in that comedy he'd seen with Evie at the cinema – *Father of the Bride*. Evie's prettiness was more homely, with her short brown hair clipped back behind her ears, her natural complexion and her girlish figure.

Reluctantly his thoughts turned to the task ahead of him at the Carters'. Best get it over with, and he'd be pleased to help allay Evie's worries if he could. She was a darling girl and she shouldn't have to be worried about her father owing money. He crossed over the road, went up the side to the back door and was surprised to find it closed. He gave a knock and Evie came to open it. Her eyes were red and it was clear she'd been crying.

'Oh, Billy, thank goodness you're here.' She pulled him inside and closed the door. 'It's worse than I thought. Dad's lost his job and there's all this money to find to pay that Mr Hopkins and we don't know what to do now.'

'Sit yourself down, love.' Sue poured Billy a mug of tea. 'Michael's told us the worst and it's twenty-five pounds he owes.'

'It'll never be paid,' sobbed Jeanie, wiping her eyes with an already sodden handkerchief. 'How on earth will we ever get that much?'

'We need to know a bit about this Mr Hopkins,' said Sue. 'Evie says you've heard of him.'

'I have, Mrs Goodwin.' Billy glanced around to see if Peter and Robert were within earshot but there was no sign of them.

'I've sent the boys to their bedroom,' said Sue, correctly understanding him.

'It's not good news, I'm afraid. Mr Hopkins runs a card game upstairs at the King's Head. I've heard the stakes start low, but once you're drawn in they soon get a lot higher.'

'The King's Head?' gasped Jeanie. 'Michael, you told me you went to the Lord Nelson with Brendan as usual. I thought this was something to do with the horses. How many other lies have you told me?'

'I did go to the Nelson with Brendan,' said

Michael. He added in a small voice, 'But I hadn't had much luck with the horses lately so when I heard there was a card game at the King's Head I thought I'd give it a go. I didn't mean to get in deep. I thought if I went on a bit longer my luck would change and I'd be on to a winning streak.'

'Pathetic!' said Sue wrathfully. 'Go on about this Hopkins, lad.'

'Well, he tends to win at the cards and then he makes a point of collecting his debts.'

'You mean by force?' asked Michael, looking even more worried.

'By any means he can. He'll bring in bailiffs to take your furniture, and he's been known to be violent if he thinks you're withholding what you could be paying him. And I've heard that once he starts adding on the interest it's difficult to clear the debt.'

'What are we going to do?' sobbed Jeanie. 'We'll be ruined . . . '

Billy looked down at his hands, reluctant to agree that this was exactly the situation. A miserable silence settled on the five of them as they tried to think of a solution.

'When did you say the money is due?' asked Billy.

'Friday,' said Michael, nervously.

The silence resumed. Billy was beginning to see the only possible course of action but it seemed so drastic that he was unwilling to suggest it.

'Nothing for it but to leave,' said Sue.

Billy was glad she had been the one to voice what he was thinking.

'What, leave our house and the washing and everything, and go right away?' said Jeanie, aghast.

'It isn't our house, it's rented,' said Michael. 'And we'll be out of here anyway if we can't pay the rent.'

'So whose fault would that be?' Jeanie screamed. 'I married you for better or for worse, Michael Carter, but I never thought the worst would be this bad. You'll have us all homeless. I can't believe what you've brought us to.'

'C'mon on, love. No need to get hysterical.'

'What do you expect me to be when it looks like I'm going to lose everything I've got and it's all your fault?' She had bitten her tongue for years but now everything was pouring out. 'Where were you when Mum and I were washing and ironing half the night to make ends meet? I'll tell you where: down the Nelson, drinking your wages and putting bets on half-dead three-legged nags that should have been at the knacker's. Or was it down the King's Head, playing some card game you probably didn't understand against some crook with marked cards?'

'It was bad luck—' Michael began.

'It *was* bad luck all right,' screeched Jeanie. 'It was bad luck for me that I ever set eyes on you!'

She got up and rushed out, slamming the kitchen

door behind her. The others heard her stomping upstairs and then the bedroom door crashing shut.

Evie and Billy exchanged embarrassed glances.

'I'll go up when she's had a chance to calm down,' said Sue.

'I'll go . . . ' said Michael, rising from his chair.

'You've done enough. Sit down and stay here until we've sorted this out,' Sue barked, and Michael slumped in his chair, defeated.

Evie cleared her throat. 'What do you think, Billy? Is Grandma right? Is running away the best thing to do?'

'I'm afraid it is. If you can't pay Hopkins what you owe, he'll dog you until you do, Mr Carter. The only way to be free of him is to leave and go somewhere he doesn't know. That means right away from here, to another part of the country.'

'Leave not just our home but all our friends? But this is all we've ever known,' said Evie, looking pleadingly at Billy.

'It'll be hard, love, and I wish I could say different, but I think it's the only way. Is that what you're thinking, Mrs Goodwin?'

'I'm afraid so, Billy. We'll have to keep quiet about it, too, as we don't want Hopkins after us where we've gone. And we'll have to go soon before word gets round about Michael losing his job or Hopkins' men will be here to take what they can sooner rather than later, if they think that's all they'll be getting.'

Billy nodded. Evie's grandma had grasped the situation exactly.

'But where will we go?' Evie asked. 'We don't know anywhere but here. We don't even have any relatives we can go to.' She looked as if she were about to cry again and Billy passed her his clean handkerchief.

'Don't fret yourself, Evie. At least you'll all be together.'

'But I won't be together with all my friends, and if it has to be a secret I won't be able to tell them where we've gone either,' Evie sniffed. 'I won't be together with you,' she added.

'I know, love, but I won't lose sight of you, I promise. I'll know where you are and I can keep a secret. Your gran's right: it would be better to tell as few folk as possible and to go as quickly as you can before Hopkins gets to hear.'

'Then it had better be straight away,' Michael said, getting up and prowling around the kitchen worriedly. 'By Monday all the folk at the brewery will know I've been sacked.'

'Right, well, I've been thinking,' Sue declared, 'and I think we should decide where we're going this evening. We can't just set off empty-handed and with no idea where we're heading.' She took a lined writing pad and a chewed pencil of Robert's from a drawer behind her. 'Let's make a list of what we know.'

Evie looked blank. 'I don't know anything, Grandma.' Michael was shaking his head, too.

'Nonsense,' said Sue. 'Buck up, the pair of you. And you, Billy. Let's put our heads together and see what we can manage.'

'Right,' said Billy, determined to rise to Evie's grandma's expectations. 'As I say, it'll have to be somewhere far enough away that Hopkins doesn't know it. You'll have to sort of . . . disappear. North is what Hopkins knows. So that means going south.'

'Good thinking,' Sue muttered, writing it down. 'And we'll need to find somewhere to live and then some work.' She looked up and gave Michael a meaningful stare.

'We don't know about those things, but I've an idea who might be able to help,' said Evie. 'Mr Sullivan.'

'Aye, Brendan can be trusted to keep quiet and he has family all over the place,' Michael said. 'I'll go over and get him, shall I?'

'You do that,' said Sue, 'but remember not to say anything while you're there. The Sullivans are good folk but you don't want to let slip our business to the entire houseful in case it accidentally gets passed on.'

Michael collected his boots from where he'd thrown them out of the back door, put them on and went to fetch Brendan.

~

It was late that night that Evie let Billy out through the back door and the Carters went wearily to bed. To Evie it felt as if years had passed since she'd gone to Mrs Russell's that morning with Grandma Sue.

There wouldn't be another wash for Mrs Russell, though. When Annie came with the bundle on Wednesday she'd find the house empty and the family gone. Evie felt sorry to be letting down the kindly widow and the other loyal customers.

Brendan had shown himself to be a true friend that evening. He'd listened to Michael's account of how he'd been kicked out so unfairly from his job and commiserated wholeheartedly. He'd been less sympathetic about the card game and the debt to Mr Hopkins – 'I told you not to go near the King's Head, Michael. You may as well be playing cards with the devil himself as that Hopkins fella' – and then he got down to practicalities in a way that made Evie think how lucky Mary was to have such a clear-thinking and sensible father.

Not only had Brendan got a cousin with a big van, who could transport them and as many of their belongings as could fit in it, but he also had a friend who lived well over a hundred miles south. Brendan's friend Jack knew of an empty property that he thought the Carters would be able to rent, at least until they found something better. Jack had his ear to the ground and he said he'd look out for any jobs going for Michael, too.

Brendan fixed all this up from the public telephone box outside Mr Amsell's shop, waiting for incoming calls to learn the facts and confirm the details, and writing them all down. The arrangements for renting the empty place were hazy, to say the least, but the Carters had the address and Brendan's word on the reliability of his friend. In the circumstances, even such vague progress felt like something to be positive about.

Not long after Brendan came over, Jeanie had been persuaded to come downstairs and she'd brought the boys down with her to join in the discussion.

'They're in this with us. It affects all of us, and Peter and Robert need to know what's going to happen . . . and why,' she said, looking at Michael with her eyes narrowed.

'You're right, lass,' said Michael. 'It's all going to be an exciting adventure, eh, fellas?'

Robert nodded dumbly, not really understanding. Peter, his mouth a tight line, looked away, ignoring his father.

Brendan had brought a couple of bottles of Guinness across with him 'to help things along', which pleased Michael, who emptied and refilled his own glass with remarkable speed.

By the end of the evening Sue's bold handwriting covered several pages of the writing pad and the plan for the Carters to move had a timetable. Fergus

Sullivan, Brendan's cousin, was bringing the van at dawn on Sunday morning and the family were to have everything they wanted to take packed ready and piled by the front door, to be loaded quickly and discreetly.

'I'll come over and give you a hand,' Billy said. 'It's my day off and I'm used to getting up early.'

'Thank you,' Jeanie said. 'What will we do without you?'

'Oh, Mum . . . ' Evie's heart was heavy with her grief. 'We're going to have to find out, that's for sure.'

Now, as she climbed into bed in the stuffy attic room and wished Grandma Sue a goodnight, she felt hot tears running down her face. One more day in this house, the only home she had ever known. Even now she could hardly believe it. And in about . . . she totted it up quickly . . . thirty hours she would be parted from Billy.

Please, let it not be for ever, she whispered.

CHAPTER THREE

'IT'S HERE,' SAID Peter, who had been looking out of the front window for Fergus Sullivan's van.

It was four o'clock on Sunday morning, the summer daylight pale. To the Carters, the air felt unusually clear. All the previous day they had packed their belongings, choosing carefully what was essential and what could be left behind. Even some of the furniture was to remain here because, as Sue reminded her family, the van would need to be loaded as fast and as quietly as they could do it so they could make their escape.

'Escape' – as if from a prison, Jeanie thought. As if staying here would be a punishment instead of the life she had made for herself and her family. She was finding it difficult to be civil to Michael even now, though she'd tried to encourage her children to pack up their belongings and clothes with light hearts and a sense of adventure. Evie and

Peter were old enough to pretend they were excited for Robert's sake, but as Robert was not a naturally light-hearted child anyway they soon abandoned this pretence.

Evie was in charge of extracting suitcases from under beds and she helped Robert to fold his clothes into one of them. There was so much to do in so little time, and keeping busy helped prevent her from becoming more upset. She knew Mum and Grandma Sue were furious about the move but it was no good stoking the flames of their anger with her own.

Peter had been very quiet since the decision to go had been made. He'd packed a duffel bag with his few treasured possessions, and silently helped bring items downstairs until the front room was full of boxes, cases and bagged-up bits and pieces, mainly chosen by his mother.

Sue, with Evie's help, had been busy finishing the washing. Luckily, it was the end of the week, so they weren't due to take in any new bundles. All that remained was collected by the owners, who came to the back door, so there was no need to hide the evidence of the approaching early morning flit piled high in the front room. It was an uncomfortable lie to call a cheerful 'See you next week' to loyal customers, but there was no alternative.

Now, as a large dirty white van pulled up in front

of the house, it was time to move. Evie had imagined a huge removal lorry but this was half the size and had no name painted on the side.

Fergus was let in through the front door and greeted Michael, Jeanie and Sue with a friendly handshake and a smile.

'Right, let's be having you,' he said, speaking softly so as not to disturb the quiet of the sleeping street. 'Beds first and we'll see what else we've got room for after that.'

'What! I'm hoping to take the settee and the chairs and table, at least,' said Jeanie. 'And the mangle has to go.' She was realising it was the size of the van that would dictate what went with them and what was left, not the speed of loading it.

'I'll do what I can, Mrs Carter, don't you worry,' beamed Fergus.

During the next hour it became clear to Evie that this was his answer to everything, and his smile never faded.

Brendan came over to help and the men began to load the heavy items while Sue supervised them and ticked items off her list. Evie packed up some smaller things that they'd needed the previous day, and Jeanie got weepy and wrung her hands.

As Evie was wrapping the last of the crockery in newspaper, being extra careful with Grandma Sue's precious cup and saucer, there was a tap at the back door and Billy let himself into the kitchen.

'Hello, Evie. Let me take that box through to the front,' he said quietly, coming over and giving her a hug. 'You all right?'

'Oh, Billy, thank you for coming to help. I'm that glad to see you.'

'Now don't get upset. You know why this has to be done.'

'We're going away from everything and everybody that we know and care for.' Her heart felt as if it was going to burst.

'You've still got all your family around you. That's what your grandma always says, isn't it: it's family that's important. As long you have each other, nothing else matters.'

'And *you*, Billy. *You* matter to me. I won't have you where we're going.'

'I'll be waiting for your return, never fear, Evie.'

'You mean that, Billy? You'll wait for me to come back? But what if I never do?'

'You will. Here is where you belong, Evie. You'll know where to find me when you come home to Lancashire. But even supposing you don't return here, you can be sure that I'll come and find you where you are. We won't be apart for ever.' He wrapped her in his strong arms and kissed her tenderly. 'In the meantime, we can write to each other. We'll write often. I've never been south and I should like to know what it's like,' he smiled.

'Yes . . . of course. I'll send a letter with the address

when I know we're going to be staying there and not moving on at once.'

'Then do it as soon as you can, my darling, 'cos I'll be looking for that letter every day.'

He gave her another hug and wiped a treacherous tear away from her face with his thumb.

'Now, to work. As I came past I saw all the beds are stowed, and your gran and mum are organising the men moving furniture from the front room. I'll take this box while you make sure you've got a couple of pans packed up, and the knives and forks.'

'Gone already,' said Evie with a brave smile. 'Come on, you can help Dad, Brendan and Fergus with putting the big stuff in the van and I'll help Grandma tick off what's done on her list. Remember, keep your voice down. We don't want half the road in on the act.'

~

As the van got ever fuller, final decisions were made about what had to be left, and the time to depart grew closer, Evie dreaded having to say goodbye to Billy. She was taking a last look round upstairs when she heard the voice of Brendan's wife, Marie.

'Just wanted to wish you luck, me darlin',' said Marie. 'You're in safe hands with Fergus. Don't forget to let us all know how you're doing. It won't be the same round here without you.'

'Thank you. We'll miss you too, Marie,' sniffed Jeanie, who was looking sadly at all the furniture left behind with no room in the van.

'Thanks for everything,' said Sue, hugging each of her neighbours, including Brendan. 'You've been right good friends to us and I won't forget that.'

'Yes,' said Michael. 'Thank you. I'm sorry to have put you to all this trouble.'

'Go on with you,' said Marie, just as Sue said, 'I should think so, too.'

'Goodbye, Mary,' Evie whispered to her friend, hugging her close. 'You're the best friend a girl could ever have – and the cleverest. I'll write, I promise.'

'Dear Evie, there'll be a hole in my life when you've gone. I shall miss you dreadfully.'

'And I'll miss you, Mary.' Evie tried to smile. 'Who's going to teach me long words now?'

'Come on, we'd better get going.' Sue gathered up her handbag, which was bursting at the seams. 'We'd better get off now before we attract unwelcome visitors,' she added meaningfully.

As Michael pulled the door to and posted the key back through the letterbox, the family moved towards the van and their neighbours went back over the road. Billy and Evie turned to one another for the last time.

'Goodbye, Billy,' said Evie, hugging him tight. 'I'll be in touch very soon, I promise.'

'Bye, my Evie,' Billy said, his voice raw with emotion. Then he bent down and kissed her mouth and their tears mingled.

'Don't forget me, will you?' she pleaded.

'I said I'll be waiting,' he reminded her as they drew apart.

'I love you,' Evie whispered, but he'd already turned away to hide his tears and she wasn't sure he'd heard.

It was a terrible squash to fit everyone in the van, although there were big extra seats that folded down behind, sideways on to the front ones. Sitting there meant finding room for your legs around the luggage, however, so it was hard to get comfortable. Peter and Evie were sharing a seat and Robert had to sit on Jeanie's knee. Fergus started the engine and all the Carters waved to their friends congregated outside the Sullivans' house to give them a silent send-off.

Evie fixed her eyes on Billy's face, but within a few seconds it was lost from her sight. The van turned the corner at the end of the road and Shenty Street was gone.

As Fergus happily negotiated the streets heading to the road that would take them south, the Carters sat nursing their regrets. Jeanie was openly sobbing and even Sue was tearful, which set off Evie, and Robert was crying, too. Michael was subdued but, wisely for once, decided to say nothing. Evie, squashed up beside Peter, took his hand in hers to comfort him, but when she looked into his face she saw not sadness but such fury that she felt a strange and terrible foreboding and withdrew her own hand in shock.

The van reached the southern outskirts of the town and the blackened industrial buildings gave way to houses with gardens and, soon, green fields. The Carters dried their eyes, made themselves as comfortable as they could and accepted the inevitable. The old life was gone and a new one, whatever it held, lay ahead of them at the end of this journey.

'I still wish I'd been able to say goodbye to Mrs Russell,' said Grandma Sue over her shoulder to Evie, who sat behind her. 'And Dora Marsh. I've known Dora . . . must be forty years. We were young brides together.'

'There are a lot of folk I'd like to have said goodbye to. Seems rude just to go, like they meant nothing to us,' Jeanie agreed. She paused for a few moments and then added: 'I wish I'd been able to say cheerio to Harold Pyke.' Then she started laughing rather shakily and soon everyone joined in, even Robert, who didn't know what was funny.

The mood lifted as they drove on and the sun rose higher on the promise of a beautiful day.

After a while Robert piped up: 'I spy with my little eye something beginning with . . . '

Sue and Evie caught each other's eye in the wing

mirror and pulled faces. It was going to be a long journey.

~

'Where are we?' said Peter, waking from a deep sleep. Sue and Evie had also nodded off, and Robert was still asleep on his mother. 'It must be the sight of those mattresses that sent me to sleep. They look so comfy compared to this seat.'

Everyone gazed out of the windows at the countryside they were passing through. In the strong summer sunshine the scene was glorious.

Evie wished she hadn't slept and missed seeing some of this: on either side of the road hedges grew tall and green, dog roses twining through them. At breaks in the hedges, through field gates, she could see cows and sometimes horses grazing. It was all so huge and so green that she couldn't quite believe her eyes.

'Countryside – there's just so much of it,' said Peter. 'I'd no idea it was so big.'

'And the air smells different – sort of nice,' said Sue, winding down the window.

They continued travelling south, amazed at how green everything was and how clean. Sometimes they passed through a town or village and Jeanie would point out a pretty house and wonder aloud if they were heading for one like that.

Eventually Sue looked at her watch and declared

it was 'dinnertime' and if Fergus would like to find a suitable place to stop they could have something to eat. Fergus turned off the road in the next market town and pulled up in a car park where there was, everyone was pleased to see, a sign for public lavatories. The little town was quiet on a Sunday lunchtime and the shops were closed when Jeanie took her children for a short walk to stretch their legs after enduring the cramped seats.

When everyone was back at the van and standing around in the sun, Sue got out a cake tin, which was filled with rather warm sandwiches, and when they'd eaten those, another in which there was cake, and Jeanie poured lemonade from a flask. Michael produced a bottle of beer with a flourish, which Fergus declined to share because he was driving. Evie noticed that her father drank it all himself then.

The sandwiches and most of the cake eaten, the Carters and Fergus climbed back into the van and set off again. There was a stop at a petrol station, where Sue paid for the van to be refuelled and bought some boiled sweets, but by mid-afternoon the novelty of the journey had worn off and everyone was bored, fidgeting and eager to arrive. They had long since passed signs for the city of Birmingham and still they headed south.

'Not too far now,' said Fergus when Robert asked for the tenth time if they were nearly there. 'We'll be there before nightfall, don't you worry.'

'Thing is, Fergus,' said Peter, reasonably, 'it isn't dark until nine o'clock, so that's quite a long time yet.'

'It could well be,' said Fergus, vaguely. 'We'll have to see how it goes . . . '

'Do you know what this place is like, Fergus? Have you ever been there before?' asked Jeanie.

'No, I haven't, Jeanie. I just said to Brendan that I'd take you in the van. I think it might be quite a small village as I've never heard of it and I had to look up the way on a map. I don't think Brendan knows much about it either. But he trusts his friend Jack Fletcher so it'll be all right, don't you worry.'

'But it is all right for us to be there?' asked Jeanie, beginning to get anxious. 'We don't know this Jack Fletcher, and Brendan's a long way away now.'

Seeing Jeanie quietly wringing her hands, Evie picked up her mother's mood and began to worry too. What if there had been a mistake and there wasn't an empty house after all? What if someone else was living there? Or maybe there'd been a mix-up and they'd been given the wrong address? Or he could have been misled by the owner of the house . . .

Peter, sensing her distress, nudged her gently with his elbow. 'C'mon, Evie, it might even be nice,' he whispered bravely.

~

It was late afternoon when Fergus drove past a shabby-looking farm and slowed down at a sign announcing a village.

'Here we are,' he said. 'Church Sandleton.'

Everyone sat up and peered out to try to get the gist of the place. There was an assortment of old and new houses lining the road, a pub and a couple of shops.

'Slow down, Fergus, and let's remind ourselves what it is we're looking for,' Sue said, fishing the writing pad out of her handbag. Then she had a rummage around for her reading glasses and Fergus pulled into the side of the road while she found them and put them on. 'The house we're looking for is called Pendles, so keep your eyes peeled for that name,' she said.

'Pendles . . . ' Michael murmured, looking to the right and left, while Evie, Peter and Jeanie craned forward in their seats to see the nameplates on gates as Fergus drove slowly on.

Jeanie caught sight of a cottage with a garden full of blooming roses and lavender. 'Slow down, Fergus. Is that it?' She squinted hopefully at the sign on the gatepost, then saw it said Lavender Cottage. 'No . . . ' Disappointed, she sat back.

'Wait, wait, what's that one?' said Sue, pointing over to Fergus's side of the road where a fine square house was set back with a black front door and steps up to it from a wrought-iron gate. 'P . . . It's

P-summat, I can't quite see . . . ' She couldn't keep a note of hope from her voice.

'Prospect House,' said Fergus, and everyone sighed and subsided in their seats.

'It must be on this road somewhere because the address is "High Street",' said Sue.

'Brendan told me that Jack Fletcher said it's towards the end of the village. I thought we'd find it easily,' Michael added.

The end of the high street was in sight as the buildings became more widely spaced and gave way to hedges and fields ahead of them. Evie felt a flicker of panic. What if there was no such place? Would they end up living out of Fergus's van? She dismissed the ridiculous thought immediately but her stomach was now churning nervously.

'It's just a derelict shop this side and what looks like it might be a market garden over there,' said Sue. 'We must have missed it. Let's turn round and go through again.'

'No, wait,' said Michael. 'There! Over the shop. It's called Pendle's. It must be that.'

'It can't be,' breathed Jeanie faintly. 'No one said anything about a shop. We're looking for a house.'

'It has to be that,' insisted Michael. 'Stop here, Fergus, and let's have a look.'

Fergus pulled up and Michael climbed stiffly out and went to the front of the boarded-up shop. There was a door at one side with wood planks nailed over it and a heavy padlock securing a hasp. Next to it was a large expanse of window, also covered in planks. The paintwork around the window, what was visible of the door and on the fascia, was a dull green. The deep fascia spanned the whole of the front and on it in peeling gold capital letters was painted the name 'PENDLE'S'.

There was no doubt this was the right name, Jeanie saw. She hoped it wasn't actually the right building, that there would somehow be another place called Pendles, and it would look more like, if not Prospect House then at least that cottage with the pretty garden they'd passed earlier.

'Brendan said the key would be here, is that right, Sue?' called Michael, looking up at the building, his back to them all waiting in the van.

Evie guessed her father was disappointed too and hiding his face until he was ready to put on a brave show.

'Round the side, under a brick, apparently,' confirmed Sue.

Michael went up the side of the shop, saw a ruined-looking wooden door, lifted the sneck and disappeared through it. A few moments later he reappeared holding up a key.

Oh dear, thought Evie. That means it really is the right place. And it's going to be awful, I know it is.

She could hardly bear to watch as her father fitted the key to the padlock and it opened. Everything

now had a dreadful inevitability. He removed the
padlock, eased open the door with its planks
attached to the frame and went inside.

'Come on,' said Sue, heavily, climbing out of the
van. 'I think we're home.'

~

The Carters and Fergus stood in the shop part of
the building. The good news was that the electricity
was on so they could at least see how awful the place
was behind the boarded-up window. There was long
counter parallel to the interior wall and floor-to-
ceiling drawers and shelves against the far wall. They
were empty and dusty, a few dead flies littering the
surfaces and the front window, and mouse drop-
pings on the floor. There was no indication what
Pendle's had ever sold or how long the place had
been empty, but the smell was stale as if it had been
abandoned a while ago.

'God save us,' muttered Jeanie, her voice trem-
bling. 'A shop. Not even a proper house.' Her face
was white with tiredness and disappointment.

'You stay here. I'll go and look upstairs,' said Sue.
She thought she'd better learn the worst and break
it to Jeanie gently rather than risk her kicking off
unprepared. It had been such a long day, it didn't
look like they would be able to get to bed for ages
yet and Sue had the unhappy idea that Jeanie's fuse

might just be ready to blow. 'Come with me, Peter, Evie, and let's see what we can find.' She opened the door behind the counter and sure enough it led to a hallway with two rooms opening off and a flight of stairs to the floor above.

'Right, you two,' Sue began when the door had closed on weighted hinges behind them. 'Your mum's had enough and I don't blame her. Let's see what works, what we can get working this evening, and decide where everyone's going to sleep. Everything else can wait until tomorrow.'

'Are we really going to live here, Grandma?' asked Peter. 'Did Dad know it was a shop?'

'I don't know and I don't know, Pete, but we're here tonight and the main thing is we're all together. So far as I know no one on earth has ever heard of Church Sandleton, so we're most likely safe from that Mr Hopkins.'

As she spoke she led her grandchildren into the first of the downstairs rooms behind the shop. It was a large sitting room, empty of furniture, with a dirty wooden floor and a bare light bulb suspended from the centre of the ceiling. Evie tried the switch and the bulb glowed dimly. Through the unboarded window they could see into a small backyard, paved but with weeds peeping through between the slabs. There was a little brick building at the end, which they all guessed was a privy.

'It'll do,' said Sue stoutly, looking round the room.

'Your mum and I will know what to do with this, I reckon.'

Evie smiled, feeling less dismal, and she saw Peter was bucking up, too.

'The kitchen will be the other room,' said Sue. 'It's make or break there, I reckon,' she added, leading Evie and Peter back to the cramped hallway and into the room next to the sitting room.

'It can be put right and your mum will come round to it – if we're allowed to do as we like, that is. It's not our place, don't forget. I haven't had a chance to work it out yet, but I think we're renting it from Jack's friend, and we don't even know who he is yet . . . Oh, this is big. It must be twice the size of Shenty Street's kitchen. Needs a lot of cleaning, though,' she added, looking at a solidly built but very grubby cream-coloured electric cooker.

Evie opened a door at the back and found a pantry with a cold slab and a vent to the outside to keep the air cool. It was empty except for a cardboard box on one of the shelves. It looked like a recent addition, being free of dust, and she opened it and gasped in astonishment.

'Look, Grandma,' she said, bringing it out and putting it on the built-in dresser. 'There's a note with Dad's name on it and a loaf of bread and a packet of tea. Who can have left this?'

'One way to find out,' said Sue, unfolding the

lined sheet of paper and holding it at arm's length because she'd left her glasses in her handbag in the shop room. 'It's no good, Evie, you'll have to read it to me. Never mind it's addressed to your dad.'

Evie saw that the letter was elegantly written with a fountain pen:

Dear Mr Carter,

I hope you have had a good journey. I am sorry about the state of the shop. Jack Fletcher says you are a friend of his and need a place to stay, so I hope it will do for now.

The electricity is working. Please accept the bread and the tea.

I look forward to meeting you shortly.

Yours sincerely,

Frederick Bailey

'Well I never!' exclaimed Sue. 'Our first piece of good luck, and I'm hoping not the last. 'Course, we've never met Jack Fletcher, but let's not fret about details. Obviously Brendan has some influence with folk, even down here. Maybe things aren't as bad as we thought.'

'I'll go and show Mum,' said Evie.

'You do that, love. It might just pull her back from the brink. Peter and I will go and look upstairs and see if we can cope, eh? Whoever this Frederick Bailey is, at least he knows this place is a shambles. Mebbe

he'll be round in the morning to sort it all out.'
Though I wouldn't bet on it, she thought.

Upstairs was pretty grim, too, but there was an
electric water heater over a wash basin, and even a
working lavatory. The three bedrooms were bare of
furniture, dusty and stuffy in the heat, but there
would be room for all of them, as there had been
in Shenty Street.

'I think we're staying, at least until we sort out
summat better, don't you?' Sue asked her grandson.

'I reckon you're right, Grandma. Let's go and tell
Fergus we can start unloading the van. It's going to
be dark soon and I'm that hungry I can hear my
tummy singing.'

'Good thinking, young fella,' said Sue. 'I won't
put up with an unclean house, but just for tonight
I think I may have to break that rule.'

~

The van was unloaded far quicker than it had been
packed up that morning. Fergus and Michael took
the bedsteads and then the mattresses upstairs
between them while Jeanie and Evie carried in the
chairs and the boxes for the kitchen. The mangle
went into a corner of the kitchen.

Fergus was invited to stay the night, Peter agreeing
to double up with Robert so as to leave his bed free
for the helpful Irishman, but Fergus said he'd rather

be getting home. He didn't mind driving late at night if it meant his own bed at the end of it, and his wife, Kate, waiting for him, so Sue made him a cup of tea and gave him some of the cake left from earlier, and then the Carters waved him on his way with heartfelt thanks and love to be passed on to Brendan and the family.

The sun was setting in a red sky as the forlorn family watched the rear lights of Fergus's van disappear down the road and they waved until he was out of sight. Then they filed back into the shop through the boarded-up door and Sue, Michael and the boys went to make up the beds.

'We won't unpack more than necessary,' said Jeanie to Evie, leading her into the kitchen. 'I don't know as we're staying, despite that Frederick Bailey's letter.'

'But it will be better when we've cleaned it up and got our things where we want them, I'm sure, Mum. And at least we've got Dad away from Mr Hopkins.'

'Thank the Lord.' Jeanie looked around the big filthy kitchen and shook her head. 'You know, Evie love, I'm really trying to see this as the start of a new life, a hope that things will be good for us from now on in a different place. That's what your grandma would be saying to you.'

'And she'd be right, Mum. We've got somewhere to stay, at least for now, and Mr Bailey must be a good sort, don't you think, as he thought to write that note and leave the tea and bread?'

'Yes, love, but we don't know him, do we? We've never even met Fergus's friend Jack, who arranged this with Mr Bailey. And if we do stay here we'll have to pay rent. Your grandma and I have a bit of money saved from the washing but it won't go far. We've lost our laundry business now, and your dad'll need to find a job straight away.'

'I know, Mum, but didn't Brendan say Jack Fletcher has an ear to the ground and might come up with something? And Dad can start looking tomorrow. I know he's been a bit . . . daft with the betting, and then this card game with Mr Hopkins, but mebbe he's learned his lesson.'

'I want to think so, love, I honestly do. But somehow I can't see your dad changing, and that's what's worrying me. I've seen the road he's been going down for a while. Mebbe it's too late for him to be any different.'

Evie wanted to argue that their lives *would* get better now they had a chance to start again, all of them together in a new place, but they'd lost so much by running away – all their friends, not least – and she couldn't bring herself to lie to her mother. In her heart she knew that Mum was probably right: Dad would never change. She only hoped he wouldn't drag them down further.

She thought about Billy – how he had kissed her

farewell and told her he'd wait for her to come back. Was it only this morning? It seemed like days ago.

Quietly contemplating their new lives, she felt furious with her father. Stupid man! Stupid and selfish. His selfishness had caused his family to lose everyone they knew and cared for, everything Mum and Grandma Sue had worked for, and their little home in the town where they belonged. Now they had only each other.

For a moment she stood breathing deeply until her anger subsided.

'We've got each other and we always will have,' she said, trying for a smile. 'Together, who knows what we can manage?'

CHAPTER FOUR

As Evie woke up very early in a strange room, the light streaming through the uncurtained window, and remembered the upsets of the weekend and her parting from Billy, she was comforted to see the familiar bulk of Sue in her own sagging bed close by.

'Awake, Evie?' Sue smiled. 'New home, new life, lass. Shall we be up and at it? I'm keen to see what that shop part is like. I had a few thoughts about it in the night. Let's get your dad busy taking down the boards and we'll see better what's what.'

'Gran, you always know how to make the best of things,' Evie said, feeling less anxious. 'So much to do . . . I'll go down and make a pot of tea while you get up.'

It was impossible for Evie to feel miserable for long with Sue's remarkable energy and enthusiasm rallying her.

Sue and Evie were up and making toast when Peter appeared, playing a cheery ditty on his penny whistle.

'You're in a good mood,' Evie remarked to Peter, as he smiled at the music, quietly tapping his toes.

'No school,' said Peter simply.

'But you'll have to go sometime.'

'Not for ages and ages. It's the summer holidays from the end of this week. Mum and Dad won't send Bob and me to school for one week, will they, Grandma?'

'They haven't even had the chance to think about school, Pete,' Sue replied. 'I reckon you're safe now until September.'

'Yippee! Though I won't tell Bob just yet. Let him stew, like.'

'Don't be cruel,' laughed Evie. Within five minutes it was smiles all round. The music was jolly and lifted their spirits.

'You can help your dad with those boards and let some light into the front,' said Sue, as Michael and Jeanie came running in.

Peter gave his father a look that said he'd rather not help him but his words belied that. 'Of course,' he said. 'I'm good on ladders – if we have one, that is?'

'Saw one round the side yesterday when I fetched the key,' Michael told him. He took a piece of toast and went off with it to find the ladder and his tools.

All their things had been unpacked so quickly from Fergus's van the previous evening that it was difficult for everyone to remember where they'd put their belongings.

'You sound keen to get on,' said Jeanie to her mother, sounding anything but keen herself. She looked as if she hadn't slept at all and her eyes were red.

'No point in delaying,' Sue replied. 'You never know what you'll find.'

'You're right, Mum, of course,' Jeanie pulled herself up, 'though it'll have to be an awful lot better than I think it's going to be if we're to stay here. The place is rundown – and a shop, for goodness' sake!'

'I'll have no defeatist talk,' Sue answered, though she was smiling. 'We don't even know who owns it, and we've yet to meet Brendan's friend Jack Fletcher, either. Or maybe he owns it? I'm confused about that, I admit.'

'Me, too,' said Jeanie. 'I expect someone will appear to tell us – especially if they want some rent,' she added.

'Come on, get that toast down you – and you too, Peter,' Sue commanded, passing over mugs of tea. 'It could be our lucky day.'

'Give over, Mum. No need to go overboard,' said Jeanie, but she winked at Evie and Peter.

'Maybe there'll be buried treasure,' said Peter, as

he led the others through to the front, bringing the plate of toast with him. 'A secret cellar full of gold.'

'Aye, and I'm the Queen of Sheba,' said Jeanie. 'Where's Bob? Is he getting up?'

'Sort of. He said his stomach aches but I told him to stop whingeing and see if it felt better when he came down,' said Peter without a trace of sympathy. 'I think he's worried about going to a new school. I haven't told him yet we're not going,' he grinned.

'I'll go and tell him and see if he's all right. You know what he's like with his sensitive stomach.'

~

It took most of the morning for Michael and Peter to remove the boards from the window to the street and stack them out of the way, while Jeanie and Evie found some dusty curtains in the attic and tried to get the place cleaner and more comfortable, and Sue unpacked their boxes. The whole family went to view the unboarded shop from the pavement, eager to see if it looked more promising than it had the previous evening.

'At least we'll be able to see out,' said Michael. 'And it's a big room.'

'A big room for what?' snapped Jeanie, her anger with him not yet dampened down. 'And everyone else can see in now, too. What are we going to do there, sit having our tea like goldfish in a bowl?'

Robert started pulling fish faces, his mouth silently working like a guppy until Peter gently cuffed him round the ear.

'No, love, I only meant—'

A young woman with a baby in a pram and a toddler clutching her arm came along the pavement and the Carters moved aside to let her pass.

'Good morning,' the woman said, smiling. 'Nice to see the old shop opened up.'

'Morning,' said Michael. He peered into the pram, turning on the charm in front of the pretty lady. 'Now that's a bonny baby . . . We're new here and know nowt about the place. What was the shop, do you know?'

'Yes, I can hear you're not from round here,' said the woman, but kindly. 'It was a general household store. Mr Pendle sold buckets, brooms, seeds, string – you know the kind of thing. There's still a call for it but people go to the new shop in the village now. Mr Pendle was old and couldn't keep the business going when his health started to fail. That was a while ago. I'd heard that Mr Bailey was talking about finding new tenants.'

'Mr Bailey?' prompted Sue.

'Frederick Bailey. The owner.' The woman looked puzzled, evidently expecting Sue to know that.

'Oh, aye? Well, Mrs . . . ?'

'Lambert. Josie Lambert.' She held out her hand to shake Sue's.

'Mrs Lambert, we're all very pleased to meet you.' Sue introduced herself and her family. 'Would you care for a cup of tea? I'm sure we can find summat for the little 'un, too, though I'm afraid we've nowt suitable for the baby,' she added. 'It's nice to meet new folk and we know no one around here. If you have a few minutes we'd be glad to learn about the old place and this Mr Bailey.'

'Yes, I can spare a few moments. Thank you.' Mrs Lambert parked the pram and lifted the baby out, murmuring to her and smoothing her fine blonde hair. 'Come along, Archie,' she told the toddler, smiling.

'Archie – that's nice,' said Evie, taking the child's hand and leading him in, though he clutched his mother's skirt in his other little fist.

'Excuse the mess. We only got here last night,' said Jeanie.

'It's all right,' said the friendly woman, though she perched rather tentatively on the chair in the dismal kitchen. 'So how did you come to be here if you don't know Church Sandleton?'

Michael and Jeanie exchanged looks.

'A friend of a friend had heard of a job hereabouts that might suit,' said Michael vaguely. 'It's a pretty part of the country . . . good place to bring up children,' he improvised, looking at young Archie and his baby sister.

'Would that be the job at Clackett's market garden?' asked Mrs Lambert, accepting a cup of

Ribena for Archie and tea for herself. 'I heard Mr
Clackett was looking for some help.'

'If the job's still going,' said Michael. Having been
working all morning at the front he couldn't have
failed to notice the sign for Clackett's a few yards
further down on the other side of the road.

Sue gave him a meaningful look. 'So do you know
Mr Bailey?' she asked Josie Lambert. 'We haven't
met him yet.'

'Oh, no, I don't know him personally. He lives in
Redmond but he's seen about the village sometimes.
Drives a smart car and owns here and a couple of
other properties.'

'Well, no doubt he'll be round before long,' said
Sue, and, having extracted what information she
could about the landlord, she changed the subject
to the village generally while Jeanie cooed over baby
Nancy and little Archie.

As soon as Josie Lambert had waved goodbye with
promises to call again when Jeanie was settled, Sue
turned to Michael.

'Right, you get over to that market garden, lad,
and see what this job's about.'

'But I know nowt about growing vegetables,' he
protested.

'Who said you'd be growing the veg? You won't
know if you don't go.' She shooed him out of the
door, then turned to Jeanie. 'Now, I've an idea about
the front room. Come through and see what you

think. You, too, Evie. It was us women that held the place together in Shenty Street and we can make a go of it here with luck and a fair wind. And as I said earlier, this could be our lucky day.'

'It's looking that way so far,' Peter said, grabbing his whistle and playing a jaunty fanfare. 'Come on, Bob. I'll wash, you dry, and Grandma can think up ways to make our fortune.'

~

Billy immediately recognised Evie's neat round handwriting on the envelope Ada Taylor had left on the kitchen table for him to find when he got in from work. He snatched it up as he called out to her that he was home, then went upstairs to read it in private.

Pendle's
High Street
Church Sandleton
Near Redmond

Thursday

Dear Billy,
    I hope you and your mother are well. I'm missing you like mad and I hope you're missing me, too.
    I can't believe so much has happened since we waved off Fergus Sullivan on Sunday evening. Dad's

got a job – the first one he tried for! It's at the market garden across the road and he's helping to pick the crops. There's a huge amount of them at the moment and Dad says it gets very hot in the glasshouses. He says it's backbreaking work, especially the strawberries, but luckily they're nearly finished. Another really good thing is that Mr Clackett, the owner, gives Dad some of the stuff he says won't sell so we're eating lots of very ripe fruit and vegetables.

The boys are on holiday from school and play outside all day. Pete is making friends with Mr Clackett's son, Martin, and Bob usually tags along with them. There are miles of fields for them to play in around here as it's proper countryside.

Where we're living is an old shop, which makes a strange house with the shop window, but Grandma has hatched a plan for her, Mum and me to open a little business. I'm so excited that we'll be working together again. We've looked around the village and there's no one advertising their dressmaking services or doing alterations and repairs so we think we may have found what Grandma calls 'an opening'. We need to get in touch with Mr Bailey, who owns the building, to see if that's all right, but so far we haven't met him.

It's nice here but it doesn't feel like home and I don't know if it ever will. It's so different from everything we know and love in Bolton. The people in the village are friendly but we're all missing you and the Sullivans and Mrs Marsh – our kind of people.

Please give my best to your mother, and write soon.
I shall look for your letter every day. Remember not
to tell anyone the address, just in case.
  With lots of love,
  Evie xxx

So, Evie was missing him 'like mad' – which was exactly how he felt about her. How he longed to see her pretty face, with her pointy chin and big hazel eyes. It seemed far longer than five days since he'd waved her goodbye and he'd been thinking of her constantly since then.

Billy reread the letter, then changed out of his postman's uniform and returned downstairs.

Ada had a pot of strong tea brewing and a toasted teacake waiting for him – 'to put you on till teatime, love.'

'Thanks, Mum. You'll have guessed the letter was from Evie. Guess what: seems her dad has a job already.'

'Well, bless me, who'd have thought it?'

'It's great news. Things will turn out better for them all from now.'

'I wouldn't bet on it with that Michael Carter. I reckon Jeanie Goodwin has long rued the day that she married him. She's a bonny woman and could have had her pick. What she wanted to choose him for I don't know. I'd have thought Sue might have talked her out of it, but no.'

'Sounds like he's doing all right now, anyway.'

'That's if he can keep this job, whatever it is,' Ada muttered darkly. 'He'd do well to change his ways and be a bit more reliable. What news of Sue and Jeanie?'

'Mrs Goodwin wants to start a dressmaking business. Seems they live in an old shop so there are ready-made premises for customers – I expect that gave her the idea.'

'Well, Sue was always a hard worker, and a talented seamstress, too. It's a step up from taking in washing, but if anyone can make a go of it, she can.'

'Evie is going to help her, she's good with a needle, and a fast learner. She worries about getting things just right and she'll apply herself to it. She has the same eye for a job well done as her grandma.'

'They'll be all right with Sue in charge,' said Ada confidently. She looked carefully at her son. 'Sounds like they're making a whole new life for themselves down south.'

'I think Evie's missing everyone here,' Billy replied. 'It's not the same as where she was brought up and what she knows. And I reckon we're all missing her, too,' he added boldly.

'You say that now, Billy, but she's not been gone long. Sometimes folk move on, love, and it's not a good idea to be wanting everything to be as it was. She's not here now and probably won't come back. You've got to accept that or be disappointed.'

But Billy wasn't at all ready to accept that Evie was gone for good. He'd never forget the promise he'd made to her that they wouldn't be apart for ever, though he decided not to share this thought with his mother.

He'd write a reply to Evie that evening. After they'd had their tea his mother liked to doze while listening to the Light Programme on the wireless so there'd be a chance then for him to write a long letter full of news about Evie's friends in Bolton. And to send her his love.

~

'I can't believe we've been here over a week and still haven't met this Mr Bailey,' said Jeanie as she chopped some of the twisty-shaped carrots Michael had returned with that evening. Sue, Evie and Peter were busy in the front room, cleaning it in preparation for a coat of paint.

'Well, that's good, isn't it?' said Michael as he scrubbed soil from under his fingernails at the kitchen sink. 'At least he hasn't come asking for any rent.'

'We'll have to pay him eventually,' Jeanie replied. 'And Mum is full of ideas for our little business and wants to get started. We'll need to have enough money for the rent when the time comes, and there's no one else offering a sewing service in Church

Sandleton. So far, anyway. We can't be the only ones with a sewing machine and Mum's worried someone may pip us at the post if we don't get started soon.'

'Can't she set up business without asking Bailey?' Michael sank into a chair to watch Jeanie work.

'I expect so, but it *is* his property, after all. It's only polite to tell him what we want to do, see if it's all right with him.'

'Why would he object, though? It's not like you're opening a – I don't know – a pub or summat you'd need legal permission for.'

'Or an undertaker's,' piped up Robert, at the far end of the kitchen table. 'That would be horrible and creepy. You'd have dead people in the front room and, Dad, you'd have to wear a tall black hat.'

'Good grief, Bob, I don't know where you get such ideas,' laughed Jeanie, pulling a quizzical face at Michael. 'Anyway, I've decided that if Mr Bailey's not coming to us then I'm going to him. Mum looked out her sewing machine this morning, oiled it and everything. Evie's written a neat little notice to pin up in the shop, offering alterations, curtain- and dressmaking, and mending. Once that's up we'll need to be ready for our customers.'

'I'd leave it if I were you, love,' said Michael. 'Wait and see what happens. We're living rent-free at the moment – no use courting expense and creating problems for ourselves.'

'If you think it's rent-free here then you're dafter than you look,' said Jeanie wearily. 'Come on, Michael, we've lost so much, but let's start as we mean to go on. The laundry and mending business was what kept us going many a week in Bolton. The boys will need new school uniform come September and we can't live for ever on what Mum and I saved from the washing.'

'I do my bit—'

'Picking tomatoes!'

'But we get given vegetables, too.'

'Mr Clackett's been very generous, and I'm grateful, but we can't eat nowt but vegetables.'

'By heck, Jeanie, you're a grand cook and few others could make them veggies taste as good as you do, but what I wouldn't give for a helping of hotpot.'

'Evie and I are to catch the bus to Redmond in the morning and we shall find Mr Bailey, introduce ourselves and make sure our plans are all straight and above board with him. What if there's been some mistake and he doesn't even know we're here?'

'You're right, of course . . . ' said Michael, getting up and stretching his stiff back. 'I'll just go out and take a stroll up the street while you're making that carrot thing.'

'Don't be too long, love. You're looking tired and the veg doesn't take much cooking.'

Michael grunted as he went down the hall, past Sue, Evie and Peter still scrubbing the walls, floor and ceiling of the front room. He stepped out into the street and turned towards the Red Lion, thinking he'd already left it far too long to make the acquaintance of his new local.

~

Jeanie and Evie got off the bus in the market square in Redmond. It was market day and on this sunny July morning the place was thronging with shoppers carrying baskets, women pushing prams and traders shouting their wares from the brightly coloured stalls.

'Oh, Mum, let's have a quick look,' begged Evie.

'A look won't hurt,' agreed Jeanie, 'but we won't buy anything until we've found Mr Bailey and seen about the rent and if we can go ahead with the sewing. Look, there's Mr Clackett behind that stall. And Martin's helping him.' She waved and the market gardener called out cheerily to her.

'Let's see if there's a fabric stall or a haberdasher's,' suggested Evie. 'We can report back to Grandma if anything looks good.'

'Aye, your gran has high standards,' said Jeanie, 'though we may have to make do to start with and work our way up to best quality as we earn a bit of money.'

'It sounds like you think Grandma's idea really will work out.' Evie's smile lit up her face. 'I'm so glad, Mum. The washing was hard, but it was nice when us three were all working together. It'll be like that again.'

'From oldest to youngest, we all stick together,' Jeanie agreed.

'It's going to be brilliant. I can't wait to get started.'

They soon spotted a stall heaped with bolts of cloth, but the prices were high compared to those the Carters were used to up North.

'No mill shops here either,' said Jeanie. 'Well, I suppose we couldn't expect it to be as cheap as it is straight from the factory. That lace is nice, though.'

'We'll remember to tell Grandma. Come on, let's go and see if we can find Mr Bailey.'

They had already made a plan. The public library was a grand-looking building on one side of the square and they went in and found the reference library where a sign instructed 'SILENCE'. Josie Lambert had mentioned that Frederick Bailey drove a smart car so it was highly likely he was the kind of man who also had a telephone in his house. Jeanie and Evie quickly found the local telephone directory and in less than two minutes were coming out of the library with the addresses written down of two people: 'F. Bailey' and 'F. W. Bailey'.

'We've no way of knowing so we'll just have to try one, and then the other if we have to,' said Jeanie.

'Maybe look out for a policeman – they always know where places are – but we'll ask Mr Clackett in the meantime.'

They went back over to the market and had to wait while Mr Clackett did a brisk trade in salad before he was free to give them his attention.

'Woodfall Road – don't know that, I'm afraid, Mrs Carter. Eh, Stanley,' he called across to a man selling sausages. 'Woodfall Road – ring any bells?'

Stanley scratched his head. 'Off the main road out towards Church Sandleton,' he said eventually.

'What about Midsummer Row?' asked Jeanie.

'Oh, that's just behind here,' said Mr Clackett. 'Next to that shoe shop there's a side road that goes down into a little square.'

'Thank you,' beamed Jeanie, and she and Evie set off for the nearer place.

'Oh, I suddenly feel quite nervous,' said Jeanie as they walked through into the pretty square with trees in a tiny central garden and tall thin town houses overlooking it all round.

'Perhaps he'll be really nice,' suggested Evie, though she, too, was anxious and her stomach was churning.

'Do I look all right?' asked Jeanie. 'I don't want to appear down at heel. I want Mr Bailey to think we're respectable folk who can be trusted.'

Evie stopped walking and pulled her mother round to face her. She tipped her straw hat a fraction further forward and brushed a tiny speck of dust off the lapel of her floral print jacket. It was old but Sue had made it from quality cotton spun and woven in Bolton and, with its eye-catching colours and sharp tailoring, it had stood the test of time and was a fine advertisement for Sue's dress-making skills.

'Mum, you look lovely,' Evie told her mother truthfully. 'Now let's see which one's Marlowe House.'

They walked round the square, reading the names on smart plaques beside the front doors, and soon came to the right one. Evie opened the iron gate and Jeanie led her through and up the steps to the front door.

She took a deep breath and had just put her hand out to ring the bell when the door was flung open and a furious-looking woman, wearing an overall and with her hair tied up with a scarf, erupted out of the house.

'You can keep your flipping job, you old bastard!' she yelled back through the open door. 'Don't you threaten me with the police. Years I've slaved for you, and poor thanks I've had for it. I've seen pigs keep themselves cleaner. You can stew in your own muck. I deserve better and I only took what should have been mine. I've had enough!'

She picked up an ornament from a side table beside the door and hurled it back down the hall. Evie and Jeanie heard the tinkle of shattering china and unconsciously they clutched each other as the harridan, oblivious, stomped past them, down the steps and through the gate, leaving it open in her wake.

Evie's heart was pounding as she turned to see her mother was white with shock.

'Oh, Mum, whatever can have happened? I think we ought to go. I don't like it here at all.'

'Me neither, Evie. Come on . . . '

As they began to retrace their steps a calm and educated voice called behind them, 'Please don't mind Mrs Summers. She can be a bit ill-tempered, though, truth be told, she was a very good cleaner. Pity she wasn't a more honest one.'

Jeanie quickly tried to gather herself as she turned back to see who had spoken.

He was a tall, very lean and good-looking man in his fifties, his greying dark hair in need of a cut. He was wearing a moth-eaten old cricket pullover, and a kerchief – such as a pirate might wear in an adventure story, thought Evie – knotted round the frayed neck of his collarless shirt. Jeanie looked him up and down in astonishment and thought without a doubt that he was the most untidy – and the handsomest – man she'd ever seen.

'Mr Bailey?' she asked, suddenly feeling strangely breathless.

'I am Frederick Bailey,' the tall man replied with astonishing dignity considering what his ex-cleaner had just called him in front of strangers.

'Er . . . I'm Ginette Carter, and this is my daughter, Evelyn.'

'How do you do,' said Mr Bailey. 'How can I help you?'

Oh dear, he doesn't seem to have heard of us. Living at Pendle's is all an awful mistake. Or maybe this is the wrong person and we should be at the other Bailey's house? As this thought flashed through Evie's mind she saw her mother's puzzled face reflecting the very same thing.

'I . . . I'm wondering if you might be our new landlord,' Jeanie persevered. 'Pendle's? In Church Sandleton?'

'Yes, I suppose I must be, if that's where you're living,' Mr Bailey replied vaguely. 'Come in, please . . .'

He stood back to let Jeanie and Evie pass through the smart front door and into the hall where shards of pink and white porcelain lay strewn across the floor.

'Pity about the shepherdess,' he said. 'I'd got a buyer lined up for her, too. Still, there we are . . .'

Evie caught Jeanie's eye behind the man's back and shrugged nervously. This man wasn't like anyone she had ever met, and though the coarse, shouting woman had gone she still didn't feel at all comfortable here.

Jeanie, too, felt out of place in this strange house, with this odd man, but as she looked around the elegant little hallway Mr Bailey turned to her and smiled, and it was a smile she understood.

CHAPTER FIVE

FREDERICK BAILEY SHOWED Evie and Jeanie into a beautifully decorated room overlooking the square. Evie realised she was gaping at all the ornaments on every surface and quickly closed her mouth.

'So, Mrs Carter . . . Pendle's. I do hope everything is all right. I haven't been over to the old place for a long while. I've a man who sees to things like that for me.'

'Oh, yes, I haven't come to complain,' said Jeanie, sitting down in an armchair that Frederick Bailey indicated. 'But we've been there more than a week now and hadn't heard from anyone, and I was wondering . . . that is, we wondered . . . about the rent . . . '

When her mother seemed to have ground to a halt, Evie continued, 'And my grandmother is a very talented seamstress and wants to open a sewing business in the shop part. We thought we'd better make sure that was all right . . . that you'd allow it and that we can paint the place and make it more suitable.'

'You may do as you like,' Frederick Bailey said. 'I'm not a man for strict rules and regulations.'

'So we can go ahead?' asked Evie eagerly. She couldn't help her wide grin – this was exactly what she had hoped for. 'Thank you.'

Mr Bailey laughed. 'Well, I'm glad about that,' he said.

'What about the rent?' prompted Evie. She looked sideways at her mother but Jeanie seemed lost in thought and was gazing around the room with real interest. 'We mean to make a go of the sewing, and my dad has a job, too, so we can pay what's fair.'

'Ah, so there's a Mr Carter . . . I was wondering about your father,' said Mr Bailey. 'What is it he does?'

'He works at Clackett's market garden, across from Pendle's.'

'Does he indeed?' Mr Bailey paused to think. 'Well, how about ten shillings a week? How does that sound?'

'Oh, Mr Bailey, that's marvellous! Ten shillings? Are you sure that's all?' gasped Evie. Again she looked at her mother, but she was still distracted by the unusual room and gave no reaction.

Frederick Bailey waved a hand as if to dismiss the subject. 'I'll have my man, Jack, collect the payments.'

'Jack? Would that be Jack Fletcher? We haven't met him yet but it was he who arranged for us to come to Pendle's.'

'Yes, Jack Fletcher works for me. No doubt you'll meet him soon. There's nothing for you to worry about, Evelyn.'

'It's all becoming clearer now.'

Evie realised how anxious she'd become about their new home and these people none of them had met. What a relief it was to have it all sorted out. Coming here today had been exactly the right thing to do.

'Thank you, Mr Bailey,' she said. She nudged her mother, who was still occupied with her own thoughts. 'Mum . . . ?'

'Thank you, Mr Bailey. That's right good of you,' Jeanie said, smiling up at him.

'Please, call me Frederick. Now, forgive my manners, I should have offered you tea, but I'm without Mrs Summers, as you know only too well.'

'Let me help,' Jeanie said without hesitation, throwing off her distraction. She was on her feet instantly.

'That's uncommonly kind of you, Mrs Carter.'

'Jeanie, please.'

'Jeanie. Why don't we all go down?'

He led the way into the hall, pushing fragments of the broken ornament aside with his foot, then down a curving staircase at the end to a basement kitchen that looked old-fashioned and equipped very much as Mrs Russell's was, to Evie's eye. She could imagine Annie being quite at home here, though Annie wouldn't have had the dirty breakfast crockery piled up in the sink. The cups Mr Bailey set out were a strange mix: a pot mug and a couple of delicate teacups of different sizes with mismatched saucers. Didn't he have a tea set to use when visitors came, Evie wondered.

'This is pretty,' she said, taking up one of the fine cups to admire it while her mother saw to the kettle.

'Yes, but almost worthless without its own saucer, I'm afraid,' said Frederick. He searched absent-mindedly for the tea caddy, which Jeanie found in an obvious cupboard next to the stove, then asked his two visitors about their plans for the sewing business while the tea was brewing in a brown Bessie pot, just like the one at home.

'My mother's idea,' said Jeanie.

'It's Grandma who's the expert,' said Evie proudly. 'She's brilliant at sewing and can do all sorts of things – make clothes and do alterations and mending, too. She made that jacket Mum's wearing.'

'Evie . . . ' tutted Jeanie.

'Very pretty,' said Frederick, looking at Jeanie, who gazed straight back at him, smiling.

'And she can make up a pair of curtains in no time.'

'She sounds very special, your grandmother,'

Frederick said, handing round the china cups and saucers and taking up the mug of tea himself. 'And are you both going to work with her?' He looked at Jeanie when he asked this but it was Evie who answered.

'Oh, yes. Grandma wouldn't have it any other way,' she prattled on. 'She's a great one for family sticking together.'

'Well, I've been thinking about that,' said Jeanie quietly but firmly. 'It's you and Grandma who have the eye and the patience for sewing. I never helped with the mending in Shenty Street. I reckon you could get on fine without me.' She ignored Evie's open mouth of astonishment. 'What I was wondering, Frederick, was if you think Mrs Summers has left for good and whether you are in need of a cleaner? Or . . . ' she looked around and then back to him with her pretty smile, ' . . . a housekeeper?'

Frederick began laughing quietly.

What on earth was funny? And what was Mum on about? Evie felt her heart thumping loudly. Starting the sewing business had been decided, hadn't it? She looked from her mother to Frederick Bailey and suddenly felt something was happening here that she didn't understand.

Jeanie was standing waiting quite calmly for him to answer her.

'A housekeeper . . . Do you know, Jeanie, I think you'd be quite perfect,' he said eventually.

'But, Mum, what about the sewing?' Evie didn't want to question her mother in front of Mr Bailey but she *had* to say something before it was too late. 'It was going to be the three of us working together, same as in Shenty Street,' she reminded her, her voice almost pleading. Where had this new idea come from? It wasn't part of the plan at all. And what would Grandma Sue have to say?

'Well, Evie, we're not in Shenty Street any more. It's different now,' Jeanie said. Though she spoke quietly her tone was very sure. She smiled at their new landlord to show there was no criticism in her words and then looked around at the pile of unwashed dishes, the newspapers strewn across the kitchen table and the loaf of bread left out drying among a pile of crumbs.

'You've grasped the situation precisely,' Frederick replied, sounding delighted. 'When were you thinking of starting?'

'Tomorrow – would that suit you? Shall I do mornings and see how we get on?'

Evie gasped. She couldn't believe what she was hearing. Even Grandma Sue didn't take the lead like that without discussing things first.

'But, Mum—' she started.

'I don't doubt we'll get on brilliantly, Jeanie,' said Frederick, extending his hand to shake hers.

~

'So what happened then?' asked Sue, pouring cups of tea to wash down their lunchtime sandwiches. Michael had returned to Clackett's for the afternoon, pleased with the news of the low rent and his wife's new job, and the boys had gone out to play somewhere.

Jeanie and Evie were telling Sue more about their morning in Redmond. The way her mother recounted the events once she and Evie had entered Frederick Bailey's house lacked some detail; so much so that Evie thought it was just one version of the meeting with their landlord and she might have told it in altogether another way. Nonetheless, it was a sort of truth.

'He showed us round the house so that I could see exactly how much work it's going to be. He's an art and antiques dealer – buys and sells old things like paintings and ornaments, pretty but useless – and the house is full of the stuff. It's everywhere and it all needs to be dusted. He says some of it is quite valuable and I'm to be careful.'

'Must be odd to live in a house that's full of things you mean to sell,' said Sue. 'I wonder he doesn't become fond of them and want to keep them.'

'He may, for all I know. It's nowt to do with me,' said Jeanie with a shrug. 'But I think this job will suit me better than sewing. I was never one for stitching – you know that.'

'I know no such thing,' said Sue, sharp as a

tack. 'But I reckon you've made your mind up. And at least you got the rent sorted out, so that's one good thing.' She looked at Evie. 'Come on, love, let's decide on the colour for the walls now we've got the front room all prepared. We can get on since we've got permission, even if it's only us two.'

They went through to the front, leaving Jeanie to wash up.

'We'll have to choose a nice light colour. I can't be sewing anywhere dark with my old eyes,' said Sue.

'I'd like yellow,' said Evie. 'A light shade of yellow – like primroses. Do you think that would be all right for your eyes, Grandma?'

'I reckon it would, lass. We'll see what we can find. Now tell me, you're not too sorry your mum's not to be working with us after all, are you?'

Evie knew better than to deny it but she was surprised at the surge of disappointment that swept through her once again as she said, 'I wanted it to be like it was in Shenty Street – all us women together, like you said. I couldn't believe it when Mum said to Mr Bailey that she could be his house-keeper without even asking me if I minded – or if I thought you would mind either.'

'I'm disappointed, too, love, but your mother will go her own sweet way. She always was one for getting what she wants. It was the same when she first set eyes on your dad. Nowt I could say would change her mind – not that I haven't got used to him and his ways,' she added kindly.

~

'You've another letter from Evie,' said Ada, handing it to Billy as he came in from work. 'She's a keen writer, I'll say that for her.'

'I'm glad of that,' Billy grinned.

'Well, just remember what I've said. I know you're fond of her but Evie doesn't live here any more,' Ada advised. 'It's hard to keep up a . . . a friendship in letters. She might not always be so keen to stay in touch, lad. You don't know what folk she'll meet in the south. She's Michael Carter's daughter, don't forget, and we all know how reliable *he* is.'

'Yes, Mum, but she's Sue Goodwin's granddaughter, too, and there's no one more sound than Mrs Goodwin. I'm thinking of getting a train down one weekend and meeting up. It'll be lovely to see her and nice to see where she lives.'

'Oh, aye? Well, don't go getting your hopes up, our Billy. There's girls round here, too, you know.'

'Yes, Mum, I know there are girls round here,' said Billy patiently, and took his letter upstairs to read in peace.

Dear Billy,

Thank you for your letter. I always look forward to hearing from you. Your letters are the best thing to happen and I can't wait for them to arrive.

I hope you've had a good week.

Grandma and me have been really busy getting ready for our first customers. I've put a notice up in the village store and our shop is painted now. It's a sort of cream colour. We wanted yellow but we couldn't find anything nice so we went for the nearest. Pete and Bob helped. Pete did the ceiling, bless him, but Bob just made a mess. I suppose he is only little.

Mum is enjoying being housekeeper to Mr Bailey. She's started taking more care of herself and is more cheerful – I'd got quite worried about her in Shenty Street when we were working so hard on the washing – and though I saw for myself that Mr Bailey's house is a big job she doesn't look too weary when she gets home. It seems odd that Mr Bailey pays Mum and then Mum pays Jack Fletcher, Mr Bailey's man, who comes for the rent!

We all like Jack. He's very friendly and knows all kinds of people. He found a big table for the shop, which will be useful when we're cutting out or making curtains. He even delivered it to us.

Jack and Dad sometimes go together to the Red Lion in the village. I'm glad Dad's got someone to go with and see him home in good time, although if Jack isn't around Dad goes on his own and tends to stay later.

Mr Clackett doesn't hold with drinking, he says, though Dad sometimes goes to the Lion at dinnertime instead of coming here for his dinner. There aren't card games or bookies' runners at this pub so I'm hoping no harm will come of it.

I know Sundays can be difficult travelling by train but you said you were thinking of coming down. It would be lovely to see you, Billy. Let me know when you can manage it, and make it soon, please!

Lots of love,

Evie xxx

Billy read the letter twice through, laughing at the thought of the kind of mess Robert would have made with the paint, and happy that Evie and her grandmother were about to open for business after all their hard work to make the premises smart.

It wasn't good news that Michael Carter was drinking during the day but at least it was unlikely that he'd get into the kind of trouble he had with Mr Hopkins.

At that moment there was a knock at the front door. He opened it to find Geraldine Sullivan standing there, looking lovely in a flowered summer dress and clutching a packet of custard creams.

'Hello, Gerry,' Billy said. 'This is a nice surprise.'

'All right, Billy? Your mum was at the shop earlier and left these on the counter by mistake. I only noticed after she'd gone.'

'Ah, Geraldine. Nice to see you, love,' said Ada, appearing from the kitchen. 'Come in. I've just boiled the kettle.'

'Oh, thank you, Mrs Taylor, but I won't stop,' Geraldine said. 'I only came round to drop these off for you.'

'Thank you, love. Isn't that kind of her, Billy?' said his mother. She took the packet of biscuits without so much as glancing at them. 'Are you sure you won't have a cup of tea, love?'

'No, thanks, Mrs T. I'd best be getting home. Bye, now. See you around, Billy.' She beamed her glamorous smile at the Taylors, then turned and click-clacked down the street on her high heels.

Ada looked put out and Billy followed her into the kitchen to find the teapot already under the cosy and three cups and saucers on the table.

'Expecting a visitor, were you, Mum?' he asked pointedly.

Ada couldn't hide her discomfort that she'd been rumbled though she tried to make the best of it. 'I thought Geraldine might bring my biscuits round when I found I'd come home without them,' she said.

'You could have gone and got them, Mum. It's only down the street.'

'I know, but she's so friendly – and works so hard at Mr Amsell's . . . I just thought – she's a lovely girl, isn't she, Billy?'

'Geraldine Sullivan is a right bonny lass, and a nice one, no one could deny that.'

Billy sat back in a kitchen chair thinking his mother wasn't cut out for scheming. If only Evie's father were so easy to read, the Carters would have had a far smoother ride.

That got him thinking about Evie's letter. He'd write back tonight and tomorrow he'd look for a pretty card to send with the letter to congratulate Mrs Goodwin and Evie on opening for business. It wouldn't be too long before he got to see them for himself and he couldn't wait!

~

'Looks a bit bare,' said Evie, surveying the sewing room. The only relief from its plainness was a colourful card with a bunch of flowers on the front, which Billy had sent. 'If only our fabric had arrived.'

Sue had written to Marie Sullivan to ask if she'd choose some fabric in autumn shades for her from the mill shop near Shenty Street. She'd sent Marie a postal order to cover all her costs and Marie had been only too pleased to help, but the parcel still hadn't arrived. Evie was feeling anxious about that – its absence seemed a big setback on top of her mother deciding not to work with them.

Peter had made an 'OPEN' sign and hung it on the front door. They'd closed the door in the passage so that the house part was private but Evie thought they needn't have bothered about that. She hadn't imagined a stampede of customers this first morning of business, but nor had she thought she'd be sitting here twiddling her thumbs.

'What you need,' said Peter, 'are a few props.'

'Props? What on earth do you mean?' asked Sue.

'Like in a theatre. They set the stage with things to make it look like what it's supposed to be. This looks like an empty room with a big table and chairs in it to me, so what you need is to make it look like a dressmaker's. It doesn't have to be real, it just has to look as if it is.'

'Clever lad.' His grandma was impressed.

'When did you get to be so wise?' laughed Evie, nudging her brother with her elbow.

'We need fabric,' said Sue, getting the idea at once. 'It needs to look like we're already working on summat – busy, like. Right, you three, go and find anything you can think of to drape about the place. But make sure it's clean,' she added as her grandchildren disappeared into the house.

Half an hour later the room had been transformed. The bedroom curtains were folded neatly and stacked on the shelves like bolts of fabric, Jeanie's best dress was displayed on a hanger hooked over the dado rail, and a pile of used paper dress patterns in their envelopes were arranged on a corner of the table opposite Sue's sewing machine.

Leftover trimmings and spare buttons that Sue had saved over the years were displayed on Jeanie's pretty cake plate, and finally Sue's workbasket was placed prominently in the window, open and with spools of thread cascading colourfully over the edges.

'That's more like it,' said Sue, standing back to survey their handiwork.

'And you can hardly see where I spilled the paint,' said Robert, drawing everyone's attention to the stain, just as they were beginning to overlook it.

'Ideally I would place a pile of fashion magazines over that,' said Peter seriously, 'but we don't have any.'

They were interrupted by the arrival of the postman, wearing a uniform so like Billy's that Evie's heart gave a little skip. He pushed open the door and brought through a huge box wrapped in brown paper.

'Mrs Goodwin? Delivery for you.'

'Ooh, looks like Marie's parcel, right on cue. Thank you,' she said to the postman, and let the boys cut away the wrapping. 'Save that brown paper and string. You never know when they will be useful,' Sue, for whom wartime habits were still second nature, reminded them. Then they opened the cardboard box to reveal what Marie had come up with.

There was much oohing and aahing from Evie and Sue over the printed cotton remnants and end-of-rolls that Marie had found. Sue had been a bit unsure about shelling out for fabric without specific commissions, but now she knew she'd done the right thing. These pieces hadn't cost much at the mill shop but the quality was second to none.

'Pete, Bob, get those bedroom curtains back upstairs, and we'll put these pieces in their place,' instructed Sue.

She and Evie had no sooner finished folding the remnants into a pretty display when the door opened and Josie Lambert came in carrying a bag.

'Thought I'd get in early before you get busy,' she said. 'I've left Nancy and Archie with my mother. Oh, the shop looks lovely. You've got a good eye, Mrs Goodwin. Do you think you could take in this frock I wore when I was expecting Nancy? It's too good to throw away and I like the colour.'

'I can completely refashion it for you, if you'd like,' offered Sue, getting into her stride at once. 'There's yards in this front panel – what kind of dress were you thinking of . . . ?'

Evie let Sue do the talking but listened carefully to what she was saying, while Peter went to make a pot of tea, bringing through a cup for Mrs Lambert, too. All Evie's worries about starting up the sewing business were evaporating. Sue looked happier than she had for weeks and Evie saw how confident and in control she was at being her own boss again.

Then she thought about the arrangement Billy had made to come to see her on Sunday and she felt happiness bubbling up inside her. The fabrics had arrived and they were beautiful, she and Sue had their first customer, and Billy was coming to see her – it was all just about perfect.

∼

Jeanie arrived home from Redmond early in the afternoon as usual. She came into the workroom to see how Sue and Evie were getting on, and was impressed with their efforts and also with the fabrics Marie had chosen for them from the mill shop.

'Not thinking of joining us after all?' asked Sue without rancour.

'I'm getting on fine at Frederick's, thank you,' said Jeanie with a big smile. 'Oh, but I can understand why that Summers woman thought it a big job. You should see his study! Luckily he was out all morning at an auction so I was able to get on in the sitting room at least.'

'He trusts you with the run of the place and his precious things, then?' Sue enquired. She'd yet to meet Frederick Bailey and Evie suspected that for some reason Sue hadn't formed a very high opinion of him so far, despite the low rent he was asking.

'And why wouldn't he?' said Jeanie. 'I'll get on and make us some sandwiches. I got a bit of cheese from Mrs Sutton on the way home so they won't be just salad today.'

'The day's getting better and better,' said Sue as Jeanie went to make their lunch.

'Mum's in a very good mood,' said Evie. 'She's a lot more cheerful altogether these days.'

'Mmm . . . ' Sue replied noncommittally, taking her tailor's shears to Josie Lambert's maternity dress.

~

Michael didn't come home to eat the sandwiches and Sue tutted that he must have gone to get some chips and a pie at the Red Lion, which cost pennies that they didn't have. The boys went off to play in the field at the back of the market garden with Martin Clackett, leaving Sue and Evie in peace to work. Evie watched and learned as her grandmother turned Josie Lambert's vast garment into a swathe of fabric, which Evie pressed and then Sue recut into a stylish new shape. Evie machined the seams as directed and the afternoon passed, Evie feeling more settled than she had in weeks.

They were interrupted by Mrs Sutton from the village store, who came to ask about having some curtains made.

'I've seen a few people reading your notice, Evie,' she said. 'It wouldn't surprise me if you weren't rushed off your feet before the summer's out.'

'We'll cope,' said Sue, winking at Evie. 'Now, are

you wanting them lined, Mrs Sutton? I would recommend it . . . '

'Two customers already,' beamed Evie when Mrs Sutton had gone.

'It's a good start,' Sue confirmed. 'What d'you reckon? Will we manage without your mum?'

'I still wish she was in here working with us but we've had a lovely day, just the two of us, and Pete was such a help putting the finishing touches to the shop.'

'And you've also got Billy coming to visit next weekend – something for you to look forward to, love.'

'He'll be at Redmond station on the first train of the morning, and he's getting a train back in the late afternoon, so we won't have very long, but he wants to see us all and the village, too.'

'He's a grand lad,' said Sue. 'We'll make sure there's more than vegetables for his dinner,' and Evie hugged her.

~

Michael was woken by someone shaking his arm. He opened his eyes slowly, blinking in the glare of the sun through the greenhouse windows. He must have dozed off for a moment in the heat . . . Distantly he could hear the sound of children playing. What time was it now . . . ?

'Michael! Michael Carter! What do you think you're doing, asleep on the job?'

Mr Clackett was leaning over him, looking furious.

'Oh, Mr Clackett, it's the heat in here . . . made me a bit sleepy, like.'

'Heat? Beer, more like. I can smell it on your breath, and your clothes smell like the inside of the Red Lion. You've been drinking, haven't you?'

'Well, it was only a couple of pints. It's thirsty work in these glasshouses—'

'Couple of pints! And how is beer better than good honest water when I'm paying you to pick tomatoes? I don't hold with drinking, Michael, and I certainly don't hold with slacking. If you're paid to do a job I expect you to do it. If you don't then I'd rather employ someone else. There's a ton of veg to be picked and you're not doing your share.'

'I'm that sorry, Mr Clackett. I must have dozed off for a minute, that's all.'

'It's two hours since you left at lunchtime. It's not fair if you take your wages but don't do the hours.'

'Two hours? Oh, surely not,' said Michael, trying to jolly his boss out of his outrage. 'Can't possibly be that long. Tell you what – why don't I stay a bit later to make up? I'll do that as a favour, seeing as there's so much to pick.'

'A favour! You'll do it to make up for sleeping away half the afternoon at my expense, never mind any favours.'

'Oh . . . that's what I meant,' said Michael sheepishly.

'And let me tell you this. I'm a fair man and I don't hold with taking and not giving in return. If I find you asleep on the job again you won't be working here any longer.'

'No, Mr Clackett. And I'm sorry. It won't happen again.'

'If it does it will be the last time,' Mr Clackett reiterated, shaking a finger at Michael. He turned and walked away, muttering, 'Favour indeed . . . ' and the sound of his heavy boots faded into the distance, leaving Michael with a dislocated feeling.

The afternoon was silent, save for the hum of bees among the tomato plants. The children's voices he had heard earlier had faded away at some point and he wasn't sure what time it was or exactly where he'd left off what he'd been doing. He pulled himself upright and stretched, feeling seedy and weary, and regretful of his pints at the pub.

Still, Mr Clackett hadn't actually sacked him. And there was no reason why anyone else should hear of this . . .

~

When Michael came in at the end of the afternoon he looked worn and weary, and he grumbled that he had a headache coming on.

'Hard day, love?' sympathised Jeanie as Michael sat down at the table. 'Never mind, I've a delicious vegetable stew for you.' She laughed lightly because she made the same joke every evening, but today Michael could barely raise a smile.

'I've had it up to here with vegetables,' he said.

'What d'you mean, love? You've not been there more'n a few weeks, and Mr and Mrs Clackett have been very generous towards us with the rejects. I don't know what we'd have done without all this food.'

'Aye, you're right, of course, Jeanie, but I don't know as the job suits me all that well.'

Peter was scowling into his stew and Robert began bouncing on his chair as if he wanted to say something but his mouth was zipped shut.

'What do you mean, Michael?' Jeanie looked anxious. 'It's only picking vegetables – there's nothing about it to suit or not suit. You just do it.'

'I don't know . . . might be looking for another job.'

'That's exactly what Mr Clackett said!' burst out Robert, then clapped a hand over his mouth as if to silence himself as Peter gave him an almighty kicking under the table.

'What!' shrilled Jeanie. 'Boys, Evie, take your stew into the yard, please,' instructed Jeanie, and there was a scraping of chairs and a gathering of bread, spoons and bowls as they did as they were asked.

'All right, you two,' said Evie, when they'd made themselves as comfortable as they could in the shady backyard on a rotting garden bench and an upturned flowerpot. She put her bowl of stew down on the ground. 'What have you heard? Pete?'

'We were playing out the back of Clackett's with Martin late this afternoon and we overheard Mr Clackett giving Dad a warning. It sounded like he'd spent the afternoon asleep in one of the sheds instead of doing his work. Mr Clackett said he'd sack him if he did it again.'

'Yes,' said Robert, his eyes huge with the importance of his news. 'And Mr Clackett said Dad wasn't to go to the Red Lion at dinnertime and then go back to work the worse for drink *ever again.*'

Evie raised her hands to her face in horror and tears sprung into her eyes. The thought of Dad losing this job so soon after the last one, especially now the family were working so hard at making a new life, and with everyone in the village having been so friendly, was more than she could contemplate. People might not be nearly so kind if the Carters got a reputation for being unreliable. It could even mean she and Grandma Sue would lose potential customers before they'd even got their business started. That would be so unfair. Evie pulled the boys into her arms, and as the row started indoors, they huddled together wishing they were back home on Shenty Street.

CHAPTER SIX

Evie walked as quickly as she could to the railway station in Redmond. Billy's train wasn't due for half an hour but already she couldn't stop smiling at the thought of seeing him. Her stomach was doing a little dance of anticipation. She'd chosen to wear a pretty cotton frock that Sue had made her and which Billy had once told her looked nice.

Redmond station had only two platforms so there was no problem for Evie finding out where Billy's train would be pulling in. In the way of all stations it felt draughty, even on this hot July day, so Evie decided to sit in the ladies' waiting room. There were a couple of other women in there but when the northbound train was announced they left, so Evie had the place to herself, which was just as well as she was finding it impossible to sit still. She got up and walked about the room, then sat down again, swinging her legs, frequently glancing at her watch all the while until she made up her mind not to, to make the time go quicker.

At last the southbound train was announced and she jumped up and hurried out. With a shrill whistle it approached, gigantic wheels turning, the familiar smell of soot thick in the air and smoke engulfing the platform. The train halted, steam hissed fiercely, and then slowly the fug cleared and Evie looked up and down, smiling widely, ready to greet Billy. Doors were opened and a few people climbed out. No sign of Billy yet. No doubt he'd be collecting his things off the luggage rack, making sure he hadn't left anything. A few doors were slammed and Evie focused on those that remained open. He'd be here any second now . . .

Then the stationmaster went down the train shutting the doors. Evie's heart started to thud and she tried not to panic as she began to walk quickly along the platform, looking in at the carriage windows. Where was Billy? What was going on? He'd said he'd be on the ten thirty train. She checked her watch again but she knew she wasn't mistaken. This was his train, but where was he?

When she got to the last carriage the guard leaned out, seeing her looking worried. 'You all right, miss?'

'I was supposed to meet a friend on this train but he doesn't seem to be here,' she said, thinking she might disgrace herself by bursting into tears of disappointment like a little child.

'Maybe your friend has missed this train. There's

another southbound in forty minutes. Why not get yourself a cup of tea and wait for that one?'

'Thank you,' said Evie, though she thought it unlikely that Billy would have missed the train if he could possibly have helped it. What was more important than their meeting up? They'd planned the whole day so carefully: going back to Pendle's café for dinner, which was going to be special and not just vegetable stew. And then afterwards a lovely walk around the village and by the pretty stream that ran through the woods bordering the fields at the back . . .

Right now though, the stationmaster loudly blew his whistle and the guard waved a flag. There was a piercing answer from the driver's whistle and with a lot of hissing and rumbling the train pulled away, leaving Evie feeling very lonely on the platform all by herself.

Now what? Better wait for the next one, and if Billy wasn't on that then she'd have to decide whether to go home or wait longer. She returned to the ladies' waiting room, subdued now, and sat despondently in the corner, prepared to wait for the forty minutes until the next train was due. So, she sat and waited and worried, constantly glancing at the big old station clock on the wall.

The distant chime of the bells of the parish church sounded at eleven o'clock, and then there was a station announcement. Evie managed to make out from the very loud yet strangely unclear voice that the southbound train had been delayed and was going to be twenty minutes late.

She sat back with a deep sigh, wondering how this morning would end. Would she ever get to meet up with Billy? She'd started off so excited and so hopeful; now she was just fed up.

Everyone had a little grumble as the late train eventually rolled in with a huff and a puff and a loud whiste. It was half-past eleven and Evie was on the platform again, looking and hoping. Again, passengers alighted and a few people boarded, the whistles were blown and the huge wheels turned, gathering speed and leaving Evie alone.

Except she wasn't alone this time. From the very last carriage Jack Fletcher had climbed down with Monty, his terrier, on a lead.

'Hello, Evie. What brings you here?' asked Jack. 'Is something wrong?'

'Hello, Jack. I'm that glad to see you. I was supposed to meet a friend off the train before this one and he still isn't here and I don't know what to do. I don't want to go home in case he turns up, but I can't stay here all day.'

'So how long have you been here?' asked Jack.

'Since well before half-past ten. We've been planning today for ages and he's not the sort to let me down.'

'Maybe he hasn't been able to help it. Perhaps he's been delayed through no fault of his own?'

Evie thought about this and decided that Jack was right. Billy was always so reliable that there could be no other explanation. She couldn't help the hot tears of disappointment that started to form, and she tried to sniff them away.

'Now, come on. I've got the motorbike rig parked round the back. Me and Monty can give you a lift home, if you like.'

'Oh, but you'd be going out of your way. You're nearly home.' Evie knew Jack lived on the edge of Redmond, where the countryside ended and the town started.

'It's no trouble. Can't leave you looking miserable, with a long walk home. How could I face your grandma if I left you here? Come on, we'll get you home by dinnertime.'

'Thank you,' Evie smiled. She blew her nose, straightened her shoulders and her spirits lifted slightly as she went with Jack and Monty round behind the station where a few cars and Jack's motorbike and sidecar were parked.

'Hop in, Evie,' Jack offered his hand to help her climb into the sidecar. 'Thing is, you'll have to share with Monty.' He indicated to the restless dog by his leg.

Evie looked at the long-haired Jack Russell. Monty was, she noticed now, absolutely filthy, with dirt drying in his curly coat, the comical brown patch over one eye and ear less distinctive now the little dog was mostly brown all over. She looked down at her pretty dress, then at Jack's kindly face and the cute way Monty had of looking at her with his head on one side. What does it matter about the dress? she thought. It isn't as if Billy is here to see me in it.

Giving a little shrug, she climbed into the sidecar and made herself comfortable. 'Come on, then, Monty.'

Monty sat on Evie's lap, and gave her a big lick.

Evie laughed, past caring about her dress now, as Jack started the bike and drove her home, Monty sitting up on her knee with the wind in his ears and pride on his face at a morning well spent.

~

Monty leapt out of the sidecar when Jack parked the rig in front of Pendle's. Evie climbed out after him and brushed the dirt off her dress as best she could. She'd enjoyed the journey home on the hot day, the rush of air through her hair and the different view of the countryside from so low down had been special. This must be how Monty saw life, she thought. She was trying hard to overcome her disappointment over Billy's failure to show. As Jack had said, there would be an explanation.

She'd had plenty of time to study the back view of Jack as he carefully drove the motorbike – rather slower with her as a passenger, Evie suspected, than he usually did. He was wearing an old waxed jacket, despite the heat, with many pockets. She wondered how old he was. Older than Dad, no doubt, but not as old as Grandma Sue. Maybe about the same age as Mr Bailey? But Jack had such an easy way with him that he was almost like a much older brother or an uncle. All the Carters liked him.

Jeanie was at the door.

'Oh, Evie, but what's happened? Where's Billy?'

'He didn't come, Mum,' said Evie, her voice wobbling with threatened tears again. 'I waited and waited, and then I saw Jack and he gave me a lift.'

'There'll be a good explanation, don't you worry, Evie,' smiled Jack.

'Oh, no, what a shame, Evie! You were that excited about Billy coming here today. Come here, love,' said Jeanie, giving her daughter a big hug. 'We were all keen to see Billy again and we were hoping he'd bring news of Shenty Street and all our friends, too.' She sighed heavily, also disappointed. 'Well, we're one less for dinner, Jack,' she said. 'I've cooked some brisket and you're very welcome to have some.'

'Jeanie, my dear, that would be perfect,' said Jack. 'If I can just wash my hands . . . Monty and I have been busy this morning and neither of us is fit to be seen.'

Jeanie laughed and welcomed them in, and in a few moments she could hear greetings all round, and Peter and Robert making a fuss of Monty.

'Sorry, love,' she said to Evie, and hugged her

again. 'As Jack says, there'll be a good explanation. Billy would never let you down. I wouldn't be at all surprised if there wasn't a letter from him, come Tuesday, explaining everything.'

Dear Evie,

I'm so very sorry not to have got down to see you as we'd planned. I hope you weren't waiting a long time at the station before you realised I wasn't coming. I am that disappointed that I couldn't go at the last moment and it was impossible to get word to you. I expect you were a bit upset and I was, too.

Mum was taken poorly with one of her migraines on Sunday morning, early, just as I was getting ready to leave. It struck her down very quickly and she was quite helpless so I had to help her into bed and stay to look after her. She said she thought she was going blind, and she'd been sick in the night, too, and knew that one of her heads was coming on then, but I have to admit I must have slept through that. Poor Mum, she did seem very bad and I was going to go for the doctor but she insisted I wasn't to. She was much better in the afternoon, though. I really couldn't leave her, when she felt so ill. I'm sure you understand.

I'd been looking forward more than anything to our day together and I wouldn't have let you down if I could possibly have helped it. Please apologise to your parents and Mrs Goodwin, too, who I know had planned their day around me being there.

We must make another arrangement soon to make up for this one falling through. I truly am very, very sorry.

Missing you lots.

Love from Billy xxx

Evie sighed. 'That was bad timing. Poor Mrs Taylor. I do hope she soon recovered,' she said, having read the letter through for a second time aloud while Sue tacked a replacement zip into a skirt for Josie's mother.

Sue's mouth was a thin line and she didn't look particularly sympathetic. 'Oh, I expect she did,' she said dismissively. 'As you say, love, bad timing. Now, Evie, let me show you how to get a zip in invisibly . . . '

They got down to work on the skirt and then Sue turned up the short trousers of Robert's new school uniform, which were completely covering his knees, while Evie machined together some curtain widths, stopping frequently to check that the pattern matched exactly.

'Come here, Bob, and let's see how these look,' called Sue. He came in dragging his feet and hunching his shoulders. She held the short trousers against him. 'They'll do,' she decided.

Robert looked even more miserable.

'What's the matter?' asked Evie. 'You look like someone's done you a bad turn.'

'It's school,' said Robert glumly. 'I don't want to go. I want to stay here with you and Grandma.'

'Don't be such a baby,' Sue replied. 'Whoever heard of a boy your age stopping at home with his grandma and sister? Why, I bet little Archie Lambert won't be making such a fuss when he starts school. It's not as if you haven't been to school before, either.'

'Yes, but, Grandma, I won't know anyone,' whined Robert. 'Pete and Martin are going to school in Redmond and I'll be all by myself at the village school.'

'You'll soon make friends,' Evie assured him. 'You won't get to meet new people if you don't go, will you?'

'S'pose not . . . '

'And it is only down the road. And you'll be home by the middle of the afternoon.'

'S'pose . . . '

'No "suppose" about it. Get on with you and put the kettle on,' ordered Sue, giving him a wink to show she understood but was taking no nonsense anyway.

'Do you think he's all right?' asked Evie, once Robert had disappeared to the big kitchen.

'Just nerves, I reckon, though I've noticed he's made no friends of his own over summer. Martin Clackett is Pete's friend and they let Bob tag along with them. And Pete's been playing music with those

Thomas boys next door to Josie, but Bob doesn't go there any more. I think he was soon bored because he can't play an instrument himself.'

'Well, he's always been a bit of an odd one out,' said Evie. 'I'll make a cake or summat for after school on the first day. That'll cheer him up.'

'Good idea, love.' Sue raised her voice. 'Bob, put the cups on the tray to bring them through, please. And I think there's a packet of biscuits in the tin.'

'Biscuits, Grandma! We must be doing well,' laughed Evie, and she pedalled the sewing machine treadle furiously to race to the end of the seam.

~

Jeanie was enjoying her work at Frederick Bailey's house. She liked that it was something she was doing on her own, away from her family for once. She, Sue and Evie had worked well together at their little laundry but, though she loved her family dearly, now that Robert was no longer a child she wanted to get away from them sometimes. The thought of working on her own – working here – had come to her all of a sudden on the day she'd met Frederick Bailey. It had felt so exactly the right thing to do: something she'd chosen for herself when the new life in Church Sandleton had been forced upon her by Michael. She'd just had to be bold for once. And it had worked out fine. Maybe she'd be bold a bit more often from now on.

She laughed aloud at that thought as she opened the ornate gate and walked up the steps to Frederick's smart front door. Of course, she'd swapped one lot of domestic chores for another, but here was cleaning such as she'd never done at home!

It was nice to come to such a pretty house. Nothing here was ordinary. She felt her shoulders straighten as she produced the key Frederick had given her and let herself in. At such moments she could almost pretend that this was her own house. The hall floor was polished wood and the central light was a brass lantern with shiny glass. They were so perfectly suited to the space that Jeanie thought she would have chosen to have exactly the same, if this were her house. But what had happened to the painting that hung on the wall next to the sitting room? The wall was bare and Jeanie noted a trace of cobwebs where the frame had rested at the top.

'Frederick – hello,' she called.

'Ah, Jeanie . . . ' He came out of his study at the back, reading glasses perched on the end of his nose. 'Thought we'd have a little outing today, if you're agreeable?'

'An outing?' she smiled. 'But I'll need to tackle those cobwebs, and give the kitchen a once-over.'

'Cobwebs and kitchen be damned. There are

more important things in life than cleanliness,' he replied mildly. 'Rise above it all and see what's important in life.'

'A clean kitchen is important,' said Jeanie, pretending to be severe. 'That's what you employ me for.'

'Ah, but today, I shall take you out of the kitchen and on a trip to a place of beautiful things.' He spread his hands like a showman, looking faintly ridiculous with the baggy knees of his worn trousers and his fraying shirt, but a little bit dashing, too, with his red kerchief knotted at his throat. He looked a jolly, peculiar little man with a smile wider than his face.

'Don't talk rot, Freddie. Just tell me where we're going. I'm not sure I'm dressed for anything but cleaning.' Jeanie was learning to give as good as she got, which Frederick evidently appreciated. She wore a pretty summer coat that Sue had made for her out of a remnant, but underneath were her everyday worn slacks and a cheap sleeveless blouse. These were quite good enough for cleaning Frederick's kitchen but possibly not the right outfit for any form of outing.

'Actually,' Frederick said in his normal voice, 'there's an auction in Kingsford and I thought I'd take *Flora* along. There will be other paintings of the period and I suspect a few experts will be in to have a look.'

'Sounds exciting,' beamed Jeanie. 'So long as you don't mind the mess waiting until next time . . . '

'Excellent. You make us some coffee and I'll go and put on my glad rags.'

Jeanie left her coat and bag on the hall chair and went down to face the electric coffee percolator, which she'd learned to operate but which still made her nervous. Frederick drank mostly coffee in the mornings and Jeanie was getting a taste for it.

In a few minutes Frederick appeared in a sports jacket and flannel trousers that Jeanie had pressed for him the previous week. His shirt was clean and tidy, and he wore a natty silk tie.

'*Flora*'s already in the boot,' he said. 'Drink your coffee and let's go.'

He led Jeanie out and through a narrow ginnel at the back of the square, which opened out into garage space.

'I wondered where you kept the car,' said Jeanie. 'I did know you had a car. A friend in the village mentioned it.'

'Oh, yes? And what else did this friend say?' he asked casually.

'Nowt really. Just that you have some properties in Church Sandleton and you drive a car.' Jeanie felt defensive. She wasn't a gossip.

'Best not to believe everything you hear,' he said, looking pointedly at her. Then he beamed his handsome smile and opened the garage to reveal a little red car. Surprisingly, considering the volume of stuff in the house, aside from the car the garage was completely empty.

As he drove to the auction, Frederick explained that he'd decided to submit the painting only at the last minute and they had to be there early so it could be included in the viewing. 'I know the people there, so it'll be all right,' he said.

Kingsford was about the size of Redmond, and the auction was to take place on the premises of an auctioneer who occupied a grand building behind the town hall. Jeanie hadn't been to Kingsford before and she looked around eagerly as Frederick parked right outside the auctioneer's and took the painting, wrapped in brown paper, out of the boot. She felt a world away from Shenty Street and all she knew, and that felt exciting and scary all at once. Jeanie took a deep breath and followed him inside and went to wait in a room where there were other paintings on view and some precious objects in cases, while he saw to business. There were pretty pieces of jewellery and great piles of crockery, and some gloomy old paintings that Jeanie wouldn't even consider buying if she had a home like Marlowe House to furnish. She'd have only beautiful things, she decided. She saw a whole dinner service decorated in a way that looked very like the pattern on Sue's precious cup and saucer that she had been given by her employer when she got married. Jeanie must remember to mention that when she got home . . . Then there was a glass case of brooches, some small and neat, others big and gaudy. A tiny one was shaped like a bow, the loops and tails set with shiny white stones. Jeanie traced a finger over the glass of the case: *so pretty* . . .

'Nice,' said Frederick, suddenly beside her. 'You've got good taste.' He gave a little chuckle. 'Aren't folk strange, eh?'

Jeanie laughed. She'd never heard that she'd got *any* taste before.

'Right, I'd like to see how *Flora* does, and I might have found something interesting that will replace her, at the right price, but the sale won't start for a while so let's go and have something to eat.'

'Lovely – thank you,' said Jeanie, pleased she was wearing the summer coat. At least she hadn't got her pinny on! She wasn't worried about getting home to feed her family. Now the boys were back at school, dinner was a more casual meal.

~

Jeanie finished her lunch and sat back, feeling full.

'Thank you, Freddie,' she said. 'That was delicious. I've never had fish with grapes before. Perhaps I'll try it at home, see what Michael thinks of it.' She laughed, then stopped suddenly, feeling disloyal.

'Good. Glad you liked it,' Frederick said. 'I'll pay the bill and then we need to get to the sale, or there will be nothing left worth having!'

'What do you do at an auction?' asked Jeanie as the waitress, wearing a black dress and frilly white apron, came over with the bill on a plate.

Frederick barely glanced at the total, just put down a note and some coins, then helped Jeanie on with her coat, which she slid into without properly standing up, in order to hide her work clothes.

'Hmm? Oh, sometimes I bid but often I just look and make a note of what's selling. You need to know the market in this game. Then I'll perhaps sell a piece privately at a good price.'

'I don't understand,' Jeanie confessed.

'That doesn't matter. So long as I do,' he laughed. 'You'll soon work it out. But remember not to make any gestures that could be mistaken for a bid.'

They sat in a large and stuffy room where rows of hard chairs were set out. Frederick acknowledged a few people with nods and smiles. Most of the chairs were occupied but when the auction got under way people wandered in and out between the lots.

Jeanie tried to concentrate on everything at first but after a while she started to get bored. The room was hot and she wanted to take off her coat but was too ashamed of her work clothes to do so.

After what seemed like hours of countless dreary paintings and ugly vases, relieved only by the occasional piece of any beauty at all, her attention was grabbed by the sound of a familiar name.

' . . . portrait . . . thought to be Flora MacDonald, the heroine of Skye . . . '

'Your *Flora!*' Jeanie whispered.

'Indeed.' Frederick squeezed her hand and they settled down to listen to the bids.

At first the bidding was slow and Jeanie was disappointed. It seemed few people were interested in *Flora*, after all. But then a few started to show interest and the price rose more quickly. Soon Jeanie was jiggling in excitement in her seat like Robert did when there was a sponge pudding, and she found herself clutching Frederick's arm in excitement. He gave her hand a squeeze and smiled into her happy face as the bids came thick and fast.

When the portrait sold for £150 Frederick declared himself well satisfied and Jeanie felt as if her eyes were on stalks at the sum.

They went outside for some fresh air then.

'That's better. It's getting a bit crowded and airless,' Jeanie said. 'Oh, but that was fun! I felt as if I was holding my breath with the suspense.'

'Why don't you go and get a cup of tea? There are a couple of things I might be interested in, which are coming up shortly, and I've got to sort out the business with the portrait, too. There's a teashop over there. I'll come and find you in a little while, if that's all right?'

'Thank you,' said Jeanie, glad to stretch her legs.

When Frederick joined her it was rather longer than 'a little while' and she'd lingered over her tea for so long that the miserable-looking waitress had asked her three times if there was anything else she wanted. Jeanie, however, refused to be cowed by her surliness. *Be bold,* she told herself. That was going to be her touchstone from now on. Michael had imposed this new life on her but she was determined to make of it what she could. And if that meant sitting waiting in a teashop, then that's what she would do. She had as much right to be here as anyone else.

The doorbell tinkled and Frederick was there, dominating the room, turning every head. The waitress approached but stepped back as he strode over to Jeanie's corner table and helped her to her feet as if she were a princess.

'I'm sorry to have kept you waiting, Jeanie,' he said. 'If you're ready, shall we go home?'

'Thank you, Freddie. Oh, but the bill . . . '

'Allow me.' He left a ten-shilling note on the table and they made for the door.

'Thank you so much,' said Jeanie graciously to the ill-tempered waitress, who was now simpering at Frederick, having seen the fortune on the table.

Jeanie emerged into the street, laughing. Frederick looked down at her with a twinkle in his eye as he took her arm and led her to the car, and Jeanie knew that he understood her exactly.

'Did you bid for anything?' he asked.

'I did.' She felt proud.

'And were you successful, Freddie?'

'I was. You'll see all in good time.' He gave a satisfied grin.

The drive back in the golden light of late summer was a treat for Jeanie. It had been an extraordinary day and she didn't want the drive to end. She'd thought she'd be scrubbing the kitchen and dusting the books this morning, instead, she'd been on an adventure.

'I shall take you home,' said Frederick.

'Thank you. That's kind. I'm a lot later than usual. But Mum and Evie will have fed themselves earlier and Michael goes to the Red Lion if he doesn't like the sound of what's for dinner.'

As Church Sandleton came in sight, she turned to him and said, 'I've had a lovely day, thank you. It was a bit of a holiday as I haven't done a scrap of work, but I have done all sorts of interesting new things instead.'

'My pleasure,' said Frederick, driving down the main street and pulling up in front of Pendle's.

'I'll see you tomorrow,' said Jeanie, grinning. 'Better tackle that kitchen then.'

Frederick came round and opened the car door for her, then gave her his hand to help her out. 'I've had a good day, too, Jeanie,' he said. 'Thank you.' And then he bent and kissed her hand.

As she stood gaping in astonishment he got back into the car and drove away without a backward glance.

Well, I never . . . Jeanie watched him go, her hand raised in a wave he didn't acknowledge. Jeanie gave a little chuckle, and quickened her steps as she went.

Robert came to the door, having heard the car.

'You're late, Mum. Who is that? What kind of car is that? Where have you been all this time?'

'I don't know, love,' she said vaguely, not really listening, watching the red car until it was out of sight. She felt as though the day had been rather good, and that she would love to do it again.

CHAPTER SEVEN

'YOU'RE LATE,' SAID Sue, echoing Robert.
Jeanie knew her mother was much too sharp
to let the wool be pulled so easily. Yet she felt she
didn't want to share the whole day with her family.
What was the point of her going to work to make
her own way if she had to account for herself every
time she came home, she muttered softly.

'Out with it,' Sue said, peeling some carrots, while
the boys did their homework at the end of the table,
just like they had in Shenty Street.

'Frederick wanted to sell a painting and he took
me with him to the auction, that's all,' she said, grinning as she remembered the excitement of the sale.

'An auction?' Peter looked up, his face full of
interest. 'Tell us what it was like, Mum.'

'Hot and smoky,' she laughed. 'But it was exciting
when the bidding started. The picture went for quite
a lot in the end – I mean, *we'd* think it quite a lot

– and Frederick was pleased. That's how he makes his living.'

She wouldn't mention the lunch at the hotel, she decided, and nobody asked whether she'd eaten earlier.

'Tell me about your day,' she asked Sue to distract her. 'Where's Evie?'

'Oh, we've had a good one,' said Sue. 'Evie's getting to be a neat hand at stitching a hem. She's upstairs writing to Billy. She's still disappointed about the other week when he didn't turn up.' She and Jeanie exchanged meaningful looks. They'd keep their views on Ada and her convenient headaches between themselves for the time being.

'So what are you working on?' Jeanie asked, laying her coat over a chair back and putting on her pinny.

'I've a fancy blouse to make out of one of those lengths from Marie's fabric parcel, and tomorrow I'm going to go and measure up some curtains at Lavender Cottage.'

'Oh, aye? That's the one I spotted the day we arrived here, isn't it? On the way into the village – looks really pretty?'

'That's right. Miss Richards, she's called. Nice woman, fifty-ish, sensible shoes and good clothes. I'll be sure to give you a full report of the house,' laughed Sue.

'I shall expect nowt less,' Jeanie replied. 'Not a lot gets past you, Mum.'

'You're right there, lass,' said Sue, and gave her daughter a sideways look. 'At dinnertime Michael said he's going to be a bit later this evening. Something about a lot of marrows . . . '

'So how was school today, Bob?' Jeanie asked.

Robert had sunk lower and lower in his chair as Peter talked about what fun he was having at school. He'd watched how quickly Peter had done his homework, too, even though it was maths. And he had noticed earlier, as he sat reading a comic in the shop window while Sue and Evie worked, that Peter had got off the school bus with a whole group of other children, some of them older than he was, and they'd all been chatting and laughing. Robert had walked home from school along Church Sandleton High Street alone, as usual.

''S all right, I s'pose,' he mumbled.

'Only all right?' questioned Jeanie. 'Why, what's wrong with it?'

'Nothing . . . '

'Have you found someone to play with at playtime?'

'No . . . They all know each other already. They don't want to play with me,' Robert said.

'Early days yet,' said Sue. 'You've not been there long, love. Just stick with it and you'll be all right.' She gave him a hug and he emerged from her well-padded pinafore with tears in his eyes.

'There, love, don't take on. Do you want me to

speak to your teacher – what's her name again?'
Jeanie asked.

'Miss.'

'Her *name*, Bob?'

'Miss Grainger.'

Robert shook his head and Jeanie decided she'd
try to speak to Miss Grainger anyway before the
week was out.

They were disturbed by a thumping noise from the
yard behind them and everyone turned to look
through the window. Michael had come in down the
side passage and was dragging something heavy with
him.

Jeanie went to the back door. 'What the . . . ?
Good grief, Michael, what on earth are those?' She
looked in horror at the contents of a large wooden
box. 'They're not . . . ? Oh, please, tell me they're
not all marrows?'

'They are indeed,' said Michael, straightening his
back with a groan. 'Mr Clackett says it's a bumper
year for them and he's got these to spare so I thought
you'd be able to do something with them.'

'Oh, you did, did you?' Jeanie gave him a hard
stare. 'Like marrows, do you, Michael?' she asked
meaningfully.

He looked taken aback. 'Well, it is all food, Jeanie.'

'They're *marrows*, Michael. No one likes marrows,
as far as I know,' she said, shaking her head at the
stupidity of her husband.

The others all crowded round to see and the boys lifted a few out of the box to test the weight of the monstrous vegetables.

'This one's as big as Bob,' said Peter, raising one above his head like a weightlifter.

'This one's as big as Grandma,' laughed Robert in turn, his tears forgotten as he tried and failed to lift the biggest marrow in the box.

'Oh, Michael, I hope you like marrows,' said Sue, 'because you're going to be eating an awful lot of them. And it was you that made such a fuss about having to eat so many vegetables over the summer.'

'Well, you know what you can do with these marrows,' said Jeanie, a smile playing about her mouth.

She caught Peter's eye and they spoke in unison. 'Stuff 'em!'

~

After they'd eaten their evening meal – possibly the last one for a long time that wouldn't include marrow – Michael took himself off to the Red Lion, as he so often did, saying there was a chance he'd be seeing Jack Fletcher there.

'So,' said Sue, as she and Jeanie sipped cups of tea at the kitchen table, 'seems a funny sort of job, gallivanting off to auctions when you reckon to be a housekeeper?'

'It was only a little trip. I think Frederick wanted some company on the drive to Kingsford and he asked me, that's all.'

'And does he intend paying you for a day's work while you provide him with "company"?'

'Don't you make it sound like something it's not,' said Jeanie. 'I expect he'll pay me for my time. I'll be there tomorrow cleaning and getting in a bit of shopping for him, and doing all the work I usually do. Don't make more of it than it was, please.'

Sue reached out and patted Jeanie's hand. 'I do understand why you want to make a bit of a life for yourself after being a wife and a mum and a washer of other people's clothes, but you won't forget that you're still a wife and a mum, will you?'

'I won't be forgetting that ton of marrows,' Jeanie sighed wearily, looking with distaste at the box of the vegetables now taking up a lot of space in the kitchen.

'We can store some of them. If they're kept dry they'll last a long time,' Sue said.

'We'll need a saw to get through them by November,' Jeanie smiled. 'They'll become armour-plated if we leave them too long. Don't you have a recipe for marrow jam somewhere?'

'Aye, lass, I believe so.' Sue heaved herself to her feet and went to find it, leaving Jeanie feeling happier now that her mother's attention was distracted from herself.

It has been a lovely day – not like any day she'd ever had before – and if Frederick asked her to go on another such trip with him she wouldn't hesitate to say yes. Why should every day be alike, stretching ahead for ever, just the same old thing and so little fun? Why shouldn't new and exciting things happen, even to her?

~

Evie and Robert made a miserable pair as they skirted a field of stubble, the greying stalks scratchy against their legs above their ankle socks.

Evie had been pleased to receive the letter of explanation and apology so quickly from Billy. It really hadn't been his fault that he'd had to stay to look after his mum, and Evie would have thought very badly of him if he'd taken the train and left Mrs Taylor feeling poorly. But it was such bad luck – the one day they had arranged to meet . . .

Since then they'd exchanged a few letters but it wasn't the same as meeting up, and Evie was missing Billy so much that it felt like a weight in her stomach. The only good thing was that the sewing business had taken off even better than she and Sue had hoped. People had been friendly when they came to the little dressmaker's premises and it felt like the family was beginning to settle into village life. Only Robert was finding it hard.

Evie looked at him now as he slouched along, hands in pockets, shoulders hunched, a look on his face that would sour milk.

'What is it, Bob? Is it just school that's bothering you?' she asked.

'*Just school? Just?* School's everything – it's all that happens to me, and it's awful, Evie.'

Robert mooched along in silence for a few minutes, his eyes fixed on the dusty field. They climbed a stile into the woods, which was a favourite place they'd discovered over the summer. Now, the first leaves were beginning to show gold in the evening sun, and the pathway they liked to take felt cool and damp.

'Let's go to the stream,' suggested Evie, remembering happy times in the summer holiday when Robert had gone there fishing with Peter and Martin Clackett.

Robert grunted and let himself be led along the rough dry track to the stream. In summer the water level had been low, but with the arrival of autumn it had started to rise. They sat down on a fallen tree trunk and watched the stream flow by, alive with insects, midges dancing in the golden light.

'Look,' whispered Evie. She raised her arm slowly and pointed to a rabbit on the path down which they'd come. It was nibbling on some plant in the verge, then hopped away. It made her smile.

Robert looked up into Evie's face, smiling.

'Brilliant,' he said. 'That's something we didn't see in Shenty Street.'

'Too right, Bob.'

'Though I think I prefer there to here.'

'Do you, now? Why's that, then?'

''Cos Pete and I went to the same school, and . . . I knew what it was like there. It's different here.'

'Can't stay the same for ever, Bob. You know that. But we've still all got each other and that's not going to change.'

'Well, I don't have any friends. At home . . . Shenty Street . . . I had Paddy, Niall and Cormac Sullivan to play with.'

'You'll make new friends—'

'No I won't! The other children are horrible. They talk different and they make fun of me.'

'How?' Evie was concerned.

'By pretending to talk like I do – like *we* all do – and making fun of it.'

Evie sighed. 'I think they must be daft,' she said. 'Folk speak like us in Lancashire, and here they speak differently. Who's to say who's better? If they were in Shenty Street they'd be the odd-sounding ones, I reckon. We know that, and if they don't then I think they're a bit stupid. If they keep on at you, you've got to tell Mum or Grandma.' Robert looked happier but he mumbled something about not wanting to be a sneak, which Evie ignored.

As they lapsed into daydreaming about Shenty

Street, the Sullivans and Billy, a water vole swam up the stream right in front of them. They both saw it at once and remained completely still and silent until it disappeared.

'Time for us to go home, too, Bob,' said Evie. 'It's getting damp.' She shivered, then took his hand. 'Come on,' and she ruffled his hair as they set off home together.

~

For a while, as everyone chatted, the clock ticked and the day grew closer to evening, everyone set about their business and the house grew quiet.

~

The children and Sue had gone to bed by the time Michael staggered his way home down the main street from the Red Lion, but Jeanie was up waiting for him. She'd spent the evening looking out recipes for cooking marrow, but then her mind wandered and she'd gone over every moment of her day with Frederick from when she'd first let herself into Marlowe House and daydreamed it was her own.

'Oh, Michael! You look like you've had a busy evening . . . ' He stumbled inside, beer on his breath, and Jeanie quickly locked the front door.

'I have that,' said Michael with a hiccup, taking

the cup of tea from her hand. 'We had a few games of darts.'

'Get up to bed and keep your voice down. The children and Mum will be asleep by now.'

'You comin' with me?' Michael asked with a leering kind of smile.

Jeanie turned her head away from the beer fumes in disgust. This was not a fitting end to such a lovely day.

'Yes, I'll be up in a minute,' she told him, and pushed him in the direction of the stairs.

'Ah, come up with me now, lass,' slurred Michael, turning back and flinging an arm heavily around her waist.

'I'll be there in a minute, love,' she said, unwinding herself from his clumsy embrace. 'You go and warm the bed.'

He grinned then gave another hiccup. 'Good idea . . . warm the bed,' he said, and clumsily made his way upstairs.

Jeanie thought she'd give it several minutes so there'd be no danger of his being conscious when she went up.

She climbed into bed ten minutes later, moving slowly, careful not to wake Michael, though there seemed little danger of that. He was flat on his back and snoring like a pig. She lay beside him, sighing, filled with disgust. At least he wasn't a violent drunk, merely a pathetic one.

She pulled the blankets round her ears to block out his snoring and closed her eyes, remembering her elegant lunch at the hotel, the excitement of the auction, the happy journey home in the red car, neither she nor Frederick needing to say much, and most of all, she remembered how Frederick had helped her from the car at the door, and kissed her hand. He was unlike any man she had ever met before.

And what about tomorrow? she thought. Work, of course! I am, after all, his housekeeper, and nothing got done today. Well, *no work* got done today, though a lot did happen. And I don't mean that pile of marrows . . .

She sighed, thinking of the monster vegetables, wondering whether she could just get rid of them, even though they were food. No doubt Sue would object . . .

One thing is clear, though, Jeanie decided, remembering sitting in the hot auction room, trapped in her coat by her shabby clothes beneath. I'm not going to work *wearing* my work clothes again. I'll take them in a bag – mebbe leave them there. Just in case there's to be another outing . . .

CHAPTER EIGHT

EVIE PICKED THE post off the doormat. No letter from Billy today, but there was one addressed to her, from Mary Sullivan, if she wasn't mistaken in the handwriting. She opened it immediately, eager to hear about her friends in Shenty Street.

'What news?' asked Sue, who was washing up the breakfast things before beginning work.

'Mary says Geraldine is having a big birthday party and they've invited me to be there!' Her heart lifted for a moment. 'Oh, can I go, Grandma? Could we afford the train? I could go up on Saturday and come back on the Sunday.'

Sue looked at the hope in young Evie's face, and knew she'd work night and day to make this trip happen. 'You can get all the news and give our love to everyone. Yes, of course you can go, Evie. No doubt Billy will be there so you'll have a grand time.' She looked up and beamed at Evie, giving her a wink.

'But I don't know if I'll be able to afford the train fare and a present for Gerry, and I'll have to arrange somewhere to stay as well . . . ' Evie was beginning to worry already.

'Don't fret yourself, love. I'll give you the train fare, and in return you can do summat for me while you're up there.'

'Of course, Grandma. Anything!'

'I think we could make use of a few lengths from the mill shop, so if you go up on the Friday you'll have time to see everyone – including Billy – and do a bit of shopping for the dressmaking as well. It can be a sort of business trip and we'll put the train fare down to expenses. How does that sound?'

'Thank you, Grandma, that sounds brilliant, if you're sure I'll get the right things.'

'Of course you will. Why wouldn't you? The Sullivans' house is bursting with folk already, but if you stay at Dora's next door you'll be able to help Marie and the girls prepare for the party. Dora's always had a soft spot for you. She'll be glad of the company, too, her being by herself so much. I'll write and ask her if you can stay there for the two nights.'

'That would be nice. Though, of course, I could stay at Billy's, if Mrs Taylor wouldn't mind.'

Sue thought for a few moments, then said carefully, 'If Ada offers to put you up that would be fine, of course, but I wouldn't ask to stay there, and I wouldn't go there unless Billy says she's suggested it herself.'

'Oh . . . '

'It would be rude to ask if the offer's not already there.'

'But you said you'd ask Mrs Marsh – isn't that the same thing?'

'No, Evie. It's quite different,' said Sue firmly. 'Now let's get the kitchen tidied up before I go to measure up for Miss Richards' curtains. And I'm wondering how your mum's got on seeing Bob's teacher this morning, though we'll have to wait till she comes home from Redmond to find that out.'

'Those mean kids – they want their heads knocking together,' said Evie.

Sue nodded her agreement, then, turning to the sink, she glanced into the corner where the box of marrows stood. 'Blessed marrows,' she muttered. 'Do you think we can give them to the Harvest Festival, Evie?'

'To our village church and several others, Grandma,' Evie said. 'Tell you what, though, I'm not lugging any of them marrows up to the North on the train!'

And they both burst out laughing.

~

Jeanie arrived at Marlowe House carrying a cloth bag with her work clothes rolled up inside. Today she wore a carefully chosen dress under the summer coat – an old favourite but not something she would be ashamed of if there was another outing.

At the thought she pulled herself up. She had a job to do and yesterday had been a one-off. Frederick had wanted company on the drive, that's all, just as she'd explained to her mother.

She let herself in the front door with her key and, as always, her heart lifted at the elegance of the place. The space where the painting of Flora MacDonald had hung was still bare, the cobweb draped exactly where it had been the previous day.

'Frederick?' Jeanie called. 'Hello?'

No answer. She knocked on his study door, then tried the handle and peeped in. No one there. This was not unusual as he often was absent 'seeing people' and left her to get on. She didn't need supervision, after all.

But today, after the unlooked-for treat of the previous day, Jeanie felt strangely disappointed to find she was alone and firmly back in her house-keeper's role.

'Idiot,' she chided herself aloud. 'What exactly did you expect?'

But that was a question she preferred not to try to answer.

She took her work clothes up to a spare bedroom,

changed into them and came down determined to catch up on her chores.

~

Sue walked down to Lavender Cottage in the autumn sunshine. The lavender in Miss Richards' garden was long over, but the roses still graced the front of the house and the scent reminded her of visits to Mrs Russell. She wondered how that gracious lady was, and wished once again that she could have confided in her before the Carters had fled from Shenty Street.

~

It wasn't Miss Richards that brought the heavy curtain fabric down the road to Pendle's that afternoon, it was Letitia Mortimer, Miss Richards' niece, which pleased Sue. Although the young woman had an unusually confident manner, she had seemed a nice sort of person, and it had occurred to Sue when Evie had said that Robert was finding it hard to make friends, that Evie herself had no new friends her own age. The customers tended to be older than Evie – women with young families. To Sue's mind, Evie was continuing to look back to Shenty Street and her friendships with the Sullivan girls and with Billy Taylor, and not really making a new life for herself here, for all she had thrown herself into the sewing business.

Letty opened the shop door.

'Hello, Mrs Goodwin. I've got the curtaining in the bicycle basket – I'll just get it.'

She went back outside and returned carrying the thick chevron-patterned fabric in both arms. 'Shall I put it here? Ooh, I love the shop! Aunt Margaret said you'd got it set up nicely.' She turned to close the door, then back to Evie, who was hand-stitching a skirt hem. 'Hello, I'm Letty Mortimer.' She extended a hand and shook Evie's shyly proffered hand firmly.

'I'm Evelyn Carter – Evie,' said Evie, standing up and putting her work aside. 'Grandma says your fabric is lovely – may I see . . . ?'

Then there was the showing and admiring of the bold fabric, and then Letty looked through the dress patterns and commented on the styles, and she and Evie exchanged views on various cuts of skirts. Then Letty had to look through Sue's collection of lace and buttons, constantly asking where they had come from and drawing out the stories behind them – 'as if she really cared to know,' as Sue said afterwards – and so the afternoon passed, punctuated by cups of tea and laughter.

Robert came home from school and Letty even drew him into the conversation, asking about his school, which he said had been 'better than usual' that day, and then going with him to admire the ridiculous box of marrows.

'We're having summat called a fête at school,' Robert announced.

'Oh, yes? What happens there?' asked Letty, giving Evie a wink.

'I don't really know . . . I think it's part of Bonfire Night but with stalls to raise money. They want to get new curtains for the front of the platform in the hall so that we can do plays and stuff.'

'Well, we all know who can make curtains,' said Letty.

Sue smiled. 'It's the first I've heard of it, but I'll go in and see Miss Grainger. I reckon me and Evie could run up summat simple for free if they brought me the fabric.'

'So what are you going to do in this fête, Bob?' Evie asked. 'Got any fund-raising ideas?'

He looked downcast. 'No . . . they all want to do the Tombola. That's the best. Some of them have done this kind of thing before and know all about it, but I don't.'

'There's time yet to think of summat,' said Sue.

'And I must be getting back or Aunt Margaret will be thinking I've gone missing,' said Letty. 'Thank you for the tea and a wonderful afternoon. It's been the most fun I've had since . . . for ages.'

'It's been nice for us, too, love,' said Sue. 'Do come again.'

'Try keeping me away,' Letty replied, beaming. 'See you soon!'

Through the front window they saw her pushing off on the bicycle and she gave a wave and big smile as she passed.

For a moment Evie, Sue and Robert sat in silence as the air sort of settled and the habitual peace of the sewing room returned.

'Blimey, that girl's a whirlwind,' laughed Sue.

'She's lovely,' said Evie. 'I do hope she comes here again.'

'Oh, she will, living in a village this small – that is, I *think* she lives at Lavender Cottage. For all her chatter, I didn't quite learn whether she lives with Miss Richards or she's only there for a bit.'

'Mebbe we'll find out next time she comes,' said Evie. 'I do hope that will be soon.'

'Yes,' agreed Sue, 'but not too soon. Do you know, I haven't got owt done this afternoon.'

'Me neither,' said Evie. 'But we've had fun, haven't we? Sometimes it's good just to have a laugh.'

'Aye, I reckon you're right, love,' Sue replied. And she thought: Mebbe that's what our Jeanie was doing yesterday, going to that auction with Frederick Bailey. Mebbe she only wanted a bit of fun. And after all that's happened, I can't say I blame her.

～

Since Jeanie had had a word with Miss Grainger, Robert was no longer being teased by his classmates, but he still came home in the afternoons heavy with the burden of having spent every playtime alone.

Evie tried to jolly him out of his misery, while trying not to make much of his loneliness in case he became more upset. If the weather was fine she and Robert had taken to walking along their favourite route round the field and into the wood, though as autumn drew on they needed to remember coats and gloves.

Letty came to visit them again and one day Evie and Robert took her with them.

'It's a bit gloomy,' said Letty, standing by the stream, which was now deep and cold-looking. 'The way those branches creak is creepy, and, look, that one is like a skinny hand – like a witch's hand.'

'Oh, don't, Letty,' Evie said, looking sidelong at Robert to indicate what she meant. When Robert had gone to collect some acorns she said quietly, 'Poor old Bob – he's not made any friends at school yet and coming here is one of his best things to do. I don't want him to become frightened about being in these woods. It would leave him with so little if he didn't have here to enjoy.'

Letty clamped her hand over her mouth in dramatic fashion. 'Oh, I'm so sorry, Evie. Me and my big mouth! I didn't think. Poor mite. Has he thought of anything he wants to organise for his school fête yet?'

'I don't think so. We've suggested a few things but he's not keen. It has to be summat nice for him to do, not a chore.'

'I've got it!' said Letty. 'I've just had the most brilliant idea! What about Guess the Weight of the Marrow? Heaven knows, you have plenty to choose from. The prize can be the marrow itself, so you'll have one fewer to get rid of.'

'Ha-ha, that is a good idea, except do you think Bob will have any takers if the marrow is the prize? Who'd want it?'

'Well, we could have a proper prize for the nearest guess – chocolate or a cake or something – but still have Guess the Weight,' said Letty.

'*We?*'

'Yes, *we*,' insisted Letty. 'I'm determined to play a part in this fête and not leave little Bob all on his lonesome with his marrow.' The girls both snorted with laughter. 'Peter and I can provide some entertainment to attract the punters and Bob can take the money and keep a note of the guesses. What do you think?'

'It sounds grand,' said Evie. 'Thanks, Letty. Hey, Bob, you'll never guess what Letty's just thought up . . . '

~

Billy was delighted that Evie was coming home for Geraldine's party. The Sullivan parties were always crowded, loud and generous, all their guests chipping in with food and drinks. He only hoped there would be a chance to see Evie properly – to really talk to her, not just at the party, where, if past Sullivan events were anything to go by, the noise would be incredible. Everyone in Shenty Street would be invited because no one would be getting any sleep that night.

' . . . arriving in Bolton on the Friday so that I can get a few things at the mill shop for the sewing business . . . ' Evie had written.

'Mum,' began Billy, one evening, as he brought her a cup of tea and placed it next to her *Woman's Weekly* on the side table. He turned down the radio and sat on the footstool beside her. 'I've been thinking, would it be all right if Evie came to stay the weekend of Geraldine's party, please?'

'What, stay *here*, you mean?'

'Well, yes.'

'Oh, I don't think so, Billy love. That wouldn't be possible at all.' Her tone implied that was the end of the matter.

'What do you mean, Mum?'

Ada looked at him as if he were daft. 'Where would she sleep, for a start? We've only got the two bedrooms.'

'Yes, Mum, but I could sleep on the settee in the front and Evie could have my room.'

'Oh, no, lad. I don't think that's a good idea,' said Ada, picking up her cup and sipping her tea. She turned the radio up to indicate the conversation was over.

Billy turned it down again.

'Why not?'

'You won't want to be sleeping on that lumpy old settee, Billy. Not with your back. Why, you could be crippled by morning.'

'Don't be soft, Mum, there's nowt wrong with the settee. And it would only be for the Friday and Saturday nights. Evie will be going home on the Sunday.'

'With your back! Whatever next? I've never heard nowt like it.'

'Mum, I wish I knew what you are on about. What's wrong with the settee? And what's wrong with my back, come to that? I only ask that we be hospitable to a friend, that's all.'

'But there'll be all the extra bedding to wash, love, and you know there's only me to do that. I don't know how I'll cope with a load of extra work at my age.'

'Your age? Goodness' sake, you're only fifty-two,' Billy muttered, beginning to lose patience.

'Don't you go bringing my age into this. I don't want you telling folk how old I am,' Ada grumbled. 'A lady's age is her own concern and no one else's.'

'Who's talking about your age, Mum? You are –

that's who. I'm talking about having a friend to stay for two nights so she can go to a party, that's all. If you don't want Evie to stay here just say so. At least I'll know where things stand.'

'Right then, she's not staying, so let that be the end of it,' Ada snapped.

'Fine.' Billy got up quickly and turned the Light Programme up to near-deafening volume, then went out leaving the door open, because he knew the draught from the passage annoyed Ada.

He put on his coat and went for a stroll down to the Lord Nelson to see who was there to join him for a pint, feeling that he'd been mean and childish to his mother. But then, she'd been mean first. He knew she regarded Michael Carter as unreliable, but it was Evie coming to Geraldine's party, not Michael, and she was the sweetest girl he could imagine.

He cheered up, thinking about Evie and how he would see her very soon. She'd written that her grandma had thought she'd ask Dora Marsh to put her up, so at least she'd be staying with a friend, and nearby. Of course, that wasn't as good as having her to stay at his own home, but he'd still see her most of the weekend . . . and he could hardly wait.

~

'I can't help noticing that your study is getting in a right old state, Frederick. Would you like me to clean it this week?' asked Jeanie. She hadn't been invited to clean the study yet, nor even to set foot in it. It was chaotic and, although Frederick hadn't said so, more private than the other rooms in the house.

Frederick looked around the small room at the back of the hall as if he didn't see it every day. Cobwebs festooned the tiny crystal chandelier and the fringed rug was rucked up by the desk, its pattern almost invisible under a layer of dust and balled-up scraps of paper that had missed the waste-paper basket.

'If you're going out, I can do it while you're gone so you won't be disturbed,' suggested Jeanie.

'Jeanie, the way you disturb me has nothing to do with vacuuming the rug,' said Frederick, 'but I have lost a receipt I need to file so I think it would be a good idea if we have a tidy-up.'

'We?' asked Jeanie, but wondering more whether she'd heard the first part correctly. *He surely didn't say that?*

'Of course *we*. My dear Jeanie, you may be the best housekeeper on this earth but there's no way I'm allowing anyone loose in my study unsupervised.'

'Oh . . . I . . . '

'It's not that I don't trust you, but only I know

what things are and where they go, and, despite how it appears, there is some order here.'

'Oh, aye? I'll take your word for that,' said Jeanie.

'We can start now, if you like, as I do need to find that receipt,' suggested her employer.

'Right, we'll remove all the paper to a safe place and you can go through it while I get rid of the dust. Would that suit you?'

'Perfectly, Jeanie. You're a woman in a million. Now please go and make us some coffee and I'll get started on the paper.'

Jeanie went down the winding stairs to the basement kitchen to face the complicated coffee percolator, trying to make sense of what Frederick had said earlier about her disturbing him. In the end she decided she had misheard and she calmly brought up the coffee, stopping to admire the new painting that had taken the place of *Flora* in the hall.

Suddenly it occurred to her how different her life was now from how it had been in Shenty Street. Here she was, a housekeeper to a nice man in a posh house, drinking coffee, of all things, surrounded by beautiful items that came and went as Frederick bought and sold them, so there was always something new to admire and to wonder at. Even the smallest of these treasures would be like the very best thing she owned if it were removed to Pendle's. Who'd have thought that Jeanie Carter of Shenty Street, up to her elbows in other folks' washing, would, just a few months later, be working here – and for such a kind man?

Michael, with his charm and his twinkly-eyed smile, had turned out to be a right slacker, there was no doubt about that. Her mother had warned her but Jeanie wouldn't listen and she knew that was down to her and no one else. He'd been lazy and a drinker when she'd met him, and he hadn't changed a bit. But this time his stupidity seemed, against all odds, to have landed them all on their feet. She worried about Michael, but then she probably always would. He was bound to get into another fix before long. But the others were all doing all right.

And what about Evie? She was less anxious about everything since Letitia Mortimer had come into her life. Letty was such a nice girl. It was sad about her parents, though, killed in a car crash at the beginning of summer, and the poor child orphaned and now living with Miss Richards, her mother's sister. Letty hadn't decided what to do with her life just yet, and who could blame her after that amount of upset?

With a sigh Jeanie took the coffee through to the study where Frederick had put all the loose paper and files into three enormous random heaps.

'Now, we can take all these piles of paper into the sitting room and you can sort it out while I get to work on those filthy windows,' she said.

'Jeanie, you're an angel. I bet you can clean the entire room before I've sorted the filing, though.'

'I bet I can,' she laughed, looking at the tottering heaps of files. 'Just take that waste-paper basket with you, will you? I reckon you'll need it . . . '

They worked all morning in adjacent rooms, calling across to each other occasionally but mostly busy in silence. Jeanie was very careful with the chandelier and the little pictures. Early on, Frederick had given her a special brush to stroke the surfaces and she took it slowly, knowing she'd never be able to pay for any breakages.

Eventually, Frederick emerged from the sitting room into the hall and held up his hands, which were black with dust. 'I'll just go and wash my hands and then we'll have some lunch. How do you fancy going to get some fish and chips?'

Jeanie held up her own hands, laughing. 'Snap! And I bet my face looks the same.'

'Jeanie, your face looks lovely,' he said seriously, and as her heart started to beat with a furious excitement he stepped forward and gently kissed her mouth. Before she knew it – before she had grasped a rational thought – he had wrapped her in his arms and was kissing her fiercely, with a passion she couldn't help but return.

'I've wanted to do that since the moment I set eyes on you,' he said.

And in that moment, Jeanie's decision that would change her family's life forever was made. There was no turning back.

CHAPTER NINE

ROBERT WAS JUMPING up and down on the spot
with excitement as Evie locked the front door of
Pendle's and the family set off together for the school
Bonfire Night celebrations and fund-raising event.

'Have you got your gloves, Bob?' asked Jeanie.

'Yes. And Dad's going to carry the marrow because
it weighs—'

'Shush! We don't want to know. There may be
spies about and this is secret information known
only to you,' said Peter.

Robert covered his mouth with his hand briefly.
'My lips are sealed,' he announced.

'I've got you a tin for the takings,' said Evie,
holding up an old sweet tin.

'And I've got the chocolate cake for best guess,'
said Jeanie, picking up her basket.

'And there's some pennies for toffee apples in my
pocket,' said Sue. 'So I think we're ready.'

Streetlamps lit the way down the High Street. As the Carters neared the school gates they slowed with the throng of people heading into the school grounds, which were illuminated with electric lanterns hung on wires.

'I'll go on ahead with Bob and we'll find his table,' said Michael. 'I'll be glad to put this blessed marrow down.'

'You'll need the tin,' said Evie, handing it to Robert.

'Look, there's James and Brian,' Peter said, pointing out the Thomas twins. The boys were carrying violin cases. Peter had only his penny whistle as he'd declared his guitar playing, a recent interest at school, not yet up to public performance standard. 'And Letty and Martin, too. I'll see you all later.' He went off to join his fellow band members. Letty gave the Carters a big smile and a wave and then the musicians disappeared to get themselves ready to play.

'We'll give Bob a few minutes to set up his stall – he can manage that, or at least he can with his dad's help – and then I'll go and pretend to guess the weight to start him off,' said Jeanie. 'I'll hang on to the cake – he'll only lose it or step on it or summat – and the prize-giving isn't until after the fireworks.'

'Look, there's Jack,' said Evie. She ran over to greet her friend. 'What are you doing here, Jack? Aren't there fireworks in Redmond?'

'Hello, Evie. You look snug in that hat. Yes, there are, but I'd a bit of business for Mr Bailey out this way today and Mr Clackett said he'd like some help with the bonfire, so I've been here most of the afternoon building it up with last-minute contributions. People have been generous with their old timber,' he laughed. 'Mrs Clackett made the guy and it's pretty life-like.'

'Ooh, I must go and see it before you light the bonfire,' Evie said, and Jack gallantly extended his arm to escort her to the field behind the school.

Just as they approached the band struck up 'The Irish Rover', Letty playing her guitar and singing as purely and sweetly as Evie had ever heard anyone sing. Peter played a tune between verses, the Thomas boys lent depth and heart on their fiddles, and Martin shook and tapped his tambourine and sang harmony to Letty's lovely voice.

There was plenty of applause at the end and Letty said, 'If you like what you hear, guess the weight of the marrow. It's only a penny a go.' A queue formed at Robert's table and for a minute he looked panicked, but he gathered himself and loudly instructed every punter to 'Write your name and the weight clearly, please.'

Letty smiled and waved at Evie and then counted the band in for the next number, a song Evie had never heard before about . . . a gigantic marrow! She guessed it had been written by Peter because familiar names were mentioned: Mr Clackett and Michael Carter, and the chorus had a catchy tune about a marrow that 'grew and grew'.

Evie was laughing so much by the end that her sides ached, and the queue in front of Robert was enormous.

~

Jeanie had met up with Josie Lambert, who had brought her children but lost her husband in the crowd.

'Never mind,' she said, 'he'll turn up. Gives me a chance to ask you . . . ' and she started to ask about solutions to baby Nancy's teething problems, which Jeanie didn't mind at all because the baby was so cute and she loved to hold her.

Sue wandered off to see what she could make of the stalls. She didn't often go out after dark these days and she'd noticed as soon as she left the house how difficult it had become to see where she was going without proper light, and to make out who people were. She could hear Peter's band distantly, sounding very professional, and she thought that Peter's talents would take him far from them before very long.

The fund-raising stalls were either games with prizes, or food and drink. There was treacle toffee, shattered into pieces with a hammer and sold in paper cones for a penny ha'penny, and toffee apples, too. There was mulled ale on a stand run by the Red Lion – Michael was standing there with a large beaker of it – and the Tombola. Sue looked at the prizes but decided she didn't fancy winning any of them, but she did buy toffee apples for Robert and Peter.

She had just turned away when her ears pricked up at the mention of a familiar name. Two women were standing close by, obviously unaware of Sue in the dim light.

' . . . owned by Frederick Bailey, you know, him that lives in Redmond and drives a red car.'

'Oh, yes? I've heard mention of his name. Sells this and that, I gather.'

'Antiques – overpriced bric-a-brac, I expect. But his real claim to fame is the number of times he's been married.'

'Oh, the poor man. Widowed more than once? I gather he's not old.'

'Not widowed,' said the gossip. '*Divorced.*' She hissed the word with horror in her voice. 'Three times, no less.'

'No!'

'Yes! And the second and third Mrs Baileys were someone else's wives before they took up with him. Lured them away from their husbands, so I heard.'

'Who'd have thought? So he isn't still married, then?'

'No, I told you, divorced the lot of them. Men like him should carry a sign to warn women what they're like, dangerous. You wouldn't catch me keeping him company.'

At this Sue, whose stomach was flipping like a pancake, chanced a peek over her shoulder to glimpse the gossip: a hugely fat woman in her early seventies, with a face like an unplumped cushion. If she hadn't felt so upset Sue would have dealt the gossip a put-down. As it was, she moved away to calm herself and have a quiet think.

Could it be true? And even if it were, what had it to do with her – with Jeanie? Sue had to acknowledge now what she'd tried to ignore these past weeks: that Jeanie was obviously fond of Frederick Bailey. But was there more to it than that? Jeanie could be wayward and Sue knew that, as her only child, Jeanie had been a bit spoiled and allowed much of what she wanted. She was still very pretty, and recently Sue had been pleased to see that Jeanie was looking after herself much better than she had in Shenty Street. She'd started doing her hair in a new way and she now walked with a spring in her step that had not been there in recent months.

Sue looked across to where Michael was buying himself another beaker of mulled ale, laughing with Jack, who now had Letty beside him. Michael's face had coarsened over the years and he was less obviously charming and more obviously lazy these days.

Could it be Michael that was bringing the roses to Jeanie's cheeks? Somehow Sue doubted it.

'Mrs Goodwin? Are you all right?'

It was Miss Richards.

'I'm fine, thank you, Miss Richards. Just getting away from the crowd for a moment, that's all. Your Letty's got a lovely voice. I had no idea she was such a talented singer. I saw quite a gathering where the band was playing. It's good of her to support Robert that way.'

'She loves an audience,' said Miss Richard indulgently. 'It's good that she's doing something so cheering after all her troubles.'

'Your troubles, too, love,' said Sue, giving Miss Richards' arm a squeeze. 'Come on, let's go and see this bonfire being lit.'

'Good idea – and I still haven't had a go at Guess the Weight . . . '

The bonfire was lit and was soon blazing fiercely, then the stalls were closed while the fireworks were set off so that those doing the fund-raising could enjoy them along with everyone else. There was much oohing and aahing from the crowd and applause at the end. Then the stallholders returned to do more business or announce the results of the games. The Red Lion's mulled ale was going fast, and already over-tired little ones were being taken home to bed.

Robert took a long time to go through all the

entries for Guess the Weight of the Marrow, so Jeanie helped him in the end and the winner of the chocolate cake was declared to be Mr Clackett. Jeanie privately thought he'd weighed more than a few marrows in his time so had an advantage over most people, but he had paid to have a go, so that was all that mattered.

'I think I'll just go and see who's in the Lion,' Michael told Jeanie, and shuffled off out of the school gate.

'Aren't you going to stop and help us with . . . ?'

Too late, Michael had wandered away and seemed not to hear.

Jeanie and Sue tidied up Robert's stall and made sure the tin of money was safely in Jeanie's basket while Evie and Peter said goodbye to their friends.

Jack approached Jeanie and Sue as they were wondering what to do with the marrow. 'Have you seen Michael?' he asked. 'Mr Clackett and I could do with a hand taking down the lanterns and making the fire safe before we go.'

'Oh . . . he said he was going to the Lion,' said Jeanie, embarrassed. 'I'm sure he didn't mean to abandon you.'

'I'll help,' said Peter. 'Here, Mum.' He handed Jeanie his penny whistle. 'I'll see you at home.'

'The more help we have, the quicker we'll be,' said Jack. And he and Peter went off together to tackle dismantling the lighting.

'I can't believe Michael's not here,' Jeanie fumed. 'It's blinkin' typical of him these days. In fact, it's typical of him altogether.'

'Well, he was never a grafter, love, you always knew that.'

'I did, Mum. Somehow I never used to mind.'

'And you do now?'

'Mmm . . . The rest of us – we're all doing our bit. And you and Evie are doing amazing with the sewing, and I've got my own job, too. But Michael – he's content to do as little as possible. He can hardly even manage his job properly. I haven't forgotten Mr Clackett giving him that warning. For goodness' sake, Mum, he only has to turn up and do as he's asked. It may be cold and mucky now it's autumn but it's not exactly difficult, is it?' She realised she'd raised her voice and she looked around to make sure no one else had heard. 'Sorry, Mum, but I lose all patience with him sometimes.'

'And how are you getting on with "your own job"?' asked Sue. 'Do you know, I've yet to meet Frederick Bailey? What's it like, working for him?'

'It's fine, Mum. I've told you, I do a lot of dusting and tidying up. He's very untidy and tends to lose things and leave the place in a mess, but it's clean dirt, if you know what I mean. The kitchen's the worst because he has no idea about washing stuff up and putting it away. In fact, I meant to tell you, I've said I'll cook his dinner – lunch, he calls it –

and wash up afterwards, so I shan't be home so early from now on. And he wants me to get the shopping in, too, which means the job's a bit more interesting than just keeping the place clean.'

'Oh, aye?'

'Yes, and I've organised a system for his post. He was always losing his letters and receipts and stuff, but I put it in a special tray when it arrives and he works through it.'

'You sound very organised,' said Sue. 'I gather there isn't a Mrs Bailey or he wouldn't need a house-keeper,' she ventured.

'No, he isn't married.'

'*Was* there a Mrs Bailey?' Sue persisted, trying to find a way of telling her the truth. 'I wonder a man who seems to have so much doesn't have a wife. And he's not bad-looking – Evie told me that.'

'It's none of my business, Mum,' said Jeanie care-fully. 'I've never asked him. But you're right, there certainly isn't a Mrs Bailey these days. Maybe she died or summat. I don't like to ask.'

'Oh, I'm sure Frederick wouldn't mind you asking,' Sue said. 'After all, if you knew the full picture you wouldn't put your foot in it by mistake. It isn't like you'd gossip about him or anything. But you'd know not to say the wrong thing, then.'

'I hope I wouldn't say the wrong thing anyway,' said Jeanie. 'All I know is, there's no Mrs Bailey at Marlowe House, and that's all I need to know.'

'All right, love. Just wondering, that's all,' Sue replied. 'Now let's get some cocoa on. It's getting cold and I think Peter will want some after helping with the clearing up.'

'Good idea,' said Jeanie. They were now back at Pendle's and she pushed the door open and went through, calling out to Evie.

~

'I must sing "The Marrow Song" to Billy when I see him – only six days to go!' said Evie. 'He's been that amused by the saga of the marrows in my letters.'

'Maybe you could teach it to Harold Pyke,' said Jeanie, deadpan. 'It's a good tune, though a bit "of the moment", so to speak. Or at least I hope it is,' she added, eyeing the only slightly reduced contents of the marrow box. 'What happened to the monster marrow, Pete?'

'I left it there, by the school gate. I reckon it will have gone by Monday,' said Peter. 'There's always someone stupid enough to pinch anything, even a gigantic marrow.' And he resumed playing the song, trying out different chords.

As the children were giving the chorus one more raucous round, Michael came slowly into the kitchen, his face screwed up, looking as if his head hurt. He sat down heavily at the table and groaned.

'Can't you kids just shut up?' he snarled. 'What

kind of Saturday is it that a fella can't have a bit of peace and quiet before he does a hard day's work?'

'You only work until dinnertime on Saturdays, as you well know,' Jeanie answered, cheerfully. 'And you'll have to get a move on if you're to get over the road on time.'

'Aye, all right. Don't go on,' Michael muttered. 'I think that mulled ale must have been a bit stronger than I thought.'

'Should have drunk less of it, then,' said Peter.

There was a brief silence. 'What did you say?' said Michael menacingly.

'Shush, Pete . . . ' said Sue, who was making toast. 'Just leave it, love.'

But Peter was determined to get his opinion of his father's behaviour off his chest.

'I said you should have drunk less of it,' he repeated loudly and bravely. 'Then you could have helped pack up the lighting and the stalls. It was Jack and me, and Mr Clackett, and the twins' father who did it all, and we could have done with your help, 'specially as you said you'd be there at the end.'

'Don't you judge me in that tone, my lad,' Michael said, standing up, though his aggressive stance was undermined by his swaying on his feet.

'But everyone else is, Dad. Everyone else is saying that you skived off to the pub and left other folk to do all the work.'

'Is this true?' asked Jeanie. She couldn't help herself: even if she prolonged the argument she had to know what was being said.

'I wouldn't lie to you, Mum,' said Peter. 'Jack was trying to make excuses for you, Dad, but the others weren't taken in.' Then he added, unwisely: 'Mr Clackett was muttering about "the evils of drink" and Mr Thomas said . . . well, I heard him saying to Jack that you were a no-good drunk, and he felt sorry for Mum and Grandma. And I do, too!'

Jeanie's hands shot to her face in horror, while everyone started speaking at once.

'Peter, be quiet! You've said far too much,' shouted Sue.

And Evie said, 'Oh, Pete, that's awful. To say such a thing so that you overheard!'

'Come here, you cheeky bugger, and I'll give you a good hiding,' threatened Michael, starting towards Peter, but he lost his footing and sat down, nearly missing the chair, incapable of carrying out his threat.

'Michael, I can't believe you haven't learnt your lesson, you stupid man,' shrieked Jeanie. 'After everything that happened in Shenty Street . . . '

'Why should I shut up, Grandma, when it's only the truth?' yelled Peter.

Robert sat looking from one to another and then loudly burst into tears. Soon everyone was remonstrating with everyone else and the noise was terrible.

Eventually it was Sue's voice that carried above all others.

'Be quiet, the lot of you! Michael, get this cup of tea down you and get over the road to Clackett's. And take your hangover with you and don't come back until you're sober and in a better mood. Peter, Robert, go to your room, please, and don't come down until I say.'

'But, Grandma—' sniffed Robert.

'I said *go*,' snapped Sue, and the boys did as they were asked, Peter taking the guitar with him. He gave his father a filthy look in passing but he didn't appear at all contrite.

Michael got up stiffly, looking more fragile than ever, gulped down the tea, and shuffled off down the passage to the front door, grumbling and moaning in equal measure. The front door slammed and there was a sudden and deep silence.

Sue, Jeanie and Evie looked at each other.

'Well, it's better we know what folk are saying. This is a small place and if I don't learn the truth from my own family I may well hear it from others in the street or the shops, which would be far worse.'

'But here was to be our new start,' Evie said, tears spilling over. 'I thought after the to-do at the brewery and that awful business with . . . ' she automatically lowered her voice, ' . . . with Mr Hopkins, that Dad had learned his lesson and we were starting over.'

'Well, folks all know each other's business here,

so anybody steps out of line, you might as well shout it from the rooftops. If Michael can't keep sober and make an effort to be neighbourly then maybe we ought to go somewhere where we can keep our heads down more, a place where everyone *isn't* minding everyone else's business.'

'You can't mean it!' gasped Jeanie. 'What, move again? But we've hardly been here—'

'And already Michael's got a reputation for drink and idleness,' interrupted Sue.

'Oh, it's not too late, is it?' pleaded Jeanie. 'You and Evie are doing so well – I'm that proud of you – and Pete's never been so happy. He'd be heart-broken if he had to leave. And I admit I didn't like the place when I first set eyes on it, but we're settled at Pendle's now, and anyway, you're making use of the shop part. And we've got friends here. Even I have got a bit of a job of my own and I can't, I just *can't*, leave Frederick's.'

Sue sank into a chair and reached across to see if there was any more tea in the pot. Evie turned away to put the kettle on again and Jeanie could tell even from the back that she was fighting away tears. They all thought about what Sue had said for a few minutes.

Then Evie said, 'You're right about folk knowing our business here, of course, Grandma, but we can't keep running away. We had to leave Shenty Street because of Dad's debt to Mr Hopkins and it was too dangerous to stay, but if we run away this time we'll be trying to run from ourselves. We'll be taking Dad with us, so we'll be taking Dad's drinking and Dad's problems too. We could keep starting over forever, but it would always end the same.'

'Wise words, lass,' said Sue. 'Yes, you're right: better to stay where we have friends. If we move because folk know us, and know what we're like, then we'll be friendless vagabonds for the rest of our lives.'

Jeanie let out a sob and mopped her eyes. 'You're both right,' she nodded. 'And after all, no one's blaming us. Everyone here knows how hard you two work. You wouldn't be so busy if folk didn't think well of you.'

Evie refilled the teapot and, discarding the cold and soggy toast, went to find the tin of digestive biscuits.

'I've an idea,' said Sue. 'I'll have a word with Mr Clackett – or you can, if you'd rather, Jeanie, love – and see if we can get him to keep Michael too busy to think about the Red Lion. Clackett's a strict man but a fair one, and I think if he were to see keeping Michael on the straight and narrow was to his advantage, then we'd all benefit. What do you say?'

Jeanie blew her nose and gave a watery smile. 'Mr Clackett's been good to us so it's worth a try, Mum. But I reckon you're the woman to do it. He terrifies the life out of me!'

'Nonsense,' said Sue with a chuckle. 'I reckon he's soft as butter underneath. It's just that we've never got underneath to see that. I'll go over this afternoon, when Michael will have finished there for the weekend. And then we'll have to swallow our pride and rise above Michael's behaviour yesterday evening. It's the Carter women that keep the show on the road, as always.'

'And Pete and me,' said Robert, coming in to hear the last bit. 'Perhaps I can stay here with you and Evie, Grandma, and help with the sewing.'

'Perhaps you can go to school on Monday with all the money you collected for Guess the Weight,' said Jeanie.

'Oh, I forgot about the money,' said Robert. 'I haven't counted it yet.' He looked around. 'Can anyone remember what I did with the tin?'

While the others were all looking for the tin, Sue sipped her tea and thought over everything that had happened in the last day or so. Despite the upset of the morning, she found her mind returning, as it had when she lay in bed the previous night, to the gossip she had overheard about Frederick Bailey at the school bonfire. So what if he was divorced, she thought fairly, wasn't it just bad luck if his marriages hadn't worked out?

But then a little voice in her head said: And whose fault was that? It took two to make a marriage work, as she knew only too well. She didn't know anyone

181

who was divorced, though she had known plenty of unhappy marriages in Shenty Street over the years. And *three* divorces! Could that be true – could it even be possible? She couldn't forget that awful gossiping woman had said he'd 'lured' women from their husbands, then married and divorced them. And Jeanie had already as good as said she was beginning to fall out of love with Michael. Oh Lord . . .

Well, maybe it was time to meet Frederick Bailey at last, thought Sue, but she'd have to think through very carefully exactly what she would say.

In the meantime, she remembered heavily, she'd volunteered to tackle Mr Clackett about Michael that afternoon.

'No rest for the wicked,' she muttered, heaving herself to her feet, still tired from standing all yesterday evening.

'What, Grandma?' asked Evie.

'I think I'll go and press Miss Richards' study curtains,' said Sue. 'We can take them down to Lavender Cottage and hang them this afternoon before I go to see Mr Clackett.'

'I'll give you a hand, too,' said Peter, for which Sue was grateful, though she suspected that what lay behind the offer was Peter hoping to spend the afternoon with Letty rather than with his father. And she could hardly blame him for that.

CHAPTER TEN

Evie sat on the train heading north. A case of
clothes, including her party dress, and a bag
containing a handmade birthday present for Geraldine,
a little thank you posy for Mrs Marsh for accommo-
dating her, and a jolly red scarf she'd knitted for Billy,
was on the luggage rack above her. In her handbag
was Sue's shopping list for the mill shop.

'See what you can manage to carry, love,' Sue had
told her. 'Start at the top and if they've got everything
then stop buying when you're spent up or you think
you've run out of hands!'

Jeanie had seen her off at Redmond station, on
her way to work.

'Give my special love to everyone, won't you, love?
And say hello to the old house for me. But don't
forget to keep quiet about where we are. We don't
want Hopkins' man turning up on the doorstep at
Pendle's.'

'No, Mum. I'll be careful who I speak to, don't worry.'

The thought of anyone trying to get information about the Carters' whereabouts from her made Evie nervous, but she was comforted by the thought that she would be among friends. After all, Brendan Sullivan knew where they all were and he'd obviously not spilled the beans.

The carriage became full before the train had stopped at many stations, but Evie was in the corner next to the window and facing forward, which she felt was the best seat. The lady sitting opposite handed round a bag of peppermints and there was some chatting between the other passengers, but Evie preferred to keep herself to herself, nervous at being on her own. She glanced at her watch and counted down the time to the change at Manchester, when she would be within an hour of seeing Billy, who had promised to meet her train in Bolton. Her stomach did that customary flip of excitement at the thought of him.

Billy had managed to swap shifts with one of his friends at work and was free the whole time Evie would be there, which was even better than she had dreamed!

After her memory of all the waiting around when Billy had been meant to visit her, Evie could hardly believe it when she changed stations at Manchester without any difficulty, the train from Manchester

Victoria was almost on time and she stepped out at Trinity Street station and looked up and down the platform for him. Quite a few passengers had alighted and there were small crowds of people blocking her view. She scanned the scene to right and left but there was no one who looked like Billy.

Oh, please, let him be here . . .

Then the other people started to move away and Evie's stomach began to change from fluttering with excitement to the nervous churning that it had done that awful Sunday at Redmond station. Her eyes searched the platform again and she suddenly had a terrible sinking feeling.

Then, just as she thought she might be out of luck a second time: 'Evie! Oh, Evie!' and he was running towards her, waving.

Evie put down her case and her bag and ran to meet him. 'Billy!' She rushed into his arms and they held each other tightly for a long, long moment. 'Oh, I thought you hadn't been able to make it. Billy, I'm that glad to see you.'

'And so am I, Evie, love. Sorry I'm a bit late. I didn't mean to worry you. Mum started fretting over nowt and getting herself worked up, and I thought I'd never get to leave the house. In the end I just ran out.'

'Well, you're here now, and so am I, and that's all that matters,' Evie said, giving him another hug and kissing his cheek.

'Let's get your things. Would you like a cup of tea? It's been a long journey for you.'

'No, thank you. I'm all right. I had time to have a quick cup at Manchester, but I tell you what I would like, Billy, if it fits in with your plans.'

'What's that, then?'

'I'd like to get a bag of chips and we can sit and share them in Victoria Park, just like we used to.'

'Bit parky to be sitting out, isn't it?' he asked, but smiling because he, too, treasured the memory.

'Chips always taste better in the open air, and it'll give us a chance to catch up. I mean, look at you. New overcoat, is it?'

'Aye,' said Billy. 'First time on.' He brushed imaginary dust off one shoulder.

'Come into money, have you?'

And they laughed together as they left the station, Evie carrying the bag and Billy taking her case.

~

'So tell me,' said Evie, as they sat in the park and Billy unwrapped the layers of newspaper from around the steaming chips, 'what have I been missing?'

'Nowt, so far as I can see,' said Billy. 'It's me what's done the missing. I've thought about you every single day, and you look even prettier than I remember.'

Evie blushed to the tip of her toes.

'Really, Evie,' he said seriously. 'That Sunday when

it all went wrong – I were that upset and it was hard to explain in a letter. I . . . I thought if you didn't forgive me . . . if you took it badly that I'd let you down—'

'But, Billy, it wasn't your fault your mother was taken poorly. And it's impossible to say if our plans are changed at the last moment when neither of us is on the telephone. I was disappointed – of course I was – but when you wrote so quickly to explain I did understand.'

'You're a good lass, Evie. One in a million.'

'So how's your mum now? No more bad headaches?'

'She's all right, thank you, Evie. She tends to get some queer ideas into her head but it's nowt I can't deal with.'

'That good, then,' said Evie, too polite to ask about the 'queer ideas'.

'Tell me more about this Pendle's where you live, Evie. And how's your friend Letty Mortimer? I'm so glad you've found folk you like down there.'

So Evie told Billy all about Letty and Miss Richards, and how Letty's parents had been killed at the beginning of summer, but that she was being really brave about it, and then she went on to describe the Bonfire Night festivities and Robert's Guess the Weight stall, and how he'd personally raised five shillings towards buying new curtains for the school platform.

Then, as they dipped into the pile of chips, Evie told Billy about the success of Peter's band on the evening, and all about 'The Marrow Song', which made them both laugh loudly, and how Peter had abandoned the huge marrow outside the school gate where by Monday morning, it had, as he'd predicted, disappeared without trace.

'So there's someone eating marrow for breakfast, dinner and tea,' giggled Evie. 'And they're welcome to it. In fact, if they want any more I reckon Mum will be pleased to hand the wretched things over.'

'I'm glad you didn't bring me one up with you,' chuckled Billy.

'I'd have brought the whole box if I could have carried them,' Evie replied, 'but I'd have needed to take a wheelbarrow on the train. Oh, but I did bring something for you . . . '

She wiped the grease off her hands with her handkerchief, then dug around in her bag of presents until she found the scarf she'd knitted for Billy, which was wrapped in reused tissue paper.

'There. Just a little thing I made in the evenings.'

Billy unwrapped the scarf and held it out. 'Evie, it's grand – fringes at the ends and everything. You are clever. Thank you, love.' He wrapped it around his neck. 'Looks smart with my new coat.'

'You look lovely, Billy,' she said, and leaned forward to kiss him.

The kiss turned into a long one, and then it was

followed by another, so that when they drew apart Evie looked a bit shy and her face was glowing.

'I've wanted to do that since the moment we parted in July,' whispered Billy.

She nodded. 'Me, too, Billy. Oh, I've missed you so much!'

They cuddled up on the park bench and Billy put his arm around Evie and held her close. After a few minutes Evie remembered she had plans, and only this afternoon to carry them out. Tomorrow she would be busy helping the Sullivans prepare for Geraldine's party.

'I could stay here for ever, Billy, but I ought to go and say hello to Mrs Marsh, and leave my things there. She's expecting me this afternoon and she's so kind to put me up. And then I've got a shopping list for the mill shop from Grandma.'

'Then we best get on.'

Billy balled up the empty chip paper, lobbed it into a nearby waste bin, then picked up Evie's case and they set off in the direction of Shenty Street and Dora Marsh's pristine house next door to the Sullivans.

They'd just got to the top of Shenty Street – which looked to Evie as if time had stood still and was exactly as she had known it all her life – when they heard a voice calling out behind them.

'Evie! Billy!'

They turned. 'Mary!' exclaimed Evie in delight,

setting down her bag and running to meet her old school friend.

'Brilliant!' said Mary, who was wearing her school uniform and holding a bulging satchel of books. 'I hoped I'd see you sooner than later. Me and Gerry were going to come round and find you at Mrs Marsh's later. This is even better, though. Come in and have some tea with Ma and me now and tell us all about everything. You, too, Billy.'

'Oh, Mary, I'm right glad to see you,' said Evie, giving her friend a hug. 'But I need to get off to the mill shop when I've said hello to Mrs Marsh. I've a shopping list from Grandma and the shop is only open until the end of the afternoon.'

'I remember Ma getting that box of fabrics, and how pleased your gran was with them,' said Mary. 'But don't they have nice things in . . . ' she turned her head furtively to check all round in an exaggerated gesture, ' . . . you-know-where?'

'Not like they do in Bolton. It's not the same quality, and the prices are higher, too. Of course, we can't get all our fabrics here but it makes sense to stock up a bit today.'

'Then we'd best get on,' said Mary, and she took Evie's arm at one side while Billy held her hand at the other.

So Evie arrived at Dora Marsh's house surrounded by friends, and it felt just like coming home.

~

Geraldine's birthday party was in full swing and the noise was unbelievable. The party-goers seemed to include everyone Evie had ever met in her beloved home town, and she couldn't have been happier. There was so much news to share with her family when she got home that she was anxious she'd forget half of it.

Geraldine was the centre of attention, of course, and was looking particularly lovely in a silky bias-cut dress that showed off her fabulous figure and made her look very grown-up indeed. Evie thought she remembered Sue running it up for Marie a couple of years before, but it fit Geraldine perfectly and looked as good as new.

'Scrubs up well, doesn't she?' laughed Mary, who couldn't care less about her own appearance, though she had pinned back her hair with a couple of diamanté clips she'd borrowed from her sister in honour of this being a party. 'I think she's sweet on Colin Fraser, who works with Billy at the postal depot.'

Brendan appeared with a glass of beer for Stephen and proffering a bottle of dandelion and burdock to replenish the girls' glasses.

'Now, Evie, m'darlin', how's your dad getting on these days?'

Evie politely outlined how Michael's job was going at Clackett's, making no mention of the upsets caused by his drinking, of course. Then she told

191

Brendan, Mary and Stephen about the misshapen vegetables that had been the Carters' staple diet for the first few weeks, and everyone was soon roaring with laughter.

Marie was handing around plates towering with sandwiches, which she and her girls and Evie had made that afternoon, and Billy came over to join Evie, putting his arm around her.

Evie and Billy soon found themselves cornered by Mr Amsell, who was getting quite emotional on the beer he'd drunk. He was loudly declaring Gerry to be the daughter he'd never had, and the greatest asset a man who ran a busy corner shop could wish to employ, when Evie looked up and her eyes met those of Billy's mother. Ada was sitting with some of the other older ladies, including Dora Marsh and Harold Pyke's wife, and she was staring straight at Evie with an expression that could have chilled a summer's day.

Evie quickly looked away. The hostility was unmistakable, yet what could possibly be the matter? When she dared to look up again, Ada was talking to Mrs Pyke and her face was quite amicable.

I surely can't have been seeing things . . .

'You all right, love?' Billy asked, feeling Evie's tension.

'Yes . . . yes . . . '

Mr Amsell was now singing Geraldine's praises to her father, which was undoubtedly a sound diplomatic move to any proud father on his beautiful daughter's birthday, and Evie and Billy went to find Colin Fraser, as Evie said she'd heard he was a sight to behold with his Brylcreemed hair and his shiny shoes. To herself she admitted that she needed a distraction from wondering about the look she'd seen on Ada Taylor's face.

'Come on, my girl,' Billy playfully punched Evie on the arm.

'My girl'? Is that how he sees me? Yes, I reckon I am Billy's girl, but I would bet on it that his mum doesn't like to think so. Again Evie wondered what could be behind that black look on Ada's face.

' . . . Evie?'

'Oh, sorry, I got distracted. It's quite hot in here, isn't it?'

'I'll get you a glass of lemonade, if you like,' said Billy.

'Thank you.'

He disappeared and left Evie with Colin Fraser.

'I was just saying, I gather you used to live around here?' asked Colin.

'Yes, that's right,' Evie replied. 'But it's grand to come back and see everyone, especially with Gerry's birthday to celebrate.'

'Aye, the Sullivans know how to hold a party,' Colin nodded. 'Where is it you live now, Evie?'

'Oh, it's . . . it's a long way away,' she said, alarm bells suddenly ringing. This man was a stranger to her. What had Mum said as she saw her off at Redmond yesterday morning? *Don't forget to keep quiet about where we are. We don't want Hopkins' man turning up on the doorstep at Pendle's.* 'Not anywhere you'd have heard of,' she added with a smile to soften the words.

She was surprised when Colin Fraser came straight back at that. 'And how would you know whether I've heard of it or not, Evie?'

Now she felt cornered and she had to think fast. 'Because it's on the south coast,' she lied. 'Such a long way away . . . near Dover,' she improvised, remembering the name of a place on the coast from a well-known song. 'It's a very long way from here,' she repeated.

'Dover? That's nice . . . good sea views,' Colin said.

So maybe he did know Dover. Oh Lord, that was bad luck. What if he asked her about it? Evie had never been anywhere near Dover in her life! She'd simply picked the first place that came to mind.

'I think I'll just . . . go and see where Billy's got to with that lemonade,' she muttered, and backed away, leaving Colin looking puzzled until Gerry sashayed up to him and whispered something in his ear. His eyes lit up and they moved to a cabinet at the side. Soon the scratchy sound of a gramophone record rose above the already high level of conversation and a few people took partners in the centre of the room, to dance as best they could in the crowded space.

'Oh, Billy, that was difficult,' Evie murmured, joining him in the kitchen. She repeated the conversation she'd just had. 'I don't want to be unfriendly, like, but I can't be too careful.'

'You're right, of course, love,' said Billy, giving her arm a squeeze. 'I've said nowt at work about where you're living now – not to anyone – and although I've known Colin a while, and I think he's a good fella, the fewer people learn where you are, the less likely . . . ' he lowered his voice, as everyone at home always did, ' . . . Mr Hopkins is to find your dad.' Then he started laughing. 'Dover, though! That's a good one.'

'Shush,' said Evie, glancing towards the door. 'I hate lying.'

Suddenly Ada was standing in the doorway, looking fierce and disgruntled. 'Hello, Evie Carter,' she greeted her, looking spiteful. 'I think it's time we went home, Billy.'

'What, now, Mum? But it's barely nine o'clock. Party's just getting started, and I think I see a cake to cut on the side, there.' He indicated an upturned tin centred over a cake board, a pile of candles and a box of matches by the side.

'But it's that noisy now, and I'm sure I've got another of my heads coming on.'

For one terrible moment Evie felt inclined to

snigger as she pictured Billy's sour-faced mother with two heads. She decided it would be wise to keep quiet and leave this to Billy.

Evie was close enough to Billy to hear him take a deep breath. 'I'm sorry to hear that, Mum, but maybe if you have a glass of water you'll soon feel better.'

'I don't think so,' she replied. 'I don't feel up to eating cake, either.'

'Well, that's a shame, Mum, because you don't often get to celebrate birthdays with your friends, and Gerry did invite us both to join her tonight.'

'Well, Gerry Sullivan is a lovely girl, there's no doubt about that,' said Ada. 'She looks beautiful in that dress, what with her figure and her pretty hair. Always one to make an effort,' she added, giving Evie a sideways glance to dismiss her girlish party dress, which was, of course, nothing like as grown-up as Geraldine's.

'So are you staying to see her cut her cake, then, Mum?' asked Billy, trying to jolly her out of her bad mood.

Ada briefly looked again in Evie's direction and seemed to make up her mind. 'No, I reckon we've both had enough company for one evening, Billy, and it's time to go home.'

'You may well have, Mum, and I'm sorry your head's aching—'

'Oh, it is, Billy. It'll be fit to split by morning if I don't go and lie down soon.'

'—but I shall be staying a while yet. *I* don't want to miss Gerry cutting her cake—'

'Oh, I can understand that, you and Gerry being so close,' said Ada, changing tack. 'But—'

'—so I've already spoken to Mr Amsell and he's said he'll walk you to the door when you're ready to go, Mum.'

For a moment Ada looked furious. 'But, Billy—'

'That way, I get to enjoy seeing Geraldine enjoying her party on her birthday,' said Billy with exaggerated tolerance, 'and you get to walk home with someone who'll make sure you get there safely, and then you can have a little lie-down. I feared something like this might happen so I left some aspirins on the kitchen side,' he added.

Mr Amsell appeared at the kitchen door with remarkably good timing.

'Mrs Taylor, dear lady, do I gather you're ready to go home?' he asked. He leaned in close as if confiding in her. 'We old folk can't stay up so late dancing and carousing as we used to, can we?'

'Dancing and carousing . . . ?' spluttered Ada.

'Let me help you find your coat, Mrs Taylor, and I'll escort you to your door.'

'I— I don't—'

'It's really no trouble,' Mr Amsell added graciously, holding out his arm to her. 'Come, my dear, the night is young for some, and we don't want to spoil

Geraldine's party, do we? We'll just thank Marie discreetly and slip away.'

He took Ada's arm and escorted her out of the kitchen, calling, 'Goodnight, Billy and Evie,' cheerfully over his shoulder.

'All right, Billy, what's going on?' Evie asked when they'd gone.

'Let's make sure they've left and then I'll tell you,' he said, helping himself to a beer out of the crate Brendan, always a generous host.

'Yes, please. Why not?' said Evie.

Billy led her through to the main room and then out into the quiet of the passage just as Mr Amsell closed the front door behind him, Ada on his arm.

'What's the matter with your mum?' demanded Evie. 'She's been looking daggers at me and I can't think why. And how did you know she'd have a headache this evening?'

'Because I'm learning she always has a headache if she thinks things aren't going her way,' Billy replied impatiently.

'I don't understand, what's not going her way?'

'*We* aren't, Evie.' He took her hand in his and gave it a squeeze of reassurance. 'She thinks we're not suited and that it's hopeless if we . . . if we have feelings for each other and we live so far apart.'

'Not suited? Of course we're suited. We've known each other for ever,' said Evie. 'And we can't be the first folk who've been apart. I know it's difficult, and I miss you all the time—'

'And I miss you – you know I do.'

'But we write and we can meet up as often as . . . Just one minute – it was one of your mum's headaches that stopped you getting that train a few months ago, wasn't it?'

'I'm afraid it was, Evie. And I know what you're thinking. Oh, I'm that sorry. I've learned a lot these last months and I can see what her game is now. If I'd realised at the time I'd have just got the train down to see you and left her there, playing the invalid.'

Evie stood quiet for a few moments, taking all this in. 'I can't pretend I'm not angry, Billy, but I reckon you couldn't have left her. I'm trying to be fair and think if it had been my mum that felt ill, what I would have done. I can't blame you for staying to make sure she was all right.'

'But it wasn't your mum, Evie. It's my mum who's being difficult and I won't have her being nasty about you.'

'Why, what's she been saying?'

Billy realised he'd led the conversation in a direction he'd really rather avoid.

'Come on, Billy. What's she got against me? I've known your mum as long as I've known you, and she's never had cause for complaint, so far as I know.'

Billy sighed. 'It's your dad,' he said quietly. 'She thinks he's unreliable.'

'We *all* think my dad's unreliable, he's the reason we had to leave Shenty Street, after all. Most of the people in that room know about him getting the sack from the brewery, and quite a few must know about . . . ' she lowered her voice, though both were speaking softly, ' . . . about the gambling debt. Why's your mum making a fuss about him now?'

'Because she thinks I'm in love with you, of course,' said Billy, in a rush.

Evie looked at him, startled.

'And are you?' she asked quietly.

'Oh, I don't know, Evie. I think so. You're the best girl ever, and the prettiest, and I've never set eyes on anyone half as good and kind as you are . . . '

'But you can't be sure,' Evie finished for him. She knew that was true because she felt exactly the same. She loved him but was it a forever kind of love? She wanted it to be, but she couldn't yet be sure. He, too, was good and kind, but maybe he missed her so much because she was far away now. Maybe if she was nearby he wouldn't have the same yearning to be with her. She had to ask herself, of course, if the same couldn't be said of herself.

'It's all right, Billy, I do understand,' she said. 'But why should your mum mind so much if we're fond of each other?'

'I reckon she's frightened that I'll go away from

here to be with you, and leave her by herself,' Billy said. 'She's trying to make out it's because your dad begrudges going to work . . . well she says he's no good and thinks you may take after him.'

'Billy!'

'Shush, love. Hear me out. I know that's not true. She just wants me to stay with her.'

'But she must want you to have a life of your own?' said Evie. 'Children do go away from their parents sometimes – often, I suppose.'

'I know, and she does, too, but she's frightened of being left alone. She can be difficult and selfish, and she doesn't have any close friends, even though she's lived here all her life. I'm all she's got and she doesn't want to share me and she doesn't want to lose me.'

'But you can't stay in her house in Fawcett Street for ever, Billy. How old is your mum – mid-fifties? Younger than Grandma Sue. She may live for twenty or more years yet.'

'I expect she'll want the girl I marry to move in with her – with us – and look after her.'

'Good heavens, Billy, it's a good thing you've warned me,' said Evie before she could stop herself.

'Oh, so it isn't the same for your dad, living with his mother-in-law?' Billy asked angrily.

'No, Billy, it isn't the same at all. There's no one like Grandma Sue. She's kept my family on its feet through thick and thin – and it's mostly been thin, let me tell you – and she'd never stand in the way of anyone's happiness.'

'I know—'

'She's not at all like your mother. Do you think Grandma Sue would pretend to be ill to get her own way? Do you think Grandma Sue would even admit she was ill if she was? She's nothing like your mother.'

'Evie, please don't speak about my mother like that,' he said dangerously.

'Like what? Like she talks about me, you mean? Feckless? Unreliable? I'm obviously not good enough for her boy, am I?'

'Evie, please . . .'

'Well, you mustn't disappoint your mother, must you, Billy? I'm only amazed you didn't go trotting off home with her as soon as she started moaning. I wouldn't want to be in your shoes tomorrow because you'll be getting it in the neck for sure.'

'Right, I reckon it is time I went,' said Billy, 'before I hear any more of your rubbish.' He turned away and disappeared into the crowded sitting room where the heat and the noise had risen to new levels.

Evie stood breathing heavily, trying to calm her anger. Where had all that come from? She was like a woman possessed. She couldn't even remember half the awful things that had come out of her mouth. *Stupid, stupid . . .*

She waited until she thought her face was composed and then she followed Billy back into the party, determined not to spoil the occasion for anyone else. She looked around but there was no sign of him. Maybe he'd gone out the back – it really was extremely hot in the sitting room. She went into the kitchen and out to the yard but there were only smokers out there.

'What's up?' said Mary, suddenly by Evie's side when she came back indoors.

'Nothing.'

'Ah, come on, Evie. You've a face like Billy's mum. What's happened?'

'I have not got a face like Ada Taylor,' hissed Evie.

'Oh . . . I understand,' said Mary. 'That woman . . . She really is the limit, with her selfishness and her headaches. Oh, and don't think we haven't all twigged by now. She's come between you, hasn't she? Don't worry about it, darling Evie. Billy'll come round. You know what lads are like – the boys are the same with their mum. Our Cormac is only six and he's the most grown-up of the lot.'

'Oh but, Mary, I said some horrible things. And they weren't even true – well, some of them were but I still shouldn't have said them.'

'Don't fret, Evie. Everyone has a little disagreement now and again. It'll blow over. Now I think Ma is going to bring a birthday cake through in a minute. I expect she's just got delayed lighting all those candles. I hope we've got the fire brigade on standby . . . '

So Mary tried – and mainly succeeded – in jollying Evie out of her temper and the rest of the party evening passed in catching up with old friends, dancing with Stephen Sullivan – who was very like a taller, older, more Irish version of Peter, and made Evie laugh at all his tales of the scrapes he got into at work as a gardener for the local council – and keeping an eye open in case Billy reappeared.

He didn't reappear, however, and later on Marie said he'd told her he was going home to check up on his mum, which made Evie secretly cross all over again.

It was very late when Evie escorted Dora Marsh back next door and they bade each other goodnight very wearily. So sleepy was Evie that she slipped into bed in Dora's spare room with barely a thought for Billy before she was fast asleep.

CHAPTER ELEVEN

EVIE WAS READY to leave her beloved Shenty Street again. She'd already been round to the Sullivans to thank them for a lovely party and to promise to keep in touch. Mary had given her a big hug and told her quietly not to worry about Billy.

'He'll come round. It's his mother who's being awkward, not you, Evie. You wait, he'll be down to see you with a big bunch of flowers before long,' she had reassured her friend.

'. . . And give my best love to your grandma, Evie, sweetheart,' called Dora.

'I will, Mrs Marsh, don't you worry.' Evie turned at the top of the street to see the kindly widow still waving.

No sign of Billy, though.

Well, what did you expect? As Mary said last night, he's a mummy's boy at heart. Ada obviously won't allow him out by himself this morning to see you off.

Mary had also said the row would blow over, Evie reminded herself, and Mary was right about most things. Obviously it hadn't blown over yet, though, she reflected as she trudged off alone to the station carrying her case and the heavy bag of fabrics she'd purchased on Friday afternoon.

It was freezing cold at the station but the train was already waiting on the platform. Evie found a seat and sat down, hot with the burden of her luggage and the remnants of her temper.

'Evie? Evie Carter? It is Evie, isn't it?'

Evie looked up at the woman sitting in the seat opposite.

'Mrs Russell, what a lovely surprise!'

'My dear, how are you? Such a long time since I've seen you,' said Mrs Russell, as the train pulled out of the station.

She looked much the same as she had when Evie and Sue had last delivered her washing to her house in summer, the day the family had found out that Michael owed money to Mr Hopkins, but somehow she had an air of purpose about her, an energy that she had never shown in the pretty pink-and-white drawing room where she sat alone.

'I'm very well, thank you, Mrs Russell, and Grandma is, too.'

'I'm pleased to hear that. I've been worried about you. Of course, I sent Annie to see if she could find out what had happened to you so I know some of it, and the rest is none of my business anyway. But I gather you live somewhere else now?'

'We do. I'm here to see some friends, that's all. We had to go away, but Grandma's said often that she was sorry not to be able to say goodbye to you.' Evie lowered her voice. 'It was a bit difficult. We had to go quickly, like.'

'And how is Mrs Goodwin doing? I imagine she's making the best of things.'

'She's set up a sewing business: a bit of dressmaking, alterations and repairs and making curtains and stuff. I'm her assistant and we're doing all right.'

'I'm glad to hear it. Give her my very best wishes, won't you?' said Mrs Russell. 'I had a lot of time for your grandmother. As I say, she makes the best of things.'

'I will. Thank you, Mrs Russell.'

'In fact, I have your grandmother to thank for a new turn in my own life.'

'How can that be?'

'Well, I always admired the way Mrs Goodwin got on with things and made her own way. I know life could be difficult for her and fate hadn't dealt her many advantages of circumstances, but so far as she could, she influenced her own destiny. She didn't just let things happen – whether good or bad – she always did her best to bring them about to her advantage. I know it was she who decided to do mending and alterations as a sideline to the washing, and that's when I heard about her. She was using her talents, and making a success of it.'

'You're right, of course,' said Evie, proud that this kind and gentle lady should think so well of her grandma.

'Now, I played the piano quite a bit when I was younger – you may have seen my piano in the back room – but when Mr Russell was killed I rather gave up. Gave up in more ways than one, I'm afraid. I didn't want to play any more. Nobody to play for, I suppose. Anyway, my cousin, who lives in Manchester, told me about a choir that needed an accompanist and she said she thought I should apply. Of course, I was very out of practice and . . . scared – yes, that's the right word – really scared that I'd make a fool of myself. But then I thought of your grandmother. I asked myself, "What would Mrs Goodwin do?" and I knew she wouldn't sit there feeling sorry for herself. Instead she'd be using her talents to make her own way. So now you find me going to Manchester to accompany the choir, as I do every Sunday.'

Evie was delighted to hear this account, and even more pleased that Grandma Sue had played a part, even if she hadn't known it.

'Congratulations, Mrs Russell. That sounds such a lovely thing to happen.'

'It is, Evie. It isn't just that I've made new friends, and I've unearthed my old and nearly forgotten love of music, but I get out and see all kinds of people now instead of sitting at home and knowing only my neighbours. We do concerts all over the place – in churches, mainly – and it's made such a difference to my life.'

She beamed at Evie, and Evie felt she could hardly wait to get home to tell Grandma Sue.

The train pulled into Manchester Victoria station and Evie and Mrs Russell said their goodbyes, Mrs Russell looking elegant and surprisingly youthful as she strode away to her rehearsal.

Evie's spirits had been lifted by this encounter and she stepped out towards London Road station with a spring in her step.

The train south was late leaving and very crowded. Evie had to stand in the corridor and there was hardly room for her luggage. A group of men came to stand nearby, smoking heavily and making lewd jokes, and Evie shifted away so she wouldn't have to listen to them.

'Can't you see it's crowded? There are no seats further down. You might as well stay where you are,' barked an ill-tempered woman as Evie tried to get past.

'Sorry . . . excuse me, please,' said Evie, edging by as best she could, certain that the cross woman was deliberately standing in her way.

'You all right, love?' said a younger woman at the end of the corridor. 'Ain't much room here, but if you sit on your case you'll be more comfortable.'

'Yes, thank you.' Evie did as she suggested, though the catches and the handle made it an uncomfortable seat, but at least she took some of the weight off her feet, which were aching after all that standing up at the party yesterday.

She got to thinking about the party, and about the disagreement with Billy, and how they'd parted without making up or even saying goodbye. Mary had seemed to think it would all be all right between them, but would it? Evie acknowledged she could never warm to Ada now she knew she had stopped Billy coming down to see her that time. She wouldn't forget the disappointment of that miserable morning at Redmond station in a hurry.

The train chugged on, seeming to take forever. It surely hadn't taken this long to go the other way on Friday?

'Something to do with signals, I reckon,' said the young woman, as if reading Evie's mind.

Evie nodded. She'd told them at home which train she'd be on and someone was going to be there at Redmond to meet her. No doubt there would be an announcement at the station of how late the train was running. She hoped whoever was waiting for her wasn't worried, and cold and bored.

'Here's my station – Kingsford,' said the young woman.

Evie stood up as the train pulled in and moved aside to let people get off and on. It was only when the train was pulling out of the station that she realised her case was no longer against the wall where she'd been sitting. Frantically she looked around, but there was no sign of it.

'Lost something?' asked an elderly man who had just got on.

'My case. I was sitting on it until Kingsford and now it's gone!'

'What's it look like?' asked the man, looking around as if Evie could possibly have missed it.

'Quite small, and covered with tweedy-looking shiny paper.'

'I saw a young woman getting off at Kingsford with a case something like that,' said the man. 'Out of this door here,' he pointed.

'Oh, no . . . '

Evie sighed heavily, wondering if there was anything she could do about it. The woman would be long gone by the time the train pulled into Redmond. Thank goodness, at least she was still holding the heavy bag of fabrics.

'Speak to the guard when you get off,' suggested the man.

'Yes, I will. Thank you,' said Evie, thinking this train journey had been horrible from the moment she'd boarded in Manchester. What with the theft and the delay, added to yesterday's row with Billy, she could hardly remember whether she'd had a nice time at the weekend at all.

The train arrived at Redmond station at last and Evie got out, making doubly sure she had her remaining bags with her. What was the point of speaking to the guard – what on earth could he do about a stolen case further up the line?

The lamps were lit on the platform and fog hung in clouds, making the globes of light dull and yellow. Evie looked along to see who had come to meet her.

'Mum!'

'Evie, love!' Jeanie came rushing up to hug her. 'So late . . . you must be tired . . . thought it'd never arrive.'

'Oh, Mum . . . ' Evie burst into tears like a small child, hugging her mother.

'Evie? What on earth's the matter, love? What's happened?'

So Evie told her mother about having her case stolen at Kingsford. This was neither the time nor the place to express her woes about Billy's mother and the row – the real cause of her tears.

Evie dried her eyes as her mother patted her back and made comforting noises, then Evie became aware of someone standing beside them.

'Mr Bailey! Oh, I'm sorry,' she sniffed. 'I know I'm being silly, it's just . . . everything . . . '

'Freddie has very kindly offered to take us home in his car,' Jeanie explained.

'Oh, but I hope you haven't been waiting for ages, as well as Mum,' Evie said to him. 'I am sorry.'

'It really is no trouble at all,' said Frederick. 'We soon discovered the train was going to be late so we quite simply went back to Marlowe House and waited in the warm until just now.' He and Jeanie smiled at each other. 'We had rather a nice time, actually. We'll speak to the stationmaster about your stolen case. You never know, it might yet turn up in left luggage, though I fear that's unlikely, and you ought to give a description of the thief, in case she's already known to the police. I hope you haven't lost anything precious or irreplaceable?'

Evie had to smile at that. She didn't own anything precious or irreplaceable.

'No, nothing like that.'

'Come on, then, let's have a word with the station-master and then get you home,' said Frederick.

It was cramped in the back of the car, and dark and not very warm, though Frederick had put on the heater. He drove carefully through the fog, Jeanie in the passenger seat beside him. Every so often she looked back at Evie and gave her a reas-suring smile so that by the time they arrived at Pendle's all danger of more tears had passed and Evie merely felt tired and reconciled to having lost her belongings and her special friendship with Billy.

Frederick helped Jeanie out, then Evie and her bag, said goodnight, kissing Jeanie's cheek, which Evie was too tired to notice, got back in the car and made sure Jeanie had the front door open before he drove away.

'What a long way he's come, just to bring us home, Mum.' Evie stood in the passage, unbuttoning her coat.

'He's very kind,' said Jeanie.

'How come Mr Bailey was at the station? Had he been on a journey, too?'

'Mmm . . . ' said Jeanie, taking a silky patterned scarf Evie couldn't remember seeing before from around her neck and absently stowing it in her coat pocket. 'Mum, Michael, boys! Evie's back,' she called.

The door of the big kitchen at the end of the passage flew open and Peter and Robert were there, firing questions at Evie and pulling her through into the warm room.

Evie gratefully took the cup of tea her father handed her and tried to answer everyone's enquiries about who she'd seen and what their news was, but she felt too tired to deal with all their excitement.

'You look ready to drop,' said Sue. 'Off you go and get in bed, love, and I'll bring you a bowl of soup if you promise not to spill it on the sheets.'

But when Sue took the soup up, Evie was already fast asleep.

~

The fabrics Evie had chosen at the mill shop attracted the attention of customers coming in with alterations and commissions for curtains or cushion covers. Once word started to get round the village that Sue Goodwin had some stylish winter dress material of top quality on her shelves, more women came in specifically to look, and she and Evie suddenly had commissions for several garments to make up in time for Christmas.

'I thought I saw your Robert yesterday morning, going through the back into the field,' said Josie one day, as she sipped tea while she and Sue looked over romper patterns for Nancy now the little girl was starting to take her first steps.

'Robert? Surely not. He'd have been in school,' said Sue.

'Oh, well, I was surprised, but I must be mistaken,' said Josie. 'Now, a bib with a pocket would be sweet, don't you think . . . ?'

As soon as Josie had gone Sue picked up on what she had said. 'He'd better not be skiving off school,' she grumbled to Evie. 'I know he's found it difficult to settle but that's no excuse.'

'Shall I see if I can find out, Grandma? Mebbe it's a misunderstanding.'

'And mebbe it isn't,' said Sue, darkly. 'But yes, please. If there's owt the matter we need to know what it is.'

When Robert came in at around the usual time

that afternoon, but looking cold and with slightly muddy shoes, Evie suspected that Josie hadn't been mistaken at all.

'Good day at school, Bob?' she asked, making him a jam sandwich while Sue continued working in the front room.

''S'pose.'

'So what did you do?'

'Nowt much.'

'How's the Nativity play coming on?'

'Dunno . . . '

She passed him the sandwich on a plate and a mug of milky tea. 'All right, Bob, the game's up. I know you weren't at school this afternoon. Why was that?'

He tucked into the sandwich hungrily, not answering.

'And I bet you didn't have anything to eat at dinnertime, did you?'

At that, he pushed the plate away and screwed his fists into his tearful eyes.

'Tell me.'

'It's horrible at school. All the others have best friends and lots of other friends, too. I've got no one.'

'Who do you sit next to these days?'

'I told you, no one. I'm by myself at the back.'

'Oh, Bob . . . '

'And I was going to be the Innkeeper in the play, Miss Grainger said, but one of the other teachers,

Mrs Kelsey, said she couldn't understand what I was saying and Miss Grainger was to choose someone who was "nicely spoken".'

'Well, that doesn't sound like Miss Grainger to me. She's always been fair to you.'

'But it's Mrs Kelsey who's in charge of the play and she's got a loud voice and the other teachers have to do as she says. She's right bossy.'

Evie sighed. 'Do you want Mum to go and see Miss Grainger again?'

'No! I don't want to go at all. I'm fed up of the others poking fun and making out I'm daft.'

'But I thought you'd put all this behind you?' said Evie. 'Weren't things better after the success of Guess the Weight?'

'They were for a bit, but then it got bad again.'

'Well, you have to go to school, Bob. It's the law. You can't hide in the woods all day, especially now it's winter. You looked cold when you came in and it'll get a lot colder yet. We'll ask Mum to go and speak to Miss Grainger again, or maybe this Mrs Kelsey, as she's the one who's made things difficult for you over the play.'

'She's big and she's always shouting. She doesn't listen to other folk.'

'Can't be much of a teacher, then,' said Evie. 'Sounds like a job for Grandma.'

~

Sue was briefed about Robert's troubles and she shared this with Jeanie, but not with Michael. He'd been unusually ill-tempered of late – Mr Clackett was keeping him very hard at work since Sue had had a word – and she didn't think it would help matters if he were to box Robert's ears and shout at him.

Sue went with Robert to school the next morning, leaving Evie to get on with baby Nancy's rompers on her own. When she came back she looked grim but satisfied.

'Well, that Mrs Kelsey might say she can't tell what Bob is saying but she certainly understands me,' said Sue, and left it at that.

Robert went into school and stayed until the end every day after that, though he was now miscast as part of the Heavenly Host in the Nativity play and didn't have a speaking part. Still, it was a small triumph for him of sorts, as not every child had a part, and Sue vowed to make sure his gown was the best-fitting of all the angels' costumes.

~

Evie hadn't expected to hear from Billy for a few days after their argument and her return home, but when she still had not had a letter by the middle of December, she started to think that Mary had been wrong and that Billy was no longer interested in her.

'And have you written to him?' asked Sue, as they sat side by side, cutting and stitching.

'No, Grandma.'

'Why's that, then? Do you think the argument was all his fault and nothing to do with you?'

Evie breathed out heavily and tried to recall exactly what had been said. Strangely, she could remember little of the cause now, only that Ada had been behind it.

'Well, it was his mum that stopped him getting the train that day, I told you.'

'That was mean, I admit, leaving you standing there on the station for hours, but if the woman's scared of losing him then that's why she's acting unfriendly. You see, Evie, as things stand, you can't both have Billy, can you? He can't be with you and with Ada.'

'True, Grandma. Thing is, I don't even know for sure that I want to be with Billy for ever and ever. It's too much to think of that yet, especially if his mother comes as part of the deal. Oh, I know that's selfish, Grandma, but you should have seen her face, and she was so rude. Maybe I'll know one day, and I certainly don't want *never* to see him again. That would be terrible! I want us to be as we were – special friends – and I do miss his letters. I was so excited about seeing him when I went north.'

'So if you could make it right between the two of you now, never mind about the future, what would you do?'

Evie thought for a few minutes. 'I'd write and say I want us to be friends again,' she said quietly.

'There's your answer, then,' said Sue, not looking up from her work. 'Why don't you go and do that now? *You* choose to make it happen. Don't wait for Billy to decide. Or his mother. He's a good lad is Billy. You can have the rest of the morning off so you can get the letter in the post box by Suttons' straight away. Then you can get the darts sewn in this blouse and the collar made by teatime.'

Evie kissed Sue's bent head and went to do as she suggested. She remembered what Mrs Russell had said on the train about how Grandma Sue influenced her own destiny, and she acknowledged to herself what a wise woman her grandma was.

Dear Billy,

I'm sorry we fell out at Gerry's party and I'm sorry for the things I said. I want it to be just like it was between us, and I hope you are prepared to forgive me. I promise not speak about your mother like that again. It was very rude and I know it was wrong.

It was especially wrong because we'd had such a lovely time until then and you'd swapped shifts to be with me and make it a nice weekend, and it got spoiled.

I've missed your letters and I hope this makes up for what I said and that we can be friends again.

With love,

Evie

How could such a short letter have taken half the morning to write? Evie wasn't entirely satisfied with it but it was the best she could do. She went down to Suttons' to post it in the pillar box outside, then nipped into the shop to buy some humbugs, which were Sue's favourites.

As she was coming out she saw further down the High Street her father disappearing into the Red Lion.

But Grandma had a word with Mr Clackett, who is supposed to be keeping Dad's nose to the grindstone so he doesn't have time to go to the Lion.

'Honestly, Grandma, if it's not Bob it's Dad,' she said when she got back to Pendle's, handing the sweets to Sue and explaining what she'd seen. 'He's like another child.'

'You've realised that, have you, love?' said Sue.

'Should one of us go and fetch him out? I don't know if he'd take any notice of me, and I don't want you to have to go. It's cold outside and a bit icy.'

'It might hurt his dignity to have his wife's mother come and drag him out of the pub in front of everyone,' said Sue. 'And I don't want to ask Mr Clackett to fetch him. That'll only create more trouble.'

Luckily, at that moment there was a knock on the shop door, which was always open for customers anyway, and there was Jack, Monty beside him.

'By heck, Jack, you're the very man I need,' said Sue. 'Our Michael's been seen entering the Lion and he's supposed to be too busy at Clackett's to be having a pint or two at dinnertime. You know how Mr Clackett doesn't hold with drinking, and Michael's already been given a warning.'

'Leave it to me and Monty,' said Jack. 'I can guess what you're going to say and I'll go there right away.'

'Oh, thank you, lad. I'm that grateful. I reckon you've come for the rent. When you've done with Michael, come back and I'll pay you and we'll give you a bite to eat, too. How does that sound?'

'I'll see you directly,' Jack said, and set off for the pub, Monty trotting along beside him.

'That was lucky,' said Sue.

'Yes, Grandma. But what on earth are we going to do when Jack isn't here to help us? Dad's been in a bad mood generally lately, and I'd hate there to be a scene in the Lion.'

'I'll have to have another word with Mr Clackett,' said Sue, getting up stiffly, then taking off her glasses and rubbing her eyes. 'So dark these days. I hate winter. I think we might need a stronger bulb in that there light. It's going to be a cold one this year, I can feel it in my bones.'

～

Having dispatched Michael to Clackett's, Jack and Monty returned to Pendle's and shared Sue and Evie's lunch, and then Letty came round to have a look through the fabrics with the idea of asking Sue to make a blouse for Miss Richards as a Christmas present.

Jack had been about to depart, but when Letty appeared he stayed on and made himself useful brewing tea and entertaining 'the ladies', as he called the three of them, while Sue and Evie worked and Letty asked questions about everything in her usual vivacious way. There was much laughter, and Sue was glad to see Evie looking happier than she had for a few weeks, now she'd got her apology to Billy in the post. Sue also noticed that Jack paid a lot of attention to Letty, taking an interest in everything she said and lending a sympathetic ear when Letty admitted that she still didn't know what she was going to do with herself next, but her aunt liked her company, and her presence at Lavender Cottage allowed them to grieve together for the loss of Letty's parents without having to explain or put on a brave face.

Then Peter came home from school and there was more lively conversation. Letty showed him some new chords on the guitar and he strummed while they both sang, Jack joining in on the chorus.

'It's better than the wireless,' declared Evie. 'Has anyone seen Bob? I haven't heard him come in but maybe he went straight upstairs. Odd he shouldn't have said hello, though.'

'I'll go and look,' Peter said.

'He's been finding school hard again lately, poor lamb,' Sue explained to Jack and Letty, 'though I had thought we'd turned the corner with that.'

'No sign of him upstairs,' said Peter, returning to the front room. 'I'll look out the back. Bob! Bob! Come and say hello to Letty and Jack. Bob . . . ?' He reappeared shortly after. 'He's not there either.'

'Odd,' Evie said, putting her work aside. 'Mebbe he's been kept in at school or summat. We ought to go and make sure.'

'I'll go with you,' Peter volunteered. 'It'll take us both to face down that Mrs Kelsey, from what I've heard about her. Shan't be long.'

They put on their outdoor shoes and coats and set off down the High Street for the school.

'You and Letty will want to be getting off home,' Sue said, as the workroom, which had been so full of life all afternoon, subsided into slightly anxious quiet.

'No, I'll wait and make sure Robert's all right,' said Letty.

'And I will, too. And when we've found him I'll take you back home in the rig, Letty,' said Jack.

A quarter-hour passed and Peter and Evie returned, their cheeks red from the cold that had descended on the village with the night drawing in.

'The school was completely shut and dark,' said Letty. 'We looked all round. Everyone's gone home.'

'Right,' said Jack, 'it's getting dark now so it looks like Robert went off somewhere after school instead of coming straight home. Now don't worry, Sue. If we search around the village it's quite likely we'll find him in no time. Could he have gone to play with one of his friends?'

'Oh, Jack, the poor lad hasn't got any friends! He never goes to play with anyone.'

Jack looked taken aback for a moment. 'He hasn't mentioned anyone's name?'

Sue shook her head. 'Has he said anything to you, Peter?'

'No, Grandma. I reckon we should start on this search quickly, though. It's getting frosty already. You stay here in case he wanders in, and the rest of us can go and ask if anyone's seen him. How does that sound?'

Peter and Evie set out to ask in the Suttons' shop and up and down the High Street. When they'd gone, Jack said he'd go to the market garden and ask Michael and Mr Clackett if they'd seen Robert playing in the field at the back.

'I'm sure they'll want to help us look, too,' said Letty.

'Of course Michael will. And I dare say Mr Clackett will, as well,' Jack said, holding the door of Pendle's open for her.

Sue went to the shop window and stood looking out, impatient for news. After a while she saw by the light of a streetlamp Evie and Peter coming back.

'Well, love?'

'Nothing. Though Mrs Lambert did say she saw Bob coming out of school this afternoon, so we definitely know he's both been and left,' said Evie.

Sue's hand leapt to cover her mouth as she stifled a sob. She sniffed back her anxious tears and visibly pulled herself together.

'You don't think . . . he could have been kidnapped by Mr Hopkins' men?' asked Peter.

'Don't be daft, Pete,' Sue snapped. 'It's Michael they're interested in, not Bob.'

'And, anyway, they don't know where any of us are,' said Evie. 'But I've just thought of somewhere else to look – down through the field and in the woods. Bob's always liked it there. Do you remember how he said he wanted to stay there for ever with the woodland creatures?'

'But why would he be there now, in the dark and cold?' asked Sue.

'I don't know, Grandma, but at least we ought to go and look. Pete, I think there's a torch in the cupboard under the stairs. We'll need that as it'll be properly dark beyond the streetlights by now.'

'Good thinking.' He went to find it and came back with two torches. 'Grandma, you stay here and put the kettle on. I reckon Bob will need a warm drink when he comes back. And tell Dad and Jack where we've gone.'

'Off you go then, you two. Take it steady; it may be slippery.'

'We will, Grandma. Try not to worry,' said Evie, giving Sue a hug before dashing off after Peter.

It was pitch-dark in the field behind the High Street. Evie and Peter were slowed by the uneven ground, but they hurried as best they could. Their breathing sounded loud and ragged in the quiet of the field.

'There!' said Peter suddenly as something shot across the track in front of them.

'Aah!' Evie cried. 'Oh, my goodness, I nearly died of fright!'

'It was only a deer,' Peter said, but his heart was hammering, too. The animal had seemed enormous, coming out of the dark so close to them.

They paused only for a few seconds to calm themselves, then moved on, over the stile at the back of the field and into the woods.

'Bob!' called Evie. Her voice sounded high and thin.

'Bob! Bob!' Peter bellowed. 'We'll have to go slower here, Evie, or we're bound to trip over something.'

They crept along, too busy concentrating on stepping over tree roots and avoiding brambles to call out. The sound of the stream grew louder and the temperature seemed to plummet as they neared the water, which was fast-flowing now, and looked black in the light of the torches.

'Bob, Bob, are you there?' called Evie. 'If you can hear us, please answer.'

No one spoke.

'I don't think he can be here,' said Peter, training the beam of his torch over the partially overgrown track in front of them. 'Bob! Bob! No, I think we're wasting our time, Sis.' He turned to retrace his steps.

'No, wait . . . ' Evie shone her torch where Peter's had just arced over the bank of the stream. It was very muddy and there were signs of shoeprints sliding down towards the water. 'Bob, are you there?' She went forward carefully, the light slightly unsteady in her shaking hand. Peter trained his torch in the same direction.

'Oh, Bob . . . ' gasped Evie.

Her younger brother was lying on his front in the stream, his face turned to one side just under the surface.

She ran forward. 'Here, Peter, take my torch. Oh, Bob, oh, you poor little fella . . . ' She lowered herself into the stream, gasping at the coldness of the water. 'Peter, for God's sake shine those torches over here.'

Peter did as she asked, though he was sobbing loudly as Evie dragged the little boy's body up from the stream, heaving it over onto the bank with Peter's help. There was a huge graze on Robert's forehead. It looked as if he'd slipped on the bank, fallen into the stream and hit his head on some stone or log beneath the water. There was no doubt, though, that he had drowned.

'Here . . . ' Evie held out her hand and Peter pulled her onto the bank where they stood and held each other tightly, weeping with all their hearts for their brother.

That was how Michael and Jack found them a few minutes later.

PART TWO

A turn in the road
January 1955–January 1956

CHAPTER TWELVE

EVIE LOOKED UP briefly from the sewing machine and waved as the postman passed the shop window of Pendle's. Then she heard the letterbox clatter.

'Aren't you going to see what's come?' asked Sue, squinting over the shirt collar she was turning.

'I don't expect there'll be a letter from Billy, if that's what you mean,' said Evie heavily, continuing with her work.

'Oh, I'll go then,' said Sue, beginning to heave herself to her feet.

'No, Grandma, it's all right, I will.'

Evie came back with two envelopes, neither of which was addressed to her. She resumed treadling and the two women continued their work in silence for a while.

Since Robert's death, Pendle's had often fallen into silence, and in the dark days of late January, no one's spirits could be lifted. The women went to their work quietly because they must, and Michael spent every evening drinking away his wages or being bought rounds by men who felt sorry for him, often returning home drunk and morose, or being brought home by Jack, or the local policeman if he happened to be around.

As she worked, Sue allowed her mind to wander. She couldn't see a way out of this and she wondered if they would ever be happy again. She thought back to the autumn when the sewing business had taken off so well, when Jeanie had blossomed in her new job, and even Michael had worked hard with Mr Clackett keeping him in order; when Peter had entertained them all with his music and his excitement about the band, and little Robert had been the hero of the Bonfire Night fête with the success of his fund-raising. It felt like a lifetime ago now – almost as if all those things had happened to a different family.

The sewing business was still going well. Evie was working hard, but there was not much laughter in her these days. Often Sue would look up while they stitched and catch Evie with red eyes, silently weeping for her brother.

Billy had not been in touch since Evie's trip to Bolton for Geraldine's birthday party. Evie had written that day Robert died and then again just before Christmas, with a card and a letter breaking the awful news, but she'd heard nothing from him. Sue thought that strange; she wouldn't have had Billy down as someone to bear a grudge. His mother, on the other hand, was exactly that kind of person, and Sue had her suspicions about Ada's role in Billy's silence. But again, she had felt too worn down with her sadness to do anything about that.

Peter was hardly here these days, and Sue knew Evie missed him. They all did. He'd practically moved in with the Thomas twins, Brian and James, and taken his music with him. Mr and Mrs Thomas had welcomed him and were glad to offer him a second home and a place where, Mrs Thomas had confided to Sue, he could be away from being reminded too much of Robert and get over his brother's death in his own way.

'How are you doing with those curtains, Evie? Will they be ready for Mrs Cooke by tomorrow afternoon? She wants to hang them herself, she says, so she's collecting them.'

'Only the hems to do once I've finished this bit, Grandma. Would you like a cup of tea?'

'I'll do it, lass. I could do to rest my eyes for a minute or two,' said Sue, getting up and shuffling through to the big kitchen.

She sat down heavily at the table while the kettle boiled, and wondered what on earth she could do to get the heart back into the family. She and Evie were fairly busy most days, and glad of the commissions, although those had tailed off a little since Christmas, but somehow they worked automatically now, without the enthusiasm and drive they'd had before Robert . . .

Sue put her head in her hands, overtaken for a moment by her sadness, and shed a few quiet tears. Then she sat up, wiped her eyes and stood up to make the tea. While it brewed she thought about Jeanie and Frederick Bailey.

Never in a million years would Sue have guessed she would meet Frederick Bailey for the first time at her grandson's funeral. Mr Bailey had sat near the back of the village church but afterwards he'd made a point of coming over to express his sympathy to the whole family and remind a tearful Jeanie that she need not go back to work until she felt up to it. Jeanie hadn't stayed away long, though.

Sue had taken a great interest in this man she'd heard so much about, and a fella who'd been divorced three times, if the gossip was true, though Sue was ashamed of listening and then remembering what she had heard – but an interesting man, with flair and imagination. Mostly what she saw, though, was a man who was clearly in love with Jeanie, and with whom Jeanie was equally clearly in love. At least, it was clear to her mother. Sue was pleased to think that no one else, especially Michael, had noticed the signs that she saw all too well.

Oh dear, what to do about that? She'd pushed it

to the back of her mind, what with feeling so tired . . . and the awfulness of Christmas, and now it was dark nearly all day and her eyes weren't so good in poor daylight.

She put the cups of tea on a tray and took it through to the front room. Evie was just finishing her seams and she stopped, smiling up at her grandmother.

'Grandma, do you know, I don't think I ever told you about seeing Mrs Russell on the train, did I? I sort of forgot, what with Billy, and having my things stolen.'

'What, you saw her when you went to Gerry's party?'

'On the way back. She was sitting opposite me and she looked really well and happy. It was lovely to see her, but the best thing was what she told me, and that it was all down to you.'

'Are you having me on, our Evie? How could I have made any difference to Mrs Russell?'

Evie related the story of how Mrs Russell had been inspired by Sue to gather her courage and rediscover her talent for playing the piano when she thought her life held so little, how she'd used her skills to make new friends and to bring something better and more interesting into her life.

Sue laughed. 'I'm right pleased for Mrs Russell. She's a lovely woman and it's a shame she lost her confidence to play the piano, but I think she might have found her way back to her music in the end anyway, without me. Though it's nice of her to say I helped.'

'No, Grandma, she really thought it was all down to you, and how you made a go of the washing and then the fine mending and alterations. She said summat like . . . ' Evie thought carefully, ' . . . "Mrs Goodwin influenced her own destiny. She didn't just let things happen to her, she always did her best to bring them about to her advantage." Summat like that, anyway. I were that proud of you, Grandma, and Mrs Russell isn't the kind of lady who would tell lies or flatter a person, is she?'

'Well, that's true enough, Evie, love. I'm glad you've remembered you saw her. That's given me summat to think about while I finish this collar.'

'Aye, me, too, Grandma,' said Evie. 'I've felt ever so down lately—'

'We all have, lass.'

'But if we don't raise ourselves up, who's going to do it for us? Oh, I know Miss Richards and Letty couldn't have been kinder – and Jack, too – and everyone in the village has done their best to help, but in the end it's down to us, isn't it? We have to decide if we're going to sit here being sad for ever or . . . ' she looked round the workroom, at the lengths of cloth on the shelves and the partially finished curtains, ' . . . or whether we're going to move this business on.'

'You're right, love. I've been trying not to think about it, but soon everyone in Church Sandleton who wants new curtains will have them, and then what will we do? The mending and alterations don't bring in much, and though we've made quite a few garments recently there doesn't seem to be a call for a lot of dressmaking in the village now Christmas is over. We need new customers.'

'And it's up to us to find them, Grandma,' said Evie. 'We can't sit here feeling sorry for ourselves.'

'And no one wants to keep company with miserable people,' said a merry voice at the door. 'Hello, Mrs Goodwin, Evie.'

'Letty!'

'Just passing. I won't stay long and disturb you.'

'Come in, love. Evie and I were giving ourselves a talking to, telling ourselves to snap out of it,' said Sue. 'You and your Aunt Margaret know better than anyone what it's like, and we admire how you've both coped with your sadness.'

'That's kind of you to say, Mrs Goodwin. I know it's helped Aunt Margaret a lot that she's had her articles to write for the newspaper. There's nothing like a deadline to keep you focused, she says.'

'If Grandma and me take on some new customers, we'll be that busy we won't have time to mope. But we need to find them first.'

'I think you should advertise,' said Letty, pulling off her hat and gloves, helping herself to a chair and putting her elbows on the table. 'I'm sure there's a market for a top dressmaker in Redmond. Why don't you put an advert in one of the local papers?'

'I suppose we could do, if it doesn't cost very much.'

'I can't think it would in the local paper or the parish newsletter. Why don't you decide which paper your clients would most likely read and then, if you want, I can ring up from the cottage and find out what the advertising rates are?'

'Oh, Letty, thank you. That would be grand,' said Evie.

'Provided we can get a few commissions outside the village we'll have enough to keep us afloat if we've not got much from Church Sandleton folk. I think in a few weeks we could be really busy,' said Sue. 'People like to have new clothes for the milder weather.'

'I'll gather a few different newspapers and magazines when I'm next in Redmond and that can start you off,' Letty offered.

'You're an angel,' said Sue. 'But I think I might take a trip into Redmond on the bus and have a look around, see what's what, like.'

Evie felt her heart lift at this news.

'I'll come with you, if you like, Grandma. Shall we go this afternoon?'

'We'll go tomorrow morning,' Sue decided. 'You've got Mrs Cooke's curtains to finish. Mustn't forget our loyal customers.'

'I'd never do that, Grandma.' Evie found herself smiling.

'So exciting,' said Letty, while Evie began on the hand-stitched hems. 'I just wish I had an idea of what I can do.'

'Well, you've already come up with some ideas to help us,' said Sue. 'And I know you're a real help to your auntie because she told me so.'

'She lets me organise her office – I mean, as if I'm her secretary,' said Letty, 'but I don't think I want to be a real secretary. Aunt Margaret is easy to work for and, anyway, I like to play in the band and that takes up a lot of time.'

'Speaking of the band, how's Peter doing?' asked Sue. 'We don't see so much of him these days. He seems to have gone to live at the Thomases. I'll have to pay Mr Thomas Peter's keep if he doesn't come home soon.'

'I think he likes it there,' said Letty carefully. 'He doesn't want to be reminded of Bob all the time, as he would be here. The Thomases have got masses of room and Peter fits in so well. I heard Mrs Thomas telling Aunt Margaret how much she likes having him around and what a nice boy he is. And he doesn't have to see his father there.'

As soon as the words were out, Letty flushed with embarrassment. 'I'm sorry, I didn't mean to be rude.' She got up and pulled on her knitted hat and gloves. 'I should be going and let you get your work done. Let me know how you get on in Redmond tomorrow, won't you?'

She waved and blew kisses, laughing, as she left.

Evie sat sewing intently for a few minutes and then she said, 'Letty was only saying what we already know, Grandma, wasn't she? Pete still hasn't forgiven Dad for us having to leave Bolton. He doesn't like Dad at all these days, and he thinks that everything that's happened to us since we got here – all the setbacks, not the good things like our work here and Mum's job – are Dad's fault because we're here because of him.'

'So what are you saying, Evie, love?' Sue got up and draped the finished shirt over the ironing board in the corner. 'That Pete blames your dad for what happened to Bob?'

'Yes, Grandma. I'm afraid he does. After all, if we were still in Shenty Street, Bob wouldn't have slipped into the stream in the woods.'

'But it was just a horrible accident, Evie. *You* know that, don't you?'

'Yes . . . yes, and I don't blame Dad for what happened, but I can kind of see what Pete means. And . . . oh, Grandma, he's so angry with Dad. He has been for a long time now and I don't see it getting any better.'

~

It was evening and Michael had come back from Clackett's and then gone out again to the Red Lion, as he did most days since Robert had drowned. His neighbours in the pub felt sorry for him that his younger son had died and there were always plenty of drinks bought for him. Sometimes he even bought rounds in return, though not often. His main currency was tall stories about bets won and lost in the pubs of Bolton, how he'd single-handedly saved the brewery from crisis on several occasions, and about the toughness of life up north in general. Then, as the drink took effect, he'd descend into maudlin stories of his 'little lad' and reminisce about what a wonderful son Robert had been.

Jack Fletcher came into the Red Lion that evening, and saw that Michael had had a skinful.

'All right, Michael, maybe it's time to go home to that lovely wife of yours,' suggested Jack after a few minutes.

'Oh, there's time for another one,' said Michael, putting his empty pint glass down heavily on the bar. 'Who's for another?'

There were one or two takers, but the locals generally respected Jack, both as a good man and as Frederick Bailey's man, and they weren't going to undermine his sound suggestion.

The beer was bought and drunk, more rambling stories were told, and then Jack announced that it really was time to get off home now. 'Jeanie will have your dinner on the table, Michael, and you don't want to keep Sue and Evie waiting for theirs after they've been hard at work all day.'

'Aye, Jack, lad, that's all I ever hear: Jeanie this and that, Sue and Evie this and that . . . '

'Well, they are your family, Michael, and Jeanie's a good cook. She'll have made an effort.'

'A house of women, that's what it's become. Outnumbered, I am, and by women, with their own jobs to go to. Work that they think is better than mine.'

'I'm sure that's not true, Michael,' said Jack, taking Michael's pint and putting it out of reach on the bar. Then he steered Michael towards the door and Monty followed them. 'They work hard, but they appreciate what you do, too. You know that.'

'I know no such thing,' declared Michael. 'They all look down on me, and even my own son has left home to avoid me and gone to live with Mr pompous Thomas and his snide opinions. It's them Thomases that have bad-mouthed me to Peter – it started at the Bonfire – and now he's gone to live with them.'

'I think young Peter is having a hard time getting over his brother's accident,' said Jack quietly, 'and it's his way of coping with it.'

'We're all having a hard time getting over Bob's accident,' said Michael, raising his voice. 'One son dead and the other left home to go to live with other folk, not his family. And when I get home, what do I find? Women! Women everywhere, talking about curtains and cleaning, and other women's stuff.'

'Well, I don't know about that,' said Jack, 'but from what I know of Jeanie, she'll be happy to hear about your day and what you've been doing at Clackett's. And I'm sure Sue and Evie will be, too. You've got good women, there, Michael, and I think you should treasure them.'

'Do you, Jack? Do you?' snapped Michael. 'And what do you think I've got to tell them about my day, eh? Up to my knees in mud and nearly frozen some days. Do you think Jeanie wants to hear about that?'

Jack thought it would be wise not to answer since it was obvious that nothing he could say would smooth over Michael's drunken anger.

'And there's Jeanie going off to work as some jumped-up cleaner – *housekeeper*, she calls it, if you please – and wearing her good clothes, and her hair all nice, and, from what I see, spending her money on ladylike stuff that she'd never have worn in Bolton. Fancy scarves and bits of jewellery! She's getting above herself, that one, sorting through the post for Mr bloody Bailey, and gallivanting off with him to auctions and God knows what.'

'Michael, I don't want to hear your opinion of Mr Bailey,' said Jack. 'He's your landlord and my employer. I won't hear or speak ill of him, and I suggest you don't either.'

Michael subsided, muttering, while Jack and Monty walked him to Pendle's and Jack tapped on the front door.

Sue answered. She took in the situation at once.

'Thanks for bringing him home, Jack,' she said. 'I can see a bit of help was needed and I'm grateful.'

'I'll be getting on home myself, Sue,' said Jack as Michael shuffled past her and disappeared in the direction of the kitchen. 'I think he's missing his boys,' he said quietly.

'I know.' Sue sighed heavily. 'It's hit him as hard as any of us. We've all been feeling down but we're going to try to rise above it and it's going to take all of us, pulling together, to make a life without Robert. We can't leave Michael behind, grieving and . . . well, I tell you, if he's intending to make a habit of this he's going to come home one day and find things have changed, and in a big way.'

Jack raised an eyebrow and opened his mouth to speak.

'I'll say no more, lad. I may be wrong. But please, if you're in the Lion and you see Michael pouring his wages down his throat – and other folks' wages, too, I don't doubt – then you've got my permission to give him a kick up the backside and get the others to help you bring him out.'

'I will. You have my word on that, Sue. I think I'll tip off Frank Davis, the landlord, too, if it's all the same to you? I know he wants to sell his beer but he's a good man and he wouldn't want you Carter ladies to be upset after all that's happened.'

'Thank you, Jack. That's right good of you.'

'I'll see you next week for the rent then, Sue.'

'I'll have it ready.'

And maybe I'll invite Letty over the day the rent is due, thought Sue. She and Jack are good fun together and their company will help keep our spirits up . . .

They said goodbye, and Jack and Monty strode back to the pub where Jack's motorbike rig was parked at the back. As they went, Jack thought about Michael's resentment of the Carter women making their own way in life, then he thought about what Sue had said.

'Well, Monty,' he murmured as he put on his biking gear and made sure the little dog was safely tucked down in the sidecar, 'if Michael Carter's going to make a habit of this, and if what I suspect is true, then I bet you Jeanie won't be around to cook his meals come Easter at the latest.'

~

It was a bleak dinner with Michael sitting morosely at one end of the kitchen table, staring unhappily into his hotpot and glowering at the others while they tried to pretend he wasn't casting a pall over their evening.

Jeanie had wept for many days after Robert died but she was trying to make an effort now, and Sue didn't like to see her spirits brought low by Michael's behaviour, especially as she'd returned from work that day looking happier than she had for a few weeks.

While they'd made the hotpot together Sue had shared her plans for expanding the sewing business to take in customers from Redmond, and Evie, peeling potatoes, had chipped in with her thoughts about the level of dressmaking she felt she could take on under Sue's guidance. Of course, they knew Michael had gone to the Red Lion after changing out of his muddy work clothes, and they also knew when he was later home than usual that he would probably not reappear sober.

'Eat up, love. I thought Lancashire hotpot was your favourite,' said Jeanie, trying to jolly Michael out of his mood.

Michael made no reply and the women chatted on, eventually forgetting about his mood as they exchanged gossip. Until Michael, getting to his feet, snarled, 'Can't a man sit and have his meal in peace without you lot gabbing about dresses and curtains, and fellas with "a bit of dash"?'

'But, Dad, we're only discussing our plans, that's all,' said Evie, hoping her calm voice would smooth his drunken ill temper, as it used to do in Shenty Street. Mostly there, though, he'd been a happy drunk. Now he was always fierce and snappy. 'Why don't you tell us about your day instead, then?'

'Don't talk to me as if I'm a child, Evie, or you'll feel the back of my hand,' said Michael. Nonetheless, he sat back down: 'What do you know about the mud and the rain and the cold at that market garden, and Clackett laying on the work so hard I've hardly time to catch my breath?'

'I'm sorry, Dad, I didn't mean—'

'And one of my lads dead and the other gone to live with strangers. And all I hear is you women talking about *fabrics* and *customers* and *advertisements*, and other fancy things that don't matter a bit—'

'Michael, they're my sons, too. You're not the only one with the right to feel sad. We're *all* heartbroken about what happened.'

'Are you? Are you really?' shouted Michael, getting up again and pushing his plate to one side. 'Well, you don't look very heartbroken to me – any of you.' He looked at each of them in turn, pointing with his knife.

'It's not a competition to see who can be the saddest and who can feel worse, Dad,' said Evie quietly.

'Evie, shut up. I've heard enough from you.'

'Well, you haven't heard enough from me,' said Jeanie, both fury and resolve suddenly written all over her face. 'Because I'm fed up to the back teeth with your drunkenness and your selfishness.'

'Me, selfish?'

'Yes, you, you pathetic drunk. You haven't come in sober one evening this year and it's nearly February and I've had enough. I've kept quiet till now because I hoped you'd feel better about Bob after a bit and I wanted to be understanding about how you felt, but you're getting worse, not better. This isn't about Bob dying any more, it's about you drinking too much, as you've always done . . . as you did in Shenty Street, and look where that got you!'

Michael opened his mouth to reply but Jeanie had got into her stride now.

'Be quiet! I'm speaking! Don't you think my heart is broken, and Mum and Evie's, and Peter's? But we're trying – we're really trying, Michael – to make something of our lives because *we have to*! Because if we don't, no one else is going to do it for us. Mum and Evie have made a whole new life for themselves with their own talents, with their own efforts, no one else's, not propped up by beer and self-pity, and what do you do?'

'I—'

'You sneer at them, like it isn't the money they make that's kept us all going. Like it isn't the respect they've won in this village that has made it a nice home for us against all odds, and though we knew not a soul here when we arrived.'

'I'm doing my best—'

'You've just been brought back from the pub again by Jack. Every evening this year you've been there, drinking away your wages, and going over to Clackett's every morning looking like death warmed over. How that poor man gets a day's work out of you I'll never know. It's time for you to sober up, Michael, and start behaving like a man because, I'm warning you, I'm getting very near the end of my patience. Oh, in Shenty Street we all bowed down to "the man of the house" – but all the time you cared more for your drinks and your bets than you did for us. And in the end, how did you repay our loyalty? With an enormous debt to some violent card sharp, that's how. And so we're here, where we never chose to be, and we're all trying to do our best. Except you. You don't even know what doing your best for other people is. Because you're a bone idle drunk, Michael, and I've thought so for years now.'

'How dare—'

But there was no stopping Jeanie as years of anger were now pouring out. 'I've earned the right to speak out, Michael, that's how I dare. Because once I was too busy having babies and running about after little ones to think life could be any different. I thought I'd made my choice and I had to put up with it. But now . . . now, well, I've seen you for what you are.'

Michael sat speechless for a few moments, as if he couldn't believe what he had heard, and then he got up and lurched towards the door, slamming it behind him. Jeanie, Sue and Evie heard his uneven tread up the stairs and then, inevitably, the bedroom door slam, too.

Then there was a long, long silence during which Evie and Sue looked at each other in open-mouthed astonishment and Jeanie pretended to eat her dinner until her tears flowed and she couldn't continue. She pushed her plate away and put her head in her hands, sobbing.

Sue got up to put the kettle on the hob, patting Jeanie's heaving shoulder as she passed.

Evie went to put her arms around her mother and they held each other tight and then Sue enveloped them both in her sturdy arms, kissing the tops of their bowed heads.

'It's all right, Mum. You've got us . . . you've got us . . . ' whispered Evie, stroking her mother's hair.

Jeanie cried all the harder then, shaking her head, too upset to find any more words.

CHAPTER THIRTEEN

THE NEXT MORNING Evie kept out of Michael's way. A night's sleep hadn't improved his mood and he was quite clearly in a foul temper, seething with anger and nursing a hangover as he sat sullen and glowering over his breakfast. Where had her once cheeky and cheerful father gone, Evie wondered. Having to leave Shenty Street, the loss of his son and his disappointment in the hard work required of him at Clackett's seemed to have broken him.

After he had staggered off to work Evie heard her mother moving about upstairs and went to see if she was all right and whether she wanted some toast before she went to her job at Frederick Bailey's house in Redmond.

'Mum, what are you doing?' Evie looked askance at Jeanie's suitcase on the bed and the piles of folded clothes beside it. Among them were some pretty things she only half remembered seeing before: a brightly coloured scarf that looked as if it was silk, some fine suede gloves and a little brooch shaped like a bow of ribbon with shiny white stones set into it.

'I'm packing my things, Evie. I'm leaving.'

'What? Mum! You can't leave us! Where will you go? What will we do without you?'

By now Sue had come to stand in the doorway, and she shuffled into the room and put her arms around Jeanie.

'I guessed this would happen. In fact, I *knew* it would, though I tried to pretend it wouldn't, but when I saw how you were with him . . . '

'Grandma . . . ? Mum . . . ?' Evie looked at them, completely at a loss. 'What's happening? Please tell me.' She felt as though something important had been discussed and decided behind her back and she'd missed out on what everyone else knew all about.

Jeanie pushed her mother gently away and faced her and Evie. 'You're right, Mum,' she said. 'I made up my mind a while since, but after last night I've decided not to wait any longer.'

'What? Tell me, Mum, please.'

'I'm going to live at Marlowe House . . . with Freddie.'

'With Frederick Bailey?' said Evie, thinking she must have misunderstood.

'We're in love and he's asked me to go to him. At first I said I couldn't, but now I think it would be better if I did.'

'In love with Mr Bailey? Mum, don't leave us, please! How is it better if you're not here?'

'Don't get upset, Evie. You and your grandma have got a right good little business going in the front room. Peter doesn't live here any longer and, honestly, I don't see him coming back, not with the way he feels about his father. I went to see him a few weeks ago on my way back from Redmond and he's happy with the Thomases. He's got everything there he wants.'

'He hasn't got his mother,' said Sue quietly.

'He's always got me whenever he wants me,' said Jeanie firmly. 'I just won't be living here. Same goes for you two. You know where I am and you can come to me at any time, but I won't be living here with Michael any more, and nor do I want to.'

'So you knew all along that Peter's not coming back?'

'Frederick has been paying Mr and Mrs Thomas for Peter's keep since the beginning of the year. That's what will happen for as long as Peter wants to stay there and for as long as the Thomases are happy to have him.'

'But, Mum, please don't go,' said Evie again. 'There's only Grandma and me here now with Dad. Bob's . . . gone, and then Peter left, and now you.

There are fewer and fewer of us. We were all together when we left Shenty Street, and I thought we'd manage in this new place because there *were* all of us, but now there's only Grandma and me. And Dad, of course.'

'Oh, love, I haven't been happy for a long while but I thought I could put up with it because it was how it was going to be. I thought I had no choice. But then Frederick gave me a choice. At first it was out of the question that I could ever leave you all and go to him, even though I wanted to, but then Bob died. And then when Pete went to the Thomases – that was his decision and no one made him go – I could see that the moment would soon come when I'd know it was time to leave – when my family didn't need me any more. And that moment is now.'

'But *I* need you, Mum!' Evie cried, wringing her hands. 'What about me? Please, please, don't go.'

'Shush, our Evie. Don't take on, lass.' Sue sat down on the bed, her weight toppling the neat piles of clothes beside Jeanie's case. 'Well, Jeanie, love,' she sighed, 'I can't say I approve, but nor do I approve of the way Michael's behaved. You always were one to do exactly as you wanted, and I know nothing I can say will change your mind. You were just the same with Michael, don't forget. I warned you not to be taken in by his charm, and now it seems that his charm was all he had, and he hasn't even got that any longer. You chose him then, my girl—'

'And now I'm choosing someone else, Mum. I made a mistake with Michael but it's not too late to change that.'

'But you've still got two lovely children with him, Jeanie. You can't just forget them and start again.'

'Who said anything about forgetting? I'll always be a mum to Evie and Peter – even if I live in Marlowe House with Frederick, and even if Evie lives here with you and Michael, and Peter lives with the Thomases.'

'But, Mum, you won't be *here*,' said Evie. 'And I really, really need you.'

'Well, you may say that, love, but you're nearly seventeen now, and getting quite grown-up, and it may not be long before you want to go away and make a life of your own – maybe with Billy Taylor back in Bolton, or maybe with someone else.'

'Not with Billy. That's all over, Mum. I doubt I'll see him again.'

'Well, sorry, love, but I'm making a life for myself.'

'I'm not sure marriage is to be thrown off so quickly, Jeanie,' said Sue. 'You vowed to take each other for better and for worse.'

'I know that, Mum. And I'm not making this decision lightly. I wish I loved Michael as I used to, but I don't. It's Frederick I love now, and I can be so much happier with him. Don't you think I'm allowed to put my mistake behind me and be happy again?'

'I want you to be happy, Jeanie, you know I do. But I just wonder if you've thought about this properly. Michael's behaved badly on so many occasions, but maybe there are better times ahead if you stick together. It's not all bad with him.'

'I've thought about nothing else,' Jeanie said desperately. 'When we came here it was to a new life that Michael had made us have. We didn't choose it. But when I went to Marlowe House to find Frederick that day, I realised that I could have a better life.'

'Mum,' said Evie, visibly pulling herself together, 'I don't want you to go but I don't want you to be unhappy either.'

Jeanie held out her hands and took both of Evie's, pulling her towards her. 'Love, you're a good girl, and I promise I'm not abandoning you. I'm leaving Michael but I can never leave you – or you either, Mum.'

Jeanie hugged her mother and her daughter, and then they drew away from each other and wiped away their tears.

'Evie, off you go down and make us all a cup of tea,' said Sue. 'Your mum and I need to get this case together.'

Evie did as she was told.

'All right, Jeanie. I can see you're set on this,' said Sue quietly as the sounds of Evie's footsteps faded down the stairs, 'but I have to tell you summat that's been bothering me since I heard it at the Bonfire Night do. Frederick Bailey might be a good man, for all I know – and he's shown us nowt but kindness, what with the low rent, and not standing in my way over the sewing business – but is it true that he's been divorced three times?'

'Good heavens, Mum, where on earth did you hear that?' asked Jeanie.

'Gossip, love, and I shouldn't have listened, but I know what I overheard and I can't unknow it. So, is it true?'

'You shouldn't be gossiping about Freddie,' Jeanie said sharply.

She turned away and started to pack her clothes into the case.

'What is the truth then, lass?' Sue was growing impatient.

'It's nowt to do with you.'

'It is if you're leaving Michael to go to live with a fella what's had three wives,' snapped Sue, pulling Jeanie round to face her by her cardigan sleeve.

Jeanie shrugged her off. 'He has had three wives—'

'So it is true—'

'But the first one died, and the second one ran off with someone else – a so-called friend of his who'd got a lot of money, and Freddie did divorce her, but can you blame him? – and the third left him too.'

'Doesn't sound like Frederick Bailey is so lucky with his women, Jeanie. Do you really think this is the man you want to spend the rest of your life with? Because I'll tell you summat for nowt, my girl, you won't want to come back to Michael – even if he'll have you – after you've got used to living the kind of life Bailey seems to lead, and which you've clearly taken to. What happened to the third wife? Did he divorce her, too?'

Jeanie looked away. 'No, Mum,' she said in a small voice. 'He's married to her still. She lives somewhere else, not nearby, by herself, I think, and she's some sort of potter.'

'Good heavens, you mean she works at a pot factory?' asked Sue, distracted from the point by this information.

'No, Mum, she's an artist. She makes special pots, one at a time, I gather, and people buy them to display rather than to use.'

'Well, I never! And you say they're still married?'

'They are.'

Sue took a few moments to digest this. 'But, Jeanie, love, to go and live with a man you can't marry, and who is someone else's husband? How do you know this woman isn't going to reappear at any moment to move back in with him? What would happen to you, then? You'd be out on your ear, because I reckon she'd have every right to return if she wanted to. You'd be the one in the wrong because you'd be living in her house. With her husband!'

'It's not like that, Mum, really it's not,' said Jeanie. 'She's been gone for years. She's never coming back. Don't you think I haven't asked Freddie about her and where I stand? Honestly, Mum, there are different folk in the world than those that live in Shenty Street. It was all we knew until we left there, but it was only one way of living – for people like us.'

Sue was silent as she watched Jeanie slowly finish putting all her clothes in her case, and gathering her second pair of shoes into a paper carrier bag. Sue thought back to her life in the big house where she'd been a lady's maid until she'd met and married Albert and left to be a housewife and then a mother. She remembered the lives of the people there, the secrets and the romances, even the scandals. She'd seen all kinds of folk there – high-born and low-born – and she recognised that poor people had less choice, less licence. Then she had got used to living a smaller life in Shenty Street and almost forgot that she had ever seen anything any different. Maybe the values of the people she knew there were sounder than those of folk with more money and more choices, or maybe ordinary working folk were long-suffering and prepared to put up with unhappy marriages because there was nothing for them outside of that and nowhere to run to.

'You go, then, lass. I only hope you're choosing

the right road. I won't put up with gossip about you but nor will I lie to our friends. I just want you to be happy.'

'Thank you, Mum.' Jeanie hugged her close again.

'All I ask is that you tell Michael. Don't leave it to me to tell him. And I want you to say it to his face, not leave him a note.'

'I've told him already, Mum. I don't know if he believed me, but he knows, and when he comes home and finds me gone, he'll believe me then.'

'And you'll see the children, won't you, lass? And me? Please don't leave us completely, Jeanie,' Sue begged quietly. 'You're the heart of this family – what's left of it – and we won't survive without you if you leave us and we never see you.'

'No, Mum, I promise.'

Then Jeanie tied the pretty scarf around her neck in a dashing new way she seemed to have copied from Frederick, pinned the bow brooch to her cardigan, picked up her case, her bag of shoes, her handbag, her coat and the beautiful fine gloves. She gave a look around the shabby bedroom one last time and then walked down the stairs with her back straight and her head held high, leaving her mother, bowed under the weight of her worry, to follow behind.

~

Evie and Sue were too upset to go to Redmond as they had planned that morning, so they stayed in working on some mending. Mrs Cooke's curtains were ready and waiting for her, and, as they sewed, the two of them spent the morning in silent worry, dreading Michael's return, with his inevitable anger.

'It feels like us two alone now, Grandma,' said Evie. 'Do you really think we'll see Mum again?'

'Not only do I think we'll see her, I *know* so,' Sue replied staunchly. 'Because I shall make sure we do. I've never been to Frederick Bailey's house, but I mean to visit my daughter there from now on and you can come with me. I can't imagine a place where everything's got a price label on it, but I expect I shall soon see what it's like.'

Evie smiled. 'It's not like a shop, Grandma. There aren't the prices on the things, it's just that Mr Bailey lives among stuff that he buys and sells. Some of it is lovely.'

'How does he know what's his and what he's got to sell on?' asked Sue.

'Does it matter?' Evie said. 'I don't suppose he has to sell anything he wants to keep. Say he bought a nice tea set and he decided he really liked it – provided he didn't need the money I expect he'd just keep it and use it.' She remembered the odd cups with no saucers. It seemed that Mr Bailey hadn't yet found a tea set he liked enough to keep. She said as much to Sue.

'Mmm . . . ' said Sue, wondering if Frederick Bailey
had found a woman he liked enough to keep, and
hoping, if Jeanie was as much in love with him as she
appeared to be, that she was at last the one he wouldn't
pass on. But Jeanie had said that one wife had died
and the next two had left him, so maybe his being
tired of her was not something to be worrying about.
The thing was, though, there were always two sides
to any story, and a man who'd had three wives couldn't
be entirely blameless for that situation. Could he?

~

In the days after Jeanie left, Evie couldn't stop
thinking about what her mother had said about
choices and making her own luck. She worked at
the sewing machine in silence, turning her mother's
words over in her mind, and Sue darned alongside
her, also silently.

By the beginning of February Evie felt she was
somehow waiting for something to happen. Maybe
it was the arrival of a letter from Billy, which never
came, she decided. If Billy wouldn't reply to her
letters then maybe she should get in touch via Mary.

Dear Mary,
I'm sorry it's taken me a while to reply to you. I was
really pleased to get your letter with your kind words
about our Bob, and the good wishes of all your family.

I know your mum also wrote to Grandma Sue, Mum and Dad, and they were made up by her thoughts and a funny little story she told about him. Christmas wasn't much of a celebration, as I expect you can imagine. We were pleased to get the card from you all, though.

It's not too good here, but Grandma Sue and me are doing our best and are working hard at the sewing. Mum has left us and has gone to live elsewhere, though she's nearby and we will see her soon. I think she just got fed up when Bob died and now that Peter's gone to stay with friends in the village.

Evie read through what she had written and thought it just awful. How could she spread all this misery around? Her heart wasn't in sharing her news, especially the actual truth of it. She tore the letter up and threw the pieces on the kitchen fire. *Stupid, stupid, stupid . . .*

If only Billy would get in touch. She'd been silly to spoil the weekend when she'd gone to Bolton for Geraldine's party but now it seemed that she would never hear from him again. She felt hurt that he hadn't even written to say anything about Robert, but she'd done her best with the two difficult letters she'd sent him. He'd always been so reliable and kind, but it was clear now that he didn't want to keep in touch with her. Maybe, a bit like her mother, he'd found someone else he'd rather be with, who was kind herself and didn't fly off the handle, and who was fond of his mother and didn't say mean things about her. Maybe, more to the point, he'd found someone Ada liked, someone who Ada thought was good enough for her only son . . .

The more she thought about it, the more Evie decided that this was exactly what must have happened. How could she not have worked it out before now? How undignified. He was simply no longer interested . . . when he was probably already in love with someone else and had forgotten all about her. Someone who was all pretty and glamorous and wore fine stockings with seams in them instead of ankle socks like a schoolgirl, and maybe had red lipstick and a swirly skirt like the ones pictured in her magazines. Evie picked one up, a treat at Christmas that she had thought would help lift her spirits and inspire her and Sue with new ideas. She flipped through and admired the impossibly slim models in elegant poses, their snooty faces beneath pert little hats and offset by fur-trimmed coat collars; their slender ankles and high-heeled shoes beneath yards of well-cut skirting. She sighed again. How far they seemed from real life . . . from herself, in her thick, warm trousers and well-washed jumper with the darned elbows.

'Evie, Grandma?' It was Peter calling.

'In here, Pete.'

'He's not here, is he?' Peter appeared at the kitchen door, Letty behind him.

'No, he's at Clackett's. He won't be back for a

while. Grandma's gone down the road to measure up for some curtains. Let me pour you both some tea and you can tell me your news. We'll take it through to the front, shall we? I've been sitting here and sort of forgot all about the shop. I don't want folk to think we're not open for business.'

'You need a bell,' said Letty. 'If you're not in the room your clients can summon you.'

'Great idea, Letty. I can't think why we haven't thought of that before. We're always having to "keep an eye" on the shop.'

'Mebbe Frederick will have one you can use,' suggested Peter.

'Perhaps. Have you been to see them?'

'Oh, yes, a couple of times after school. He's got such an interesting house and Mum does seem much happier. She's much more smiley than she was here and she sort of looks different, too.'

'In what way?' asked Evie, handing Peter and Letty their tea and leading them through to the front room, taking her magazine with her.

Peter thought about it. 'Difficult to say. She's still the same old mum, and wears mostly the same things, but there's more . . . drama, I suppose, about the way she wears them.'

'Style?' suggested Letty. 'More style?'

'Yes, that's it. Bits of jewellery and stuff, and a smart new belt on an old frock, that kind of thing. Even the way she tucks her jumper into her slacks.'

'You always had an eye for what looks right, Pete,' smiled Evie. 'Remember how you set up the front room to look like a proper dressmaker's workroom?'

'It *is* a proper workroom,' said Letty, sitting down at the table and reaching for Evie's magazine. She turned the pages as Evie asked Peter about his guitar lessons and what else he was doing at school. Then Letty joined in as they talked about the band and Peter invited Evie to go to listen to a concert they were to play in a church hall. After a while he got up to leave.

'Don't want to have to see Dad,' he said, 'so I'd best be off now. Sorry to miss Grandma but I'll catch her soon. Don't forget to tell her about the concert and maybe she'll want to go as well.'

'I'll tell her. Bye, Pete.'

The front door shut and he waved through the window and was gone.

'All right, Evie, what's the matter?' said Letty.

'Oh, you know . . . '

'I know about Robert, of course, and your mum going. But Pete's seen her and it sounds as if she's fine.'

'Yes, it does, and I'm glad. But, oh, Letty, I still wish she hadn't gone. Dad's hardly around these days, what with Mr Clackett keeping him busy and then his going out every evening, and it feels so empty with just Grandma and me here all the time.'

'You're missing the others, that's all, Evie.' For a

moment Letty looked sad and Evie knew that of course she understood.

'But it's something else as well, Letty. I've been thinking a lot since Mum left and what I'm really fed up with is being me,' said Evie. She looked down at the shapeless and slightly itchy trousers, at the jumper felted with wear, an old and fraying shirt underneath it. 'I wish I looked more like these women.' She pointed to the magazine, which Letty had left open on the table. 'No wonder Billy's probably found someone new – who would want a girl looking like me on his arm?'

'Good heavens, Evie, where on earth has all this come from?' asked Letty. 'You're lovely.' She laughed then. 'Though I have to admit that your clothes aren't! But then mine aren't either, and I don't care.'

'Well, I haven't got much to spend on fancy clothes – and certainly not stuff like that.' She indicated the gorgeous suit in the fashion spread. 'And anyway, at the moment it's all about keeping warm.'

'You're right there,' agreed Letty. 'I have at least five layers on most days. The forecast is for snow again, too. But everyone has to have new clothes, and there's no reason why you shouldn't have something that looks a bit more like . . . Well, take that dress, for example. I expect you and Mrs Goodwin could copy that design and come up with something similar.'

'Such a lot of fabric in it, though, Letty. I'm not sure we could run to that just for me.'

'Nonsense, Evie. You'd be a walking advertisement for the business. Or how about one of those straight skirts? No excuse about too much fabric in that. When people see how well-dressed and smart you look, and how well made your clothes are, they'll want something the same. Before you know it, there'll be commissions for all sorts – no more kitchen curtains!'

'Aye, Letty, love, I can see what you mean,' said Sue, coming in to hear the last bit. 'No use me getting done up in sharp tailoring: I haven't got a sharp figure. But I reckon it's time our Evie had a few new things, summat more grown-up and suitable for a working woman, and you're right about needing to show off our skills. Who's going to believe an old woman and a scrap of a girl could make them summat nice to wear? And Evie's the one to show off our style.'

'Hello, Mrs Goodwin.' Letty got up and kissed Sue's cheek. 'I'm so glad you agree. You see, Evie, *we* agree so *you're* outnumbered. And I've just had the most terrific idea.'

'Not another one?' laughed Sue, sitting down and unzipping her boots.

'Yes, but I'll have to ask Aunt Margaret first.' Letty got up and buttoned on the layers she'd hung on the back of the chair. 'Don't worry, I'll be back tomorrow.'

'Ask Miss Richards about what?' said Evie. 'You can't leave us guessing.'

'Oh, but I can!' laughed Letty, pulling on her knitted beret. 'Don't sit there being miserable about your clothes any longer because I may have thought of the perfect solution.'

She departed laughing and blowing kisses, and the air settled as it always did behind her liveliness.

'*The perfect solution*, indeed,' smiled Sue. 'Well, we'll see, but she's a good 'un, is Letty Mortimer. Now, let's get the kettle on and then I'll make a start on these curtains while I can still read the figures I wrote down.'

'I'll copy them out larger for you, Grandma, if you like? And while the kettle boils I can tell you what Peter said when he was here earlier, about how he's doing, and about Mum.'

'I can see from your face it's good news. Not such a bad day, after all, then?'

'No, Grandma,' said Evie, following Sue through to the kitchen. 'And I've been thinking all the time about what Mum said that morning she left.'

'Oh, yes?'

'About making her own luck, and choosing what she wanted and not what she was given.'

'And what about you, Evie? You'll be seventeen in a few days, old enough to begin on your own path through life. What destiny will you choose, love?'

Evie paused to get her thoughts in order. Then she said carefully, 'I'm choosing to link my destiny to yours, Grandma. But I won't be the same little Evie any longer. If we're to make something of this sewing business – make a success of it and grow it, not just make it something we do day in and day out, for ever, without it going anywhere – we need to make some changes. We should look for new customers, as we said we would, and take on dress-making rather than household linen and mending so that's what people get to know us for. No more boring old kitchen curtains! Our customers can bring their own fabrics, but we need to find a source nearby of nice trimmings and some lengths for smaller garments. The mill shop in Bolton is too far away and we can't keep calling on favours from old friends, nor expect them to choose the fabrics for us. It's time to make some big decisions together – you and me, Grandma – and I reckon we can make a real go of it.'

Sue smiled. 'I like the sound of all this and you're good enough at the sewing now to take on some ambitious garments.'

Ambitious. Evie thought about it. It wasn't a word she'd ever applied to herself before. But things were going to be different from now on.

'Let's get that tea made and we'll raise a cup to toast the future and big decisions,' she laughed, and Sue agreed.

CHAPTER FOURTEEN

THE NEXT MORNING Evie and Sue got up with a renewed sense of purpose and set about finishing their current sewing tasks as quickly as they could so they could start to concentrate on exciting new projects.

Michael had gone to work quietly and dutifully on time. His anger seemed to be spent, to be replaced by sadness but also a misplaced sense of hope that Jeanie would return.

'She'll not stay away for long, I reckon,' he'd said to Sue as she poured him a mug of tea, and she smiled and offered to pack him up some sandwiches for midday in case he was too busy to come back over the road to eat. He thanked her politely and accepted, leaving meekly a few minutes later.

'It's as if his spirit has been quite crushed, poor Dad,' said Evie.

'Don't worry about him, lass,' Sue replied. 'I'll

see him mend his ways before he gets much of my
sympathy . . . '

Halfway through the morning Letty appeared with
a big smile, and a huge pile of clothes in her bicycle
basket.

'I've asked Aunt Margaret and she isn't upset if I
do what I want with these,' she announced, bringing
in the first armful of garments, then going back out
to the bike to get the rest.

'What are they?' asked Evie, getting up to look.
'My goodness, Letty, these are lovely. Where did you
get them?'

'Mum,' said Letty simply. 'Oh, it's all right, don't
get all sad about it. It's my idea to get rid of them.
I can face it now. It's time.'

'But they're so pretty and . . . well, I think they
were quite expensive. Your mum must have looked
smashing.'

'She did,' said Letty. 'But I won't ever wear these,
and I don't need them to remind me of her. I've
got some photographs of her in them. Aunt Margaret
has kept a few things, including a nice warm coat,
and I've got one as well, and a couple of dresses
that I may wear when I'm performing with the band,
but all these are spare and just taking up room in
the cottage. As you know, I don't care much about
clothes. I thought that maybe you could use them
somehow . . . if you want?'

Sue was feeling the quality of the fabrics and then

she held up one of the dresses. She could see it was a bit too wide and a lot too long for Evie.

'Would you mind if we altered them, even cut them up a bit?'

'No, of course not,' said Letty. 'I would expect you to. They're yours if you want them.'

'Oh, we do, we do!' said Evie, laughing and hugging Letty. 'You are such a love.'

'Letty, lass, you're an answer to my prayers,' said Sue. 'I've been awake half the night wondering how I can get together a few smart outfits for Evie to show off our skills without spending any money.'

'I would have explained yesterday, but I had to ask Aunt Margaret first. The clothes are mine to do with as I like but I didn't want her to be upset by my giving them away.'

'Quite right, love. You're a good girl.'

'And there are more, but I couldn't get them on the bike.'

'More?'

'Oh, yes, this is only a fraction.'

'Your mother must have been as smart as the Queen,' said Evie, holding up a light red evening dress with a row of tiny pearl buttons down the front. 'Oh, Grandma, look at this!'

'Not really, but Dad used to get asked to a lot of functions and Mum needed to look nice, too.'

'It all sounds very grand,' said Sue. 'What did your father do?'

'Oh, something in the government,' said Letty vaguely. 'Not the kind of thing I understand . . . Anyway, if you can use them I'm really pleased. Now, I'll leave you to look through these clothes and I'll bring the rest along soon.'

'Thank you, lass.'

'Yes, thank you, Letty. You've made our day,' said Evie.

'Made our year, more like,' said Sue. 'And if you need anything you're keeping altered or refashioned, I'll be glad to do it for you. Same for your auntie, tell her.'

'Thanks, I will. Bye, then.'

'That is so generous,' said Evie after they'd waved Letty off, her expert hands sorting through the lovely materials. 'It seems a shame to cut them up.'

'Well, they're no use to you if we don't,' said Sue sensibly, 'because they're probably all too big for you. I think we should go through them piece by piece and see what's what.'

'Good idea. Oh, Grandma, it's like Christmas,' said Evie, feeling a lightness in her heart for the first time in a long time.

~

The snow that had fallen in Bolton back in January turned out to be nothing compared to the amount that fell over the whole country in February.

Billy was unable to go to work because the roads were blocked and, anyway, the post wasn't getting through to be sorted and delivered, so he spent his days with a working party of local men – and some women, too – clearing the roads and making sure his neighbours were all right.

They met at the Lord Nelson, and at first there was a worry that the pub would run out of beer, but the snow-clearing gang knew where their priorities lay, and the roads between the brewery where Michael Carter used to work and the pub were among the first to be cleared. There would be beer for as long as there were barrels ready to deliver to the Nelson.

Billy wasn't a big beer drinker but clearing the roads was thirsty work.

'I'll have a half of mild, if you've got it, please,' he told the landlord, stopping by one lunchtime.

'Make that two, please,' said a soft Irish voice behind him.

'Brendan, hello. I've not seen you for a bit. You all surviving?'

'Just about, Billy, but I tell you, the house seems very small when we're all there all day long.'

'I bet it does, with the lads not at work and the schools closed.'

'I thought I'd join the working party this afternoon for a bit of peace and quiet. Only our Gerry's at work, and I reckon Mr Amsell will have to close the shop in a few days if he can't get any deliveries. He's running on what's left on the shelves and then that's it.'

'Mebbe there'll be a thaw before then. I hope so, or we all might run out of food. Gerry OK, is she?'

'Oh, yes, though she says it's colder in the shop storeroom than it is outside!'

It was then that Billy, whose thoughts were never far from Evie, was reminded again of the disagreement at Geraldine's birthday party.

'Has anyone heard from the Carters?' he asked casually.

'Marie and Mary are the ones for writing letters but I haven't heard that they've been in touch with Jeanie and Sue or Evie recently. Not since before Christmas. I think that bad business with Robert hit them hard. It's difficult to write when you've lost heart.'

Billy set his glass down slowly. 'What bad business? What's happened to the little 'un?'

'Oh, dear Lord, lad, have you not heard?'

Billy was filled with dread. 'No. Tell me, Brendan. What's happened?'

So Brendan told Billy all about Robert drowning, and that the Carters were in pieces over his death.

Billy listened, shocked and pale.

'She never wrote to tell me, Brendan. How could she not have written with such news?'

Brendan knew Billy was speaking of Evie, and he

also knew from Mary something of their falling out at Geraldine's party, but he hadn't realised the rift between them had never been healed. It was clear to him that Billy had thought Evie would write eventually, but that Evie had washed her hands of the poor fella. He wasn't all that surprised. Evie was still only about seventeen and the family had been gone for months now. It was no wonder that the youthful romance between Billy and Evie had died a natural death, particularly when the Carters had so much to deal with in their new lives. But it wasn't for him to voice this opinion and he didn't answer.

'I haven't heard from Evie since . . . since Gerry's party,' Billy went on. 'Poor little Bob. What an awful thing to happen.' Downcast, he finished his beer, said goodbye to Brendan and went to collect his shovel from the pub's porch.

While he cleared snow he thought long and hard about what Brendan had told him and reached the same conclusion that the kindly Irishman had: Evie no longer wanted to keep in touch with him.

That afternoon, when Billy returned to Fawcett Street in the muffled and strangely white twilight, his face was glowing with the effort of his snow clearing, but inside he felt cold.

'I'll make a pot of tea and we'll open them biscuits I've saved from Christmas,' said Ada, seeing the weariness in his face.

'Oh, Mum, I've heard the most terrible news,'

Billy told her, as he pulled off his wellies and padded into the kitchen in two pairs of thick socks, the scarf Evie had knitted for him around his neck.

He told his mother about Robert Carter's accident. 'I haven't heard a word from Evie, so I'd no idea. How could she not have written to tell me?'

Ada had her back to him, making the tea, and she didn't dare turn round in case her face gave her away as she said, 'What an awful thing. Poor lad. But those Carters don't seem to have much luck, do they?'

'Well, that's true enough, Mum.'

Ada, who was genuinely sorry about Robert, and had heard the news from Dora Marsh at Christmas, came over then, looking sad, and hugged Billy to her where he sat on a kitchen chair. 'It's a bad business, true enough. I reckon they've got friends down wherever it is they live now and no need to share the news up here.'

'But Brendan Sullivan told me,' Billy pointed out. 'The Carters have been in touch with Marie and the girls.'

Ada thought quickly before she undermined her own point. 'Well, I know Sue Goodwin has always been one to share her news. It's a generation thing, love.'

'Maybe . . . but Evie used to write, Mum, as you know. I don't understand why she wouldn't let me know about young Bob.'

'It looks like she's stopped writing, love,' said Ada, well aware that Evie had indeed stopped writing since the two letters she'd sent after she'd visited Bolton and at Christmas – and which were in Ada's sideboard – had of course gone unanswered.

Ada hadn't opened and read them – that would have been dishonest, she reckoned – but she could guess what was in the first after Geraldine's party, and when she'd heard the sad news about Robert from Dora she knew what was in the second. No need to be bothering Billy with any of that. Though, now she thought of it, it was hardly a surprise that someone should have mentioned the little lad's accident to him eventually.

'The Carters have been gone a long time, Billy, and Evie's got new friends now, I'm sure,' said Ada. 'As I've said before, she's a long way away and she's only young. She'll know all kinds of different folk down there and it's hardly surprising if she's too busy with her new life to be thinking about Bolton.'

'Yes, I reckon you're right, Mum,' Billy said. 'But still, I thought she'd have let me know about this. We all liked poor little Bob.'

'Mmm,' said Ada, who had thought Robert an awkward child, sad though the news of his death was. 'Well, I think this proves I'm right,' she said, and Billy couldn't really argue with that, having reached the same conclusion.

'Sit down and have your tea,' she went on, pouring out a cup.

'Thanks, Mum. I think I'll take it upstairs with me,' Billy replied, and wearily went to his room to think through what he had learned.

Ada spent the rest of the afternoon alone, and the conversation over the tinned soup she heated that evening – taken from the enormous hoard she'd started to store in the larder at the sight of the first flurries of snow in January – was on her side only. Billy washed up and, as Ada settled beside the wireless to listen to the weather forecast, he came through with a cup of tea for her and declared he was very tired with all that snow shifting and he thought he'd get an early night, leaving her feeling quite alone in her own company.

~

In Church Sandleton the February snow was just as heavy as it was in the north. Michael was kept busy helping Mr Clackett to clear the market garden and lending a hand to their neighbours. The schools were closed so Peter was around, but he kept away from his father, shovelling snow with Letty and Miss Richards at Lavender Cottage at the far end of the village, the rest of the time playing music with the Thomas boys.

Evie and Sue didn't mind the snow. They were

working on refashioning the treasure trove of garments Letty had given them to make smart new clothes for Evie, and altering the ones Letty and Miss Richards had chosen to keep for themselves, in return for the generous hoard of beautiful clothes.

'You look gorgeous, Evie,' enthused Letty, when Evie put on a newly finished tailored two-piece to show her friend and Miss Richards what she and Sue had made from an old outfit.

'Good fit, Sue,' said Margaret Richards, inspecting the back of the neat jacket. 'You've done wonders with that old costume.'

'What you need now, Evie,' said Letty, always full of ideas, 'is a new hairstyle. Not that you don't look pretty as you are, but maybe something a bit more grown-up . . . ?'

'I don't know if I can afford anything very different,' said Evie. 'I usually just have the ends trimmed.'

'Well, why don't you ask your mum to pay?'

'Letty!' tutted Margaret. 'That isn't for you to suggest.'

'I know, Aunt Margaret, but I saw Mrs Carter in Redmond before the snow and she had such a lovely new hairstyle. Maybe she could pay for it for your birthday – if you asked nicely, I mean,' Letty laughed. 'With the lipstick and bits Auntie and I gave you, your lovely new outfits and smart hair, you'll have all the ladies in Redmond looking at you and asking where you get your clothes.' She pushed the ever-open fashion magazine towards Evie. 'If this model had long hair and a fringe like yours, it wouldn't really go with the dress, would it?'

'Letty, you are so rude,' said Margaret, laughing.

'But she's right, Miss Richards,' Evie agreed, and Sue was nodding, too.

'I reckon Jeanie will be all for that,' she said, 'and anyway, it's time we went to see her. Soon as this wretched snow's gone we'll get the bus to Redmond.'

~

As soon as the roads were open and the buses to Redmond were running again Sue and Evie embarked on an expedition to see Jeanie. Evie wore her two-piece with one of Letty's mother's coats over it, which Evie had turned up but otherwise was perfect for covering any number of layers in the cold weather. Her shoes rather spoiled the effect but there was nothing she could do about those until she and Sue started earning again. The snow had been bad for business even if it had been good for Evie's wardrobe.

They alighted in the market square. It was market day but what few stalls there were were a sorry-looking lot in the bleak weather. The fabric stall Evie had seen with Jeanie in the summer wasn't there, which was disappointing, but then they didn't have much money to spend anyway.

'I've had an idea,' said Evie. 'You remember how Mum and me found Frederick by looking in the telephone directory? Well, I wonder if there are any fabric shops or haberdashers in Redmond. We could look them up and see.'

Sue agreed and Evie led her across the square to the imposing library. They sat at desks in the reference room and carefully wrote down two names and addresses in Redmond and one in Kingsford. Then, in a whisper, Evie asked the librarian where the local streets were and she and Sue listened carefully to the directions.

'Let's go and see Mum first, though,' Evie suggested as they came out into the cold. 'I've missed her so much.'

'Me, too, love. Now where's this Midsummer Row . . . ?'

Evie could tell that her grandmother was impressed with the neat railings and steps up to the front door of Marlowe House, though Sue didn't say anything.

Evie rang the bell, remembering how the fierce, angry woman had rushed out just as she and Jeanie arrived that first day. How much had happened since then. Now Jeanie lived here!

The smart front door opened and Jeanie's smiling face greeted them. In a moment she was holding Evie close in a big hug, and then Sue.

'Oh, Evie, love . . . Mum, I've missed you both so much. I was beginning to think with all that snow that I'd never see you again. The roads have been terrible here and I expect they were even worse in the village.' She stepped back to let them in out of the cold as she spoke.

The first thing Evie noticed was how lovely her mother looked. She did indeed have a new hairstyle, as Letty had said, but there was something else about her. Evie thought hard about this as she gazed at her mother: less worried, not too thin any longer, and her face was a healthier colour, though that might have been the subtle make-up she wore as well. Her clothes were warm and casual – a hand-knitted jumper and trousers – but she wore them with style.

'Mum, you look so pretty,' Evie gasped.

'Thank you, love,' said Jeanie, accepting the compliment with a confidence she never used to have. 'Come in and have a hot drink. Or you could stay for lunch. I've made some soup and there's plenty.'

'We won't put you to any trouble,' said Sue.

'It's no trouble. I'd like you to stay. We've got a lot to talk about.'

Evie and Sue looked at each other and smiled. 'Yes, please,' said Evie. 'There's so much to catch up on, Mum!'

Frederick came out of a room at the back of the

hall and was delighted to see the unexpected visitors.

He hung up their coats, then showed them into the sitting room, where interesting-looking things stood on every piece of furniture.

'Why don't you and your mum go and make us that hot drink, Evie,' suggested Sue, 'and Frederick can show me some of these treasures?'

Evie and Jeanie did as they were asked.

'Now then, Frederick Bailey,' said Sue in her forthright way as soon as they'd gone downstairs to the kitchen, 'I can see my lass is looking happy here, but I've heard there have been a few Mrs Baileys and I want to be sure you mean to do right by her.'

'Well, Mrs Goodwin, I certainly mean to love and to cherish your beautiful daughter,' Frederick replied, indicating an armchair for Sue and sitting down opposite her. 'But it isn't possible for me to marry her – at least not at the moment.'

'Aye, she told me you're already married,' said Sue. 'To the *third* Mrs Bailey, isn't that so?'

'It is indeed, Mrs Goodwin. Truth be told, I don't actually know where the third Mrs Bailey is. I haven't set eyes on her for years.'

'Not know where your own wife lives? I thought I'd heard it all in my time . . . '

Frederick smiled. 'I have to agree with you, Mrs Goodwin. I've rather let matters slide. But Jeanie, of course, is still married to Michael Carter, so there are two reasons why we can't be married,' he added pointedly, but with another disarming smile.

'Well, I can't argue with that,' said Sue.

'I have been married three times, though my first wife died, and I am still married to the third, and . . . well, Mrs Goodwin, I'd maybe have done things differently if I'd known how they were going to turn out. But this time I'm certain I've chosen right.'

'But she's Michael's wife, Mr Bailey. She wasn't free to be chosen by you or by anyone else.' Sue couldn't help raising this although she knew it was water under the bridge and there was no way Jeanie would suddenly remember her obligations to Michael and decide to go home.

'You want her to be happy, though, don't you, Mrs Goodwin? She is happy here.'

Sue knew there was only one answer to that, and it wasn't about asking Jeanie to honour her wedding vows.

She sighed heavily. 'She's gone against her vows and left her family for you, it's up to you to make sure she never, ever regrets it. Because she won't want to go back to Michael – I can see that, and he's certainly not been the best husband. But she's left her children and if she hasn't got you she won't have anything.'

Frederick stood and took Sue's arm to help her to her feet. 'Yes, Mrs Goodwin, I mean to keep

Jeanie with me for ever. I shall do my best to make sure she never regrets coming here,' he said quietly. 'I don't know if we shall ever be free to marry, but she is as dear to me as anyone can be and I dare to hope that she feels the same.'

'Then,' said Sue, 'I think you had better call me Sue, because whatever she is and whatever she does, Jeanie will always be my daughter.'

Frederick looked into Sue's formidable face and saw strength, kindness and good sense written there.

'Thank you, Sue, and I shall be pleased to see you – and Evie and Peter – whenever you care to visit. Now I think Jeanie said something about a cup of tea, or even soup, and you and she and Evie can catch up with all your news while you have it.'

~

When Evie and Sue eventually left Marlowe House it was late afternoon and starting to get dark. There had been so much to say that the hours had flown by and Sue had lost all track of time.

Jeanie had said she'd book an appointment for Evie at her own hairdresser, and pay for her daughter's new hairstyle and also some shoes with maybe a bit of a heel. They'd make a day of it next week and have some fun together.

Jeanie was full of praise for Evie's new outfit and the plans for expanding the sewing business into more ambitious projects. 'You should go into tailoring and make a suit for Freddie, Mum,' she grinned, looking sideways at his frayed shirt collar and trouser hems.

'No, I'm not that good. I only do dress patterns,' said Sue. She could see that although Frederick was shabbier than anyone with no money, such as those that lived in Shenty Street, it was almost an act, a kind of statement of style rather than through necessity. Kind of as though he is dressing up, she thought.

The Carters talked about Peter and shed a few tears over Robert, which they couldn't help because they all missed him so much. Jeanie wrote the date of Peter's concert in a smart diary by the telephone and promised to try to go if there was no danger of Michael being there.

'I don't want any awkwardness in public,' she said, 'and there'd be no avoiding him in a church hall.'

'I don't suppose Peter wants him there either,' said Evie.

'I've just had an idea,' Jeanie said, pen still in hand. 'You could do with a telephone at Pendle's, what with taking on customers in Redmond, couldn't you?'

'Ooh, Mum, I hadn't really thought. It would be a great help, wouldn't it, Grandma, so we'd be able to arrange fittings and tell them when their clothes were ready?'

'Yes, you're right, love,' Sue agreed.

'I'll ask Jack to arrange that for you,' said Frederick.

'Oh, thank you,' beamed Evie. 'We'll be like a proper business, with a telephone and everything.'

'It *is* a proper business anyway,' said Jeanie, smiling at Sue and Evie, 'and I couldn't be more proud of you.'

~

That night, Evie lay in bed thinking about the day and how much she'd enjoyed seeing her mother. It wasn't just that she missed Jeanie, but her spirits were raised by what she had found. She remembered how she'd begged Jeanie not to leave them, but now it was obvious that it had all been for the best. Jeanie had been different . . . happy, despite still grieving for Robert. Evie couldn't remember ever seeing her mother that happy before. She was clearly very much in love with Frederick – and he with her – so that even the house felt like a happy place to be. It was almost as if the walls had been smiling.

Evie shrugged off her fanciful notion while accepting that here was a lesson for the new Evie to learn. The new Evie was now a seamstress who was about to launch a proper business with an expert needlewoman, Sue, and she had some beautiful outfits to show off their talents and style. They were even going to have a telephone installed. All they needed was to put in some hard work and everything would be fine. It was all down to them.

The only thing the new Evie wasn't sure about was whether she would ever be as much in love as her mother and Frederick Bailey were, and as Grandma Sue and Granddad Albert had been in the old tales Sue told about how they had met and married. Billy Taylor was no longer a part of her life. He'd made his choice and she had to go along with that. Maybe he had never been the one for her. Now she'd never know. But there must be someone else out there for her. How long before she found him?

CHAPTER FIFTEEN

Evie had never been vain. However, she couldn't help but notice with satisfaction how, since she'd started wearing the beautiful clothes she and Sue had sewn, and had her hair cut in a new style, total strangers sometimes turned to give her a second glance in the street. This morning, in Redmond, one lady, wearing a smart outfit herself, even asked where Evie had bought her suit, and Evie was able to give her one of the business cards she and Sue had had made with their names and the number of the newly installed telephone on it:

Goodwin and Carter, Dressmakers
Telephone: Church Sandleton 325

There had, of course, been no time to find the fabric and haberdashery sellers, the addresses of which they'd noted in the library, on that first visit to Jeanie at Marlowe House – far too much catching-up to do – but Evie and Sue were back in Redmond on this spring-like morning in early March especially to seek out the shops. Disappointingly, neither of the places was anything special, but it was useful to know where they could buy all the basics nearby. The vast amount of thread and buttons that Sue had brought with her to Church Sandleton was beginning to run low.

'We've been spoiled by the quality of the cotton prints from the mill shop in Bolton,' said Sue, as they came out of the second shop with only some tacking cotton and a card of press studs.

'You're right, Grandma,' Evie replied. 'Do you think it's worth looking out this place in Kingsford?'

'I reckon we should. Be a pity if we didn't and it turned out to be worth the effort.'

'You're not too tired, are you, Grandma?'

'No, lass. We'll take the train as it's quicker, so I'll have a sit-down more comfortable than on the bus. Come on, I gather it's only the next station.'

Neither Evie nor Sue had been to Kingsford before and they were pleasantly surprised by the pretty little town.

'"G. Morris, Market Passage",' Evie read from the shorthand notebook into which she'd copied the addresses she'd found in the library. She'd taken to carrying the notebook these days, and with so many prices to remember it was proving to be essential this morning. 'It must be off the marketplace.'

They walked slowly around the marketplace, admiring the shops and checking the names of the side streets.

'Here we are,' said Evie, and she and Sue walked arm in arm down a narrow cobbled side street, treading carefully on the uneven surface. 'My goodness, Grandma, I wasn't expecting this,' she gasped, gazing at two long windows filled with draped fabrics to either side of a blue shop door. 'It's enormous.'

'Best get in and see what it's like,' said Sue, looking pleased.

A bell tinkled loudly as Evie opened the door and they entered. Fabrics in every colour and pattern she could imagine were stacked on shelves, and there were racks of braid, ribbon and lace, zips in a huge variety of lengths and colours, and then buttons and threads in cabinets with glass-fronted drawers – everything a dressmaker could need.

'It's like being back in the North,' laughed Sue. 'I reckon we might be able to do a bit of shopping here.'

'Good morning. How can I help you?' A middle-aged man with thinning hair and tortoiseshell glasses came out from behind one of the polished counters.

'We've just come for a look round at the moment,' said Sue. 'My granddaughter and I are professional dressmakers and we're keen to find a source of quality fabrics and trimmings.'

'Professional?' asked the man. He eyed up Evie's stylish suit. 'So I see,' he said, admiringly. 'Well, Mrs . . . ?'

'Goodwin,' said Sue, dipping into her handbag for one of the business cards.

The man took it, looked at it and turned to Evie with a smile.

'Evie Carter. How do you do?' said Evie, offering her hand. That was what Letty would say, she thought.

'George Morris,' said the man, shaking it gently, then offering his hand to Sue. 'Well, please have a look around. The prices are retail, of course, but I can offer you a trade discount as you're in the profession.'

Sue and Evie beamed at each other. *Trade discount?*

They spent the rest of the morning oohing and aahing over the fabrics and trimmings, discussing what they could do with them. The prices, though, were much higher than they were used to and they soon realised that they wouldn't be coming away with bagsful of purchases, even with the promised trade discount.

'I love this midnight blue,' whispered Evie, 'but I don't know if we ought to buy any without a specific commission. We can't afford to buy even half a yard too much at this price.'

'I was wondering about that, love,' murmured Sue. 'I reckon it might be worth the risk for a blouse and a dress. We know well enough what most patterns take. That green broadcloth is summat special. I wonder what sort of a discount Mr Morris offers to the trade.'

'We'll have to ask him,' said Evie. 'But then he'll cotton on that we've just started out and mebbe he'll take advantage.'

'Mmm . . . ' Sue frowned, thinking hard. Luckily two other customers came into the shop and George Morris, who had been packing up some brown paper parcels for the post, became busy with them while Sue and Evie thought what they could do.

'I didn't expect there'd be so much choice,' said Evie quietly. 'But we haven't got a lot to spend and "trade" probably means buying quite a bit.'

'Yes,' said Sue, 'we'll just have to do what we can. Don't forget he's already offered a discount. Where's that notebook?'

Evie pulled the shorthand notebook and her propelling pencil out of her bag. She noted down the prices of the fabrics they liked best, and also of some lace and some special beading.

'So, Mr Morris,' said Sue, when the other customers had gone, 'you've got some nice stuff here. The thing is, we're from the north, as you can probably tell, and northern folk are canny shoppers. Now, you mentioned a trade discount, did you not?'

'I did indeed, Mrs Goodwin.'

'And might I ask how much this discount would be? You see, Mr Morris, we're mainly buying from the mill shops – and as you know, Lancashire cotton is the best in the world – so not only are we used to buying quality, but we always get a good trade discount at the mill. It's the personal service, you see. They know us up there and they know how to keep us going back.'

George Morris looked taken aback at Sue's forth-right words, but he quickly regained his cheerful smile.

'But if you're a regular customer of the mill shops, Mrs Goodwin – and I do agree with you about the quality of Lancashire cotton – why would you need to shop here as well? I can't compete with the mill shop prices.'

'Because you're local to us now, and if we were to shop here we'd be able to choose not only the fabrics but also all the special trimmings that are such a feature of our work, and all in one place, Mr Morris,' said Evie. 'The mill shops don't have these kinds of things, and we're having to buy them elsewhere . . . in London,' she said, inspiration suddenly striking. She indicated the racks of lace and decorative bindings. 'We'd rather buy local, if the price is right, and we'd be able to recommend that *our* regular clients come to you to choose their fabrics and trimmings for themselves, though, of course, you'd be selling to them at full retail price.'

'Yes . . . I can see that would be beneficial to both of us.'

'And we're *two* dressmakers, don't forget,' smiled Evie, 'so that's twice as many customers to send to you than if there was only one of us.'

George Morris raised his eyebrows. Never in his life had he seen a pair of women like these two. The nerve of the girl! Still, that suit was a work of art – if they had indeed made it themselves, that was.

'So mebbe we can talk about the discount . . . ?' suggested Evie with what she hoped was a winning smile.

She really has got a very pretty smile, though, thought George. Suddenly he didn't want Miss Carter and her formidable grandmother to leave.

'How does five per cent sound?' he asked, testing the water.

'What about twenty-five?'

George clutched the counter for support. He looked like he might actually faint away.

There was a long silence. Just as Evie was about to lose her nerve, George Morris cleared his throat.

'Fifteen per cent?' he offered, his voice sounding as if he were being strangled.

'Agreed,' beamed Sue, taking his hand and shaking it hard. 'Evie, write that down now and then we'll not forget,' she suggested pointedly, and Evie did as she was told.

'I'll be right glad to do business with you, Mr Morris,' said Sue. 'I wonder if we might have two and a half yards of that midnight-blue voile, and four yards of the green broadcloth, please, to be going on with? Our clients will be asking where we got those, don't you worry.'

'Certainly, Mrs Goodwin,' said George, unsure whether these two unusual women were in fact dressmakers or merely pretending to be. Mrs Goodwin looked old-fashioned and a bit shabby, but that didn't mean she wasn't a skilled seamstress, of course. The granddaughter, Miss Carter, looked amazing, and certainly someone had made that suit to fit her perfectly. It was difficult to place them as he'd never seen anyone quite like them before.

As he measured out the fabric an awful thought occurred to him. Perhaps they were con artists? A double act? No, that couldn't be right. If it were so then why would they be asking for a discount from a draper? It made no sense . . .

He cut the fabric lengths, folded them neatly, wrapped them in brown paper and tied the parcel with string. Then he totted up the total, deducted fifteen per cent – Sue leaning over the counter, her glasses on her nose, checking the sums from upside down – and announced the sum owing, writing out a receipt and putting his carbon copy on a spike by the till.

As Sue handed over what seemed like a large sum

even with the discount, Evie tried not to think how many remnants and blouse lengths she had bought for less than that at the mill shop in Bolton.

'Thank you, Mr Morris. A pleasure doing business with you,' said Sue graciously, folding the receipt into her purse and handing the parcel to Evie.

'We'll see you again soon,' smiled Evie, turning with a deliberate swish of her well-tailored skirt as she went towards the door.

George nipped out from behind his counter and rushed ahead to open the door for his customers. He still didn't know what to make of them but he knew for certain that they'd got very good taste. The fabrics they'd chosen were among the best he stocked.

Sue and Evie waited until they were back in the marketplace before they dare let their social smiles turn to mirth.

'Heck, love, if this is the new Evie you spoke of, I approve of her!' grinned Sue. 'You did well there, lass. I thought the old miser was going to go back on his word about a discount for a moment. And at his prices he ought to be offering fifty per cent!'

'Oh, Grandma, I have to laugh. I could see he was thinking he'd never seen owt like us before.'

'I don't know as we'll be shopping at "G. Morris" all that often,' Sue said, sounding regretful.

'I don't see why not, Grandma. I rather liked him, and we've secured a discount for the business. If we want to build a reputation for quality we'll have to get the good stuff from somewhere, and it's a long way to Bolton!'

'And a long way to London, too!' Sue laughed loudly. 'London, indeed!'

Evie joined in the laughter as they walked slowly back to the station.

~

Sue and Evie's raised spirits from the success of their shopping in Mr Morris's shop were lowered on their return to Pendle's. Evie went upstairs straight away to change out of the precious suit and put on her old clothes, which felt baggy and shapeless after a morning spent in the perfect-fitting jacket and skirt, though her feet were glad of her socks and plimsolls after so long in the elegant court shoes Frederick and Jeanie had bought her for her birthday.

Then it was back to letting down hems on summer school uniforms for a couple of children in the village, which reminded Evie and Sue of Robert and altering his school uniform, and this deflated them even more.

'I wish the telephone would ring, Grandma, and someone would ask for a blouse in midnight-blue voile,' said Evie, eyeing the lovely fabric on the shelf.

'So do I, love. I thought when we placed those adverts in the *Redmond Gazette* that we'd be turning folk away. Almost every last penny went on that ad.'

'Maybe Mum will mention us to someone. Frederick seems to know a lot of people – that is, he gets around and Mum goes with him to so many places now – and she did say she'd put a word in for us if the chance came.'

But two weeks went by and the telephone didn't ring once. Sue and Evie swallowed their disappointment and carried on with their mundane tasks. At least they still had those, though it didn't look to them as if they would be revisiting Mr Morris any time soon. Funds were getting low and every day they were more glad of the mundane work while their dreams were put on hold. They started making cutbacks at home and this further dampened their spirits. It was back to meals made of Mr Clackett's leftover vegetables, which drove Michael out to the pub in the evenings, where the locals would buy him a pint or two.

~

By the beginning of April the days were lengthening so fast that Sue declared she thought her eyesight was improving. She'd spent the dark winter peering under a table lamp as she stitched, and on a couple of occasions she'd had to ask Evie to finish something for her.

'It's sometimes difficult to get a sharp focus,' she said, 'but I reckon I'll improve with these longer days.'

Evie wasn't so sure, she worried terribly about her grandmother, but she knew better than to say anything. Evie was thinking she needed to take over some of her grandmother's work as her fingers always got stiff and swollen in the cold. She had pressed the fabric and laid it flat on the big work table when the door opened with a crash and her father stomped in with a furious look on his face.

'What's the matter, Dad?' checked Evie kindly, just as Sue said, 'Out! Get them mucky boots out of here at once, Michael Carter.'

Michael strode out without a word, almost slamming the door to the big kitchen in Evie's face as she followed him, all concern, and Sue heaved herself to her feet with a sigh and went to see what the matter was now.

When Sue saw Michael hurling his boots through the back door she had a horrible feeling she knew exactly what he was going to say.

'Go on, tell us, lad.'

'I've left Clackett's,' Michael announced, slumping down on a chair.

'Left?' she said wearily, going to put the kettle on.

'Yes, left. Clackett gave me my notice so I told

him I'd not be working it and I'd rather leave straight away.'

'But why, Dad? What's happened? I thought you were getting on all right there these days.'

'Well, you thought wrong,' he shouted. 'Seems Clackett were only keeping me on until that Martin of his were old enough to go to work there. Martin's leaving school this summer and so there'll be no job for me.'

'Oh, Dad, I am sorry,' said Evie. She went to give him a hug, which he shrugged off.

'You could have worked your notice, Michael. At least you'd have been paid until summer.'

'I'll get summat else, don't you worry,' said Michael, though he didn't sound as if he believed it.

'You could always go and tell Mr Clackett that you've changed your mind,' ventured Evie.

'I'll not set foot on that bugger's land again. He wants blood, sweat and tears for his bit of money and I've done with the mud and the cold. I don't care if I never see another cabbage.'

Sue made a pot of tea, her brain whirring with options that Michael might consider. Because there was one thing she was sure of: he wasn't going to sit here in the kitchen doing nothing while she and Evie sat stitching all day.

'Now that the days are getting warmer, it might be better there?'

'Perhaps you could ask around the village, Michael—' began Sue.

'Just shut up and let me drink my tea in peace for a minute,' Michael said wearily. 'It's all right, I'll be out of your hair before long. I won't be in the way of your precious sewing.'

Sue chose not to answer and the two women slipped away back to their work, which they took up in silence, the only sound the grind of Evie's shears through the fabric.

'Shall I go and ask Mr Clackett to give Dad his job back until Martin joins him in the summer?' asked Evie.

Sue smiled a sad smile. 'No, love, don't waste your breath. Do you think he'd go if you did?'

Quiet work resumed. Evie felt sick with worry, where was their next meal coming from if they didn't have Clackett's leftovers?

Suddenly the door opened and there were Jack and Monty.

'Hello. What's up? You two look a bit gloomy,' said Jack.

'Our Michael's lost his job at Clackett's.'

'I'm sorry to hear that,' said Jack, frowning. 'It wasn't more trouble about him being at the Red Lion, was it?'

Sue explained about Mr Clackett wanting his son to come into the business full time when he left school in the summer.

' . . . So Michael's taken umbrage and left now,' she concluded.

'Where is he? Shall I go and see him?' Jack wasn't keen but he felt he should offer support.

'I wouldn't, lad. He's in the back, but with you being Frederick's man and all, I don't want you getting caught up in something you can do nowt about. I've noticed you've not been round here of an evening, and I don't suppose you came by today to see Michael, did you?'

'I had expected him to be over the road.' Jack was keeping his voice down now. 'I came by with a little something for you that Jeanie found in a junk shop. She and Frederick thought it'd be useful so I've brought it round in the van.'

'Well, bring it in, lad,' Sue said, looking at Evie in excitement.

Jack disappeared while Monty came over to be petted by Evie. Jack reappeared a couple of minutes later with . . .

'Good grief, Jack. It's a dressmaker's dummy.'

'It certainly is,' said Jack, carrying the figure in and placing it on its castors in front of the window. 'What do you think? Jeanie was a bit anxious you wouldn't want it when she'd bought it, but Frederick said in that case you are to send it back with me and he can sell it on.'

'Oh, no, it's perfect!' Evie gasped. 'Exactly what we need. Thank you for bringing it, and please thank Mum and Frederick for thinking of us, won't you?' She felt sad that her mum hadn't come around but was pleased she'd thought of them.

'Of course, Evie.'

'Thank you, Jack,' Sue joined in. 'I've never had one of these before. I never thought I would have either,' she smiled.

With a cheery wave, Jack was gone, his loyal dog following at his heels.

Evie went over to inspect the dummy. A medium size, it was covered in a fawn-coloured calico.

'I've got an idea,' Evie said, and disappeared upstairs, returning shortly with the tailored suit. 'If we dress the dummy it can show off the clothes we've made – when it's not being used, that is.'

Sue watched as Evie did just that, her young fingers working quickly and confidently.

'Looks lovely. If only we had some folk in to see it.'

'Grandma, it's only a matter of time, I know it. In the meantime I'm going to get this blouse made and then the dummy can wear that, too!'

'We'll have to visit your mother to thank her.'

'Will you tell her about Dad?' asked Evie.

'I suppose we'd better, love,' she replied sadly.

~

It was Easter at the end of the week, and time hadn't improved Michael's temper. Evie guessed the news would be all around the village now, and her dad said he'd been asking around, but he always seemed to end up in the pub.

~

Michael had just been to a farm a couple of miles outside the village where he'd heard they needed a cow man, but when he told Evie and Sue about the muck and the smell, even he had to join in their laughter at the thought of him working with a herd of cows.

'Smell was terrible,' he said.

'Well, of course it was, Dad,' said Evie. 'We may live in the country now but we're townies. I don't think farm work is for you, but I suppose you needed to go to find that out. I heard Miss Richards wants some help digging her garden – maybe you could help her?'

'Oh, that Miss Richards is a good sort,' said Michael, 'but I'm not sure I want to do any more digging.'

'You don't have much choice,' Sue said, firmly, turning Michael back out through the door. 'Don't throw away her kindness.'

That night, as she lay in bed, Evie worried greatly. Now her brothers had been gone so long, Sue had moved into what had been the boys' room so Evie had a bedroom to herself. She could hear Sue's distant snoring and she got up and went to the window, which looked onto the backyard. The sky was black and cloudless, and she shivered. Evie couldn't help thinking of that cold dark evening when she and Peter had gone to find Robert, and tears filled her eyes. She would never get over it, but was starting to learn to deal with it. But she missed her brothers and her mum so much. And all the folk on Shenty Street. Billy especially. With that thought, Evie climbed back into bed and cried herself to sleep.

The sun had barely risen when Evie made her way downstairs, hoping to get a head start on work. But Sue was already up and a little unsteady on her feet as she stepped around the kitchen making some breakfast.

'Just tired eyes, love, that's all,' she assured Evie. 'I'll be better after a good night's sleep.'

But Evie was not so sure. She'd noticed that Sue was still stitching by the light of the lamp, even during the sunnier days, and she'd had to ask Evie about colour-matching some thread several times. Evie had been too worried about the lack of work to think much about it, but now she vowed to keep a more careful watch on her beloved grandmother.

As they worked on their stitching, Evie kept a watchful eye on Sue. When Michael came in at the end of the afternoon, he declared he'd had a good day at Lavender Cottage. He looked happier than he had for months.

'Margaret only wants me to help her do the boring bits, she says,' he smiled, 'so there's a bit of digging, pots to wash and the paths to sweep. She does all the clever stuff herself, but she did show me how to do some pruning. She says I made a decent job of it.'

Evie was delighted to hear her father so cheerful. She couldn't remember him expressing any interest in his work since they'd left Bolton – and possibly long before that.

'I'm so glad, Dad,' she said. 'She and Letty are such good friends to us. We're lucky to have them.'

'We are, that,' he agreed. 'Now what's for tea? I'll peel some spuds, if you like, and you can make a start on it.' Evie had never known her dad to help, but she'd been so busy with her sewing . . .

'Oh, no, I forgot all about tea, Dad! I don't know if we've got anything much. Now that you don't get the vegetables given, we've sort of run out. I'm not used to buying them.'

She was fearful for a moment that Michael's good mood might evaporate, especially when he fell silent.

Then he said, 'Well, it's lucky I've got some pennies from Margaret. Here, Evie, you nip over to Suttons' before they close and choose summat for tonight.' And he gave her some coins.

Evie flew out without even her coat on to catch the general store, which was open every day, bank holidays included, arriving breathless.

311

She looked at the goods on the shelves and in the fridge and chose a minced beef pie and some carrots and potatoes.

Mrs Sutton put them in a paper carrier for her, enquiring, as she always did, about Sue.

'She all right, your grandma?'

'Yes, thank you, Mrs Sutton. Her eyes get tired with all the stitching but then she's getting old and I think mebbe she needs new glasses.'

'It's just, well, the last time she was in here she was finding it hard to see what she wanted on the shelves, though it was right in front of her and as plain as could be to me.'

'Oh? She never said.'

'I helped her out and she said she hadn't spotted it, but then she went out right past Mrs Lambert without a word. Oh, don't worry, Mrs Lambert said she thought Mrs Goodwin was preoccupied and hadn't noticed her. She's a nice woman and not one to take offence.'

'No, of course not . . . ' Josie had been polite enough not to mention it, but Evie was puzzled and not a little worried. 'Thank you for telling me, Mrs Sutton.'

She went home with her pie and vegetables, full of new worries.

After they'd eaten and washed up, Michael went to the Red Lion with some of the money Miss Richards had paid him and Evie made a pot of tea.

'You all right, Grandma?' she asked, sitting down beside Sue at the kitchen table.

'Never better, lass. Why?'

'Well, I've noticed you seem to be having trouble with your eyes. You've always got the lamp on, even during the day, and you've asked me a couple of times about matching a colour, and I think you're finding it hard to see what's right in front of you.'

Sue was silent for a few moments. Then: 'You're right, love. It is getting difficult to see to sew, but mebbe I just need new glasses.'

'Are your eyes hurting at all, Grandma?'

'No, lass.'

'No headaches – you would tell me, wouldn't you?'

'My head's fine, Evie.'

'Shall we go and see if we can get you some new glasses?'

'I'm sure I'm all right, love. I'll think about it.'

~

The following day Evie took a few coins out of the tin Sue kept to cover small expenses and went over to Suttons'. As she approached, she could see a couple of women gossiping outside the shop. Hearing the name 'Carter', she stood quite still behind the pillar box to listen.

' . . . heard their mother ran away and now lives with her fancy man in Redmond: only Frederick

Bailey, if you please, he that owns their place and those two houses further down.'

Evie didn't want to listen but she couldn't help it.

'What, him that's had all those wives! I don't believe it. I thought I hadn't seen her around but I'd no idea she'd done a runner. Always thought she was flighty. Far too pretty for her own good.'

'Disgraceful, if you ask me. One child dead, one living with other people, and that scruffy-looking urchin now dolling herself up and going off on the bus to Redmond. What's she doing there dressed like that, I'd like to know. It's plain to me that the mother hasn't kept her on the straight and narrow. Like mother, like daughter I should say.'

Evie was torn between running away and giving the gossips the tongue-lashing she felt they deserved. But then she remembered she was now the new Evie. Grown-up and with the courage to face the gossips down with dignity, not run away crying like a child.

She swallowed down her anger while taking note of what these two middle-aged women looked like. She knew neither of their names, but she vowed to find them out. Then she drew herself up to her full height to give herself courage. She stepped forward and they turned to see her. If she hadn't been so cross she'd have laughed at the looks on their faces.

'I think you'll find,' Evie said, 'that people who know us – people who aren't gossiping in the street like fishwives – are very pleased for my grandmother and me to be running a successful dressmaker's, and if you think wearing a nice outfit is somehow immoral, I expect you'll be making saints, the pair of you.' Leaving the gossips open-mouthed and silent in astonishment, she went into the shop.

'Hello, Evie, dear,' said Mrs Sutton. 'What can I get you?'

Evie asked for her few essentials and Mrs Sutton helped her.

'Who are those women I saw just now in front of the shop?' asked Evie casually.

'Oh, Mrs Bradshaw and Mrs Pinnock, I think you mean,' offered Mrs Sutton.

She decided not to tell Sue what she'd heard in case it upset her, but when she got back to Pendle's Sue could sense Evie buzzing with energy at the encounter.

'You all right, love?' Sue asked. 'Only you look like you're bursting with summat to say.'

'No, Gran, I'm fine,' said Evie. 'But I overheard one woman in the street saying I looked flighty, like my mum.'

'Oh love, don't you listen to them.'

'You don't think everyone is saying that, do you? I couldn't bear it if folk or you thought badly of Mum and me when we've done nowt wrong.'

'Don't you worry, Evie. No one who matters thinks badly of you at all.'

But whatever her grandmother said, Evie felt sick that everyone was thinking bad of her family. She felt that no good would come of this.

CHAPTER SIXTEEN

'I've got a job!' Michael beamed. 'I start tomorrow. It's a small place just outside Redmond, bit of a walk from the bus, though.'

'What do you have to do?' asked Evie. 'Is it difficult?'

'No, lass, I'm only sweeping up and fetching and carrying at a shoe factory, as far as I know. There's no skill involved.'

'Mebbe you'll work your way up to do the shoe-making.'

'I doubt it, our Evie. It looks to be quite a skilled job. Lots of stitching, but bigger machines than your grandma's.' He laughed loudly. 'Still, it's indoors, which has got to be better than Clackett's.'

'You won't forget to let Margaret Richards know that you've got a job now and won't be going there to help her in the garden, will you, Michael?'

'Well, Sue, I was thinking, mebbe when the

weather's fine, at weekends, I could go down and see what she wants doing, if that suits her.'

Evie and Sue looked at each other in astonishment. This was a turnaround!

'Good idea, Dad,' said Evie, when she'd managed to compose her face.

~

Suddenly it was just Evie and Sue alone all day at Pendle's and the atmosphere lifted slightly. They worked hard, hardly stopping to eat at lunchtime, and the workroom was abuzz with the sound of the treadle machine and the grind of scissors through fabric. Working on a client's clothes by herself, Evie sensed for the first time in her life that things had turned a corner and she felt the flutterings of happiness.

On the Thursday they took the bus to Redmond to look at the market, and to go to the doctor, as Sue's eyes were getting worse. They shuffled into the consulting room, Sue looking as if she was going to her execution and leaving her coat with Evie, who sat nervously waiting.

Time passed slowly and Evie started to worry: did it usually take this long? Eventually the door opened and a white-faced Sue emerged.

'What is it, Grandma? Tell me,' whispered Evie, her heart hammering.

'It's a *degeneration* thing, love –' Sue pronounced the word carefully '– something to do with my age, and the rest is just bad luck. It's only in one eye, though, and if I have new glasses then I'll be able to see through the other one better than at present.'

'Oh, Grandma! Oh, I'm sorry. Will it get worse? Will you . . . you won't go blind, will you?' The very idea filled her with horror.

'No, love, but it might get worse.'

Tears sprang to Evie's eyes. Just when their lives were beginning to improve at last, too! It was so unfair! Better go and tell Jeanie the bad news while they were here.

~

'Er, we wondered if we could beg a cup of tea, Mum, please? Grandma's been to the doctor's and it's not good news.'

Jeanie was at once all concern, and led Sue down the winding stairs to the kitchen.

'There's nothing to be done.' Evie explained the sad situation. 'Grandma's only sixty-four and we've got such plans for the dressmaking. It's starting to take off, and bring some money in. If Grandma can't see to sew then I shall have to do all the work myself. I don't know if I'll be able to manage that. I'm worried about Grandma and I'm worried that it might all be too much for me . . . ' She sniffed and mopped her eyes with her hankie.

~

Ada Taylor had a bit of a summer cold. She claimed she hadn't really felt well since the snow in February and now, towards the end of June, she was petulant, moany and demanding.

Billy had done his best to tend to her, and had even gone to the surgery to ask the doctor to come round. The doctor had done so, then declared Mrs Taylor had only a mild summer cold and a severe dose of self-pity, and he told Billy not to waste his time bothering him again unless she took a turn for the worse.

Billy, too, was feeling the effects of his mother's illness – not in his own health, but in the demands she made of him. For the last week she'd taken to staying in bed for much of the day, saying she was too ill to get up and do the housework. At first Billy tried to take on the chores himself when he got home from work, but then Ada fretted he might not have cleaned the kitchen well enough, or that the shopping he'd bought entirely at Mr Amsell's on the way home from work was more expensive than taking a trip to the bigger shops in the nearest high street. There was no pleasing her.

Billy had to leave her by herself all day to go to

work, which meant making her a sandwich before
he left and leaving it under a plate, in case she really
did feel too ill to make her own. At least there
seemed to be nothing wrong with her appetite. The
food was always gone by the time Billy arrived home,
the plates left for him to wash.

'Are you sure you're not well enough to get up,
Mum?' he asked eventually. 'If you can manage the
afternoons you could do a bit of light housework
then, something to occupy you, like, and it'd be to
your own high standards.'

'Billy, you wouldn't ask it of me if you felt like I
do,' Ada moaned, coughing into her hankie.

'Would you like me to ask someone to visit you,
Mum?' he suggested. He racked his brains. He
thought of Marie Sullivan, but decided she had
enough to do with her large family. Dora Marsh?
But Mrs Marsh, though she had a heart of gold,
was of the old school, like Sue Goodwin, and
she'd probably tell Ada to buck up and get on
with it. Geraldine Sullivan? Gerry was a cheerful
sort, and he knew his mother liked her. He would
understand, though, if she declined to visit. How
he wished Evie was here; she'd look in, he was
sure.

Gerry reluctantly agreed, however, when he
popped in to ask her as he passed the corner shop.
'I'll not be able to stop long, though, Billy,' she said,
primping the back of her new hairstyle. The queues

for morning papers at Mr Amsell's were even longer than before since Gerry Sullivan had changed her style.

'Oh, Geraldine, love, is that you?' called Ada in a shaky voice when she heard the key in the front door at lunchtime. Billy had given Gerry a spare key when she'd agreed to visit.

'It is, Mrs Taylor.' There was the sound of light footsteps on the stairs and Gerry put her head round Ada's bedroom door. 'Oh, you poor thing. Is it a bad cold you've got? Here, I've brought you some sweets from the shop.' She handed Ada a box of fruit gums. 'By, it's hot in here, Mrs Taylor. Shall I open the window?'

Before Ada could object the window was opened and fresher air entered the musty room.

'How are you feeling today, Mrs Taylor?'

'Not so good, Geraldine, love. I don't know if I shall make it to Christmas at this rate.'

'I'm sorry to hear that,' said Gerry.

Billy had briefed her about his mother's mood. 'I don't know what she's after, Gerry. Sometimes she just wants some attention, so if you can bear to go and see her, at least she'll have a fresh face to look at. Mebbe she'll snap out of it when she thinks she's stayed in bed long enough.'

'Would you like me to make you a cup of tea, Mrs Taylor? Billy says he's left you a sandwich.'

'Oh . . . Geraldine, that would be so kind. I haven't

anyone to make tea for me, what with Billy out all day on his rounds. He's a good lad, though.'

He's a saint to put up with you. 'He is indeed,' agreed Geraldine, sweetly.

Ada was encouraged by this reply. 'Do you see much of Billy, Geraldine, love?'

'Oh, yes, Billy and I are great friends,' she beamed. 'We've known each other for years and . . . well, you grow closer over time – you know what I mean?' she added artlessly.

Ada perked up for a moment, forgetting she wouldn't make it to Christmas.

'If you make me that tea, love, we can have a little chat,' she suggested. 'Have a cup yourself,' she added.

'Thank you, Mrs T. I'll just go down and do it.'

A few seconds later Gerry called up, 'The tea caddy's empty, Mrs Taylor. Have you another packet?'

'I keep it in the sideboard in the front room,' called back Ada, her voice surprisingly strong.

Gerry went to find it and was astonished when she saw the size of the hoard of tea. Saints above, the woman must be mad! It looked like she'd withstand a siege. How many were there? Out of sheer naughtiness she quickly pulled the packets of tea out to count them. If nothing else it would make a good tale to confide to her mother. Twenty-five!

And what was this? She reached in and extracted two envelopes that had been right at the back of the cupboard behind all the tea. Both of them were addressed to Billy and neither had been opened. Strange . . . She looked at them carefully. There was something familiar about the hand-writing . . . Mary had had letters in the same round schoolgirl hand. Suddenly Geraldine knew. There was no doubt these letters were from Evie Carter, and no doubt either that Billy's mother had taken them and hidden them from him. After all, why would Billy himself have not opened them, and why would he hide them in the sideboard, which was definitely his mother's territory?

For a moment Geraldine debated with herself whether to put the letters back where she'd found them and forget all about them. They were, after all, nothing to do with her. But she knew that Billy had been out of sorts since his split from Evie, and Brendan had said that the poor lad hadn't even known about what happened to Robert. A quick glance at the dates of the postmarks confirmed these letters had arrived last winter and Geraldine would have put money on it that they contained the vital news.

She quickly put all the packets of tea back in the sideboard, arranging them as they were but with a gap at the front to show she had taken one out. Then, as she went back into the kitchen, she slipped the letters into her handbag, which she'd left in the hall. It wasn't stealing, she told herself. It was Ada

324

who was the thief. These were Billy's letters and she would be simply delivering them into his hands at last.

Her conscience clear, Geraldine made the tea, found the sandwich on the kitchen table and took Ada's lunch upstairs for her. Out of sheer devilment she'd put three spoons of sugar in the tea.

'Here you are, Mrs Taylor. It really is hot in here.' Fanning herself, she went to open the window even wider. 'Nothing like fresh air to bring colour to your cheeks.' She smiled kindly at Ada.

'I don't know about that—'

'So how long have you felt bad, Mrs Taylor?'

'Ooh, weeks at least. I've not been right since the snow.'

'And have you seen the doctor?' Geraldine had been told all about the doctor's visit but she was feeling spiteful since she'd found Billy's letters.

'Hmm. He was no use.'

'Oh dear, whatever did he say?'

Ada looked abashed. 'He said it's only a summer cold and we weren't to waste his time again,' she muttered.

'Oh dear, how cruel! And there's you suffering. Maybe you should get a second opinion, Mrs Taylor. Perhaps you should go up to the hospital and demand to see one of the doctors there, what with you doubtful about making it to Christmas. Still, that's six months yet,' she added cheerfully.

Ada was at a loss how to take this suggestion so she decided to move the conversation on from her health.

'So you and Billy have grown closer, you say?' she asked.

'Mmm. He's a grand lad.'

'And you're a lovely lass. You know, Geraldine, I always dreamed of having a daughter-in-law like you, someone right pretty and knows how to dress herself well. Any man would be proud to have you on his arm.'

'Well, thank you, Mrs Taylor.'

'And I reckon, with all them brothers of yours, that you know how to do things properly around the house. I'm sure you'd fit in well here, love. I'd leave you a free hand at the chores and I've never been one for eating fancy food – just plain cooking – so there'd not be owt complicated for you to learn.'

'Now, I best be getting back to the shop.' Geraldine got up, cutting Ada off. 'I'll let myself out and give Billy the key when I see him.' *And his letters, you miserable old woman.* 'I'm sure you'll be feeling better soon.'

She went downstairs, leaving the window in Ada's room wide open, rinsed out her cup and the teapot, and called a cheerful goodbye up the stairs.

Out in the street she vowed to deliver the letters to Billy at the soonest opportunity. It might be awkward to explain how she'd come by them but she could work round that. It was Ada's conscience that should be worried, not her own.

~

'It's so beautiful here,' breathed Evie, walking slowly along the track around the fields at the back of Clackett's market garden.

'Bliss,' smiled Letty, stopping to raise her face to the sun.

'It's good of Grandma to give me a bit of time off. Two women arrived with babies in prams, wanting little frocks made for them, so as Grandma likes to do the baby clothes I was pleased to leave her to it. The workroom was beginning to feel a bit crowded. The babies were good as gold but the mothers always fuss something terrible.'

They sank down onto some soft grass and Evie idly started a daisy chain.

'I didn't really notice how peaceful and nice it was last summer, what with us only just arriving here and everything to sort out,' Evie went on. 'Pete and Bob liked the other side of the road, the path that leads to the woods. I don't think I shall ever go there again, though.'

'I don't blame you, Evie. I'd feel the same.'

Letty looked down shyly. 'I think I may be a bit in love with Jack. He's just the kindest man I've ever met.'

'He is kind. I don't know where we'd be without Jack's help this last year. But I've seen the way he is with you, and how you seem . . . I don't know . . . to understand each other without owt being said.'

'Yes, it's true!' gasped Letty. 'That's exactly how I feel. It's such a special thing.'

Evie was delighted. 'And does Jack feel the same?'

'I think so. He's taken to coming round to Lavender Cottage more often, and Aunt Margaret was asking me only the other day if we had any special feelings for each other.'

'And she wouldn't mind if you fell completely in love with Jack, and he with you, would she?'

'Good heavens, no. Even though he's more her age than mine, and has all sorts of odd and part-time jobs running together, I don't think she'd care in the least if I was happy.'

'She is lovely, your aunt, and Jack's lovely, too.'

'And so am I, and so are you!' Letty giggled. 'We're the loveliest people in the entire world.'

'What are you two giggling about?' asked Peter, coming up the path unseen.

'Ah, here's lovely Peter,' said Evie, and she and Letty roared with laughter.

'Idiots,' he muttered affectionately.

'Just girls' talk. You wouldn't understand, Pete,' said Evie.

'I came with a message from Grandma,' said Peter, sinking down on the grass next to them. 'You know,

I blame Dad for everything – us having to leave Shenty Street and all our friends, and then about . . . about Bob, and then Mum going, and then losing his job, and making it so that poor Grandma and you had to work every hour to make enough money, Evie, but now I can see that Mum leaving was the best thing for her. We all want her to be happy, don't we? I went round yesterday after school and Mum and Frederick are so very happy. It's strange, but I can feel it the moment I go in the house.'

'I've felt that, too,' said Evie. 'Of course I miss her, but you're not here any more and I'm working so hard with Grandma that I feel now we can let Mum go and be glad for her. That's something else I thought would be awful but turned out right. Mum deserves to have a nice life after looking after all of us and everything she put up with in Shenty Street.'

'Dad, you mean?'

'Well, yes. But he's doing all right with his job at the shoe factory – that is, he goes to it every day and stays there until it's time to come home, and I expect he does some work in between. He's bought himself a bicycle to save the bus fare to Redmond and then the walk to the factory. He doesn't say much about the job, but at least he doesn't moan like he did about Mr Clackett.'

Letty chipped in. 'He's being a huge help to Aunt Margaret. She was saying only last weekend how pleased she is to have your father to help her keep it tidy.'

'Well, that's good,' said Peter. 'Mebbe he's found a job he can manage not to mess up. Anyway, this message from Grandma: could you pop round to see Mr Harris, please? He hasn't got something you ordered but he's got something else instead. I expect it will make sense when you speak to him.'

'It doesn't sound very urgent,' said Evie.

'It is if you want to catch him this afternoon. It's getting on for five o'clock.'

'Oh, no, I've lost all track of time. I'd better hurry. Bye, Letty. Bye, Pete. See you soon.' She rushed away down the track.

'There she goes, all in a flutter, expecting the worst,' laughed Peter. 'Will she ever learn?'

'Oh, don't be so unkind, Pete. It's worrying about getting things right that makes her such a good seamstress. If she didn't care about the details she'd be hopeless.'

'You're right, of course, and I didn't mean to criticise. I only wish . . . I don't know.'

'What?'

'I just want Evie to be happy. She holds the weight of our family on her shoulders.'

'Well, who knows what's round the corner?'

'True. Even Billy let her down. I know she was disappointed when Billy didn't reply to her letters, especially when she told him about Bob. Whatever their differences, the way Billy treated her then was bad. But she's over it – and over him – now, I think.'

'She never mentions him, that's for certain.'

'So it would be nice if she were to find someone who suited her so well that she'd never have to worry again.'

'Why, Peter Carter, you old romantic! I'd never guess you're only a schoolboy. Perhaps Evie *has* found someone who suits her,' suggested Letty with a naughty glint in her eye.

'Who are you thinking of?'

'This Mr Harris, of course. Oh, but imagine if she were to marry him. She'd have all the fabrics in his vast shop to choose from and she'd never have to negotiate a discount again!'

Peter couldn't help laughing at the idea. 'Let's hope Evie's luck is about to change,' he said.

CHAPTER SEVENTEEN

Billy sat on his bed and read the two letters Evie had sent him way back at the end of last year. Geraldine Sullivan had said they'd fallen out of the sideboard when she was fetching a packet of tea for his mum, and she thought Billy had maybe put them down and forgotten about them and Ada had tidied them away by mistake. Well, full marks for invention to Gerry, and she was sticking to her story even if it didn't hold much water.

The first letter was a simple and heartfelt apology for Evie's part in the argument at Geraldine's party. When he'd read the letter, Billy thought back to that evening when he'd last seen Evie and the stupid argument that had divided them. He tried to remember who had said what but, in the way of most arguments, the subtlety of both sides' words had become lost in time. He did remember their differences had turned on something Evie said

333

about not wanting to live with his mother, and now he wholeheartedly agreed. How could he have thought anyone would want to live with such a woman? He didn't! Oh, he'd always known she was selfish, but this . . .

Then he read the other letter and was surprised to find tears in his eyes at the account of Robert's death. The page was smudged in places and Billy thought that Evie had also shed tears as she wrote it. It was such a brave letter, and included in the envelope was a pretty Christmas card with glitter and a robin on the front, wishing both Billy and his mother a merry Christmas. At the sight of that Billy could contain his misery no longer and he gave himself up to weeping for that lovely girl and her dead little brother.

Eventually he pulled himself together. What must she have thought of him when he hadn't written back?

There was a tap at the door and Ada, who seemed to have rallied since Gerry's visit, called, 'Billy, love, your tea will be ready in ten minutes.'

Billy considered not answering her, but he didn't want her to know anything about his having the letters yet. He'd decide how to play this in his own time.

'Thank you, Mum,' he called back with little enthusiasm for the prospect of having her company over his evening meal.

C'mon, Billy, think! What's should we do about this?

Was there anything to do about it? All kinds of things could have happened in six months. Maybe the Carters weren't even living in Church Sandleton any longer. Perhaps when Robert died they couldn't face it there and had moved on. After all, there had been nothing to take them to the village in the first place except a need to escape Shenty Street, and it was just somewhere that a cousin of Brendan Sullivan's knew about.

Even if they were still there, Evie's circumstances could have changed dramatically. She was six months older – seventeen, now – and she might well have a new boyfriend. A boyfriend who lived nearby and was able to see her all the time. A boyfriend who didn't argue with her and who hadn't got a spiteful mother.

Dear God, how had he even imagined Evie would *ever* want to come to live with his mother? The idea was ridiculous! Her arguing, far from being the thoughtless response of a young girl, now appeared nothing more than common sense. It was he who had been stupid, not Evie.

But then maybe Evie hadn't got a boyfriend at all – maybe she'd got a husband! The thought, though unlikely in so short a time, was terrible, but Billy couldn't help niggling at it like a bad tooth. Soon his imagination was running riot. If Evie was married – very happily married – and lived in her own house, not at Pendle's, then if he wrote to her, Jeanie would be quite justified in withholding the letter from her. What newlywed would want a letter from an old boyfriend forwarded to her blissful new life?

All through that awkward evening meal Billy's mind churned with various imaginings, some bizarre and others credible, until he no longer knew what was plausible, or what to do about it.

He went back up to his room as soon as he could escape Ada, and then to bed, but he couldn't sleep with his thoughts in turmoil.

The next morning he got up even earlier than usual for work and went off while Ada was still asleep, leaving her a note to say he was going out that evening and she was not to cook him any tea or wait up.

After work he went down to the Lord Nelson for a pie and a pint, and the hope of catching Brendan Sullivan. Billy's friends at the postal depot were good fun but he drew the line at confiding this whole sorry story to any of them for their advice.

'All right, Billy, lad?' asked Brendan, coming in and seeing him looking miserable and nursing his pint by himself.

'Ah, Brendan.' Billy brightened. It was Brendan who had masterminded the Carters' flit from Shenty Street, and a good job he'd made of it. Plus, he was the father of two daughters around Evie's age, and possibly he even had sisters of his own. Brendan was the best man to help him sort out this mess, no question.

'What are you having? This one's on me, Brendan, and if you've got the time, I could really do with some advice,' said Billy.

Brendan agreed. He sat down with Billy and listened to the tale of woe, from the argument at the party last November to the letters Billy had been handed only yesterday by Brendan's own daughter.

'Gerry meant it for the best when she gave me the letters,' Billy finished. 'I might have found them myself one day and, as it is, they're six months old, but at least they've not been hidden from me for years. I'm only hoping it may not be too late to do summat about being reunited with Evie.'

Brendan had to smile at Gerry's part in the tale. She was a bold girl who didn't put up with any nonsense, and Ada Taylor was a bigger fool than she'd yet shown herself to be if she thought she'd have had an easy time of it had Gerry and Billy married. As it was, Gerry was seriously involved with Colin Fraser, who suited her in every way.

'Well, lad, I'm fairly certain that young Evie Carter isn't married, at least,' Brendan said. 'Sure, Marie and Mary would not have let that golden nugget of news escape circulation. I also know that most of the family still live in Church Sandleton, or they did when my womenfolk last heard from them, which I think must have been Easter. Just a card and a brief letter with good wishes. It's hard to keep in touch at such a long distance as the time goes by, but I know Sue Goodwin, bless her, would have tried to let us know if they'd moved away or something big had happened in the meantime . . . as she did when that poor lad of theirs died, and when Jeanie left home.'

Billy looked surprised. 'Evie's mum's gone?'

'Aye, lad, some while ago. Don't know the details.'

Oh no, it looked as if things were going from bad to worse for the Carters. First, that awful business with Robert, and then Jeanie leaving. What must the others be feeling? Billy knew how important her family were to Evie and he started to imagine her all alone and grieving for her brother and her mother, which – he really must stop this and behave like a rational man – was absurd.

'So I don't know quite how things are with them at the minute, Billy, but circumstances have definitely changed since Evie wrote to you at Christmas.'

'What do you think I should do, Brendan? I don't want to blunder in where I'm not wanted, but how do I even know . . . ?'

Brendan ordered another couple of pints and he and Billy sat thinking on a course of action.

'There's only one thing for it, so far as I can see, young fella,' said Brendan eventually. 'You'll have to go down there, find Evie and speak to her. If you write, you can't be sure she'll get the letter, and even if she does she may not reply straight away, and in the meantime you'd be left wondering. I can see already that you can hardly live with yourself, not knowing.'

Billy acknowledged this, thinking he also had to live with his mother while he sorted this out, however long it took. At present, this was not a happy prospect.

'You're right, Brendan. I'm owed some holiday from work so I'll take time off and sort this out. Mum wants to go to Blackpool, but she can go on her own, for all I care.'

'That's the spirit, Billy, though I don't mean about your ma.'

'I'll arrange it as soon as possible – next week, even. You're right: if I explain to Evie, to her face, then I shall know once and for all.'

'Well, I hope it works out for you, Billy, I really do. Evie Carter's a grand girl and we were all sorry when you two fell out.'

'Thank you, Brendan, and thank you for your advice.'

Billy and Brendan chatted on, finishing their pints, then Billy took a stroll the long way home in the light June evening. When he let himself into the terraced house in Fawcett Street he could hear the sound of the radio coming from the sitting room, so he called, 'Goodnight, Mum,' as he passed and left Ada to her own company.

The next morning Billy went to work early again, eager to arrange a couple of days off as soon as he could. His holiday was agreed for the beginning of the following week, and he decided to withhold this information from Ada for the time being.

By the time he got home that evening Ada had worked out that something had happened to put Billy out of sorts, but she was at a loss to know what.

'What's up, love?' she asked, pouring him a cup of tea.

'Nowt, Mum.'

'Oh, but I think there is, Billy. Is it summat I can help with?'

'No, Mum. I told you, it's nowt. Thank you for the tea.' He took the cup of tea upstairs with him and spent the time before eating feeling both resentful and a bit triumphant at having secretly arranged his days off.

It was a hot evening and Ada had prepared a salad of tinned sardines, which further fuelled Billy's keenness to get away, however briefly. Ada wasn't making much of an effort domestically these days. Billy thought she'd got used to lying in bed and out of the habit of cooking. The unappetising meal passed mostly in silence, and then Billy washed up and went up to his room.

On the Saturday evening Geraldine Sullivan came calling after tea.

'There are a whole lot of us going to the pictures this evening, Billy. Would you like to come?'

Billy was delighted to accept – he didn't mind what the film was – and he quickly gathered his wallet and jacket, wished his mother a goodnight and left her alone with her wireless.

'Don't wait up,' Billy called, pulling the door to behind him.

There! Let her spend her time in her own company. Folk who stole other folk's letters didn't deserve any consideration, he thought.

It wasn't until Sunday evening, over another dismal meal, that Billy decided to tell Ada that he was getting a train south next morning to go to see Evie. He was about to come straight out with the information when Ada started talking about her hopes for a holiday.

'I've been thinking, Billy, you've been looking a bit tired of late, and not quite yourself,' she began. 'What you need is a holiday away from here.'

'I certainly do,' agreed Billy.

'Where shall we go, love? Do you fancy Blackpool again this year? Or we could go to Southport, which I always think is a bit smarter, like.'

'I fancy neither,' said Billy.

'Oh . . . ' Ada was put out. 'But we always go to the seaside. I thought you liked Blackpool.'

'I shan't be going anywhere with you, Mum. You go anywhere you fancy, but you can leave me out of your holiday plans because I've made plans of my own.'

'What? Billy! You might have said. I've been looking forward to my holiday.'

'Well, as I say, Mum, you can go on your own. Don't let me stop you.'

'But, Billy, where . . . ? What . . . ? Oh, I can't believe you've made plans and not even told me.'

'And why can't you believe it, Mum? It's the truth. After all, you took Evie Carter's letters and didn't tell me, and that's the truth, too.'

Ada looked flabbergasted. For a moment she sat there with her mouth opening and closing and no sound coming out at all.

Billy was grimly satisfied. If, for even a moment, he had thought his mother could possibly be inno-cent of the theft of the letters, her reaction was proof of her guilt. He sat waiting to see what she would say.

'I . . . I never—'

'Oh, but you did, Mum, didn't you?'

Silence.

'How else did they get into the sideboard? Hopped in there by themselves, did they?'

Ada was backed into a corner. 'Well, I was only protecting you, Billy, love. That girl showed her true colours at Geraldine's party and I didn't want you to be hurt by her any more. Those Carters are unre-liable folk and Evie's plainly as bad as her father.'

'It's not your place to steal my letters and make decisions about my life,' snapped Billy, his voice rising.

'It's my place when I can see you coming to harm, Billy.' Ada's voice was getting louder, too. 'It's a mother's role to keep her child from being hurt.'

'I'm a grown man and I can make my own mind up. I don't need you poking your nose in where it's not wanted and keeping me from the girl I love.'

'Love? I didn't see much return of love when that little madam went off back down south and didn't write for weeks, leaving you miserable. I decided then that if she could treat you like that it was better you didn't know her.'

'You decided? What right had you to decide? Don't you reckon I'm old enough to make up my own mind? You'd already taken against her before then. I haven't forgotten you wouldn't even welcome her as a guest in our home, and I'm downright ashamed of that. So you couldn't let us make up our differences – you had to stick your spoke in. You say you didn't want me to be hurt – well, how hurt do you think I feel to learn that Evie's little brother died, and she wrote to tell me and I didn't even know? How hurt do you think I am to discover that Evie wrote to make up our quarrel and I didn't know that either?'

'I only meant it for the best, Billy, love.'

'You meant to keep Evie and me apart because, you say, you don't like her father.'

'But can't you see it's over between you now? She's miles away and she's got her own life to lead down south now. She's never coming back here. You'll be hurt some more if you try to take up with her again. And leopards don't change their spots, son: she'll always be Michael Carter's daughter. She's hurt you once *and* she's shown herself to have a nasty temper—'

'Now you really are talking rubbish. The real reason you don't want me to be with Evie is because you're afraid I'll leave and go south and you'll be left here on your own. That's the truth, isn't it?'

'No, I've told you—'

'And I'm now telling you. You were never so against Evie when she lived in Shenty Street, but when you thought there was any chance I might one day go to be with her and not be here all the time, looking after you when you take to your bed for days, taking on the chores when I come home from work, listening to your moaning—'

For a moment Ada looked stricken but she had gone too far to retreat.

'I was ill, Billy. It's time for you to move on, find a new girl, someone who suits you better.'

'Someone who suits *you*, you mean. You just don't understand, do you? This is the girl I hoped one day to marry. I've booked a couple of days off work.

I'm taking the train tomorrow morning. I only hope I'm not too late. And if I am, it's all your fault, Mum, and I don't know how I'll ever forgive you.'

'Billy, don't speak to me like that,' lamented Ada. 'I can't bear it.'

'Well, Mum, you might just have to "bear it". Because you've brought it on yourself.'

With huge dignity Billy got up, scraped the remains of his lunch into the kitchen bin and went upstairs to pack a few things into his duffel bag.

~

The next morning Billy was still seething with anger, which fuelled his energy to be gone. He gathered the remainder of his belongings for the journey in his bag and put on his jacket.

There was no sound from Ada's room. Should he knock and say he was going now? He didn't fancy renewing the argument this morning, or listening to Ada's self-pity that she would be left alone. He wouldn't be gone long, anyway. That was a comfort: one way or another, this would be sorted out very soon.

He left the pot of tea he'd made under the tea cosy for her. Then he called up the stairs, 'Bye then, Mum. See you soon.'

When there was no reply he guessed she was

sulking and he wasn't going to waste time dealing with that.

He closed the front door carefully on the silent house and set off to find Evie.

~

The bell tinkled merrily at G. Morris as Evie entered the shop.

'Morning, Evie. My word, you look a picture in that striped cotton,' beamed George, coming round from behind the counter to greet her with a hand-shake, holding on to her hand a little longer than necessary.

Over the past weeks Evie had become a regular at the smart draper's shop and she and George were now very friendly. Evie sent her clients here if they wanted to choose their own fabrics, and she came here to choose them herself if the client preferred.

'Thank you, George. It's come out well, hasn't it? Stripes are always fun to work with.'

'Show me the back, then,' George asked, and Evie did a twirl to show off how she'd worked the stripes on the back of the bodice. 'Very nice indeed. So how are you, dear? And how is Mrs Goodwin?'

'We're both well, thank you, George. It's better for Grandma's eyes in the summer when the light is brighter.'

They exchanged more pleasantries and, as there

were no other customers in the shop, George brought out a tray of tea from the back room, and a plate of biscuits. Then they began the business of the day, Evie perched on a stool while George unfurled bolts of fabric and cards of trimmings to show her what was new while she drank her tea. Other customers came and went but although George served them all with his full attention and courtesy, no one else was privileged to the special treatment he offered Evie.

Evie chose some pretty prints for a summer two-piece and a blouse commissioned by Mrs Smedley, a client who was fast becoming a favourite: easy to fit, choosy but not fussy, and, best of all, she paid top price on delivery. This meant that Evie and Sue had money in hand to buy more fabrics, and so the small business ran smoothly. They made payment on delivery the rule now, having learned a lesson about that early on.

There had been an awkward business with Mrs Smythe, who had said she'd settle the invoice at the end of the week 'as is the usual way', and had shown Evie to the door of her house without paying. Evie had had a sinking feeling about this and she knew Sue would have demanded the money there and then, but maybe this was the way better-off folk did things. A fortnight later Mrs Smythe had still not paid and Evie had had to telephone to remind her.

'Oh, I didn't realise you were so in need of money,

dear,' said Jean Smythe, implying nastily that they were on their uppers, which, of course, they were.

'And I didn't realise it would be a problem for you to pay,' replied Evie, who'd rehearsed what she might say. 'You can always pay in instalments, if that would make it easier for you.'

There was a sharp intake of breath. 'That will not be necessary,' Mrs Smythe said haughtily.

'Then I shall expect the cheque in tomorrow's post,' said Evie. 'The address is on the invoice, or would you like me to remind you of it?'

'No thank you. I have it here.'

'Good. Then you have everything you need and I shall expect the cheque tomorrow,' finished Evie, and put down the phone. Her heart was thumping. What an awful woman Jean Smythe had turned out to be.

'She won't order anything more, I reckon,' she said to Sue, who had heard Evie's side of the conversation.

'Do you know what, love? I don't care,' Sue had replied. 'There's a name for those what take and don't pay and it's not a nice one.'

'Oh, I expect she'd have paid eventually.'

'We don't need clients like that, love. No use working and not being paid.'

The cheque had duly arrived the next morning.

'Now, Evie,' said George, parcelling up the fabrics in brown paper, 'I was wondering if . . . if you weren't too busy . . . and I can quite understand you might be . . . if, well . . . '

'Yes, George?' asked Evie. What on earth could he be trying to say?

'Well, that is . . . I was wondering if you'd care to go out to tea with me on Sunday? There's a little place that serves tea in the park, but the main draw is that there's a bandstand on Sunday afternoons in summer.'

'Oh, George, what a lovely idea.' Evie was delighted. 'Thank you for asking me. I'd be really pleased to go with you. I haven't had a day off for ages.'

George looked relieved. 'I'm so glad. I'll meet you at the station if you telephone me which train you'll be on. The music usually starts about three o'clock, but people come and go all the time.'

'I think we should try to get there at the start,' said Evie.

'I agree.'

She paid for the fabrics, put them carefully in her basket and, with a merry wave and a big smile, went to the door.

'I'll look forward to Sunday. It'll be a proper treat.'

'Goodbye, Evie, dear.'

George quickly went to open the door for her, then stood on the doorstep watching her walk over the cobbles and into the marketplace. Evie Carter really had got the prettiest smile . . .

∽

Evie hadn't seen her mother in weeks so she decided to drop in. As always when she approached Frederick's tall pretty house down the tiny Midsummer Row, she remembered the first time she had come here with her mother, and how that awful woman had stomped shouting down the steps. How much had happened since then! On this glorious June morning, the square was peaceful and the garden in the middle blossomed with flowering shrubs.

Evie rang the bell and Jeanie opened the door, looking beautiful but a bit flushed.

'Hello, love, how lovely to see you. You scrub up well,' she said, indicating the striped dress as Evie went inside.

'A Goodwin and Carter special, Mum,' laughed Evie. 'I've just had Mr Morris admiring it, too.'

'I reckon that draper's soft on you, love.'

'Nonsense, Mum. He must be three times my age. He likes to see a nice bit of sewing, that's all,' laughed Evie.

'Ha, it's all right, I'm teasing. Now come downstairs and I'll make you some lunch.'

It seemed her mother was more comfortable down in the kitchen than the posh parlour, Evie pondered. She wondered how happy her mother really was.

'Thank you, Mum, I'd like summat to eat, though we're that busy now, I'd better not stay too long. Any news?'

'I do have some, but it'll wait until you're sitting down.'

~

All the way from Bolton to Manchester, and then again from Manchester to Redmond, Billy thought about what he would say to Evie. The quarrel between them was as nothing compared to Ada's thieving of his letters, and Evie had done her very best to make amends anyway. Billy acknowledged that it was he who had done badly: not writing to Evie last year to make up the quarrel but expecting her to make the first move – which, of course, she had – and then not writing when he heard about Robert's death last February. But by then he thought Evie had washed her hands of him, he reminded himself. The whole situation was a muddle. But now he meant to make it right.

Billy's train pulled into Redmond station in the early afternoon. He knew he had to get a bus from here to the village of Church Sandleton and that the bus ran from the market square, which would likely be in the middle of town.

The market square was easily found, and the bus stop for the south-travelling buses displayed a rather complicated timetable in very small print. Eventually Billy decided he had half an hour before the bus was due and standing there waiting wouldn't make it come any quicker. Better to get something to eat. He looked around and spotted a café that served plain food, and he went in and sat down near the window.

As he sat drinking his tea, he idly watched the people of Redmond passing by. They looked pretty much like Bolton folk, but no one here was shuffling down the street in carpet slippers and a pinny. He noticed a man, very tall and lean, with hair that fell into his eyes and a fine scarf knotted round his throat. He was very good-looking, kind of like a film star, for all his jacket was so crumpled. And the young woman on his arm was his equal in looks, with her pretty hair, cut short, and a stylish striped frock that showed off her slim figure, and sandals with heels.

Billy peered through the window, his eyes drawn to the glamour of the couple. Then he looked again, craning forward, slowly lowering his knife and fork to his plate, though his eyes did not leave the figure of the woman.

Good grief, that looked a bit like Evie – he turned to press his face closer to the window – looked like Evie, but yet not quite like Evie. Like Evie would look if she was the kind of girl who wore fashionable dresses and had fashionable hair, and was all sort of grown-up. Billy, his lunch forgotten, sat staring at the couple across the square. They walked past the bank, chatting, the woman holding the man's arm. His face was turned away from Billy, looking down into the woman's face, and he partly hid her from Billy's view. Then they stopped to speak to a country-looking man with a Jack Russell terrier by his side and the three stood talking. The woman bent down to pet the dog and Billy got a good view of her face at last. Oh, but she looked so very much like Evie. Could there be another with that heart-shaped face? Though this woman wore lipstick. Evie had never worn lipstick.

Billy felt confused now. Nothing he had imagined on the journey down had prepared him for this situation. He stood up, shrugged on his jacket and left what he hoped was the right money on the table as he picked up his bag and went out. He was just in time to see the couple going down a side street off the market square and he ran across the square after them, dodging traffic. 'Midsummer Row', read the sign, and it was a narrow passage. The man and woman were at the end of it now and Billy ran lightly after them. When he emerged into an attractive little square he caught sight of them going up the steps of an elegant terraced house, where the man opened the door and they both disappeared inside. 'Marlowe House' said the sign beside the door.

Now what? Billy loitered in the square, watching the house and trying to work out what he should do.

He could knock at the door of Marlowe House and ask for Evie Carter. Then if the woman turned out to be Evie he'd be able to speak to her. If she wasn't Evie he could always say he'd got the wrong house.

Oh, but that would be so clumsy. If it was Evie, and she was married to the good-looking man, she wouldn't want to see good old Billy from Bolton, the boyfriend she'd fallen out with months ago and had probably forgotten about by now. What if she invited him in that smart house and introduced her to the man – to her husband? She certainly looked very happy, and her life must have changed, what with the frock and the hairdo. And coming out of a bank! Billy would be willing to bet the Evie he had known had never been in a bank in her life. It was all so unsettling.

But Brendan had said that Evie wasn't married. It looked as though the Sullivans hadn't heard the news. Brendan said they hadn't had a letter from Sue Goodwin since Easter so all this had obviously happened since then.

As he stood there dithering and unable to decide what on earth to do, a woman with grey hair came into the square and walked up to the gate of the house across from Marlowe House. She gave Billy a long look, evidently wondering what business he had here. Billy saw a way forward and went to speak to her.

'Excuse me,' he asked, 'I'm looking for Evie Carter, though that might not be her name now. She's an old friend. I think she lives round here but I'm not sure.'

'Carter . . . Carter . . . ' The woman looked round the houses of her neighbours, thinking. 'Oh, yes, I think that's the name of the young woman at Marlowe House,' she said. She pointed across. 'You were right outside it.'

'Yes, she is a young woman,' said Billy.

'Then that's certainly her,' smiled the neighbour. 'The rest of us are all older.' She laughed lightly to show she didn't care if he thought her old.

'Thank you,' said Billy, and turned away.

Flippin' heck, Evie was living with a man old enough to be her father, and in some splendour, by the look of it. He cast his eyes over Marlowe House a last time then went slowly back down Midsummer Row, his mind once more in turmoil. Never in a million years had he imagined this situation.

He emerged back into the market square and wondered what to do now. Pointless to call on Evie, who looked so happy in her smart new life.

Face it, Billy, you've lost her. You're a part of her past now, nothing more . . .

He sat down on a bench outside the bank from which Evie had emerged only a quarter-hour earlier and thought through his options. He quickly concluded there was none. He'd just have to get the train back to Bolton and go home to his mum. What a dreary thought that was, especially after their argument. To top it all, Ada had been right and Evie, miles from Bolton, in this little southern town in the countryside, was never coming back north. She'd moved on and left him well and truly behind.

As he walked back to the station Billy was lost in miserable thought. He stepped into the road and jumped back as a red car sped by dangerously close.

No need to get yourself killed, Billy.

He continued on his way, hoping the north-bound train would not be too long.

~

Evie, sitting beside Frederick in the car, wasn't paying any attention to pedestrians, but looked up as she felt Frederick swerve.

'Oh, what was that?'

'Just some fool not looking where he's going,' said Frederick. 'Don't worry, no harm done.'

Evie glanced in the wing mirror to catch sight of the 'fool'. How strange, the slouching figure with the duffel bag receding into the distance behind them looked a lot like Billy Taylor.

Evie shrugged, settled lower in her seat and gave

herself up to planning what to do with the money in her new bank account.

~

So much for having a couple of days off, Billy thought bitterly, slowing his pace as he approached Fawcett Street. It was late evening and the sky, at the height of summer, was beginning to darken. It had been a very long day and he was not looking forward to facing his mother.

All the way home on the train the image of Evie – a new kind of Evie – had haunted his mind: the way she held onto the arm of the dashing-looking husband she gazed up at so affectionately.

Face it, Billy, she's well out of your league now, even if she wasn't married.

Might as well go back to work tomorrow, holiday or not. No point stopping at home with Mum, and I'm not bloody well taking her to Blackpool either.

He reached the house and opened the door. There were two letters addressed to his mother on the mat. She must have overlooked them. The house smelled stuffy and Billy wondered if Ada, who seemed to be allergic to fresh air, had sat in with the windows closed all day despite the warm weather.

'Mum?' he said.

Silence, but then – he glanced at his watch – she'd

probably gone to bed. It was well past the time she normally listened to the wireless.

He hung his jacket on the peg in the hall and went through to the kitchen. Strange, the teapot was still on the table under the tea cosy exactly as he'd left it many hours ago. It looked as if his mother had never got up.

'Mum!' Suddenly Billy was racing up the stairs. 'Mum! Mum, are you all right?' He barged into her room without knocking, groping for the light switch.

Ada lay sprawled untidily on her back in her bed, her eyes partially closed and her mouth slightly open on one side.

Even without touching her, Billy knew the truth. She was stone-cold dead.

CHAPTER EIGHTEEN

BY SEPTEMBER THE gardens of Church Sandleton were laden with full-blown flowers with little green apples growing on the trees. Evie stopped to admire the quiet high street before she crossed the road from the bus stop and carried her heavy load of purchases back to Pendle's. The fresh prettiness of the countryside was something that she loved – even now, more than a year after coming here – and she would never take it for granted. Maybe she'd make a country girl yet. Certainly she no longer thought about going back to Bolton, going back to Shenty Street. What was there to go back for? Here was home now.

'How did you get on?' asked Sue, looking up from her work as Evie hefted her bags through the door. 'You've got quite a haul there.'

'I know, Grandma, but wait till you see it. George had got in both the green and the blue I ordered, and some lovely prints in a woollen mix. They're quite expensive so I got only two, for those autumn dresses we've taken on. George says he'll probably not sell the others too quickly yet so I've got till the end of the month to make up my mind about them, but I'd like your view on the ones I've bought first. And I found a couple of beautiful remnants in his box at the back, which we thought would make some sweet little matinee jackets. I hope you like them. George says I can always take them back if you don't. He doesn't usually allow returns of remnants, but as it's us . . . '

'"George says . . . George says . . . " Honestly, you should hear yourself, lass. It's your opinion I want, Evie, not George Morris's.'

'Sorry, Grandma, I didn't mean to go on.'

'George is in business, same as we are, love. He's out to make a profit and he'll do so even when he gives us a discount. It's nice that he's got what you ordered, and there's no doubt that he's selling lovely stuff, but he certainly knows how to sell it to you.'

'Oh, I'm not sure that's quite fair, Grandma.' Evie was stung by the implication that she was a soft touch for the draper's sales patter. 'I do think you'll like the remnants. And the other pieces.'

Evie felt that her bubble had been burst with Sue's strictly no-nonsense attitude this afternoon. And she'd had such a good morning in Kingsford, enjoying the special treatment George meted out to his favourite customer. She admitted to herself that she liked to be seen in her well-cut suit, courtesy of Letty's mother's legacy, perching on a stool in front of one of the counters while George ran about the place bringing bolts of fabric to her to view, whereas other customers had to go to find their own unless they asked for something specific. And the tea and biscuits were welcome, too.

'See you on Sunday?' asked George as he'd opened the shop door for Evie. 'I thought we could go for a picnic, as well.'

'I shan't want to miss it, then,' Evie had said. 'Usual train.'

'I'll be there.'

Now Evie busied herself opening the numerous brown-paper-wrapped parcels and spreading the fabrics over the big work table for Sue to examine. Sue felt the woollen prints for quality and, bending close to see properly, examined the patterns.

'And how much did you say you paid for these?'

Evie produced the receipt and pointed out each item on it.

'And that's with the discount?'

'No, Grandma, George took that off the total at the end – see, here? So we've got the remnants at a discount, too. He doesn't usually do that as they're reduced to clear already.'

'I bet he doesn't,' said Sue, deadpan.

After a silent minute Evie dared to ask, 'So what do you think, Grandma?'

Sue drew a long breath. 'I reckon you've done all right, lass, but I think you need to be careful. It's lovely stuff, but I don't want George Morris persuading you to buy what's not suitable. We're only dressmakers, not fancy designers.'

'I know that. So you're saying I'm being too ambitious?' asked Evie, feeling slapped down.

'No, but I reckon you might be if you carry on down this road. Always keep in mind what folk want and what they're prepared to pay. If you aim too high you'll be up there by yourself with no one to pay for it.'

'I suppose you're right,' Evie said in a small voice.

'You know I am,' said Sue. 'All I'm saying, love, is don't carried away with what George Morris has got in his fancy shop, that's all. We started at the mill shop and on the market, and we did all right there. There's nowt wrong with giving folk what they want, Evie, and you'll soon find it's a hard life *telling* them what they want and then trying to make them have it.'

Evie bit back her reply. There was no point in arguing with her grandmother.

At that moment the door opened and a young woman with two identical toddlers holding on to her hands struggled her way in. Evie rushed over to help.

'Hello, I'm Mrs Armitage. I telephoned earlier about pageboy outfits for the boys,' the woman said.

Sue introduced herself and Evie, and showed Mrs Armitage to a chair. There was a box of toys in the corner, which Josie had suggested would help keep small children quiet while discussions took place, and Evie showed the boys the building bricks and Dinky Toys while Sue found out what Mrs Armitage had in mind.

'Oh, but this is lovely,' said the young mother, noticing the fabrics Evie had just bought. 'This print with the tiny sailboats is exactly right for the little sailor jackets.'

Evie slipped out to make a cup of tea for their customer, and to hide her smile. She just *knew* those remnants would be useful, and they'd been snapped up before she'd finished unwrapping the parcel. Well, Sue was a canny woman – no doubt about that – but she didn't know everything.

~

'I'm glad I put my coat on,' said Evie, wrapping her summer coat around her. 'It's getting a bit nippy to be sitting out in a deck chair.'

'I expect that's what the organisers thought now they've brought the season to an end,' said George. 'It's been fun, though. I've really enjoyed having you to share it with this summer.'

'Me, too. I shall miss these lovely afternoons,' said Evie.

'Will you?' George asked, looking intently at her.

Evie frowned in puzzlement. 'Mmm, I said as much. Shall we take a last walk around the pond now the band's finished?'

'Good idea. Though I hope it's not the last walk.' George got up and helped Evie out of her deck chair.

'Well, it will be for this year,' Evie replied.

'We could find something else to do instead,' George suggested.

'I suppose we could: summat indoors, though,' Evie added with a shiver at the cold wind.

'Have a think, my dear, and I will, too,' he said.

'Oh, I hope so,' said Evie. 'It's been so lovely having Sundays off – you've been so kind.'

George beamed. 'It's been a pleasure, Evie.'

He really was a very thoughtful man, thought Evie. She guessed he was probably lonely since his wife had died several years ago. He lived in a flat over the shop, which Evie imagined was very clean and tidy. George Morris was definitely a different sort of man from her father, with his flinging his boots around, and rinsing his hands in the kitchen sink when you were trying to wash vegetables. She couldn't imagine George ever raising his voice and getting into an argument, or drinking too much. He seemed to inhabit a different planet from

Michael, with his drinking and that unforgettable business with Mr Hopkins, and, Evie realised, that planet would be quite an appealing place to live. Peaceful.

Evie said she'd better go to get the train home and George walked with her to the station while they discussed the concert. He waited with her for the train and saw her safely onto it.

'I shall miss our Sundays,' smiled Evie. 'It's been fun.'

'It has. I shall miss you, too, Evie.'

'Oh, I'm not going anywhere,' she said. 'I shall be in the shop in the next week or two.'

'I shall look forward to that,' George said seriously. 'You certainly brighten a morning behind the counter.' He took her hand through the carriage window and held on to it. 'In fact, I'd go so far as to say you brighten my life.'

Evie was taken aback. She didn't think she was a part of George's life – not really. The Sundays out were just nice outings before it was back to the sewing on Mondays, so far as she was concerned.

Before she could think of anything else to reply the train exuded a cloud of steam, the whistle sounded and the wheels started to turn. 'Bye, then, George.'

But his reply was lost under the increasingly loud chug of the departing train.

Evie sat back in her seat and tried to think what

George could have meant. She knew he had a romantic nature because of his taste for the more sentimental tunes in the band's Sunday repertoire, whereas she liked the jollier melodies she could tap her foot to.

I'd go so far as to say you brighten my life . . .

Perhaps he was merely being nice at the end of a lovely afternoon. Then suddenly a big and disturbing thought rushed into her head: George Morris was in love with her.

No, that was ridiculous. He was ten years older than her mother! No, she must be mistaken. Better get that idea straight out of her mind before she said something foolish.

To banish the thought, she began thinking about the parcel her mother had sent that morning, with a bank book for the account that she'd opened for her and a note apologising for not seeing her. Evie had bought a second sewing machine for the workroom so that she and Sue could both work on their seams without delay or the bother of changing threads. There had once been a very frustrating day when both of them had left the wrong colour thread in the bobbin and each had sewn a whole seam, red on one side and blue on the other. Now Sue sat at the treadle machine near the window, the better to catch the daylight, but with her lamp by her side, too, while Evie had set up her new electric machine on one end of the big table. There had been no more mix-ups.

Jeanie had suggested that she didn't mention the money to her father, and Evie had agreed. Michael took little interest in the sewing business since he'd started work at the shoe factory, and Evie let him assume whatever he wanted about the new sewing machine.

Sue had been a bit snappy of late and Evie guessed that her eyes were worrying her more now that the daylight was fading with the onset of autumn. Sue didn't complain but Evie noticed she was working more slowly and she herself worried about it, not just on Sue's account but because the dressmaking business was so busy that she knew she couldn't manage all the work on her own if Sue couldn't go on. This thought surfaced sometimes in the small hours of the night, but Evie had confided in no one. To speak it aloud made her worry more, but the burden of not telling her mother and brother was hard. Her grandmother was so precious to her, and she realised just how scared she was.

~

Michael wheeled his bicycle down the side passage at Pendle's and parked it in the backyard. He really must get some lights for the bike now the evenings were growing darker. It wouldn't be long before he was cycling home in complete darkness.

To Michael, sweeping the floors and keeping the premises tidy, every day was exactly the same. The men and the couple of women who made the shoes in the factory hardly acknowledged his presence as they sewed and hammered, glued and polished. Though everyone was pleasant enough, Michael had made no friendships among the employees. He felt that no one even noticed him, that he was just a part of the background of the place, rather taken for granted.

He opened the back door and let himself into Pendle's. The kitchen was empty. He'd seen the light on in the big front room as he'd passed, and Evie and Sue bending over their sewing machines, the table and chairs strewn with the cut-out shapes of garments. He switched on the kitchen light and reached for the kettle, which was empty and cold. There were a couple of used cups on the side, one of them Sue's special cup with its matching saucer, but there was no sign of any preparation of food.

He changed his shoes and went to see what time tea would be ready. He was hungry and he had hoped one of them would have started on some cooking by now.

'Oh, hello, Dad,' said Evie, hardly looking up. 'I hadn't realised it's that time already.'

'Hello, love. Are you both nearly finished?'

'Well, I just want to get these darts in before I stop, Dad,' said Evie.

'And I've got this collar to do,' said Sue. 'If I stop in the middle it won't look so smooth as if I carry on.'

Michael hovered by the door.

'Make yourself a cup of tea, why don't you?' said Evie. 'We'll eat when I've finished this.'

'If you're putting the kettle on I could do with a brew,' said Sue. 'We've been that busy this afternoon . . .'

Michael went off wearily to do as he was asked. He had to admire Sue and Evie's commitment to their work, but he felt a bit put out that they seemed to have less commitment to him as head of the household, and his need to be fed after a hard day's work.

He brought the tea through.

'Thank you, lad. Just put it on the side there,' said Sue, her eyes inches away from her seam.

'Thanks, Dad. We really have been very busy today,' said Evie.

'So have I,' Michael replied, defensively.

'Good . . . good.' Evie did not look up.

Half an hour later Michael came back to see if they had nearly finished for the day. His stomach was rumbling by now.

'Almost done, Dad,' Evie said. 'If you peel a few spuds I'll come and see to our tea in a minute. You could put the oven on . . .'

Another half-hour went by before Evie came through to the kitchen. The oven was on and the peeled potatoes sat in a pan of cold water.

Evie could have been knocked over with a feather. 'I'll get these spuds on the boil.'

'I thought you'd be finished long since,' Michael said. 'I have been at work all day, too, you know, love.'

'Yes, Dad, and I'm sorry to keep you waiting, but Grandma and me are rushed off our feet this week. Maybe if we're still hard at it tomorrow you could begin cooking?'

Michael looked sulky. 'Is this what it's going to be like now – I come home and have to make everyone's tea?'

'Well, I do usually, Dad. I know you've been at work, too, but I've only just finished now. It's been a long day.'

'A working man shouldn't have to make his own tea when there's women in the house.'

'Why ever not?' said Sue, coming through, rubbing her eyes. 'Why does your work mean you can't help around the place? We're all tired at the end of a long day. Those that get to the kitchen first can start on the cooking. That's only fair.'

'Well, I've never heard of that,' said Michael. 'Jeanie always got the tea ready.'

Evie thought that maybe that was why Mum, who had always worked, had found somewhere she preferred to live and had upped and left, but fortunately she stopped short of pointing that out.

'Well, while Evie and me are so busy, let's see if you can help us out, lad,' said Sue. 'And then, when you're extra busy at the factory, we'll do the same for you. It can work both ways, can't it?'

Michael could not argue with that point, especially as Evie now had on her pinny and was spreading sausages out in a roasting tin.

After they'd eaten he took himself off to the Red Lion, feeling unappreciated and sidelined. It seemed to him that, if he hadn't come home, Evie and Sue would have carried on working until bedtime and gone without cooked food. Far from being head of the household, Michael feared he was becoming the one whose place was juggling pans on the stove, wearing a pinny. Work at the factory was very much like housework as it involved a lot of sweeping and tidying up, and now he wondered if he'd find himself being the cook in his own home. As he opened the door of the Red Lion and greeted his neighbours he felt far more at home than he had done all evening at Pendle's.

~

The telephone rang and Evie hurried to answer, her order book open and ready. But it was only George.

'What did he want?' asked Sue, after he'd rung off.

'He's invited me to tea at his flat above the shop on Sunday.'

'Oh? Any particular reason?'

'He didn't say. Perhaps he wants someone to chat with. It must be lonely on a Sunday now that the band isn't playing any more.'

'I suppose . . . Did he say who else he's invited?'

'No, and I never thought to ask. Why?'

'Just wondering.'

The phone went again and Sue heard half of another conversation, also clearly not about ordering new clothes.

'What was that about?' she asked, when Evie, grinning hugely, came back in.

'Well, I've arranged for a bit of maintenance work on the front this afternoon. There will be a couple of men with ladders. Do you think you'll be disturbed by them? You could always go and see Miss Richards if you think they may be in your light.'

'Maintenance? When was this decided?'

'It's a surprise, so don't ask.'

~

'Come and look now, Grandma,' Evie said when the painters started to pack up.

Sue got up stiffly and shuffled out of the front door to look.

'Good heavens!'

There, above the shop, where before it had said 'Pendle's', there was a newly painted sign: smart dark blue with curly gold lettering: *Goodwin and Carter, Dressmakers.*

'All right for you, missus?' asked the painter.

Evie studied Sue's face. She looked amazed but also very pleased.

'Oh, Evie, love, our own names over the shop. And so smart, too.'

Evie thanked the painters and waved them off in their van.

'Do you really like it, Grandma?' she said when they'd gone.

Sue couldn't stop gazing at the sign. 'Of course I do, love. It's . . . it's like we're a real business.'

'Well, even though there's only the two of us we stuck with it and we've made a success of it. And now we're officially Goodwin and Carter, for all to see.'

'It's grand, lass. I'm that proud of it. And I'm that proud of you, too.'

'Thank you, Grandma.'

~

'So it's come to this, has it?' said Michael grumpily, coming into the workroom from the back of the house, where he'd left his bicycle.

'Don't you like our sign, Dad?' Evie asked. 'We

think it looks nice. There's no need to have "Pendle's" above the front. Mr Pendle left here years ago, according to Josie.'

'Goodwin and Carter,' said Michael heavily. 'Well, it's nowt to do with me, is it? Why don't you two just take over the whole place with your sewing machines and your bits of stuff lying about the place? I'm surprised you've left me a bed to sleep in, the way things are going.'

'Oh, Dad, don't be daft. You know we never take our work out of here,' said Evie, disappointed. 'We've always kept to our own space.'

'It doesn't feel like it to me,' argued Michael. 'It seems to me that this whole place is nowt but a dressmaker's these days, and there's no room or time for anything else – or anybody else – at all. I feel like I'm *living* at a dressmaker's, not a home of my own.'

'I'm sorry, Dad, I don't want you to feel like that. It's true the sewing takes up the whole of the big room, but it's how we earn our living – Grandma and me – and it needs a bit of space.'

'And what if I need a bit of space?'

'Well, there's the big kitchen. We've all always sat in there of an evening,' said Evie.

'All . . . ' said Michael sadly. 'Once there were all of us Carters. Now it's only me, facing a tide of sewing stuff piling up around me—'

'No, Dad—'

'My wife has gone off with a fancy man, my little lad is dead, and my other lad can't stand the sight of me and has gone to live with folk who aren't even his relations. And now you two have claimed the place entirely as your own and announced it with a ruddy great sign outside with your names all over it. Seems to me I'm a spare part here, a leftover. Not needed and not wanted.'

'Now you know that's not true, Michael,' Sue said. 'The old sign made no sense any longer. What would you have up outside?'

Michael looked stricken. 'I'd have nowt,' he said eventually. 'I'd live in a proper house, like we had in Shenty Street, not a rented shop.'

'Well, those days are gone,' replied Sue, looking hard at him.

Evie wanted to argue with that but she knew better than to speak out against Michael when he was feeling sorry for himself.

'Yes, we know, Dad. We all miss Shenty Street. But this is our home now.'

'It's not just you who lives here, Evie, you'd do well to remember that.'

'I think,' interrupted Sue loudly, 'that I might finish up here for the evening and go and see about summat to eat.'

'I'll do it, Grandma,' said Evie, getting up from the big table. 'Come on, Dad, cheer up. It's one of Mrs Sutton's pies for tea . . . '

She and Sue exchanged glances as Evie followed Michael out to the kitchen. She'd been so pleased with the new sign and now it felt like it was a kind of showing off. Maybe she should have considered her father's feelings, but lately he was so easily cast into an ill temper that there was no pleasing him. Well, it was too late to do anything about the sign.

No point, perhaps, but that didn't stop her worrying as she lit the oven and wearily looked out some vegetables to go with the pie.

She tried to remember a time when the whole family had been all together, and happy, and she had to cast her thoughts further and further back to the beginning of that last summer in Shenty Street, before Michael had fallen into debt with Mr Hopkins.

I've tried so hard – all of us wanting the same thing, being a happy family – and at every turn it's slipped away. No sooner do I get one bit right than another part goes wrong. If only I could make everything all right for all of us, for ever . . .

CHAPTER NINETEEN

'I'VE HAD A letter from Marie Sullivan,' said Sue, coming into the workroom with the letter in her hand. 'It's good to hear from her. It's a while since we've been in touch. My fault, I suppose. I'm finding it hard work to be much of a letter writer these days.'

'Are they all well, Grandma?' Evie asked, watching her grandmother carefully. She was having one of her bad days, her eyes were bad and she was shaky on her feet.

'They are. Geraldine's engaged to be married.'

Evie's heart stopped beating for a moment. Not to her Billy?

'Oh, I'm so pleased. Who's the lucky man?'

'Colin Fraser. Marie says he's a lovely lad, very good-looking . . . '

Evie felt her cheeks pinken in relief. Life on Shenty Street and Billy seemed a lifetime ago now, and she still felt so fond of him.

'What about Mary?'

'Still at school, being clever. Marie says she doesn't know where she gets it from. And she says summat else, too. She asks if it's true that you're married.'

'What? Where on earth did she get that idea?'

'I dunno, love. She doesn't say. Just asks if it's true.'

'Strange. Maybe she's muddled me up with someone else.'

Sue shrugged. 'I reckon she must have. Oh, and she says Ada Taylor's dead.'

'Ada . . . ? Billy's mum? Good grief, she wasn't especially old.'

'Not like me, you mean,' said Sue drily. 'A stroke, Marie says. Found dead in bed by Billy.'

'Oh, poor Billy. That must have been a shock.'

'Aye, poor lad, as you say.'

Sue went back to her sewing, leaning close to her lamp, and Evie resumed making her seams.

After a while Evie said, 'I do feel sorry for Billy.'

'I'm the same, love.'

They continued with their work and then the door to the workroom slowly opened and Letty came dancing in.

'Guess what,' she demanded, planting a kiss on each of their heads. 'The very best news.'

'Best tell us before you explode, then,' said Sue.

'Jack and I – we're getting married!'

Evie clasped her hands together with joy. 'You're

right, Letty, it *is* the very best news.' She stood to give her friend a big hug. 'Oh, I'm so happy for you.'

'And then we can discuss the wedding dress while we drink our tea.'

'You want us to make it?'

'Who else? I want something pretty that I can wear later, made by my very favourite dressmakers.'

'I think, then,' said Evie, 'I'd better take you to the shops.'

~

Michael was getting used to cooking when he got home in the evenings, but that didn't mean he had to like it. Since Letty Mortimer had asked Evie and Sue to make her wedding dress, the sewing took up more time and seemed, somehow, to take up more space, too, although the materials were never allowed to spread from the workroom into the rest of the house. And every time he came home from work, there was that fancy sign proclaiming the place was a dressmaker's, shouting to the world that it wasn't his home. It didn't feel like his home now, with no wife, no sons. He wasn't needed.

After a week of cooking for everyone, Michael decided that he'd had enough.

'I'm home now, Evie, so you can stop messing about and cook our tea,' he announced, standing in the doorway of the workroom.

Sue was immediately furious. 'Evie's not going anywhere. It's our money that mostly pays the bills, Michael Carter. If we've work to do we'll stick at it until it's done. There may be days to come when there is none. It's no different from the laundry we had in Shenty Street, just drier.'

'But you never carried on of an evening with the laundry and expected me to make the tea,' objected Michael.

'I think you've got a short memory, lad,' retorted Sue. 'I remember darning and mending and altering clothes well into the evening, and Evie doing the ironing then, too. It was Jeanie who stopped to cook for everyone.'

'Well, Jeanie's gone,' he said bitterly, 'so one of you will have to do it instead. We've still got to eat. What could be more important than womenfolk providing for their men?' Michael asked crossly.

'We *are*, Dad! That's exactly what all this work is about, providing for all of us.' Evie felt what she was explaining was so obvious that Michael was wilfully not understanding.

'Well, I don't know what was wrong with the stuff you used to do – repairs and curtains and that,' he said sullenly.

'Is that really what you want us to do, Dad? Repairing other folks' old clothes so that you can get your food on time? We can do better than that – and we *are* doing. And if you don't like it, well . . .'

'Right then . . . ' said Michael. 'I'm off to get summat to eat at the Lion. You two can do as you like,' and he stomped off to the Red Lion, slamming the front door behind him.

Evie put down her sewing and took a deep breath.

'It wouldn't be like your dad to make much of an effort for very long,' sighed Sue. 'Pop a couple of potatoes in the oven, love, and we'll carry on for a bit until they're ready.'

'He could have done that for us instead of making a fuss,' said Evie, getting up resentfully, but her concentration was shattered now and she didn't want to go on.

'Will you thread this needle for me, love?' said Sue. 'I'm finding it hard to see the fine stuff now the evenings are drawing in.'

'How are your eyes, Grandma?' It wasn't like Sue to mention her difficulties.

'Not so good, love. This right eye is getting worse, I know it. It's a good thing it's only bad in the one eye or I think I'd have had to give up by now.'

'Oh, Grandma. What would I do if you couldn't do your sewing? What would *you* do?'

'Well, Evie, love, I know the answer to the second question and so do you. I'd make your father's tea.'

Evie smiled a tiny smile and squeezed Sue's hand.

'As to the first, we'd manage. I wouldn't be completely useless. We'd have to organise ourselves differently, that's all. I'd do all the cutting out and you'd do the sewing. Don't worry, love. It's not come to that yet, though I think we should be prepared.' Sue had obviously been thinking this through.

'And I think we ought to finish for today,' said Evie. The argument with her dad had left her feeling upset and now the discussion about Sue's eyes was adding to her worries.

~

Michael ate a pie and washed it down with a few pints of beer. At first some people he knew were at the bar and he forgot his anger with Evie and Sue as he chatted with them, but after a while they drifted off, leaving him with his bitter thoughts. He looked out for Jack, but Jack was seldom in the pub these days. Michael took himself into a corner with the *Redmond Gazette*.

That was a mistake. On the first inside spread was a round-up of recent events in the town. There, looking beautiful and wearing a very fitted dress, was Jeanie! His wife, pictured in the newspaper, smiling into the camera, holding a glass of what looked like wine. And next to her, of course, was that bastard Bailey she'd gone off with. The contrast between this Jeanie and the wife he'd recalled only an hour or two ago – the woman who took in washing and cooked his tea – was overwhelming.

'Mr and Mrs Frederick Bailey' read the caption. Michael could hardly believe his eyes. That woman was not Mrs Frederick Bailey and she never would be. 'Mrs Frederick Bailey' indeed! The nerve of the man. Or maybe that was what Jeanie was calling herself these days, trying to pass herself off as a respectable married woman instead of a hussy who'd upped and left her husband and children and taken up with the fella whose cleaner she was. She was behaving as if he'd never existed! Well, it was time Jeanie Carter remembered who she was and where she came from.

Michael scraped back his chair, knocking the table and slopping beer over it. He tucked the offending newspaper into his jacket pocket as fuel to his anger and lurched out into the autumn night.

'Mrs Frederick Bailey indeed . . . ' Muttering, Michael wove his way down the road back to Pendle's. Except it wasn't Pendle's any more, it was Goodwin and Carter, Dressmakers. He'd done nothing to deserve this, nothing at all. Well, he was going to put a stop to Jeanie Carter gallivanting about Redmond, making out she was summat she wasn't.

He opened the side gate and sent it crashing into the wall, then lumbered down the side passage to collect his bicycle from the backyard.

The kitchen was lit up and Michael could see Evie and Sue sitting at the table, eating, but he grabbed his bike without acknowledging them and, with just one failed attempt, wheeled it down the side of the building and out to the street.

Evie rushed out of the front door as he emerged.

'Dad, what on earth are you doing? Where are you going?'

'I'm off to get your mother,' he slurred. 'I've had enough.'

'What are you talking about? You can't bring Mum home on a bicycle. Come inside, Dad, and tell us what's wrong.'

'Perishing women, that's what's wrong,' he hissed. 'You're all as bad. Your mother—'

'What? Dad, please, come in and tell us.'

Sue came up behind Evie. 'Come inside and sober up. You can't go anywhere like that,' she called over Evie's shoulder.

Michael ignored her and pushed off on his bicycle, starting to wobble his way past the front of the shop.

Evie stepped out to grab him and ran after him but in two turns of the wheel he was away and she was left behind.

'Dad! Dad! Come back, please,' she called, but he didn't even look back.

'Where's he going?' asked Sue. 'Not far in that state, I should think.'

'He says he's going to get Mum,' Evie answered. 'He's so angry.'

'What's that there?' said Sue. She pointed to a

newspaper lying on the pavement by the side gate. Evie picked it up. 'You look, love. I can't see nowt in the dark.'

'It's the local paper.'

They went into the kitchen and spread the newspaper on the table. Sue put on her reading glasses and in no time they both saw the photograph of Jeanie and Frederick, and read the caption.

'Oh Lord, and Dad said he's going to Redmond to get her,' gasped Evie.

'He'll never get there in that state,' said Sue. She spoke confidently but they looked at each other worriedly.

'I think I'd better telephone Mum and Frederick and warn them about Dad,' said Evie. 'He's so mad that I'm really worried. I don't want Mum being upset.'

'Good idea, love, just in case.'

They went into the workroom and Evie dialled the number.

'Redmond 786,' said Jeanie. ' . . . Oh, hello, love. You sound a bit bothered – are you all right?'

'No, Mum. Dad's been in the pub all evening and now he's drunk and he says he's coming to get you. He saw a photo of you in the *Gazette*, calling you "Mrs Frederick Bailey" and we think that's what's got him in such a fury. He's set off on his bike, but he's very wobbly. Grandma and I think mebbe he won't make it and he'll see sense and have to turn back, but then I'm worried that he might reach you, and he'll do something awful. He's ever so angry, Mum.'

'Oh, no . . . oh dear. I've never said that was my name. Freddie's not here now. He's gone to Jack's.'

'I reckon you should call him and ask him to come back, Mum. I don't want you to have to cope with Dad on your own.'

'Yes, love. I'll do that. If your dad does get here, Freddie will deal with him and send him home. Thank you for warning me. You're a good girl. Don't worry, Evie.'

She rang off and Evie told Sue what Jeanie had said. Then she made a pot of tea and they sat and waited anxiously to see what would happen next.

~

Michael was hot with anger as he pedalled out of Church Sandleton and onto the Redmond road. Once he was out of the village there were no street-lamps to light the way, but the moon was bright in a clear sky and he could find his way with his eyes shut.

The countryside was fairly flat and the road a good one so he made fast progress despite some-times weaving across to the right. One time a car approached from behind and passed him, the driver slowing down and pulling out to allow Michael his wobbly progress. Then a car came towards him and hooted. Michael hadn't realised he was so close to the other side and he moved back to the left.

'Bloody women . . . ' he muttered. 'Mrs Frederick Bailey . . . Thinks she's too good for the likes of me these days . . . ' He ranted on, pedalling faster, furiously, carelessly. He was approaching Redmond now – he could see streetlights in the distance.

Another car approached behind, headlights illuminating the empty road ahead. Michael tried to steer to the side but he seemed suddenly to be a long way from the verge. He wobbled on, thinking the car would pull out but it moved ever closer. Then suddenly it was right behind. Then next instant it had clipped the back wheel of Michael's unlit bike and sent him somersaulting off the road and into the ditch beyond the verge as it sped away.

The ditch was deep and Michael landed heavily on his back, the bicycle coming to rest in a tangle of spinning wheels on top of him. The last thing he heard was the sound of the car's engine fading into the distance. Lying in the ditch, he looked up and saw the huge white and grey moon above. It looked very distant and very cold. The road was now completely silent. Then the image of the moon faded from his sight and he felt darkness closing in around him.

~

After a fitful night's sleep, Evie awoke and took a few moments to remember that Michael had set off for Redmond and she hadn't heard him return. She went to see if he was in bed, but the blankets were pulled over and it looked as if the bed hadn't been slept in. She went downstairs to see if there was any sign of him there, but the kitchen was exactly as she'd left it the night before.

Oh Lord, what to do now?

She put the kettle to boil while she tried to have a sensible think, then took a cup of tea up to Sue.

'Grandma? Here, I've brought you some tea. There's no sign of Dad. I think summat might have happened to him. Should I call the police?'

'You sure he's not gone to work?'

Evie explained. 'I'm worried he's had an accident, Grandma.'

'Mmm, it doesn't sound good, love. Yes, better call the police. Do you want me to do it?'

'No, Grandma. I will while you get up.'

'Think carefully what we know, love, 'cos they're bound to ask you about the time he left and what he was wearing and that.'

Evie went back down to telephone and recited all the facts as carefully as she could. By then she was tearful and fearing the worst, though the policeman she spoke to was sympathetic and reassuring. He took the address and telephone number and promised to be in touch as soon as he could.

It was mid-morning, and neither Evie nor Sue had got much work done, when a black police car drew up outside. The women looked at each other and Evie felt her heart sink as two policemen got out of the car. Evie sprang up and ran to the door.

'It's bad news, isn't it?' she gasped. 'I knew it! I should have tried harder to stop him setting off on his bike like that.'

'Miss Carter?' asked the older policeman. They both removed their hats as they came into the work-room. 'And you are Mrs . . . ?'

'Goodwin,' said Sue. 'I'm Evelyn's grandma and Michael Carter's mother-in-law. Tell us, Sergeant, what's the news?'

'We think we've found Michael Carter, but I'm afraid I'm going to have to ask you to come with us to the hospital. It's bad news.'

Sue guessed what was coming but she had to be sure. 'He's dead?'

'I'm sorry. I'm afraid so. But we need to be certain it is him.'

'No!' wailed Evie. 'Not Dad as well! Oh, I can't bear it, I just can't bear it . . . ' and she sank to the floor, sobbing loudly, tears streaming down her face, and wouldn't be comforted.

Eventually, Sue asked the younger policeman if he'd mind going to Lavender Cottage at the other end of the High Street to fetch their friends so that she could leave Evie and go with the police to the cottage hospital in Redmond.

It wasn't until Margaret and Letty arrived, full of compassion and common sense, that Sue was able to set off on her grim task. As she looped her handbag over her arm and stepped through the front door, she turned the 'OPEN' sign to 'CLOSED'.

Goodwin and Carter would remain closed for many days.

CHAPTER TWENTY

'I THINK, EVIE,' said Sue, 'that it's high time you
got back on your feet. I don't want to sound
hard, my girl, but I reckon you might find doing a
bit of work will take your mind off your sorrows.'

'I don't know, Grandma . . . It's all such a big
effort, and I feel so exhausted. Bob's dead and
Mum's gone, and Pete's not here any longer either,
and now Dad's dead, too. There's only us left,
Grandma. I don't think I can ever be happy again.
What if summat were to happen to you? I'd be all
by myself and I don't know how I could manage.'

'Nonsense. There's nowt going to happen to me.
It's a bad do about your dad, and it were worse
about little Bob, but you can't let your life be all
about. We all lose people we love, you know that,
but we have to go on without them. Look how you
pulled us up after Bob died. You did it then and
you can do it now. Come on, love, up you get and

come and get summat done. I need you in that workroom.'

Evie sighed heavily. 'But it all seems so pointless. What does it matter what the stupid buttons are like when everyone I love is dead or gone?'

'Now listen, Evie,' said Sue sternly, sitting down on the edge of Evie's bed, where Evie had spent much of the time since Michael's funeral, a week previously, 'it's them clothes what pays our bills. *Our* bills, Evie. Yours and mine. You can't give up and leave me to do it all – my eyes are failing and I need you.' Sue was finding it increasingly hard to focus properly on the finer sewing. 'We haven't got your dad's wages now so we're relying entirely on ourselves. Don't let me down.'

Tears sprang to Evie's eyes, as they did so frequently these days. 'Please, Grandma, just let me be. Give me a bit longer to get over Dad.'

'No.' Sue stood up and wagged a strict finger at Evie, her face fierce behind her glasses. 'If you stay here nursing your sorrows any longer you'll find it's become a habit and you'll never get up. I want you washed and downstairs in ten minutes.'

'No, Grandma, please . . . ' Evie wailed.

'And if you're not then I shall come back up here and drag you out, do you hear?'

Evie sank down in her bed and threw the covers back over her head.

'Ten minutes,' said Sue, and went down to put

the kettle to boil. Every situation could be eased with a cup of tea.

Soon Sue could hear Evie moving about. Eventually she clumped downstairs, looking red-eyed and thin.

'That's better,' said Sue with an encouraging smile. 'Here, there's a cup of tea for you.'

'Thanks, Grandma.'

'You know, Peter's been going to school all this time and trying to carry on as usual. He's not given in to grieving.'

'Pete didn't even like Dad.'

'I think,' said Sue carefully, 'you'll find that's not entirely true. He's been busier than ever with the band, too, and they've all sorts of concerts lined up. It's his way of coping, and if you ask me it's a good 'un.'

'S'pose . . . '

'Now go and get started and we'll see what we can manage this morning. I shall be glad to have someone else in the sewing room. It's been a bit lonely there all by myself.'

Evie knew Sue was trying to jolly her along. When news had got out of Michael's accident there had been a stream of visitors bringing their condolences, leaving posies of late flowers, dropping by with cards, some with cakes they'd baked. Michael himself had not had many friends in the village but Sue Goodwin and her granddaughter were popular. Even Mr Clackett had come over with a box of vegetables and a few kind words about Michael, which had made Sue laugh hollowly after he'd gone.

Evie and Sue worked all morning. Already she had assumed her lifetime habit of watching the pennies, reining in on any extras. Most evenings it was vegetable soup and bread with no butter for their tea. Biscuits, and sugar in the tea, were things of the past.

Gradually, over the following weeks, Evie pulled herself out of her sadness and – Sue was right – the work helped a lot. Yet she felt she was marking time, waiting for something to happen. She hadn't the inclination to see a way forward and make a move herself. As so often since meeting Mrs Russell on the train to Manchester, she remembered how that kindly lady had made positive decisions that led her to a new and better life.

But what am I even deciding about? Where do I go from here? Do I even want to go on with hardly any of my family around me?

'You know, Grandma,' she said one afternoon, while she was stitching some beading to Letty's wedding dress and Sue was leaning as best she could over the table, cutting out pattern pieces, 'I once thought that if we could get the sewing business up and running I'd never want for anything again. I saw no further than that. I thought that would be it – all I could possibly need in life.'

'Did you, love?' Sue stopped and stretched her

back, regarding Evie seriously. 'I don't think that life is quite like that.'

'Yes, you're right.'

'We always need more work, though.' Sue thought of the bare kitchen cupboard and how grateful she'd felt to Mr Clackett for the box of vegetables, which had lasted a good few days.

'Of course, but we're here, people know that, and we can put an advertisement in the *Gazette* or summat if we need new clients. But I can't see what happens next.'

'Well, that's what it's like in this kind of business, love. The work gets finished and then we have to look for summat else to take its place. You know that. We have to keep going because otherwise we'd run out of money – and soon, too.'

Just then the phone rang and Evie went to answer it.

'Evie, my dear. I haven't wanted to bother you too much lately, what with all you've had on your mind, but I wonder if you'd like to come round to tea again?'

'George, that's a kind offer but I'm not sure I'm very good company at the moment.'

'You don't have to put up a front among friends, you know. I'd love it if you felt you could visit.'

Evie thought quickly. A few minutes ago she'd been thinking that she was waiting for something to happen with her life – well, nothing ever would if she never left the workroom.

'Thank you, George. I'll be in Kingsford on Sunday at the usual time, shall I?'

~

After the first outing to see George, Evie felt better. She enjoyed putting on a pretty dress and her lipstick, making an effort after languishing in bed in her pyjamas for so many days, consumed with misery, then keeping a low profile in the workroom. Her weekly visits to see George were resumed, although sometimes on the train home afterwards her thoughts would turn to Michael, her heart would fill with grief and she'd cry quietly, feeling suddenly lonely and bereft. But as the weeks went by and Christmas approached, these moments of intense sadness became fewer.

She and Sue had found a few more jobs, and the work was a huge relief. It had been famine and feast since Michael's death – not enough money coming in, or now two of them working flat out – and since Sue had acknowledged the limits of her sight for fine sewing Evie was working very hard for long hours at her sewing machine. But the mood in the workroom had lifted, and Evie looked forward to her Sundays off, visiting George. Sue insisted that she stopped working for one day a week, and she herself either had a nap or went to visit Margaret while Evie was in Kingsford.

Often on the way home Evie would go to see her mother before catching the bus to Church Sandleton.

'What's happened to your car, Frederick?' Evie asked the first week, when he offered to drive her. She was opening the passenger door and noticed some scratches and a dent on the front wing.

'What? Let me have a look . . . ' He peered at the slight damage in the dim light of the winter dusk. 'Must have caught it on the side of the garage or something. I hadn't realised. I'll take it to be repaired. There's a good man in Kingsford who can fix it for me . . . '

He didn't seem very worried, but then if he hadn't even noticed there was no point in getting worked up about it now, Evie thought. Frederick was like that about so many things: he had great confidence in everything working out to suit him with the minimum amount of fuss and effort.

The next time she saw the car it was all smooth and smart again, so the man in Kingsford was obviously very good at his job.

Evie observed Jeanie carefully when she went to visit, looking to see how her mother was taking her father's death. Jeanie had wept a bit at the funeral, but had been very dignified, and, Evie thought, quite a lot less upset than she'd been about Robert. Sometimes now Evie caught Jeanie with a faraway look on her face, and maybe she didn't laugh quite so readily, but she certainly wasn't heartbroken. No, Jeanie had moved on in her life and Michael had been part of the past she'd left behind. What she hadn't left behind, despite Evie's fears that she was losing all her family, were her surviving children and her mother, with whom she was in touch most days.

~

What Evie hadn't expected when she went to tea with George that Sunday, was that he'd ask her to marry him. She could feel her heart beating fast and her stomach was fluttering like a bird. There was no doubt in her mind that George Morris was quite a catch, with his kindness and his generosity, but he wasn't like Billy.

Where did that thought come from? That was her old life.

George was waiting patiently.

'I'm very fond of you, George,' Evie began, and saw his smile slip. 'You're the nicest, kindest man I've ever met and we always have such fun together . . . '

'But . . . ?'

'I know you'd be a wonderful husband and that you would look after me, as you say, but I'm not sure I'm ready to marry anyone yet. I'm only seventeen and, well, there's quite a gap between our ages.'

'But I'm not ancient, Evie. I'm good for many years yet,' George said.

'I'm sure you are. That's not what I meant. What I should have said is that, I'm sorry, I'm not in love with you and so I don't think it would be right to marry you.'

'But do you think you could ever fall in love with me, Evie? Can you give me any hope at all?'

He looked so sad that Evie reached out and clasped his hand. Immediately he put his other hand over hers and held it tenderly.

'It would be wrong to string you along, George, but if we continue to be friends then maybe I will come to love you. I'd really like it if we could still meet up as we do, which are the times I enjoy best of all. I can't make any promises about love because that wouldn't be honest, but I can promise that I'll always be your friend.'

'And you will tell me if you change your mind – if you find that, after all, you do love me, won't you, Evie?'

'Oh, George, of course I will. If I fall in love with you, you will be the very first person to know.'

~

That night, when Evie got into bed, thoughts about George's marriage proposal ran endlessly through her head. Had she said the right thing? She thought of the neat flat above the draper's shop, which was big enough to accommodate Sue if she wanted to live there, too. Then she thought of the shop with the finest selection of materials and trimmings she'd ever seen, its polished mahogany cabinets and counters, its smell of pristine new fabric. Finally she thought of George, widowed for several years now, probably a bit lonely, always kind, sober, fun and thoughtful. What did it matter that he was ten years older than her own mother, if they loved each other? Tears sprang to her eyes as she remembered the flowers George had sent when Michael died and how he'd telephoned to see if she was all right while she'd been lying miserable and selfish in her bed, leaving all the work to Sue.

If only I could love him, George would be quite perfect.

He'd said he'd give her time, but how long would that be? Typically, he hadn't asked her for a deadline. He was prepared to wait for as long as she needed to make up her mind.

I want to be in love with him – I do – but I can't make it happen. I can't hurry it or direct it, and it would be so wrong to pretend. What if, then, I met someone else and really fell in love, and wouldn't feel alone any more?

CHAPTER TWENTY-ONE

Back in Fawcett Street, since Ada's death Billy had been miserable. It had been a terrible shock finding her lying in bed like that, especially as she'd been dead for many hours, all alone. And he'd just gone and left her without even looking in. What kind of son did that make him? It was true that Ada had been a bit of one for playing ill and faking to bed, but that was no excuse for not checking whether she was all right.

Billy missed his mother. He missed her gossiping and grumbling, and he missed the sound of the wireless of an evening but hadn't the heart to put it on for himself. Now the house was silent. He even missed her bad cooking. One of the worst things about his life without Ada was returning home to an empty house and having to get his own lonely tea after work, with no one to sit and eat it with. At first he'd taken to going to the pub, just for the cooked food and a bit of company, but he couldn't afford to go every evening, and, anyway, he felt he didn't deserve the company. Not after the way he'd treated his mother. It served him right that he was by himself now. After a week or so he stopped going to the pub.

At first Billy had not told the truth of that awful day to his friends. He was so ashamed of the way he had treated his mother, he'd never forgive himself. They had rallied round to try to cheer him up, but he couldn't set aside the feeling that he had let Ada down in her final hours, that the last thing he'd ever said to her had been in anger. Now he was being punished for it and he felt he shouldn't be looking for a good time with his friends. After several failed attempts to raise Billy's spirits, Colin from the postal depot, Geraldine and her older brothers gave up and left him to stew in his own misery.

One day on his delivery round, Billy saw a poster up outside Mr Amsell's shop, advertising an evening of music at a church hall in Manchester the Saturday before Christmas. He thought nothing of it, but then the fellas in the depot had organised a few festive events he'd turned down and he got to thinking he'd rather go somewhere where no one knew who he was – where no one knew what an awful son he'd been, letting down his mother in her last hours. At least he wouldn't have to speak to anyone in Manchester, as there was no one there he knew. And it had to be better than sitting alone at home, where he spent so much time he felt he was in danger of becoming down-right peculiar.

The day of the concert, Billy took an early train and had a look around the city. There were rows of metal and canvas chairs and the place smelled dusty and looked a bit shabby with use. He took a seat not too near the front.

'And now for a song that may be new to Manchester,' said the girl singer, who had a very assured manner, 'but we think it will soon be sung wherever marrows are grown. It was written by Peter Carter here, on guitar, and it's called "The Marrow Song".'

As the musicians burst into a lively tune Billy stretched his neck to see the composer, his attention caught by the familiar name.

Good grief, I don't believe it. It can't be . . . Yes, it's Peter Carter from Shenty Street. Evie's little brother!

Peter was older, of course, much taller and halfway to being a man, but there was no doubt it was the same person. Billy hardly listened to the song as he tried to think what on earth he would do now. He couldn't go back home as if he hadn't seen Peter. Even if Billy had never been in love with Evie, Peter was a good lad and, although he wouldn't know, it would be ridiculous not to try to say hello, at least. And maybe there'd be some news of Evie. Despite the fact she was now married to that dashing fella, Billy would like to know how she was.

The song ended and the applause was enthusiastic. He filed out of the row of seats and headed for the front of the room. The band would be somewhere behind the stage, he reckoned. Everyone was moving that way and he heard talk of refreshments. Good, that would make it easier.

Straight away he saw Peter, talking and laughing with the twins who played violins.

'Peter! Peter Carter!'

Peter looked round, surprised. Then his face brightened. 'Billy! What a surprise. I never expected to see anyone from Bolton here.'

'It's good to see you,' said Billy, shaking his hand and slapping Peter on the back. 'I've enjoyed the concert so far. Will you be playing again?'

'We will. We're appearing last. I hope you'll stay for that. Let me introduce you to the band . . . '

Billy met each of them and shook their hands, impatient to ask Peter about Evie.

' . . . and our leader, Letitia Mortimer,' Peter finished. 'Letty, this is Billy Taylor.'

'Letty Mortimer?' asked Billy, seeing an opening. 'I know your name. You're a friend of Evie's.'

'Evie's very *best* friend,' smiled the young woman. 'And I think I've heard your name, too.' She looked more serious. 'Are you the Billy Taylor with whom Evie had a falling-out at someone's birthday party last year?'

Billy didn't like the way the conversation was going now. 'That's true, I'm afraid, though I tried to make it up to her by coming down to see her.'

Letty drew Billy to one side and Peter joined them in a private huddle.

'All we know is that you didn't reply to her letters, even when she told you Bob was dead, and she never heard from you again,' said Peter, but patiently. He evidently suspected there was far more to this than a silence on Billy's part. After all, Billy would hardly be being so friendly now if he'd never forgiven Evie for her side of the quarrel.

'Oh, Peter, I did get two letters from Evie, but my mother . . . she put them aside and they got overlooked somehow . . . ' Billy still could not bring himself to blame his mother in front of these people.

'So what happened?' asked Letty. 'When you eventually found the letters, I mean.'

'It was months after Evie wrote them. I went down to see her, to tell her to her face that I was sorry about the quarrel as I know from the letters that she was sorry, too.'

'I didn't know you'd been down,' said Peter.

'Evie didn't tell me that,' said Letty.

'She didn't know. I never got to speak to her.'

'So what happened?' asked Letty, taking a cup of

tea off a passing trolley and putting it into Billy's hands.

'I stopped in Redmond to catch a bus to Church Sandleton and I happened to see her in the street there. She looked lovely – right got up – and I hardly believed it was her at first. She was coming out of a bank with an older man and they looked very close.'

'George Morris, I should think?' Letty asked Peter. 'He's a draper. He owns a shop where Evie goes to buy fabrics for the business,' said Letty. 'He's been a good friend to her, especially since her father was killed.'

'Michael, dead?' Billy's mouth was agape. 'Oh . . . oh, Peter, I'm sorry.'

Peter looked away for a moment. Then he said, 'Evie took it badly, but Grandma's got her working hard, everyone's been kind to Evie and Grandma Sue, haven't they, Letty?'

'They're very popular in the village and people always rally round their friends.' Letty said this with slight emphasis and Billy felt that in her opinion he had been found wanting as a friend. Well, that was right enough.

Just then someone rang a handbell to signal the interval was over and the audience began to troop back to their seats while the musicians gathered together and looked out their music for the second half.

'In the village?' asked Billy, confused. 'But doesn't Evie live in Redmond, in some grand house in a little square?'

'Come and find us afterwards . . . ' said Peter as Martin Clackett called him and Letty over to where he and the twins were busy preparing for their turn.

Billy sat impatiently waiting for it to end, although he could tell why The Mortimers, as the band was called, were the main draw and the last to reappear as the highlight of the evening. All he could think about was getting back to Peter and Letty and finding out about Evie – and who this George Morris was to her. It was the first time that he'd felt hope since finding his mother dead in her bed.

When the applause died away and the lights were switched back on, Billy rushed out and back to the room behind the stage.

'Billy,' said Peter, who'd been looking out for him.

Billy was bursting with questions. 'So is Evie married? Where does she live? I saw her going into a right smart-looking house in a little square in Redmond, and a neighbour said she lived there.'

'It's our mother who lives in a house like that – in Midsummer Row.'

'Yes, that's the name. But I saw Evie going there with the older man, sort of dashing and untidy, but like it didn't matter, and very good-looking.'

'Ah, Frederick Bailey,' said Peter. 'Our mother

lives with Freddie. It's his house. He's kind of like our stepfather, I suppose.'

Billy let out a long breath. Everything he'd thought about Evie and the man he'd seen her with had been of his own imagining. What an idiot he was.

'But what about Evie? You say she's still in the village? And who is this George Morris, besides a shopkeeper?'

Letty interrupted. 'Look, Billy, we have to go now to get the bus back down south.'

'Yes . . . yes, of course. But what shall I do? Do you think Evie will want me to be in touch with her again?' Suddenly he felt like a child on his first day at school, completely at a loss. These people knew all about Evie and he knew nothing any more.

'It's up to you what you do, and I can't speak for Evie. But there's one thing I do know, she's had a hard time but she's pulled herself up with the help of Mrs Goodwin and their friends, and none of us wants to see her heartbroken after all she's been through,' said Letty.

'Now hold on a minute—' began Billy.

'I only want to see Evie happy,' said Letty, 'so, please, think very carefully whether what you do is going to be the best thing for her.'

Billy was silenced for a moment by the young woman's fierceness. 'Will you tell her that we've met and I asked after her?' said Billy.

'No, I won't,' said Letty, picking up her guitar case. 'She doesn't need to know if you don't do anything about it, does she?'

She turned away and went over to join her aunt.

'Bye, Billy,' said Peter.

'Thanks, Pete . . . and mebbe I'll see you soon.'

Peter grinned and gave a wave as he went to join the others, leaving Billy with a lot to think about on the train journey back to Bolton.

~

She doesn't need to know if you don't do anything about it.

The words went round and round in Billy's head. Billy's life had been brought to a standstill by Ada's death, and he had become used to the same humdrum routine of going to work and coming home to spend his evenings alone.

In his head, he planned what he would say to Evie when he saw her. Of course, he'd also planned his previous visit but the result had been completely unexpected. He knew Evie and Sue lived in the village and that Evie wasn't married and that lightened his heart.

But then he thought about Letty's words of warning.

I only want to see Evie happy, so, please, think very carefully whether what you do is going to be the best thing for her.

Perhaps Evie had forgotten all about him. Would going to see her upset her at a time when she was recovering from the death of her father? It would be unforgivable to go stirring up feelings that may well be buried and causing her more distress.

Oh Lord, what to do?

Christmas came and went, and then the New Year. The more he tried to think what to do, the less clear it all became and the further he was from making his mind up.

Then one day on his postal delivery round he met Brendan Sullivan in the street.

'All right, Billy, lad?'

'All right, Brendan? I'm not so bad . . . you know.'

'Well, you look dreadful, if you don't mind me saying. What's the matter?'

So Billy told Brendan everything.

'What are you waiting for?' gasped Brendan. 'It was not acting quickly enough and writing to apologise for that argument at Gerry's party that got you into this mess in the first place! C'mon, Billy, if this was our Stephen I was talking to I'd give him a boot up the backside and throw him onto the train south myself.'

'I just thought—'

'Whatever you thought, you thought wrong. It may work out or it may not, but it's as certain as the love of God is there'll be nothing between you and Evie if you don't go. Is that what you're choosing?'

At that, Billy pulled himself up, shouldering his mail sack with a straight back where before he had seemed bent under its weight.

'How could I be so stupid? Thank you . . . thank you . . . ' He turned to collect his bike from where it was propped and cycled down the street, waving to Brendan, determined to finish his round and then get the first train south.

~

Evie sat back in her chair and stretched. It was a dark January morning, and cold in the house, but two cardigans helped keep out the chill. They chatted on happily while Evie resumed her stitching and Sue rested her eyes.

'You know, Grandma, despite the dreary January days and Dad being gone only a few months I do feel better about . . . everything, really. I reckon this will be a good year for us.'

'Yes, love. Now you're over the worst of your grief for your dad you've been a lot more cheerful. That wouldn't have anything to do with George, by any chance, would it?'

Evie had told Sue all about George's proposal of marriage and how she'd replied to him. It was testament to George's generosity of spirit that he and

411

Evie had become even better friends since his proposal but that he had not referred to marriage again. Sue had observed their growing closer and she thought George was a canny man who was playing a long game.

'Ah, Grandma, I shall have to see if I fall in love with him. But you know I don't want to marry anyone yet awhile. I won't be eighteen until next month and there's so much to do here. I'm not leaving you.'

There was a knock at the workroom door.

'Come in, it's open,' called Sue, as Evie, nearest but sitting with her back to it, was half-buried under yards of skirt, unable to get up quickly.

The door opened slowly and there stood Billy Taylor.

'Good grief!' Sue gasped. 'Where the heck did you spring from, lad?'

Evie turned and her mouth fell open. There was a long, long moment of silence. Then: 'Billy? Can it really be you?' she breathed.

'Evie . . . oh, lass, I'm that glad to see you.'

Sue heaved herself to her feet and went out to put the kettle on. One way or another there would be a need for tea, that was certain. And, in the meantime, a need for privacy.

'Sit down, Billy,' said Evie, gathering herself and putting her work aside. She indicated a chair and he sat and looked around the workroom.

'I found you easy enough – that smart sign with your name on it. You're doing well for yourself, Evie,' he smiled.

Evie didn't reply. She was looking at this man who had once meant a great deal to her. What did she feel about him now? She searched her heart and her mind and discovered only confusion.

'Why are you here, Billy?' she asked politely.

Billy looked at the girl he'd last seen close to well over a year ago. She was a girl no longer. She was a beautiful young woman, taller, slim but in a womanly way and, despite the layers of cardigans, he felt clumsy and out of place all of a sudden.

'I came to see you, of course, Evie,' he stuttered.

She was looking at him with an unreadable expression on her face. After a few moments she said, 'And why have you come to see me, Billy?'

Oh Lord, she wasn't making this easy for him.

What did you expect – that she'd rush into your arms declaring undying love, you idiot?

'To say I'm sorry . . . for that stupid argument we had . . . for all the daft things I said.'

Evie turned and gazed out of the big shop window, a faraway look in her eyes. Then she sighed and turned back to him. Her face still unreadable.

'It's all right, Billy. I forgave you a long time ago. I wrote to say that I was sorry and asked you to forgive me. It doesn't matter any more.'

Billy felt tears in his eyes. This was going all wrong.

413

Any moment now she'd get up and thank him for coming as she showed him to the door.

'It matters to me,' he said, dashing the tears away. 'Oh, Evie, I've been a right fool! I was too proud to write and apologise straight off, and when I knew you'd written—'

'So you do know I wrote?' she asked quietly, frowning.

'I didn't get your letters for months.' He took a deep breath. 'My mum stole them and hid them and, when I found out, we argued and I came down to see you to try to put it all right. I knew I should have said I was sorry straight away.' He shrugged helplessly. 'I saw you in Redmond, looking right pretty, and with a man I thought was your husband, and I went back home without speaking to you . . . without saying all the things I needed to say.'

Evie looked away again, eyes narrowed as if she was thinking very carefully. The silence stretched out until he could hardly bear it.

'And have you said all you need to say now, Billy?' she asked him.

'No! Never mind what happened. Never mind about my mum and your dad and all the things that took place to set us apart from each other and to keep us there. I'm sorry that we argued, and I'm more sorry than I can say that I let it go on and on and was too daft to do owt about it.'

'It's all right, Billy. I told you, it doesn't matter.'

'But it does, Evie. Because I love you. I love you more than I can say and I can't bear to think that I hurt you and you thought I wasn't sorry. I've wasted so much time when I could have been with you, loving you as I do.'

'Oh, Billy, a long time has passed since we fell out.'

'Yes, but my love for you hasn't changed, Evie. I should have listened to my heart and not given up until I'd told you, and I should have done it months ago.'

Evie put her hands over her face and Billy thought she was crying, but when she eventually looked up she was dry-eyed though she looked troubled.

'Billy, I don't think we can just take up where we left off.'

'Why not, Evie? If I love you—'

'Because my life is different now. This isn't Shenty Street and I'm never going back to Shenty Street. I know what we said that day we put all our stuff in Fergus Sullivan's van – for a long time I thought of little else. But I have made a life here, and Grandma Sue and me have worked hard to set up this place and make it a success. I'm not going to give it up. Not because it's what Grandma and me do but because *I don't want to!*'

Billy let this sink in for a minute or two.

'I'm not asking you to give up owt, Evie,' he said

quietly. 'I can see what a success you are here.' He looked around at the shelves of fabrics, the dress-maker's dummy, the two sewing machines, the pile of fashion magazines, and the fitting room screened off in the corner. 'It's marvellous what you've done. Why would you want to give it up? All I'm asking is that you let me back into your life and allow me to love you and be proud of you.'

'Yes, Billy, we can be friends again, if that's what you mean,' Evie said. 'But I think you want more than that.'

'I did hope that you could love me in return,' Billy ventured. 'Or maybe learn to love me again, as I think you did once.'

'Oh, Billy, I don't know,' said Evie, getting up and walking over to the window, biting her nails. 'It's different now.'

'Is there someone else?' Billy thought of the name Letty had mentioned, George Morris.

'There is someone who wants to marry me, yes.'

'And do you want to marry him?'

Evie sat down again, sighing. 'Not now. Not yet. But he's a good man, very kind, and he's one of my dearest friends. I've told him I'm too young to be married and I don't know if I want to marry him. He understands that and is prepared to wait. But we are close friends.'

'And what about me, Evie?'

Evie smiled a crooked smile. 'A close friend, Billy?'

'Oh, Evie, if that's what you want. If that's the best I can hope for.'

'It is just now, Billy. We've got a lot of ground to make up before things can be the same between us as they were, if they ever can, and I reckon you know that.'

Billy nodded.

Evie reached out, took his hand and gave it a squeeze. 'But I shall be glad to have you back in my life, Billy, even if you are miles away.'

'Thank you,' he murmured.

Sue made a lot of noise outside the inner door and came in with a tea tray, looking carefully at the pair to see how things were.

'Tea,' she announced needlessly. 'Where have you got to get back to tonight, Billy?'

'Home, I suppose,' said Billy. 'Though now Mum's gone I've no one to worry about but myself.'

'Yes, we heard about Ada. We're sorry for your loss, aren't we, Evie?'

Evie nodded and they drank their tea while Sue asked about old friends in Bolton.

'Right, best be off then,' said Billy eventually.

'I'll see you out,' Evie offered, getting up.

'It's nice to see you, lad. Goodbye,' said Sue, taking up the tea things and going back to the kitchen.

'Goodbye, Mrs Goodwin,' he called after her, then turned to Evie. 'Goodbye, Evie.'

'I hope it's not really goodbye, Billy,' she said. 'I

think we'd better say farewell, and I'll see you soon.' She smiled. 'We can't make up all that lost time if we don't see each other again, can we?'

Billy's heart lifted and he smiled for the first time since he'd arrived. 'No, Evie, you're right. I reckon I might give up the postal delivery and have a look around, try my hand at summat else, maybe else-where.'

'Don't rush it, Billy,' said Evie. 'Close friends, remember? Please, you need to give me time.'

'Evie, love,' said Billy, 'you've given me hope and I know that's more than I deserve.' He kissed her cheek as she stood aside to let him through the front door. 'You can have as long as you need.'

EPILOGUE

'OH, EVIE, LOVE, you look beautiful,' said Sue, as she helped Evie arrange her hair, in which she had a pretty white band with flowers on it.

'Thank you, Grandma. Is Mum here yet?'

'She's gone to the church. I think she wants a moment with your dad and Bob.'

'Of course she does. I know she takes a posy to the grave whenever she's in the village.'

'Well, we'll have no sadness today, lass. Let's get you to church.'

'Good grief, you brush up well, Sis,' said Peter as Evie came into the workroom. 'I hardly recognise you.'

'Which was exactly what I was going to say to you,' laughed Evie.

Peter grinned and pretended to adjust his tie. 'Ready, Grandma?'

'I am, love. Let's go.'

When it was the moment to leave, Evie held her bouquet of white roses tightly, thinking about all of those who wouldn't be at her wedding, sending up a prayer to her dad and wishing that he could walk her up the aisle.

~

Bells rang out as the newly married couple emerged from the church and their family and friends showered them with rose petals.

'Oh, doesn't Evie look amazing? I can hardly believe she made that dress herself, even though I lived through every decision about it and every fitting,' said Letty to Margaret.

Billy looked down at Evie's glowing face, feeling so happy, aware that he'd nearly lost her, lost everything.

Evie leaned in and kissed him on the lips. 'You are *perfect*.'

'And so, my darling Evie, are you.' Billy smiled shyly.

'But I'm the luckiest, because I've got you.'

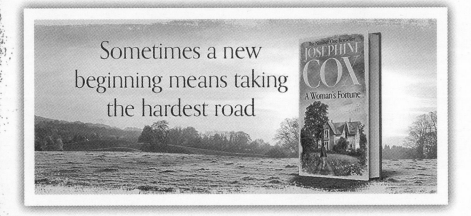

Chatterbox

All the news from Jo's life . . .
straight into yours

If you'd like to know more about Josephine Cox and her novels, then sign up to Chatterbox, Jo's free newsletter. Simply send a postcard to the address below, or email chatterbox@ harpercollins.co.uk with your name and full address details.

The Chatterbox newsletter is packed with exciting competitions, fun activities and exclusive merchandise and gifts, plus the latest news and views from other Josephine Cox fans!

And you can now access Chatterbox online. Simply head to www.josephinecox.com to read the latest issue in full.

CHATTERBOX
HarperCollins Publishers, The News Building,
1 London Bridge Street, London SE1 9GF